Winter Suns

Julie Roberts Towe

Stitched Wing Publishing

ISBN: 978-0-9908007-3-6 (paperback)

ISBN: 978-0-9908007-2-9 (ebook)

This book is a work of fiction. All names, characters, places, organizations, businesses and events other than those clearly in the public domain are used fictitiously and are the product of the author's imagination. Any resemblance to actual events, locales, or persons, living or dead, is entirely coincidental.

Stitched Wing Publishing
1719 Angel Parkway, Ste. 400-116
Allen, TX 75002
USA

Cover art and design by Anna Wand

For Jane

Allie

December 25, 1990

I know I'm running because I feel my legs moving. A dim light before me grows larger as I near it. I don't know what I am running away from, but I hear my heart pounding loudly. The sound of my heart seems to be coming from the tunnel itself. I can hear nothing else. How long have I been running?

The light from the tunnel grows brighter and other sounds emerge. Cries of a screaming baby. The echo bounces off the walls, multiplies. I can't hear my heart anymore. I can only hear the sound of crying. As I move into brighter light, all sound begins to fade. The light becomes so bright that I can't see. Then I hear nothing at all.

His face appears. His dark eyes look into mine, examining me. I remember now, and with remembering my head throbs in pain. Instinctively I reach for my forehead, but my hand is stopped short, tethered.

"It's born," Jim says.

"Angelina?" my voice is a raspy whisper I don't recognize. I need water.

Jim shakes his head. "Gabriel."

My throat tightens and tears reach my eyelids. I feel overwhelmed with simultaneous joy and pain. He is born. I want to see him. I let my tears fall. I forget to be afraid. I forget until I feel Jim's fingers pinch the flesh on the inside of my arm. He twists until I close my eyes and clench my teeth in pain. He says, "Don't you cry. He doesn't belong to you. He's God's child."

"I know," I force a smile which cracks my lip. "All things are of God."

Jim leans close. I try to hide my emotions. I try to keep still. He sneers and says, "Except for you Allie, you are cursed to Hell."

He stands up. I hear his grunt before I feel his fist slam my temple. I'm back inside the tunnel, but I still feel his fist hitting me again and again. I can't get away from it.

I run until the lights go out.

Part One

Perdy

1

June 9, 2003

"Perdy!" Ma's voice was hoarse and could barely be heard from the garden. I ran, careful not to step on the watermelon vines. My hands were shaking, holding my apron steady so the new yellow tomatoes would not fall from it.

"Coming, Ma!"

The back door of the trailer stood wide open to let a breeze through. The days had begun to feel less like spring and more like the peak of summer. The heat inside our little tin box of a home had become nearly unbearable.

The year before, I had often wheeled Ma outside under the willow tree. From there, she could see the garden. The chickens would wonder over to her. Ma had loved to scatter just enough crumbs to keep them anxious. The last time she'd been well enough to leave the bed had been in April.

I followed the sound of Ma's coughing and found her face down on the floor beside her bed. Her stained nightgown was so loose, she looked like a doll in it. Her thin arms struggled to hold her head up from the pool of blood and vomit she had just coughed up onto the blue carpet.

"Oh, Ma! I'll help you back to bed and clean you up." As I dropped to my knees, the tender yellow tomatoes tumbled onto the floor.

"No. Just pray. Right now. Oh, heavenly Father..." Ma's coughing was violent. She wheezed and gasped for air.

Taking hold of Ma's bony shoulders, I leaned her over so her head rested on my lap. Ma faced away from me, wheezing. Her fit of coughing shook us both. She was so light. My hand touched Ma's thin auburn hair and I closed my eyes, focusing my mind on the face of Jesus.

"Oh, heavenly Father, we ask that you bind and cast out the evil spirit causing Esther Billings' cancer. Satan has planted this seed inside of her. We banish that seed of evil. In your name we command that Satan leave her body and that her body is healed and made whole. Heavenly Father, we ask for your forgiveness for our sins. We turn toward your light. Let your healing light flow through my hand as I touch her now. Let your healing power enter into her body, in Jesus' name."

The words continued to roll out of me as I lost myself to Jesus. My tongue spoke words I could not know the meaning of, strange languages of God. I felt Him guide my touch to Ma's sores. My heart was pure, my faith complete. Jesus would heal my mother; I believed. I believed it with all my being.

So often, I had prayed that same prayer over Ma, but this moment was different. I felt the release of Ma's sickness. Throughout her body, I felt the divine work of God. I smiled up to the ceiling, thanking God for healing my mother. "Thank you, Jesus!"

Before I even opened my eyes, I slid my arms under Ma's small body, preparing to lift her. When I finally opened them and looked down at her, I saw her eyes were open to narrow slits. Her face was covered with blood and drool. Her mouth was full of blood, pooled there. She was dead.

"No!" I cried, "Oh, God, my God what have I done to displease you?"

2

I had never seen Daddy cry before, but I soon learned his tears were not a sign of weakness or lenience. He was angry with me. I was not supposed to have let Ma die, especially not while he was gone.

By the time he had returned home the day Ma died, I already had her cleaned and dressed for burial. Ma had given me instructions months before and had regularly reminded me which dress, how to style her hair, and to place her church shoes on her feet.

As soon as Daddy had come home, he walked into Ma's bedroom and saw her in that dress and knew. He had dropped to his knees and cried. I knew I would be in trouble if he caught me staring at him, but I couldn't look away. I had never seen him do anything like that. Tears were not permitted in his house or anywhere near Daddy.

He stayed there on his knees for a few minutes to gain his composure. Then, he screamed my name as he pulled himself up to his feet, "Perdy!"

"I'm here, Daddy," I said from the hall behind him. I wanted to comfort him, but I knew better.

He turned, his legs shaking as they struggled to balance his weight. Daddy was stout with dark hair and dark eyes. His skin was tanned brown where the sun had beat down on it over his sixty years, but beneath his clothes he was white as an onion skin. He never washed his hair like Ma and me, so it always held the shape of his hat long after he had removed it.

"You do this to her?" His voice indicating he had decided I

had.

I wasn't sure if he meant killing Ma or dressing her. Failure to answer immediately would have brought punishment. So I nodded my head yes without knowing what it would imply.

"Did you pray over her this morning? Or did you let her lie there alone because I wasn't here to make you obey?"

I glanced up at his eyes to be respectful, then dropped my gaze to his boots. "I prayed this morning and again when she called for me and asked me to pray over her. I was praying when she died."

"Did you mean it, Perdy? Or did you pray with Satan's grip on your heart?"

"I meant it, Daddy. I felt Jesus working through me. I spoke in tongues and touched her sores," I hoped he would forgive the tears in my eyes just this once. "Satan was not in my heart, only my love for God and for Ma."

Silas's lip snarled in suppressed anger, "Jesus don't work through you Perdy. Don't you ever say such a blasphemous thing again. Jesus don't work through no twelve year old girl, especially not one like you. That was Satan you were feeling inside you, you deceitful dog!" His hand landed across her cheek and his voice boomed as he spit the words at me, "Satan worked through you and killed Esther through you. He is probably in you now, bringing wrath upon this house!"

I had already felt a nagging guilt about not being able to save Ma. Daddy's words cut especially deep. Maybe he was right that Jesus would never work through me, that I was destined to bring only misery. I had certainly witnessed and been affected by enough of it in my life. I said, "I'm sorry, Daddy."

"Sorry won't bring her back! Ain't nothing going to bring her back!" He grabbed my arm and spun me around so I couldn't face him. With his hand gripping my wrist, he pulled me back against him. I had never known my punishment to come so quickly. Usually there were so many preparations I had to make. But this time he hadn't made me cleanse my body in the presence of the Lord, nor had he instructed me when I should meet him in his room. This time, right there in the hall, just feet from Ma's dead body, he had let go of my wrist to lift my skirt and immediately set to casting out my demons.

The next day, Daddy buried Ma under the willow tree.

3

July 18, 2003

The sky was clear, leaving open a direct path for the sun to beat against my dark hair, warming my head like a winter fire. Thinking about winter when it was so hot outside was a common trick I played on myself.

I pulled another half runner green bean from the vine and tucked it into my palm with the rest. The air was heavy with humidity, but it was easier to breathe outside in the garden than it was in the trailer. I filled my hand with beans and dropped them into the bucket before moving another step down the row. The dirt clots broke apart under my feet. Kentucky could have used some rain.

My hand quickly worked around and through the leaves of the vine, pulling bean after bean. I kept count until my hand could hold no more, trying to outdo the greatest number I'd ever held. Thirteen. I tossed the bundle into the bucket and started again. I kept count of the handfuls it took to fill up the bucket. 275 beans usually filled it to heaping, but the most I ever got in one bucket was 322. The game was my secret; things I found pleasurable were usually taken away or forbidden.

When the bucket was nearly full, I felt something strange happen to me. Something thick came out of me and ran down my leg beneath my skirt. I felt panicked, not knowing what it was. But, I struggled to maintain a calm expression. I didn't want to cue Daddy that something might be wrong with me.

I stood straight up and looked over at him sitting under the willow tree. He had buckets and pans set out for stringing and breaking the beans. I called over to him, barely loud enough to be heard over the cicadas. "Daddy, may I use the outhouse?"

He didn't raise his head to look at me. He kept it bowed, focused on his thick fingers as they pulled strings and snapped beans in sections. His voice boomed in his usual commanding tone, "No, ma'am. You have two more rows of beans left to pick. You can hold it."

I lowered my head out of respect and continued pulling beans from the vines, slowly at first as I tried to assess if I was going to fall over and die. When I felt the wetness increase, I squatted down by the bucket and saw blood on my work boots. I knew it was cancer like Ma had. I prayed a silent prayer to God to banish Satan from my body, then stood and repeated the prayer for the next forty-five minutes until the beans were all picked.

"The beans are done, Daddy. May I go to the toilet, please?"

"Fine. But first, bring me that bucket of beans. I'm about out." Daddy still didn't look at me.

I carried the full bucket knowing it must have had more than 322 beans in it, but I had stopped counting. I walked steadily so none of the beans would slide from the heaping pile I had formed on top. I felt more blood. Tears filled my eyes, but I shook my head to make them stop. I couldn't let Daddy know that Satan had seeded me with cancer. I held my legs close together as I walked, then gently placed the bucket beside the one Daddy had nearly emptied.

Daddy's gaze moved to my shoes and he tensed up. I wanted to run, but was afraid he would think I was disrespecting him.

"What's on your shoes, Perdy?" His brown eyes held a spark, a mix of anger and amusement.

"I... I think I have cancer."

He stared at my face for a long while, magnifying my fear. My legs were sticky and I felt ashamed. Finally he said, "Well, now, I don't think you have cancer, Perdy. I think you have become a woman. That means you are old enough to have babies and you are just twelve. A twelve year old woman. I knew all along you were marked and every day I see more signs of it. Esther showed you mercy and I let her. But I don't know if that was wise. I don't know if I'll ever get the devil out of you. And now, this. Everything is going to change. There are laws in the Bible about this. While women are bleeding, they must stay away from men. That means you stay away from me. Keep to your room until you are clean again. Seven days, Perdy. You come out of that room before seven days, I will put you out of the house like a pig in the pen. Do you understand me?"

I nodded calmly, but my thoughts were racing. I wasn't sure how to get clean if I wasn't going to be able to leave my room. I didn't dare ask Daddy because that would have been talking back.

He looked down at his fingers which were pulling strings and snapping the beans. He continued with his instructions, "This will happen every month. And every month you are to get some rags and that chipped black bucket from the side yard. Now, don't sleep on your bed, you sleep on the floor. Don't make your bed unclean. I will bring you a jug of water and a bite to eat after dark. But don't you open the door until you hear me walk away. Esther should be telling you all this, Perdy. I shouldn't even be talking to you with blood on you like that. But, she couldn't unleash her heart from Satan and neither could you unleash yours to help her. That's the way it is with women. So, she ain't here. And I ain't going to suffer for your tainted soul. I will not. So get on out of my sight and I will explain how we're going to continue on together after you bathe on Thursday."

"Yes, sir," I said, relieved to have some instructions about what to do, even though I couldn't really understand what was happening. I held out my skirt and turned to leave, hoping to keep most of the blood from ruining my only clothes. If I couldn't wash my clothes for seven days, I feared I would never be able to wash the stains away.

With the black bucket in one hand and my skirt still held in the other, I entered the open trailer door through a thick wall of heat. I walked straight to the bathroom, which had never been operable. A washbowl set nestled in the sink. I had always filled it with fresh water each morning. Cleaning rags were stored beneath the sink. I pulled nearly all of them into my arms. Quickly, I went to Ma's room and took a dress from her closet. Daddy would've probably been upset, but I feared he would be more upset to see me wearing unclean clothes.

My room was terribly hot. I hung the clean dress up on the curtain rod and undressed myself. I put my stained clothes into a pile in the corner of the room. With a cleaning rag under me, I sat on the floor naked. In a whispered chant, I repeated a prayer for forgiveness and for the bleeding to stop. I said it over and over until I entered a trance, a peaceful place where I no longer worried about the stains.

When the sun set, I tried to sleep as best I could.

4

July 23, 2003

On Wednesday, my bleeding stopped. I watched the shadows grow long and counted the minutes after the sun set waiting for midnight, waiting for Thursday. There was no way to know for sure when the hour had passed. So I waited a few extra minutes after my calculations indicated it was time, just to be sure.

All of the cleaning rags were saturated with blood and the black bucket had a horrible stench. The late summer humidity picked up the smell like a swirl of insects that flew into my eyes and nose and mouth. The tiny window did little to let in fresh air. I had never felt so dirty nor ashamed.

Confident that Thursday had officially arrived, I opened my bedroom door and walked into the bathroom. No laundry had been done in the days I had been isolated. The washcloth by the sink was dirty from a week of Daddy using it for his hands. I took it and the wash pan outside to the pump. I hoped the sound of the handle squealing with each rise and fall would not wake him.

I filled the pan with water and carried it over to the edge of the garden where there was a small patch of flat land far from the house. I washed myself there as best I could. Then I dumped the pan and filled it again with clean water for another round of scrubbing. When I believed I was properly clean, I then filled a tub with bleach water for the rags and my stained skirt which I ripped into rags to use the following month. Then I pushed them all down into the bleach water, which had quickly turned pink.

My naked body felt clean and alive as I worked to erase any

sign of the mess I had been hours before. The last vile thing I had to do was carry the heavy bucket of waste to the outhouse and dump the horrid filth down the hole.

After doing that, I dressed without fear of ruining Ma's dress. I slipped it on over my head. It was a bit small; it squeezed uncomfortably against my breasts. Images of Ma entered my mind, thoughts of her tiny frame and how much smaller she had become before she passed. Tears filled my eyes as they did every time I thought of her. Silas had said tears bring Satan. I knew I should fight them back, and I tried but couldn't stop a few from sliding down my cheeks. I wiped them away, then headed to the pump. I needed fresh bleach water for the rags.

The hours passed quickly as I caught up on a week's worth of washing. Silas's clothes, handkerchiefs, the washcloth and towel, and my bedding were all cleaned and draped over the line in the moonlight. I went inside and washed the dishes and emptied the mouse traps, reset them. I mopped the kitchen and my bedroom, then let the mop soak in the bleach water outside.

I was in the garden picking ripe tomatoes, some too ripe and cracked open, when the sun turned the skies above the mountains to a beautiful shade of pink, like wild roses. Glory be to God.

After multiple trips carrying an apron full of vegetables into the house, I had spread out enough to cover the entire kitchen table; okra, broccoli, squash, and zucchini. On my way back to the garden I heard Silas's gritty sleep-filled voice call, "Perdy!"

"Coming," I said, my heart pounding with fear that he might find me unclean. I entered his room, not the one where Ma died. Daddy had always had his own room, a small one with a large bed and very little space to move around it. He was sitting at the foot of his bed just like every other morning, his knees poking out from under his long sleeping gown. It looked in need of laundering and I felt guilty seeing it so dirty.

"Girl, have you cleaned yourself?"

"Yes, Daddy."

He stared at me for a moment, differently. I realized he was staring at Ma's dress. My heartbeat nearly deafened my ears. Finally he moved his squinted gaze up to my face. "Good girl. You did alright for your first time. But, there are other things you need to learn. Now, you's a woman. Satan will be after you like never before. Women can't resist the temptations of evil. But I am the head of this house and I forbid you to allow Satan in here. Your demons must still be cast out. You will still serve me as your father and as the master of this house. But, we don't want no babies, so we must have new ways, Perdy, more difficult ways for you. You must abide my will for the good of this house and your soul."

My heartbeat slowed to one giant thud after another. I tried to imagine what he could mean. I couldn't imagine how the casting out of demons could have been worse than it had been before. My fear made me feel weak before God. I was ashamed of my lack of faith. I was ashamed of my reluctance to perform my duties. I was terrified that Satan was inside of me, mocking my hesitation, laughing at how dispassionate I was to please the Lord.

Daddy's rough fingers curled around mine. "You were born evil, and I must stay vigilant to destroy your wickedness."

I stood in front of him, noticing his oily hair was thinning. Seeing him from that angle made me reflect on how much I had grown over the years. I remembered when I was small and would look up to see his eyes which were always piercing, forcing me to look away. I tried to remember when this casting out of demons all started, but I couldn't. I just remembered that he called me Perdy Girl then and he would twirl my long brown hair around his finger. There were only flashes of memory left of those first times. Now I had entered womanhood and the ritual was about to become even more difficult. I wanted to cry, but I didn't dare.

His voice interrupted my thoughts, "It's time to make sure you are clean. Take off your Ma's dress."

I pulled it off and folded it neatly, the same way I had done with my old dress. I set it on the floor near the doorway. I put my hands to the wall and stood with my feet apart. And just like every other time, I closed my eyes and let the blackness take over. Emptiness filled my senses as I left the Earth and floated up to the stars where I was unable to feel the suffering of my body. I abandoned my fate as a woman. I knew Satan likely lived in that darkness. But, I was a shameful girl and a coward. My body obeyed God's law, but my soul always betrayed Him.

5

Three Years Later,
November 26, 2006

Every Saturday morning, after the breakfast dishes were clean and the kitchen floors were mopped, it was my responsibility to walk through the woods to the church and clean it before Sunday services. Even if Daddy and I were the only two ever in attendance, the church needed to be made worthy of the presence of God.

I pushed my arms into the sleeves of Ma's coat. It was a thick, black, wool dress coat that she had worn every Sunday since I was a child, until she was unable. As I walked along the narrow path through the woods, I stopped every so many feet to spin. The coat flared out around me, rippled wide, made me feel big. I never twirled where Daddy could see me, but he seldom came with me on Saturdays.

The air was cold, but not as bitter cold as the heart of winter. With Thanksgiving just past, I expected our first snow any day.

The trail began mostly level, staying low through the hollow. Both sides were heavily wooded and a small stream trickled over rocks to my left. Sometimes in spring it would flood and the trail would become rutty with trenches. When that happened, Daddy and I would bring shovels and rakes up the trail and smooth it out again. To my right were the piles of rocks we had cleared in the past. Seeing them made me thankful that spring was a long way away.

As I neared the church, the trail rose higher and higher up along the side of the mountain. The tiny church was tucked around the bend on an elevated clearing that had become increasingly overgrown with shrubs and saplings. The church looked as if it had sprouted up with the mountain and been there as long as the rocks beneath it.

Daddy had said it was his family's church, a family that had dwindled to only the two of us. But a long time ago his family lived all along that hollow and on the other side of the mountain ridge. I pictured the church as a place ladies in fine dresses and gentlemen in suits had visited to worship every Sunday. Perhaps they rode in on horses with the ladies sitting side saddle. They would have packed into the church; the gentleman would have filled up the two pews and the ladies would have stood in the back and tended to the children.

But, on this day it barely held itself together. The foundation bricks had mostly crumbled. Daddy had tried to brace it up with cinder blocks through the years. There were a few holes rotted out in the floor from the leaking roof and the siding slats were in need of paint. If I had money I would have given it to Daddy to buy supplies to fix the church. But I had nothing and Daddy didn't have a whole lot more than that. The most I could've done for the church was to clean it every week and run the reel mower around the foundation so shrubs wouldn't take root. There was always less work in Winter.

The cleaning supplies were stored in a dry place just under the northern corner of the church. I pulled the bucket out and headed to the western edge of the clearing where an old pump could still bring up water from the well. When the bucket was full, I lugged it inside.

Cleaning the floors, windows, and pews took very little time. Only a couple of hours had passed and the morning frost was still on the ground. I took a moment to walk to the pulpit and pull the heavy Bible into my arms. I sat cross legged on the floor, with my heart racing, and opened the pages. Daddy had no idea I had been teaching myself to read. He certainly never suspected I had nearly deciphered every word in Genesis. It was a surprise I wanted to give him for Christmas. I wanted to read his favorite passage to him because Daddy couldn't read it himself. He used to rely on Shem to read the passages.

I knew very little about Daddy's sons, my brothers. They were gone or dead or both before I was born and were never mentioned except for Shem. I had overheard Ma say that Shem could read the Bible. But, he had drowned in the creek when he was eleven. Daddy and Ma had spoken of him often, shaming me with his perfection, reminding me that Shem had never been as evil as I. But, the other brothers were the biggest mystery. I did not even know their names or how many there had been. I only knew what I overheard in snippets. Ma used to say, "When our boys were little..." and Daddy would give her a glare until she would correct herself to say, "our boy, Shem". Sometimes I was afraid that I would end up like the nameless brothers, and Daddy would one day refuse to acknowledge I ever existed.

Of course, it was hard for me to imagine that Daddy would ever stop saying my name. He called it so often, and who else did he have to care for him?

I pulled my thoughts back to the Bible. The reading of Exodus began telling of the sons of Jacob. I was so excited to be reading it, learning how the Pharaoh wanted all the Israelite sons to be killed at birth. I forgot to check the progress of the sun. I usually watched the shadows get short then grow long and I knew when it was time to go home to prepare lunch. But I forgot about the shadows, lunch, the church, Daddy, everything.

It wasn't until I heard the door push open that I remembered. I slammed the Bible closed and cringed at the bang it made. I tried to heave it over my head and onto the pulpit.

Daddy walked around the corner and saw me sitting in the floor with the Bible above my head as if I was prepared to throw it. He grabbed my wrists, pressed his fingers into bones until I thought they would snap. My hands could no longer hold the Bible. It fell, the corner landed on my thigh before falling open on the floor. Pages were splayed and crumpled beneath its weight.

"Perdy, this is not your place!" Daddy bellowed angrily. "Women are not allowed behind the pulpit of a church. You know better. Now clean where your body has touched and get home for your punishment!"

He picked up the old Bible, the binding had broken loose even more than before. He closed it and tucked it under his arm. I blinked back my tears and swallowed hard as I listened to him walk away.

6

December 12, 2006

Opportunities were rare, but when they came, I looked for the Bible. Daddy took it to the church with us every Sunday and brought it home afterward. He would place it on his nightstand. But, every Sunday night it would be missing again. I had craved to read it, to find out what happened to the Israelites in Egypt. It was all I thought about. I couldn't believe how willing I was to sneak and disobey Daddy in order to search for the Bible. He probably thought it was suspicious the way I had been so eager to clean his bedroom. I had already searched everywhere else. There were only so many places it could have been.

The best opportunity for searching was when Daddy bought grocery staples for the month. That had been two weeks ago. I hadn't expected to have another chance until his yearly Christmas outing. I was surprised when I saw him sitting on the couch, tying up his boot laces. He wore his burgundy flannel shirt, which I had not seen on him since before Ma died. His hair was combed. I dared not ask where he was going; staring at him was dangerous enough.

When he looked up and saw my eyes on him, he gave me a look of warning. He leaned over to spit tobacco juice in the canteen beside the couch. I looked away from his piercing eyes and turned to leave the room. His voice stopped me.

"Perdy, I have to go up Caney Branch Holler. I don't know how long I'll be. Might be an hour, might be sundown. You behave and do your chores and mind your place, hear me girl?"

I turned back to face him again, keeping my head bowed. "Yes, Daddy."

"Idleness invites Satan." It was a warning Daddy gave often. I waited without moving while he stood and put on his worn brown leather coat. "Go on and get. I got nothing else to say."

"Yes, Daddy."

I walked out the back door and headed over to the wood pile. There were still pieces of wood in need of stacking where Daddy had cut up a downed tree the day before. I focused on the work of my hands and resisted exploding with exhilaration. I had most of the wood stacked when I finally heard his truck engine sputter to life. Only then did it occur to me that Caney Branch was where the midwife lived. Ms. Thorneagle was Cherokee but she was also a Christian woman. She seldom delivered babies anymore, but she still possessed a vast knowledge of the medicinal properties of natural things. She had been called on occasion to see about Ma. Daddy believed she provided God's medicines and he would rather seek care from a Cherokee Christian than a sacrilegious hospital. If Daddy was going to see Ms. Thorneagle, maybe that meant he was sick.

Mixed feelings tugged and twisted my insides. It was wrong to wish anything bad would happen to him, but I couldn't explain why the thoughts of him being sick made me happy. Maybe it was because, for once, he would have to say Satan was in his own heart making him ill. But as soon as that thought entered my mind I knew he never would think that. If Daddy was sick, he would blame me. So I kept myself from wishing it. Besides, it was also scary to think about something happening to him. There was no one else to care for me. No one besides he and Ms. Thorneagle knew I existed.

When the wood was stacked, I gathered up the remaining twigs and small branches for the kindling box. Then I carried in an armload of wood for the fire. By the time I had the logs burning in the wood stove, Daddy had already been gone fifteen minutes. I figured there were at least forty-five more minutes before he returned.

I had a plan for where I would look for the Bible next. There were only a couple of places it could have been. I went straight to his bedroom and lifted up his heavy mattress. Nothing. Next, I went to his closet which had a green and blue plaid curtain hung up as a door. For all of my life, I had been forbidden from looking in it. I had been taught to place Daddy's clean shirts and pants on hangers and leave them on his bed. He placed them in his closet himself. Snooping in that closet would mean breaking one of the most enforced rules of the house. I raised my hand to touch the curtain, rationalizing that if I had not exhausted all other options, I would not be breaking the rule. I prayed to God for forgiveness and pulled the curtain to the side.

There were shirts, jackets, pants, and coats. Lots of fabric things hung from hangers, some of the older things had a layer of dust where they had been folded over. I squatted down on the floor and saw boots in a pile, almost all were worn nearly soleless. I moved them around and saw nothing under them, no secret floorboard compartment, no boxes, no Bible. I stacked them up the way I had found them.

Next, I stood on my tiptoes to look on the shelf above his clothes. There were hat boxes that must have belonged to Ma. I thought for sure Daddy must have put the Bible inside one of them.

I pulled down a small hatbox from the front and immediately saw the Bible on top of another hatbox behind it, pushed far to the back of the closet. A smile stretched across my face. I tossed the small hatbox onto the bed and stretched to reach as far into the closet as I could. Finally my fingertips touched the strap of the hatbox beneath it. If I could pull that out, the Bible would come, too. As it neared the edge, the hatbox tipped. I caught the Bible in my arms, but the hatbox fell open on the floor.

Like a prize, I gently laid the Bible on the bed. Then I sat on the floor to gather up the hats. Four pillbox hats had been stacked in that single box. A navy blue fedora was largest, so I picked it up first and turned it over to put a pink one inside it. A folded piece of paper caught my eye. It was tucked behind the ribbon hatband of the blue hat. I pulled it loose and unfolded it. The writing was a curly script much unlike the text in the Bible. I couldn't make out all the words, but decided it would be good practice to try to read it. So I laid it on the bed with the Bible and boxed up the other hats.

With the hatbox back in the closet, I carried the Bible and the paper to my room. I slid the paper inside my pillowcase and placed the Bible on top of it so I could read it.

With only a thirty minutes of certain safety remaining, I fell onto the bed and opened the tattered book to Exodus. I couldn't read fast enough. I skimmed the story, wanting to get as far ahead as I could before my time was up. But time was difficult for me to keep track of when God's people were enslaved. It wasn't until I heard the burbling of Daddy's truck exhaust coming closer up the mountain road that I realized I had waited too long.

Bible in hand, I dashed into Daddy's bedroom. I shoved the Bible back into its place and tossed the small hatbox in front of it. I could hear his boots crunching gravel as I walked out of his room. My panic was fed by an overwhelming sense of guilt. I worried he would notice. But a solution crossed my mind and before I could think better of it, I opened the front door to greet him. It was a door I knew I was forbidden from ever opening, but I wanted to appear happy to see him. I eagerly looked at Daddy and said, "Is everything alright? I was worried."

In pretending to be his innocent little girl, I had hoped Daddy wouldn't be suspicious of me. But, I didn't know he had been crying. When he saw me standing there watching him cry, he became furious.

"Get in the house, girl!" With just one leap, he skipped two steps and landed on the porch only inches from my face. "You have disobeyed me one too many times. You bring one terrible wrath after another on my house! Go and cleanse yourself, repent of your sins, and prepare to have your demons cast out."

7

December 13, 2006

I didn't want to think about what Daddy would have done to me if I hadn't gone to wash myself and discovered it was my time of bleeding. Since I had become a woman, his force had become more intense with each punishment. The last few times it had been difficult for me to keep my mind zoned out of the experience. My body's bruises, cuts, and tears had taken so long to heal that some wounds still felt fresh when he took to punishing me again. The seven days I remained locked in my room every month had become a welcomed reprieve from Daddy's ever increasing anger. I could think of nothing different I had done to cause it. Just the sight of me, at times, would trigger his rage.

The time in my room allowed me to heal, even if it meant my housework waited and more punishments would be inevitable when I got out again. For three years I had spent my monthly time contemplating how I could be a holier woman. Any time I had asked Daddy to advise me on how to be good, he became enraged, if not at first, eventually. He said that if I wasn't so full of Satan then Ma would be here and he wouldn't have to talk to me about it. I was starting to think Daddy would be happier if I was dead. I reasoned that he beat me as if he was trying to make it so. At the end, as I cleaned him, he used to say he hoped his actions had helped. Not anymore.

I began to suspect Daddy had set a trap I could not escape. If I pleased and obeyed him by being very still, quiet, and not looking at him, he became full of rage and would lash out at me anyway. If I didn't please him, he became twice as violent. But there were no new bruises on this night. Daddy would never have laid a hand on me while I was bleeding. Still, the floor in my room was painfully cold. I thought the sun should come up within the hour, but I couldn't say for sure. I had fallen asleep early, before sundown, and now I found myself restless. My mind drifted to the paper I had found in the hatbox. I still couldn't understand why Daddy had hatboxes in his closet when Ma had plenty of space in her room. There were hatboxes already in Ma's room, a couple under her bed and one in her closet for her funeral hat. Everything in Esther's room was feminine, though much of it was stained. Everything in Daddy's room was functional and quite ugly, except the hats stored in his closet. I found that strange and my mind hung up on it.

Daddy might have bought the hatboxes for Ma but never given them to her, or maybe they had been passed down from someone in his family. For a moment, I imagined he had planned to give them to me. I pictured myself as a real lady one day in the future, wearing a nice dress with lace and the navy blue hat on my head. But the pleasure in the fantasy faded when I realized I would need to get married for it to happen, but to whom? I didn't know any boys. The last person to visit had been Ms. Thorneagle when Ma was sick over three years ago. Before her, there had been no one. My thoughts darkened, returning to their usual hopelessness. I decided I should focus on something else, like learning to read.

The sun had finally begun to peek through the window with the palest of rays. I shifted my naked body to reach into my pillowcase on the bed, which made the cold air hit all the places I had been trying to keep warm. I pulled out the paper and unfolded it again. The writing could barely be seen in the dim light. But I knew soon the sun would be high enough and I would have nothing but time to figure out this new script.

January 25, 1991
2:47 a.m.

Jute,

I thought he could heal me and make me whole. I thought he would teach me how to accept and be worthy of God's love. I put so much faith in him; a minister should be Godly. I did everything he said. I obeyed him, tried to change my heart, confessed every evil thing I've ever done or thought. But he just became angrier with me until he was filled with hate. I have no doubt that he is convinced I am Satan himself.

I should have had faith in you, Jute. I should have believed in us. Now it's too late. I have a son, Gabriel, who is the most perfect thing I've ever known. He was born exactly one month ago today. He's beautiful. But Jim doesn't trust me around him. He is paying a lady from our church to stay with us to care for the baby. Her name is Cynthia. She brings me Gabriel when it is time to nurse him, but Jim doesn't allow me to speak. Still, I can look at him and see he is safe. He is beautiful. When he falls asleep, he turns his head away from me. His lips move as if still suckling in his dreams. I love him so much.

It is hard for me not to cry when Cynthia comes and pulls him from my arms. She won't even look me in the eyes. I go days without speaking to anyone. It has been so difficult. Sometimes I want to run far away from here, but I am afraid he will kill me and Gabriel, too. I just can't risk it.

Remember when you begged me not to kiss you? You were afraid of what it would do to us. I hope you know the kiss didn't do this. My shame did this. What you and I had was love and I feel it still. I know Jim has done everything in his power to convince me that two women can not love each other as righteously as a man and a woman. But I have never been loved by a man in any way that felt righteous, not even Jim. My heart pulls to you, no matter how hard I try to change how I feel, it always wants you. I would never survive this without the memories of you. I wish I could feel you now, your touch on my scars. Even if it would damn me to Hell forever for touching another woman, it would be worth it to touch you again. I wouldn't care. I need you now. I am so sorry, Jute.

I know this letter will probably never reach you. I have no way of getting it to a mailbox, and even if I could, where would I send it? I don't even know where you are. I plan to tuck it into a hatbox and have Cynthia donate the things to the local Goodwill. I hope someone finds it, finds you. I need you to know that I am sorry for the damage I have caused. I need you to know my son's name, so that if anything happens to me, you might look in on him. I have no expectations that this will find you. I only have the tiniest hope, the very last I can hold.

Love,
Allie

8

I wanted to find her. That was my first thought, and it was so overwhelming I found myself on my feet before remembering why I had been seated on the floor in the first place. I sat back down and tried to think. I needed to see her in a way I had never felt a need for anything. My mind reeled, trying to wrap around the idea that the letter had been written by a real person somewhere out in the world. Somehow it made its way to me. Allie's hats were in Daddy's closet. How? Who was she to him? I had never seen or heard of her or any of the names she mentioned.

Maybe Daddy didn't know her either. Maybe he bought the hatboxes for Ma. Allie mentioned her plan to donate the hats and it all seemed plausible. Daddy traded things all the time. Maybe he traded something for those hats. It could have been the divine hand of God that placed the letter into my hands. Maybe I was Allie's answered prayer. Maybe I was the one meant to get the letter to Jute. These thoughts were vitalizing, but I immediately understood the plight of Job. I didn't even know where to start, and technically I was still an unmarried woman in servitude to my father. How could God have called me to do both?

My hands shook so much the letter fell to the floor. I squeezed my hands together to steady them. My mind rolled over the images conjured by the letter, images so foreign that I felt I was in a dream, in another world, an illusion. I put my hands to my head to hold it steady, but it wasn't my head that was spinning. It was the world around me. There was nothing within my power to put it back the way it was before.

Feeling conflicted and unsure about what in that letter was God and what might have been Satan, I spent nearly an hour on my knees in prayer. I asked God to guide me to the answers. How had the letter come to be in my hands? Had I been called to do something with it? My prayers were constantly interrupted by the images the letter incited. I saw two women staring into each other's eyes, fingers on scars, scars like mine. My heart ached unbearably and I had to stop praying to sob. I tried to keep quiet so Daddy wouldn't hear me crying. But I could not lessen how much I physically felt their love for each other, a feeling I had never had personally. Now that I was aware of it, I wanted it for myself. I felt guilty for that desire, and I prayed again.

The images kept coming. Not just images of love, but I also saw a man beating a woman the way Daddy beat me. It was too much. I may not have known about love, but I knew too well the pain inflicted on Allie. I had never thought of Daddy's actions as wrong. He had always beaten me, touched me in ways that hurt, said and done things that made my mind go black because the pain was too great for me to process. I had never questioned the necessity of it. But after reading the letter, I could not hold back the flood of questions. Those were dangerous questions and I felt some of them would surely lock me in the devil's grip. But I couldn't stop asking them.

I also imagined Cynthia, a woman my mind made similar to Ms. Thorneagle because I had no other references for caregivers. I imagined Allie looking similar to Ma, she was holding a baby close. It was obvious that Allie loved the baby more than she loved her husband and more than she even loved God. For me, it was the opposite. God was first, then the church, then Daddy, and Ma, and last was me, the baby. I envied the love Gabriel was given, however brief his time in his mother's arms, even though I believed the way I had been raised was the proper way. Or had it been? Maybe it had once felt that way to me, but I wasn't sure if I could still believe it, not with my whole heart. Imagining a mother loving her baby above all else made my wounds throb in contrast. Every single image conjured by the letter was held up to my own life in comparison. It all seemed to matter more than it should.

Reading the letter was like looking into a mirror, holding up someone else's pain and recognizing my own. We suffered the same isolation, denial, and rejection. I knew exactly the horror she was telling in that letter, something so much more relevant to my life than anything I had read in Genesis. I felt it and couldn't shake it from me. It made me feel justified in my terror, newly alive with fear, and also guilty for questioning how I was raised.

I wrapped my arms around my knees and bowed my head which muffled the sound of my sniffling. Allie had loved someone. Even if she had been confined to a room, people knew her before that. Jim and Cynthia were cruel, but they were not the only people who knew her. Jute had loved her. Her baby felt comfort in her arms. My heart ached at the thought of that love, something I doubted my parents had ever felt for me. All I had was Daddy and he hated me. My entire life of nearly sixteen years meant nothing to him, and meant little more to me.

I started to think maybe Daddy was right. Maybe I couldn't be saved. Maybe Satan lived in me and I would never be free. But if I could never be saved, why had Daddy kept trying? Why had he kept hitting me and cleansing me and casting out my demons if he had been convinced it was a waste of his time? Why had we kept performing the rituals to make my body holy if he knew I never could be? I feared he'd lock me away like Allie had been locked away. I feared, if ever I married, my husband would do the same. I couldn't find a single thread of hope in all those thoughts except for Jute. My mind latched onto her like a savior because of the feelings Allie had expressed for her. Surely if Allie felt hope in Jute, I could feel enough hope there, too. I needed only the smallest grasp onto goodness to keep me from losing my mind. Jute was it.

I knew I had days of isolation ahead of me. I could do nothing while in my room. But I also knew, one way or another, I was going to discover the truth.

9

December 25, 2006

It was Christmas morning. I stood at my bedroom window looking at boot-deep snow. I couldn't remember the last time, if ever in my life, it had snowed on Christmas. Ma would have loved it. I wondered what it must have been like for Daddy as he walked to the church at sunrise. All the beauty outside my window made my isolation feel even more ostracizing.

December twenty-fifth was also my birthday. I had turned sixteen. But the changes I felt inside of me had little to do with age. It had been two weeks since I had found Allie's letter. Since then, everything looked different to me. It had become more difficult to obey Daddy and I could no longer fade into the blackness when the pain came. My heart stirred with a new understanding of love, a sense of right and wrong and good and evil which had never been organically mine. Before, my mind repeated the laws set out for me and I forced myself to comply. But now my heart's voice spoke louder than my mind. They were at odds and I needed to figure out the truth.

The plan was to search Daddy's closet again. He had always left soon after his return from church. Every Christmas, he spent most of the day away. He never told me where he went and I certainly couldn't ask. When Ma was alive, he had left her with me to make sure I wouldn't leave my room. They considered it shameful to have been born the same day as Jesus. They felt my presence detracted from their prayers and devotionals. I spent my Christmases in silent prayer on my bedroom floor. But I had different plans this year.

When I heard the back door open, I shoved my thoughts away as if Daddy might hear them. I knew he wouldn't come to my room and he didn't. I stayed silent and listened to him move about the house. I heard him walk to the kitchen and move the water kettle around on the stove. He was probably making a cup of coffee. I heard the chair scrape on the hardwood floor and creak as Daddy sat in it. The more I listened in silence, the more anxious I became. I prayed to God for Daddy to hurry and go away.

I felt no shame at these thoughts, just fear and determination.

When the next sound of the sliding chair finally came, I exhaled in relief. But, I caught my breath again when I heard his footsteps walking toward my door.

"Perdy, I'm leaving. Today of all days, you are not to show your shameful face outside of this door. Don't make yourself worse in the eyes of the Lord. Your punishment will match the extent of your sin. Do you understand me?"

I put my hands together and brought them to my lips in pretend prayer as if he could see through the door. I wanted him to believe everything was normal. I said, "Yes, Daddy."

His footsteps got farther away until I heard the front door open. Soon his truck started with a rumble and a couple of loud pops like gunfire. He sat there, as always, letting the engine warm up. After a few revs, he backed up, turned around, and drove down the dirt road which led off the mountain.

As soon as the engine noise faded away into the distance, I jumped out of bed. I didn't even change out of my nightgown. I just ran straight into Daddy's room.

The first place I looked was the top of the closet where there were more boxes. I pulled down the small hatbox. I looked inside it this time but there was only a hat. I turned it over and saw nothing inside the hat and nothing else in the box. I tossed it on the bed and grabbed the larger hatbox. I already knew what was in it, so I sat it on the bed as well. There was a metal box that looked like a small toolbox. It was heavy. I nearly dropped it trying to get it down. I set it on the bed by the hatboxes and opened it up. There was a handgun inside, a small box of bullets, four old pocketknives, and some coins. The contents smelled like dirty feet. I wrinkled my nose and shut the lid.

There were two shoe boxes stacked in the back corner. I dragged a chair in from the kitchen and climbed up to reach them. The first one felt like it had shoes in it. I took the lid off and saw Daddy's brown dress shoes, which I had never seen him wear. Maybe he had been saving them for his burial. I tossed that box down from where I stood.

The last box had been for womens shoes. It was full of papers. Some looked like official documents, and others looked like scraps of paper with curly or jagged writing on them. My heart pounded at the sight. A smile stretched across my face. There was a foreign joy in my heart. Tears made everything a blur. I laughed, marveling at the unusual emotions I felt.

I pushed the other boxes aside and climbed onto the bed. With all the care I might have given an infant, I held the box in my lap. I gently removed the lid again and placed it beside me. One by one I picked up paper after paper, trying to discern what it was, why and how it came to be.

The first paper was Ma's death certificate. There were also notes from Ms. Thorneagle, recipes, and instructions. Beneath those was a clipping from a newspaper. In the first paragraph, I saw the name Allie Billings and my head felt light and dizzy. My eyes skimmed over it randomly, afraid that really reading it would be too much. The last name alone meant that it was no accident Daddy had her things. Finally, I was able to read it, all of it. Jim Billings shot and murdered Allie in a place named Nashville, Tennessee. Jute Duren was also shot and in serious condition. The article did not mention Allie's relationship with Jute, or that she had gone there to get away from Jim. But, I knew it was true. I knew what that news clipping didn't say. When I read that a baby was taken into custody, I realized there were also things I didn't know. If Gabriel survived, what happened to him?

My urgency to find Jute grew tenfold.

I placed the clipping onto the stack of papers I had already gone through. I picked up the next, a note. It was wrinkled as if it had been wadded up and then straightened out again. The handwriting was loopy and hard to read. I put it to the side and choose the next one, hoping to get through as many as I could. It was a birth certificate. Gabriel James Billings. Mother: Allison Leona Vining. Father: James "Jim" Silas Billings. Gabriel was born December 25, 1990, the same day I was born.

Time seemed to stop as I stared at the date. Emotions ran through me too fast to register them all. I felt sorry for Gabriel. Being born on Christmas seemed especially damning to him with his mother and father both dead. I also felt bad for Allie. It couldn't have been considered any holier for her to have given birth on that day. I was sad for them. But I couldn't help feeling less alone in my own situation. Gabriel and I shared a birthday. That had to mean something.

The next paper was a list of first names. It seemed that someone had added the names over time using different pens, different colors of ink. Some I could make out, others I couldn't, mostly I just scanned the list for my name. It wasn't there, but at the very bottom of the list were the names Allie and Jim. Gabriel's name wasn't there, either. I wanted to know what happened to him. The excited feeling I had earlier sank like a stone into the pit of my stomach.

All the papers remaining in the box were old, older than I was. Why was there no mention of me? Daddy had a birth certificate for a child he had never talked about. He had letters from Allie. None of these people had been mentioned in my presence. Why? Why was I nowhere in the box of papers? Nothing mentioned the name Perdy. I picked up each piece of paper one after the other, faster and faster, confirming that I had never mattered at all. Tears streamed down my face as I threw handfuls of papers back into the box, not caring that they weren't in order. I was screaming at the box louder than I had ever screamed at anything, "I am here! I have been here sixteen years!

Do I not even deserve a record of my name?"

My screaming was what kept me from hearing the stomping of boots on the porch. It wasn't until the door swung open and the winter wind whipped snow into the trailer that I realized he was home. I saw him before he saw me. There was blood on Daddy's forehead over his right eye. He must have been in an accident. He caught sight of me out of the corner of that eye and turned his head in my direction. His mouth dropped open in shock before it closed up tight with rage.

10

Daddy stepped into the room. I grabbed for something, anything, to cover my face. All I caught hold of was the bedspread and a few papers. I yanked it all up too late to block the back of his hand slapping across my cheek. The force knocked me onto my side and I hit my head on the metal box with the gun inside. I had forgotten about it, but now I was terrified he would see it and he would kill me. I shoved it off the bed and heard it land with a loud thud.

Daddy was on his knees on the bed. He grabbed my arm and yanked me around to face him. "These are not your things! They are mine and you are mine!" He was screaming at me, squeezing his fingertips into my arms. His eyes were wild with rage. "I should've smashed your head in with a rock the day you showed up here. I would have ended the curse of your mama's sins. She seeded you with evil! Esther didn't see it then, but she should see you now!"

His anger seemed monstrous. He expected me to repent as I always had; the words had been memorized by the time I turned six. But now I couldn't speak them. No sound would come out of me. I watched the rage building as he waited for the words I couldn't say. Only seconds after my eyes looked away, his other hand came down across my cheek. I looked back at his eyes, they were still hard but had grown distant. When his mind registered that I was refusing to divert my eyes, he no longer fought to control his fury.

His fists came down on my face one after the other, so quickly that I barely had time in between to form a thought. The only thought that came was that he was going to kill me. I tried to turn away, finally getting my body on its side. His fists hit my ear, the back of my head, my shoulders. There was a whirring in my head like a tornado. Behind my eyelids, flashes of light danced with every punch. I remained still, hoping he would think I was already dead. He finally stopped hitting me.

My ankles were gripped by his hands. He pulled my legs straight toward the foot of the bed. His hand ripped the seam of my nightgown from the hem to under my arm. He yanked it to rip it completely off, but it hung around my neck like a noose. I rolled toward the force to keep it from strangling me. I ended up lying flat on the bed, face down, with my head toward him. In this position, my nightgown was pulled completely off. I lied there looking at his wet shoes.

"Daddy," I said through my throbbing and bleeding lips, the taste of blood like the metal of the gun box. "Please don't."

"What did you say to me?" His voice bellowed.

I didn't repeat it because what I had said was dangerous. What I had said would only increase my punishment. But so would my refusal to answer his question.

"Answer me, you dog! What did you say to me?"

I stayed motionless, not speaking.

His voice boomed as if he was standing behind the pulpit addressing Satan himself. "God is nowhere inside you! A demon's teeth clutches your soul! I warned Esther. I said you would bring evil to this house, but she begged to keep you alive because of that damned name your mother gave you. I will tell you the truth so you can take it to your grave. Your mother was a whore. My son married your whore mother, but you are not his child. You are Satan's child, like all females. You tempt men to do evil, damn them to Hell, destroy their souls. You were supposed to have been killed at birth. But Satan whispered your name in your whore mother's ear. When they brought you here, Esther found you. I would have crushed your tiny bones and buried you in the woods. But Esther saw your name, the same name she had named every daughter she believed died being born, but the truth is that I killed every one of them. Women are only good for birthing sons, and we didn't need no other women here but Esther. But she believed God sent you as a reward for her righteousness. I told her you were evil. I beat her nearly to death to get to you. But I couldn't kill my wife, so I gave in, let her keep you. Jim should have killed you himself instead of having Cynthia bring you here! But now, Angelina," He said my real name in a high pitched taunt, "I'm going to do what I should have done long ago!" He threw back his head and laughed, "See how it is, girl… I see through your skin. I see inside you, Angelina. I know the Devil's in there. And I'm going to rip him out slow and use the power of God Almighty to crush him back into the earth!"

I had never been called Angelina before. Ma had said my name was Perdy because I was the prettiest thing she had ever seen. She had warned me that beauty was dangerous, Satan loved pretty girls best. She had said I should be extra vigilant not to show off. All my life I had been warned to keep the devil away. I had done everything they said. I trusted they were honest and only wanted to keep me safe. But, even my name was a lie. I was not even theirs. My mind took inventory of the few truths I now knew. I was Allie's child, a twin, an orphan.

The sound of a belt being unbuckled interrupted my thoughts. I began to sob, not in fear of the pain to come, but because my entire life had been a lie. I sobbed knowing it would only enrage him further, but I almost wanted to die. The only person to ever want me had been Esther. Yet, she had never told me the truth. I wondered if Allie had known the truth, or if she had assumed I was born dead. I felt certain she could not have known about me or she would have mentioned me to in the letter. I let that thought resonate; my mother had never even known I existed. My heart felt ripped out and I couldn't stop my display of misery.

"I will enjoy this," he spoke through clenched teeth as his belt came down on my back. Usually, the first strike of his belt stung the worst. My skin always went numb eventually. Usually, I blacked out before it did. But this time I wanted to feel the pain, I wanted it to stop my heart. So, I let my mind stay present. I forced my eyes open, staring off the bed and down at his shoes. Beside them laid the crinkled strip of paper with beautiful writing. The ink was smudged with melting snow. I focused on it until I could make out the words. The note said, "*Her name is Angelina. I'll leave her here. If you find her alive, please finish. I can't. - Cynthia*".

The lashes of the belt were not numbing me. He had turned the belt so the buckle would rip my skin. The force he was using would leave scars. I expected the belt would break, or I would. I marveled at the force he was using as if I stood separate from myself, my body belonged to a girl I didn't know.

I thought of Allie's letter to Jute and how my name was absent from it. I remembered the rush I had felt after reading it, how desperately I had wanted to find Jute. I knew I couldn't simultaneously be called by God to get the letter to Jute, and be expected to serve my father. Now, I had no father in which to serve. With that thought, I realized my life had a divine purpose. If I was part of God's plan, then that meant Silas was the evil one. Rage exploded inside of me. I scrambled away from him and fell onto the floor. I rolled under the bed as he dived across it to reach me. As I stood up on the opposite side, I heard him trying to open the gun box. I ran to the door and picked up the heavy cast iron doorstop. Within seconds, I stood over him, straddling him. He jerked his head around and saw me just before I slammed the black iron into the wound over his right eye. I heard a crack and watched the blood pour out of his head like a pot boiling over.

I stood up straight and backed away, not wanting his blood to stain me. I felt repulsed by him and the thoughts of all he had done to me, all he had lied about. It was his blood, not mine, which had been unholy. He was the one filled with Satan, but it ran from him now.

"In Jesus' name, amen."

11

The documents were gathered together, tied with string, and placed into a large leather shoulder bag. I had packed two of Esther's nicest dresses, a pair of dress shoes, and the best underthings she had. Nothing was without stains, but it would have to do. A pang of sadness washed over me every time I looked at her things and thought of her. What I had believed about her all of my life was a lie. My memories of her were nearly worthless. I could no longer think of her as Ma, nor as honest.

My hair was braided and pinned to the top of my head under the blue fedora. I hadn't wanted to carry the hatbox, so I only chose one hat to wear. I had Allie's letter tucked inside the ribbon hatband where I had found it. I tugged the hat low so the winter wind wouldn't blow it loose. A pair of Silas's pants were pulled up beneath the skirt of my work dress for extra warmth. A strip of cloth was tied through the belt loops to hold them up. His boots were laced up over two pairs of socks on my feet. Esther's blue sweater was added for warmth over the dress and I hoped the blood from my back would not soak through onto it. Lastly, I put my arms into Ma's heavy wool dress coat. A pair of her church gloves were in the pockets, but I pushed my hands into thick work gloves instead.

When I turned the door knob, the door resisted. I gave it a kick and the ice broke loose from the outside. I stepped out into at least six inches of snow. The sun was high in the clear blue sky overhead. The winter storm had clearly blown east, but it had left behind a mess for me to walk through. My feet sank into the top layer of soft snow before they crunched through an underlying layer of ice on the blades of grass. Where the sun shone directly, the snow shimmered beautifully.

The first place I went was to the chicken coops. I opened their doors and scattered feed on the ground. I left the doors open so they could return if they wished. I knew a few would most likely become prey before the night had passed. But it was better than leaving them to starve to death in a cage. I left them and walked toward the church, thinking of my earlier wish to do that very thing. If I had known what would have transpired to make the wish possible, I wouldn't have wished it at all.

I had never been into the mountain beyond the church. I remembered Esther mentioning an abandoned train track up that way. She had been talking about her sisters loving to watch the trains go by her house when she was a little girl. She had said, "Now all I have is that old abandoned track up over the ridge." I hoped I could find it and follow it, wherever it would lead. It was a better option than the road. I didn't want anyone to see me and ask about my face or trace me back to the trailer and discover what I had done to Silas. I never wanted to think about that place again.

No one knew I existed except Ms. Thorneagle. I wasn't sure how much of my story she knew. Maybe I could have gone to her and she would have given me all the answers I needed. But I didn't trust her. She was a friend to liars.

Lies. I felt them on me like a cross I was dragging up the mountainside. My whole life had been lies. I thought of all the things I had believed. I had believed Daddy and Ma were good. I had believed I was evil. I had believed Jesus was the son of God. I had believed I must obey the Bible or be condemned to Hell. There had been so many rules for me to follow and I had become proud of my ability to follow them. But things had changed. I was afraid to believe any of it. The only thing I had faith in was that I was meant to get the letter to Jute. Whatever else there might be to believe, I couldn't be sure until I got to her.

My feet kept moving up the mountain, but I didn't know

where I was going. I knew I was headed west, but I didn't know if west was the right direction I needed to go. The news clipping said Jute was in Nashville, Tennessee. I had seen maps in the Bible, but couldn't recall seeing Tennessee on any of them. Even if I had known how to get to Tennessee, I couldn't be sure Jute would even still be there. The news article had been written nearly sixteen years earlier. I reasoned that even if I had no hope of ever finding her, just getting far away from Silas's body was enough to keep me walking.

The train track led southwest across a number of small roads and passed a few houses. After five hours, the sun began to set and turned the sky amber. No one had seen me; or if they had, they hadn't made it known. Through the day, the sunlight on the dark wool coat had helped me tolerate the cold wind. But as the tall shadows grew longer, I knew the snow would soon freeze over with a layer of ice. As the light faded, my feet moved more swiftly and my eyes struggled to discern the old train track from wild animal trails. I wished I knew if I was headed in the right direction, or how much further I needed to go.

Darkness came as the sun dipped behind the mountain tops. The small slice of moon did not shed enough light for me to see the woods around me. Within minutes of nightfall, I sensed I had gone off the tracks. Branches seemed to be closing in around. I started to panic. I walked faster, dodging larger and larger branches, trying to find a place I could be sure was the path. The leather bag slammed against trees as I ran. I thought, if I could just get back to the track, I would rest for the night. I vowed not to risk losing my way again.

It was with thoughts of eventually sleeping under a large dense pine that I felt my foot step too low. It landed down an embankment, pulling all of me with it. I slid, clinging to my hat, trying to dig in my heels where there was nothing in which to dig. I then fell briefly through the air before landing face down on hard flat rock. I hadn't fallen far, but I was disoriented. I slowly started to push myself up from the rock when bright light filled the space around me. Blinded for a moment, I thought that it was God. But I registered the sound of a motor just before the sound of squealing tires. I realized I was in the middle of a road. I scrambled to the other side of and landed face down by a guardrail. The truck skidded to a stop a few feet away in a bank of snow on the other side of the road.

I heard a door slam and his voice filled up the night. "Oh, shit! Ma'am? Oh, shit! Are you...? Oh, shit!"

He was walking toward me, but I could only make out his silhouette against the headlights of his truck. Parts of the dense woods and the road were lit up like day. The snow ran in lines on the road, melted where tires had traveled. The closer he came, the more my eyes adjusted until I could make out his cowboy hat and heavy denim jacket. I wasn't sure if I should keep looking at him but I couldn't stop myself.

He fell to his knees beside me and grabbed my shoulders. His face was puckered in repulsion at the sight of me, but his pale eyes seemed kind as he glanced over my injuries. Yellow curls peaked out from under his hat. He looked like the angel in the painting over Esther's bed, only grown up. He shook me a little. "Are you okay, lady? Oh my God, did I hit you? It didn't feel like I hit you. Did I? Oh, God. Can you move?"

I sat up, unharmed from the fall except for bruises on my knees and elbows. He stared at me, waiting for an answer. His eyes held so much pain. It seemed to be all he could do to keep looking at my face. I was too mesmerized to say anything. I had never before known anyone to be so concerned for me. I smiled as wide as my cracked lip would allow. A handsome man knew I existed.

Part Two

John

12

Two Days before Christmas
December 23, 2006

A lady was crying in the kitchen. "Oh, Ms. Jute, he was so cruel to Hannah. I haven't told anyone..."

I put my pillow over my head and rolled over to face the wall. I needed to think of something to get me out of that depressing house for the day. Courtney. That's what I wanted to think about. Maybe Mom would let her come over and we could walk up to Dads' for a movie.

My mind tumbled into my memories of her. Every image was filled with soft skin, yellow hair, and green eyes so big that I couldn't escape their gravity. My body agreed that seeing her was a must. I sighed with frustration and hugged the pillow tighter.

"John!" Mom called through the door as her knuckles tapped against it. The door swung open before I could answer. I threw the pillow over my lap and sat up.

"Mom! Don't just barge in here!"

"I knocked," she shrugged, "And you shouldn't sleep naked. What if there's a fire?"

I didn't bother to answer because she said that same thing every morning. I just said, "It's Saturday, and way too early for you to wake me up."

"It's noon. And I need you to clean out the attic room for your sister. She's moving up here to go to Vanderbilt. We have to have that room cleared by tonight and you know I can't lift that stuff." Mom had an old injury which had never healed right. At least, that was her excuse for why I had to do everything.

"Why do you and Dads call Iris my sister when she isn't?"

"She is your dad's husband's daughter, so close enough. Besides, you argue just like siblings."

"See, there you are, calling Dawson Dad's husband when you know they aren't married."

Her lips pressed together in annoyance. I knew I was close to crossing a line. She said, "The fact that they aren't married has everything to do with the law and nothing to do with their situation. They've been living together for longer than you've been alive, and you've called both Tracy and Dawson Dad since you could talk. I'm not in the frame of mind to be messed with, John. We have guests. So, just help me out and take the stuff from the attic to the barn."

"All the way to the barn!? Can I at least pull the wagon on the back of the tractor?"

She crossed her good left arm over to hold the elbow of her bad arm. She squinted and shook her head at me like I couldn't be serious. "It's a couple of boxes. I think you can just load it into the truck and drive it through the field."

"Fine. But, if I do it, can Courtney come over and watch a movie at Dads'?"

"There isn't an *if*. You are going to do it. Why don't you invite her to help you? Hard work might do that girl some good." She was messing with me. I intended to reciprocate.

"Inviting her to hang out here might ruin our vibe. Too many crying women around." I laughed, but stopped when I saw that look in Mom's eyes.

"You know, I think the problem is that your 'vibe' isn't ruined nearly enough. So why don't you start clearing the attic by yourself while I think of some other chores to help put your misery in perspective."

"Mom!"

"You're nearly sixteen, not ten. Stop whining and help out."

She turned and left, gently closing the door so not to alarm her guests. Everything was always about her guests. We couldn't be too loud. We couldn't raise our voices when we argued. She had even started sending me to the big house with a babysitter if a guest was particularly uncomfortable with me being in the farmhouse with them.

I would have liked to have a normal life, just for a while if not forever. Many times I wished for my parents to actually live together, not just on the same farm but actually in the same house like when I was six. But when they bought this place, everyone decided that I needed to stay mostly with Mom because my Dad Tracy was out of town a lot on tour with his band and Dawson worked at night. So, I didn't get to stay in the all-guy house with the swimming pool, mini theater, and ten bedrooms. I stayed mostly with mom in the all-girl Victorian house with the endless supply of crying. Secretly, there were times I thought the house was kind of awesome because it was a hundred years old with lots of hidden nooks. It would have been much better if it had been a home for just our family and not the 24/7 abuse shelter Mom had turned it into.

I wondered why Iris was staying at Mom's and not with Dads. Usually when she came from Florida for summer visits, she stayed at the big house. When she was younger, they had hired a babysitter to stay with her while Dawson worked. But she was nineteen now, so no one cared if she stayed up there alone. I wished she would.

Ready to get the day over with, I went to my closet and pulled a random green t-shirt on over my head. It was tight on my chest and that made me happy. Helping Ellis, the man who leased our farm so it would actually be used, had it's benefits. I had started helping him clean stables and cut hay in October. Two months later I needed new shirts. Hell, yeah!

I glanced in the dresser mirror and moved my hair around with my fingers. A couple of times each year I was allowed to go to events with Dad. While there, his stylist would cut my hair. I tried to keep it the same style. But it always ended up looking too long to be short and too short to be long, hanging down in my face all the time. I pushed it to the side above my eyes and wished my hair was like dad's, dark and curly. But, I had unremarkable pale brown hair like Mom's. Thankfully, the sun had lightened it some over the summer, but it was starting to look dull again. And then there was the issue of my round face, Mom's genes again. Of course, having a face like Dad's wouldn't have been any more masculine. I just wanted to lose my baby cheeks sometime before I turned fifty. I shook my head and watched my hair move loosely back into my face. I had no idea why Courtney liked me, but damn, I wasn't going to question it.

"Hey, Mom!" I called as I headed downstairs. "I'm walking up to Dads' to get the truck."

"Shhh!" She called from behind a closed door somewhere downstairs, probably the counseling room.

I stepped into the hallway and turned right to see a little girl looking up at me. Only because I had just been thinking about it, I noticed her hair was mousy brown like mine. Her mother walked up and took her by the arm. She pulled her away from me, saying nothing, looking at the floor. They were all aware I lived there, but none of them wanted to look me in the eyes.

13

The sun was lost somewhere above the dirty gray sky. Everything on the farm looked dreary despite the overabundance of pine branch wreaths and garland. Red bows had been hung everywhere, thanks to Aunt Drew. She decorated the farm house every winter because she knew no one else would. The last few years, she had brought Devon. He and I would climb the ladders and hang wreaths from the windows as Mom paced around below. She complained to Aunt Drew that none of it was necessary or worth risking our lives over. That was my favorite part of doing it, seeing Mom worked up and worried about me. A long time ago it used to upset me that Mom never wanted to put up a Christmas tree or decorate. She stayed mad all through winter, yet somehow kept it from her guests. She really cared about them and it showed. I had seen her go from sobbing one minute to smiling the next just so they wouldn't see it. But she never did that for me. She would scream at me any time and for no reason.

Summers were different. She worked in the garden a lot and I believed working with plants made her happier. I think that's why Aunt Drew brought up all the greenery for the Holidays. She wanted Mom to be surrounded by green, hoping it would cheer her up. But I had stopped trying to make her happy a long time ago. I didn't think there was anything in the world that could have made Mom happy.

A gust of wind snapped me out of my thoughts. I wanted a heavier jacket, but not enough to go back to the house to get one. The cold air was worse walking up through the open field which faced west. I shoved my hands in my jean pockets and went back to thinking. I had two more weeks until school started back up. I thought maybe I could look for a job to get away from home for a while. Not that I didn't like helping Ellis, and he did actually pay me. But, I didn't want to say I was a farmhand. I thought about one day working for Dad, going on the road and keeping groupies off the stage. I flexed my arm muscles and felt pretty good until I saw Dawson coming out of the big house. Compared to him, I was a runt. The guy was huge, and he looked even bigger in his police uniform.

"Dad!" I yelled up to him. He looked down across the field and saw me walking up the trail. He waved with his huge brown arm swaying back and forth. I wanted my arms to be like that, the kind of arms girls would notice. I didn't know how someone like Dawson could have helped create a daughter as small as Iris. She was like a pixie and he was a giant. I called out, "I'm getting the truck!"

He was tactful enough not to yell back across the field. He waited for me to get closer.

When I had made it to the short iron gate, I reached over and unlatch it, making sure Montgomery didn't run out. He was their beagle. If they didn't keep him in the gate, he would run off into the woods chasing squirrels and not come back for days. He must have heard the sound of the latch, because he ran from around the house barking like mad.

"It's me, Monty, hush!"

"Hushit!" Dawson yelled from the porch, no longer caring about tact. "Monty, hushit!"

I guess Monty knew what hushit meant because he stopped barking and ran up to Dawson wagging his tail. Dawson got down on one knee to pet Monty quickly and all over like he was an automatic, dog petting machine. "Good boy, Montgomery. Don't you bark at John."

He stopped petting him long enough to give me that fatherly look that asks if everything is okay with me. He looked tired and I couldn't tell if he was just waking up to go to work or if he hadn't gone to bed yet. "You got big plans, big man?" He smiled at me and winked.

"If cleaning out Mom's junk from the attic so Iris can move in is considered big plans, then yes."

"Ah, Mommas. Tough love is their specialty. So Jute is cleaning out the attic, huh?" His eyes stopped looking at me and looked through me instead.

"I guess. She wants me to take the stuff to the barn. I haven't been up to the attic yet, though, so I don't know how much there is."

"Well, I'm surprised she's letting it go. But I guess it's time."

I shrugged, not really caring about a bunch of woman junk she had hoarded up. I didn't see how moving something to the barn equaled letting it go.

I changed the subject, "So, why isn't Iris staying up here with you?"

Dawson took a deep breath and exhaled with a shake of his head. "She's staying where she wants to stay. You know how we do things here. Everyone has a right to their choices and to be where they're comfortable, especially when they are adults. She likes being around Jute and the women at the shelter. I can't take that personally."

I hadn't considered that it would hurt Dawson's feelings that Iris chose to stay with Mom. I had only considered that I didn't want her down there and couldn't understand why she wanted to be around all that crying. She could have been up at the big house watching movies, swimming, or sitting up on the very top balcony watching the hawks fly along the mountain tops. That alone was proof that Iris was not normal.

"Have you heard from Dad?" It was back to our usual small talk. Dad had been on tour since August. I had stopped keeping track of his exact itinerary.

"He just left Christchurch and should be in Tokyo before the sun goes down on Nashville. He will be here on Christmas, though. I expect him home around noon. Then he'll leave again on Wednesday." Dawson's eyes looked even more tired. When Dad was gone, he missed him. As much money as Dad made, Dawson could have quit the police force and gone with him. He would have made an excellent bodyguard. But Dawson seemed to prefer having a normal life and keeping to himself.

"I don't know why he couldn't schedule the whole week here," I complained.

Dawson wrapped his arms around me and I felt like a little kid, but I let him hug me. I hated to admit that I needed it, but Dawson always knew when I did. I figured he probably needed it just as much as I did so I put my arms up and patted his back. There weren't many people who accepted or even understood our family structure. I had two dads and a mom, Aunt Drew and my cousin Devon, and Iris was Dawson's daughter which made her my... something. I always thought of her as my sister, and around my family, that pretty much made her my sister.

They had decided I should go to a private school because they believed it would lessen the inevitable bullying that came with having two dads. They probably still thought they were right. But, I didn't tell them what kids at that private school had been saying about Dads or my "crazy mom". There were some things my parents were better off not knowing.

We let go of each other. I didn't look at him because I had tears in our eyes.

"I was going to make an omelet, do you want one?" He asked, already turning to walk in the house.

"No, I need to get that work finished so I can sweet talk mom into letting Courtney come over."

"Courtney still, huh? She seems like a nice girl."

I laughed because sometimes Dawson sounded a lot like Mom. "She's hot." I said just to watch him give me the same look Mom does when I say it around her. Right on cue he raised his eyebrow. I laughed again.

Dawson said, "If you can't see her beyond her hotness, then maybe she's not the girl for you."

"Oh my God, we're not getting married, Dad! She's just a girl I like. You and Mom say the exact same shit."

He laughed then. "I'll take that as a compliment. You are lucky to have that Mom of yours. And all I'm going to say about your escapades with women is, always have their permission and always use protection. Now, if you don't want any more advice than that, you better grab the keys and get out of here."

I smiled and gave him another quick hug before running into the kitchen for the keys. I passed him again on my way back through the foyer.

"Slow down, that girl's not going anywhere!" He was laughing still as I opened and closed the door to the garage.

The truck was an avocado green 1974 Ford F-100 with rust on the fenders and a broken grill. It was simultaneously hideous and beautiful. I climbed in and hit the garage door opener. I heard the truck saying to me, "I hate it in this house, take me to the barn!"

"Yes, sir, Greenman. Let's hit it!" I said, because I sometimes gave nicknames to non-living things.

I slid the key in the ignition and the engine rattled into a purr. I backed the truck out and drove down the paved driveway until I reached the dirt entrance to the field. That was probably my favorite place on the farm to drive Greenman. The ruts were just big enough that if I hit them at just the right speed I'd be tossed around in the seat. It felt dangerous. I usually clung to the steering wheel and pretended not to be so scared. I wondered what Courtney would think of such a ride. I imagined her beautiful soft body bouncing around in the seat beside me and immediately tried to think of something else. I didn't want to arrive at the farmhouse with an erection. "Settle down", I said and adjusted my jeans.

The field exit was at the far end of our garden. There, I had to be more careful with my steering on the a narrow dirt road that curved around between the garden picket fence and the wire fence of the hay field. When I pulled the truck around to the front of the house, I saw Iris's purple Volkswagen Beetle parked in the driveway blocking my access to the front porch.

"Damn it!" I slapped the steering wheel. Mom was going to be mad that I wasn't finished cleaning out the attic before Iris showed up. And because of where Iris parked, I was going to have to walk twice as far to load the truck.

I yanked the parking brake and turned off the engine, leaving the keys dangling in the ignition. The old rusty door squeaked a little before loudly popping open. A few frightened faces looked out of the house windows.

The little girl I passed earlier was sitting on the porch swing. She was eating a sandwich that looked like cold cheese on bread. I remembered how her mother pulled her away from me like I was a monster. I forced myself to smile at her in a very non-monster way. She looked up at me, her eyes were happy as her mouth puckered in a fight to keep from grinning. She chewed while her lips stayed in that smile-resistant pucker. I considered that an improvement.

I stepped through the front door and called out, loud enough for mom to slap me if she had been standing there, "Iris Hathea Dawson, you are illegally parked! Move your damn car so I can clean out the junk in your room!"

14

Iris stormed from the kitchen with her mouth tight. I was laughing, but I had to catch my breath at her appearance. The last time I had seen her, her hair was in a million braids falling to her shoulders. But, now her hair was gone. Well, it wasn't gone. It was cut so short that her thick black hair seemed nothing more than a frame for her small pixie face. Her perfectly curved black eyebrows arched above her equally black eyes, pulling me straight into them. She was small, but she looked fierce. When the hell had that happened?

"Why are you coming in here yelling like you have lost your mind? This house don't revolve around you, John. You need to grow up and stop acting like a toddler wanting everyone to come look at him." Her lips relaxed then and her expression shifted to amusement. "Now, get over here and hug me before you get all mad."

I was already all mad, but I hugged her anyway and it halfway dissipated my anger.

"Why do you smell like onions?" I asked.

She shoved me out of the hug, "Mom and I are making sandwiches. You know how I eat mine. Do you want one?"

What I wanted was to remind her that she had a mom in Florida. She didn't need to claim mine, too. But, if she knew it bothered me, she'd have done it even more.

"Maybe a quick one," I said, "And then I have to clean out your room, which you should be doing anyway. But that's fine. I'll do it and then you can thank me by convincing mom to let my girlfriend come over."

She laughed in a high pitched giggle. "John's in love." She batted her eyelashes at me, then bent over snorting and clapping her hands to her knees. Women were weird. One minute they were crying their eyes out and the next they were laughing so hard they might pee. She straighted up and put her hand to her chest, "I can not wait to meet her. Does she have big hairy feet and horns on her head?" She bent over again, laughing until she had to sit down. I was pissed off for a second, but I could barely keep from laughing at the same time. I really didn't want to encourage her, so I stepped over her and pretended not to be amused.

Mom was in the kitchen spreading mustard on a piece of bread with a butter knife. I counted the sandwiches she had already made and felt confident that at least six women were staying with us at the moment, including Iris.

"I already made you a ham and tomato sandwich with pickles, mustard, and mayo. It's in the fridge. If you'd rather have something else, I'll eat that one and make you whatever you want."

Evidently in the world of sandwiches, I came first. I left that observation unspoken. Mom never liked my sarcasm when it was aimed at her.

"It's fine. Thanks, Mom."

I opened the fridge and pulled out the plate, carried it over to the bar and sat on a tall spinning stool. As I took my first bite, Iris walked back into the room. Her eyes were still lit up with joy or mischief, I wasn't sure which. She grabbed her plate from the table and brought it over beside mine. She silently slid into the stool next to me. Her mouth looked a lot like the little girl's, puckered to keep from grinning. I didn't even want to eat anymore.

Mom set two glasses on the bar in front of us, then filled them with milk like a waitress at a Denny's.

Iris said, "Mom, stop it. We're grown. We can get our own milk."

"John isn't grown. He's fifteen. He needs his mommy still."

She winked at me and my face blushed hot with embarrassment. I dropped my sandwich on my plate and left the room. I hated that fucking house full of annoying girls.

I should have gone to the attic, but I was too mad. I went to my room and fell face down on my bed. I reached for my iPod and played the Nitty Gritty Dirt Band song, Fishing in the Dark. I let my mind drift to Courtney, absolutely the only woman I wanted on my mind. I wondered if she had any idea how much I wanted her.

She had been to visit a couple of times. We had fished in the pond and taken a walk through the woods a few times. I had held her hand on the way back to the house and kissed her goodbye before she had left. She seemed to like it, but I wasn't the only guy after her. We weren't officially a couple, but I hoped to change that soon. I didn't want to push too hard and ruin my chances. I needed more time alone with her to see where things were headed.

The door swung open and Iris ran over and sat down on my back with her legs hanging off the side of the bed. She bounced a little to be even more annoying. She said, "Let's go, little bro. Help me move the heavy stuff and then you can ask over your girl. I already talked Mom into it. Thank me later." She hopped up and headed out my door. I heard her opening the door to the attic stairs, which was right beside my bedroom. Her footsteps were audible all the way up to the attic; I even heard her walking around above me. Great.

I sighed and tossed my iPod back onto the headboard shelf. I picked up my phone and texted Courtney. "Are you free this evening? We could look for mistletoe."

I slid my phone into my back pocket and headed up to the attic. As soon as I got to the top of the stairs, my phone vibrated. Courtney had already texted, "OK."

"Great!" I texted and said aloud at the same time.

"She coming over?" Iris asked from behind a small stack of boxes.

"Hell. Yes. Thank God, finally!"

"You mean, thank Iris. Now come over here and get these heavy ones and I'll carry the ones with clothes in them."

I walked over and lifted a box full of notebooks, probably Mom's old schoolwork. I put it onto my shoulder and felt my shirt sleeve tighten around my muscle. I thought it was coming along nicely.

"You better get that hair out of your eyes and carry that with two hands or you are going to fall down the steps and Mom will kill you if you aren't already dead."

"But, I have to build up my arms." I smiled at her and flexed the other arm.

"I am not impressed because you know who my Daddy is. So, put both of those toothpicks to use and be careful."

"Fine, but toss something else on top so I won't have to make so many trips."

She picked up an old hatbox and nestled it on top of the notebooks.

I made it to the truck without encountering any women and put the boxes in the back of the truck. I turned to see Iris walking out with a box of clothes. She said, "One more box of old records, a trash bag full of more clothes, and a box of your old toys. That's all that's left."

"Records, huh? I think I'll put those in my room. One more trip out should do it."

Iris nodded with excitement, but I couldn't see any reason for her to be. I followed her back in the house and up to the attic. As she reached down to pick up the bag of clothes, I asked, "Why do you want to live here?"

"Because it's real, John. Being in this place keeps me grounded. I don't want to forget what it means to be human."

"Watching women cry makes you feel human? How? I don't understand you girls."

She looked at me like I had just been diagnosed with a terminal illness. "John, don't be one of those men. I know I give you a lot of shit, but I've just been playing around. Right now, this is serious. How can you grow up around all this suffering and not feel humbled by it?"

"Because it is constant. Every fucking morning. Women crying. And everything I do has to revolve around them. No loud music. No loud voices. No loud sounds. I hate it here. I love helping Ellis because I can be loud and rude and he won't crumple into a soggy weeping heap on the ground. You'll see. When you move in here, you'll get sick of it."

She shook her head at me, pitying me. It made me angry. I didn't want to talk to her anymore. I picked up the box of my old toys and wasted no time getting to the truck with them. I made it back to the attic stairs before she had even come down stairs with the bag of clothes.

We passed again as I was coming out of my room from dropping off the box of records. She was carrying a broom and a dustpan. I gave her a sympathetic look, hoping to conveyed the same pity she had just put on me. Her eyes narrowed as she walked by. Her feet sounded heavy on the stairs as she stomped up to her new bedroom. If she was pissed, I had succeeded.

15

We had a horse barn, a barn that Ellis used for supplies, and another old tobacco barn we used for storage. The storage barn was the closest to the farmhouse. The damnedest things ended up in there. There was a small boat that would have sunk if we ever put it back in the pond. There was a stall with nothing but six antique doors leaned against the wall, three of which had busted boards. In another stall, there was a metal desk, cabinet drawers but no cabinet, and a few hat racks. That was the same room where Mom stored pumpkins and squash in a corner with a heap of straw around them. There were a few useful things in that barn like the rototiller, fishing poles, and a few hooks and string for hanging up whatever plant or vegetable needed drying. Oh, and there were cats. There were at least three lying around the barn at any given time, but I wasn't sure of the total number on the farm. They just showed up, Mom would catch them, have them spayed, and turn them loose hoping they would catch mice.

I looked around in the stalls. I wasn't sure where Mom wanted the boxes, but assumed she didn't want them on the dirt floor. I considered putting them in the loft that I once used as my clubhouse. That seemed sacrilegious. But, even as my mind reeled with protest, I knew that would be where I put them.

I pulled the bag of clothes out of the truck and heaved it up to the loft without climbing the old wooden ladder. I did the same with the hatbox. My old toys went in the stall with the broken doors. Two more boxes were left and I had to climb the ladder with those.

The box of clothes was lighter, so I got it first. Climbing up and seeing all my tattered hideout decor made me feel like I had lived a hundred years ago. How did I get from that little boy to the giant I felt like I was at the moment? The loft was open to the inside of the barn, but the outside wall had a small window to see out across the field. The glass was still intact inside the panes. I used to pretend to be a military guard and that window had been my lookout. Whenever I had spied Mom walking up the trail I climbed down so my clubhouse would stay a secret. She had been convinced I came to the barn to draw in the dirt with sticks, which was kind of true, just not entirely.

I was good at keeping secrets and I expected the same from my friends. I hadn't let anyone know about my clubhouse unless they passed the test. I would tell them which girl I liked at the moment. That had always been the one thing almost no kid could keep secret. If they told, it had almost always gotten back to me. If it hadn't come back to me in a couple of weeks, I knew the guy was trustworthy. Only three boys had passed that test, and only one of them was still my friend. That was Eugene Pickle, the most bullied boy in history. He was the only boy I still gave a rat's ass about and not because I pitied him. He had it rough, but not around me.

Lost in nostalgia, I sat at the edge of the loft and let my feet hang over the dirt floor below. I felt huge. I could have easily jumped from there and landed with ease. Just a few years before, jumping would have seemed like certain death to try. Unable to resist, my legs pushed off the wall below me and in mere seconds I landed on the dirt, dust flew up in a larger than expected cloud. Quickly, I got out of the barn and dusted off my jeans. By the time I had picked up the box of notebooks, the dust had settled.

Getting that box to the loft wasn't as easy. Despite the show I had put on at the house, the box was actually heavy. The ladder was nailed a bit too close to the wall, so there wasn't a lot of foot room. I balanced the box on my shoulder and turned a little sideways to make my way up. When I was high enough to be able to slide the box on the loft, I realized that I was holding it on the far side of my body and away from the loft. I laughed at myself for having made it harder than it needed to be. I was just glad Iris wasn't there watching me struggle with my coordination.

Finally, I just decided to twist and heave it onto the loft, hoping I wouldn't fall off the ladder in the process. No one was watching, so I even let out a "Huh-yah!" as I tossed it. I watched it flip on its side and slide all the way across the loft floor, leaving a line of notebooks like a trail of slug slime. That felt good. If I hadn't thought Mom cared about those notebooks, I'd have packed them back in the box and flung them across the room again.

I climbed all the way up and scooped the first few into my arms before sitting beside the box on the floor. I picked them up and tossed them in randomly, scooped up handfuls of loose papers and piled them on top. It wasn't until everything was back in the box and I had started to move it that something caught my eye.

There was a photograph peeking out from a notebook, stuck between the pages. I sat back down and pulled the photograph completely out. I had never seen the girl before. She had long brown hair and capacious blue eyes that seemed to suck me right into them, the kind of eyes I would have remembered. The longer I stared at her, the more I became convinced that I did remember her. But who was she?

I picked up a piece of lavender paper from the stack and saw that it was a poem written by Allie Vining in 1990. I grabbed another handful of papers, each of them was also a poem written by Allie Vining from around the same time. Most of the poems were about love, but a few were clearly about sex. She wrote very descriptively about the ways in which she had tried to please someone to no avail. I found myself wondering what kind of man would not be pleased by all the things she was writing about doing. I felt my face turning red and I knew I should not be going through Mom's stuff. But, I was liking what this Allie girl had to say about sex. I mean, it wasn't like I really understood what women wanted. So, it was educational and that made it okay to snoop, right?

The notebook on top was yellow. I start with it. Like the loose papers, everything in the notebook had been written by Allie Vining. Every single page had the date and time written at the bottom. Some of the poems were about her dog, Bonkers. A few entries were more like essays about her dreams, how she might become a better person, and how she wanted to be the perfect wife one day. Other pages had only one word written on them. Reading that stuff was like spying on the mind of girls. It was golden! And I couldn't put it down.

By the time I had made my way, in random order, to the fifth notebook, I started to realize that this Allie girl was into some not-even-playing-around trouble. Evidently, she felt guilty about something. She had written about deserving the "blade of his knife", and "my skin bleeds as does my heart for all the pain I cause you". I wanted to yell at her to stop being so fucking stupid. I picked up the picture again and looked at her and it hit me like a slap in the face that Allie was dead. I don't know how I knew it, but I was sure of it. Why else would Mom have had all her stuff? Maybe Allie had been a woman who came to the shelter and left stuff behind. But that happened a lot and Mom never kept anyone else's stuff. Allie Vining had to have been important to Mom.

I propped the photo up against the hatbox stacked against the back wall. I didn't know why I felt so upset. I picked up the next notebook on the stack, but let it fall back into the box when I heard the ladder creak under someone's weight. I broke out in a sweat of panic and started throwing notebooks back into the box. Before I could finish, I felt someone knock me over on my side. Courtney's blonde hair fell into my face and it smelled sweet like berries and vanilla. I rolled over on my back and she stretched out on top of me. It was quite an unexpected improvement.

She looked down with a mischievous grin. "Surprised?"

"In a good way, yeah!" I put my hands on her hips under her coat. She was warm and made me aware of how cold my hands had become. I grabbed the hem of her shiny pink coat and turned it around my hands to warm them faster. I kept my eyes glued to her face. She was heart-stopping beautiful. Her long blonde hair was held back in a sideways braid. The short holly branch clipped in her hair over her ear highlighted her huge green eyes. I was the luckiest guy in the world.

"Your mom said I could find you in the barn, in your clubhouse..." her eyebrows raised and she laughed loudly. "So, this is your little boy clubhouse, huh? No girls allowed?"

Maybe I wasn't so good at keeping secrets. "I guess I can make an exception for hot blondes."

"Hot, blondes, huh? Are you flirting with me?"

"If you don't want me to, I won't. But, if you don't get off of me soon then this might count as my first sexual experience. I'm seriously going to explode." My hands slid out from the folds of her coat to lift her hips off me. I was embarrassed by what was happening in my jeans.

She sat beside me on her knees. I watched her eying my body, satisfied with what she had caused. "Are you telling me John Duren, son of the sexy as Hell heartthrob Tracy Duren, is a sophomore in high school and has never had sex? Like, not even some girl's hand?"

She looked amused and painfully beautiful. I didn't answer her because I liked how she was looking at me and I didn't want it to stop. I smiled and raised my hand to touch her hair. She shook her head in disbelief then reached over and unbuttoned my pants. They popped open from the pressure and I was simultaneously relieved and terrified. I felt her hand slide in and her fingers wrap around me. I couldn't even breathe. I closed my eyes only because if I had kept looking at her it would have all ended sooner than I wanted.

"Impressive," she said. "Yours is probably the biggest at Wainwright Academy High, but I can't say for sure... I mean, I don't know about Eugene." She giggled. Despite my best effort, I couldn't find anything funny about it. I didn't know why she was talking that way.

"Eugene's alright," I said, opening my eyes again to see Courtney absently staring toward the window while her hand pulled and squeezed at me in a way that was uncannily similar to how I did it in the shower. When she looked down at me and saw my eyes were open again, her face went from indifference to a photogenic smile.

Her voice was full of forced cuteness, "Are you saying Eugene's cock is alright? Or Eugene himself? I wonder about you John, like maybe the gay rubbed off from your Dads or something. We've been exploring the woods…" she rolled her eyes at the phrase, "three times and you have yet to try to get in my pants."

I blinked as if doing so would clear the fog of my confusion. Her words became a slow echo of warped and droning sound. My head was swimming with disbelief and the word 'fuck' echoed through my brain until it found its way to the word 'her'. Fuck her.

I grabbed her by the wrist and pulled her hand off me. My body protested the halting of its pleasure, but I couldn't let it go on. What she said was total horse shit.

"What the fuck did you say about my Dads?" I let go of her wrist and stood up, turning away to zip my pants.

"Are you mad?" She asked defensively. I turned back around to see her sitting where she had been. She had a confused look on her, unable to find a problem with anything she had just said. I could still see her beauty, but it no longer captivated me. She said with a laugh, "Everybody jokes about it, John. It's just a joke!"

"So you aren't just a cock expert, now you are a comedian, too?" I ran my fingers through my hair to get it out of my face.

She stood up with a surprising lack of any sign of anger or embarrassment. I had once taken her lack of emotion to mean she was down-to-earth, just a country girl. But now I saw I was wrong. She was very matter of fact when she said, "No, John, your dad is the cock expert."

I shook my head, feeling sorry for her more than I had ever felt sorry for any of the women at Mom's house. I felt like a fool, ashamed for ever having liked her; but at lease I had answers.

She waited for me to say something, but I had no intention of doing so. I was just about to ask her to leave when she finally stood and said, "Well, I guess we won't be going up to your Dad's house and meeting any celebrities, huh? My friends said, 'If anyone can get us in, Courtney, it's you.' But they didn't know what a man-sized little boy you are, John. Just a damn loser. Good luck to you and Eugene." She kissed the air and turned to leave.

I heard her talking on her cell phone just beyond the barn door. "Hi, Mom. I'm leaving John's. I'm going by Ashley's now. I'll call you when I get there."

I had little doubt Courtney would start spreading rumors about me before she even left our driveway. But part of me didn't care. Mentally, I added her name to the long list of people who only see me as a way to get to Dad.

16

I chose a few notebooks I had yet to read and slipped Allie's photo into the inside pocket of one of them. I wanted to ask Iris if she knew anything about her, but I didn't want Mom to know. I couldn't explain why, other than my suspicion that Mom had a reason for not mentioning her.

I climbed into the Ford and tossed the notebooks on the seat beside me. I hesitated before starting the truck, not quite ready to face Dawson. I let my head fall back against the glass behind the seat. I was still pissed and a bit shaken about Courtney. I didn't want to be, but I was. She had made me feel so good, damn it. But it wasn't worth it. I sat up straight and turned the key. Just hearing the engine made me feel a little better. On the drive back through the field, I intentionally hit every rut I could find. Every time I bounced off my seat, I yelled out a different string of profanity. By the time I got to Dads' garage, I had invented a few new satisfying combinations.

The keys needed to go back to the kitchen. While I was there, I dropped the notebooks inside a plastic bag. I was tying it up when Dawson walked in, rubbing his eyes. He must have been asleep.

"Sorry, Dad. I didn't mean to wake you up."

"You didn't. The alarm did. I have to be at work in an hour." He yawned then smiled as if excited to be going to work.

"Well, thanks for letting me use the truck."

"It's yours whenever you want to use it." He walked past me to the coffee pot. "Oh, how did it go with Courtney?"

I tried not to sound annoyed by the question, "Terrible. She just wanted access."

He knew what I meant. We'd had similar conversations many times before. Even Mom had to deal with women pretending to need the shelter just to get close to Dad. Aunt Drew finally got that under control by only sending the worst and unquestionable cases to Mom.

Dawson bent his head and shook it in sympathy. "It's tough, man. I was hoping she liked you as much as you liked her. You're a great kid, John. You'll find the right one."

"It's no big deal. I mean Courtney Brendelson was just the most beautiful girl in the world." I laughed off my misfortune. "But she's pretty damn heartless, too."

He stepped over and wrapped his big arms around me. "That's how it is a lot of times, but not all the time. You know we love you." He let go of me and slapped my back a little too hard. "I have to go get ready. Give Iris my love when you see her. If either of you need anything else, just come get it. This is your house, too."

He smiled at me, waiting for it to sink in. I nodded, "I know, Dad. I love you both." Saying *I love you both* had become automatic over the years. Even when Tracy and Dawson weren't together, I thought of them as being connected all the time.

"Be safe." He turned and walked off through the foyer.

Outside, the sun was starting to set and the air was frosty. By the time I reached the farmhouse my fingers were getting numb from the cold. I entered the back door and walked down the hall to the stairs. No one was around. I assumed everyone was in the living room for a group session. It was the perfect time to talk to Iris.

I darted up to the attic and stood in awe at the sight of what she had done to the place. In so few hours, she had cleared away all the cobwebs and dust. It smelled like lemons and Murphy's Oil Soap, which triggered a memory I physically felt. Images played in my mind of us moving into the house years ago. I remembered how Mom and Aunt Drew had scrubbed every inch of the place while I unpacked my toys in my room.

Iris looked up from straightening the bedding on her antique wrought iron bed. The pieces to that bed had been leaning against the attic wall since we had moved. Now it had been put together near the back window. The sepia colored lace bedspread looked just as old as the bed, but I had never seen it before. It wasn't until she laughed at me that I realized my mouth was gaping open.

"I'll take that expression to mean you are shocked I could clean up this nasty place."

"I kind of expected you to throw a cot up here. I didn't know you were going for House Beautiful."

"Oh, John, really! It's a just an old bed. Stop gushing."

Despite her words, I could tell she was proud. I walked across the room, which seemed so much bigger after being cleaned, and touched the design of the iron headboard. The white paint had peeled in places leaving exposed areas of patina but it all felt worn smooth. "It's perfect. But how did you get the mattress up here by yourself?"

She stood up and put her hands on her hips. "The same way I picked your sleeping ass up off the lawn chair that one time and tossed you into the pool. Remember?" She grinned.

She was right, she had done that a couple of summers ago. "Well, I bet you couldn't do it now. Come on, pick me up!" I flexed my arm muscles.

She waved her hand like I was joking. "Why are you up here, anyway?" She feigned annoyance.

I tossed the bag onto her bed. She looked confused at the notebooks, "Weren't you supposed to take these out of here?"

"Yes, but I read a few. They're, uhm… interesting. Do you know anything about Allie Vining?"

Iris stiffened up a little. She bit her lip and tapped her finger on her cheek. It was obvious she knew something. Finally, she put her hand down, "You know, you should probably ask Dads."

"Why!?" My voice was just shy of yelling at her. "If you know, then why can't you tell me?"

She rolled her eyes and dropped to sit cross-legged on the

bed. She patted the spot opposite the bag of notebooks for me to sit there. When I did, she leaned in a little so I could hear her whispering, "Look, I was told not to talk about this at all. I mean, AT ALL. My mother used to go on tirades about this all the time." She paused to let that sink in. "She was still mad about Dad hooking up with your Dad because that proved he wasn't lying about being gay. She wanted our family like it was before. So, anything negative she could find to say about the situation, she let it fly. You know Mother can not hold her tongue."

I nodded. Thalia Dawson never hesitated to tell people if their food was overcooked or their shirt needed ironing. "So, Allie Vining had something to do with Dads?"

She looked pained at the thought of explaining it to me. "Allie Vining died the night Mom's arm was shot. Allie's husband shot them and killed himself afterward. Allie wasn't there in need of shelter that night. She was there because your Mom was her lover."

"No fucking way!"

Her hand slapped over my mouth and stayed there. Her dark eyes were wide with warning. "Shut up, John or I will yank out your tongue." She stared at the top of the stairs in silence. We both waited for any sign that Mom heard us, but she must have still been in the meeting.

"Listen, we can not talk about this around Mom. My dad forbid me from talking about it period. Why do you think Mom never got married, never dated, never had an interest in finding a partner? She loved Allie, John, she really loved her."

"Mom isn't like that, Iris. I just can't see it."

"You never knew her before, and I was just three years old when all that happened. But afterward, I remember being told to stay away from Jute and not go in her room. Mother acted like your mom wasn't stable, like she might molest me or beat me or something. Mother gave me every gory detail she knew to scare me. But, I loved your mom. I went around her anyway and I've always seen the hurt in her."

"How do you know she wasn't just upset because she was shot

and nearly killed?" Iris was making sense, but I didn't want to believe it. I had never seen Mom in a relationship, and I certainly couldn't imagine her with that beautiful girl in the photo.

"John, what is your middle name?" Iris crossed her arms and leaned back.

"Alvin...?" I watched her nodding at me as if in victory. "What does that have to do with anything? I'm named after John Lennon and Dave Alvin, two musicians. Mom likes one, Dad likes the other."

"No, you are named after Allie Vining because Mom loved her. *Loved her.* Is this getting through to you, yet?" Iris shook her head, ready to give up.

I was stunned. I had to believe it. I felt hurt and a little angry that no one had told me.

"So, why did Mom want this stuff taken to the barn if she loved this girl so much?"

"I guess because I'm in the attic. Do you think she wants this stuff up here for me to go through and start asking questions? I mean, I had no idea she had these."

Pangs of guilt ran through me. I wondered about the other things in the barn. "Do you think the clothes were Allie's?"

Iris shrugged, "Maybe, but Allie was only with Mom for less than an hour before her husband shot them. Mom hadn't even seen her in months before that. Dads say they broke up because Allie got religious and turned against Mom. Then Allie showed up one night here in Nashville with her baby. She'd been beaten pretty bad. Mom was with you and Allie's baby when she heard the first shot. You were just a few weeks old."

"So I was there?" A chill ran through me and I was embarrassed by it.

"My dad told me..." she gave me a stern look as if what she was about to say should never be repeated, "Social Services took Allie's baby into custody and Mom cried like someone took her own baby away."

"Where is it?" I was enthralled.

"Dad doesn't know. I think he would have told me if he did.

He made sure to satisfy every question I had so I wouldn't go ask your mom. Then he made me promise not to talk about it again, especially not in front of her."

"I hope the statute of limitations has run out on that promise because I don't think we have all the answers."

Iris sat up straight, pointed to herself, and shook her head. She wanted no part of it.

"Look, I'll leave a couple of notebooks with you and I'll take the rest. Read them tonight and then I dare you to say you don't want to know more about her."

"Her? You mean Allie? I thought you wanted to find the baby for Mom's sake, but this is about *her*?"

Her accusatory eyes moved from me to the bag on the bed. I could tell she was curious. Iris had always been nosy, of course she never saw it that way. She claimed she just liked to get to know people. I had to admit, I seldom heard her gossip or put people down. But, I had caught her in my room many times when she had no reason to be in there.

Without a word, she untied the bag and dumped everything out. The picture of Allie slid out of the notebook pocket. Iris picked it up and stared at it thoughtfully. She clicked her tongue, "That is one beautiful girl, John." She glanced at me warily. "Okay. But, if Mom finds out, I'm blaming all of this on you."

"Nothing new there," I laughed and winked at her.

17

December 24, 2006

My eyes sprang open. I had been dreaming. I tried to piece it all together. Allie's naked body had been lying in an open field, the sun had turned her skin bright pink. I knelt down to see if she was alive. I touched her eyelids and they opened. Her eyes were blue like the sky, pleading. I was terrified in the dream; but even after waking, my heart still raced. I thought of her body in the dream and blushed. She had been so beautiful, so fragile, and in so much pain. I felt ashamed of my physical response to seeing her. I told myself it wasn't really her, it was just a dream about a made up girl. I had no way of knowing what Allie's body had looked like.

I rolled onto my side and looked at the clock. It was 5:24 a.m., too late to go back to sleep, too early to get up. But, I got up anyway. I didn't want to risk having that dream again. I grabbed some random clothes and headed toward the bathroom for a shower. While in the hall, I smelled coffee brewing and figured Mom must have been up. Before I even made it into the bathroom, I heard her whisper behind me, "John? Why are you awake?"

I turned around to answer her, but I couldn't really find the words. I stared at her, trying to see what I had been missing. She was short, round faced, her hair disheveled and spiked every which way. I had never thought of her as attractive, never thought of her as someone's lover. She had always just been my mom and the woman who ran a women's shelter. But, now saw her as a woman who had watched someone she loved being killed. My back twitched just shy of a shiver.

She stepped closer and put her hand on my forehead. She gave me a worried look even though I didn't have a fever. She still kept her voice low, "You should come eat. I can scramble some eggs or make you toast if you want something lighter."

I just wanted to get in the shower, but I nodded my head because I wasn't finished looking at her. I had no idea who she was anymore.

Normally, she would have never let me out of my room wearing only pajama pants. But, she didn't say a word about it that morning as I followed her to the kitchen. Maybe she assumed no one else would be awake. But when I got to the kitchen, I saw that someone else was awake. Iris. We locked eyes briefly and she subtly shook her head left to right as a warning not to bring up last night's discussion. She cleared her throat and looked down into her coffee. "Morning, John." Her voice was muffled inside the cup. Her sip was louder than the words.

"Hey." I sat across the bar from her.

Mom poured some coffee into a pottery mug and set it in front of me. She eased onto the stool at the end of the bar and stared at me while I blew into my coffee. Finally she said, "Okay, I'm just going to say it. I talked to Dawson."

I glanced at her and quickly looked back to my coffee. I was fairly certain Dawson hadn't seen the notebooks, unless he had recognized them through the plastic bag. Even if he had, I didn't think he would have told her about it. But, I couldn't come up with any other reason for her to look at me with a mix of such worry and resignation. Finally she continued, "He told me about Courtney."

I glanced at Iris. She didn't look at me, but her eyebrow raised signaling her curiosity. The corner of her mouth turned up behind her coffee mug. My face grew hot. Mom said, "Dads and I were discussing that maybe it would be better for you, at this point in your life, to consider moving up on the hill with them."

"You say this now?" I slammed my mug down so hard my

coffee spilled. Iris gave me a full on glare of warning. I calmed my voice, "I mean, when I asked years ago, you said no. What changed?"

"Why are you getting upset? You've been begging to live there since they built it." She looked hurt and confused. "I just thought you might want to be around some guys to talk to about... guy things."

My face was on fire and I began to sweat with humiliation. "Just stop, Mom. I don't need to talk about... guy things." I mocked her tone at the end.

She sighed a tired sigh. I remembered again that Allie had loved her once. The notebooks I read through last night had been from the time Allie and Mom were together. They were pretty intense and would have been much better reading had they not been about my mother. I couldn't deal with the contradiction between Allie's Jute and my mom Jute.

Mom put her hands to her forehead and was rubbed in hard circles. "God, John, make up your mind. You are never happy with anything."

Iris spoke up, "Mom, I think John is trying to tell you he *is* happy. Here. With you." She touched Mom's arm. I was irritated by how easily Iris said the right thing.

"I'm going to take a shower," I grabbed my stack of clean clothes off the counter top and headed for the door. I was almost to the hall when I heard Mom putting my mug in the sink, which I should have done.

"Don't wake anybody," she said with a tired sigh.

18

It was only a little after six o'clock in the morning when I made my way up the stairs to Iris's room. I reached the top of the stairs and saw her standing in front of the dresser mirror holding earrings up to her ears. She was wearing a red sweater dress that looked like it was swallowing her up. She turned around with her hands on her hips, annoyed. "John Duren, you can not keep walking up here without knocking. I was getting dressed!"

"Oh!" I laughed. I felt a little embarrassed, but it was also funny. "So, how many times exactly have you gone into my room without knocking?"

"When you were *not there*, John! Really? It's entirely different. Look, just knock, okay?"

I channeled Mom's voice, "But, I might wake the guests."

Iris laughed. "Yeah, you might. We don't want Mom to yell at you." She mimicked Mom's worried voice even better than I had, "You are just never happy."

"Shut up. Let's talk about the notebooks before you piss me off."

"You mean you don't want to talk about 'guy things'?" She covered her mouth and giggled. I glared at her and felt my face get hot. "Oh, John. You know you're my favorite brother, right?" I was her only brother, and not even a real one.

She walked over to her desk and pulled out the wooden chair for me to sit. I sat facing the computer monitor and she stood over me as she wiggled the computer's mouse. The screen flashed on. A death certificate was already pulled up from an ancestry website.

"So, I did some research," she said. "It was worse than Dad told me. I found a news article about the murder-suicide. Allie's husband, Jim, had been trying to find her. He shot her mother in Felicity, Ohio before driving to Maryville, Tennessee to Allie's father's house." Iris pointed to a spot on a printed out map beside the keyboard. She had highlighted the route in yellow; her finger traced the lines. "But Allie had already left for Nashville when Jim got there. He murdered her dad, supposedly after getting Mom's address." Her finger tapped over Nashville.

I turned back to the document on the screen and asked, "So, how is Jim's death certificate going to answer anything?"

She grunted in annoyance before moving the mouse, "Because, right here is the name of Jim's parents. With this information, we can find out his closest relatives. One of them probably has the baby."

"You mean the 15 year old boy. Do you really think her son will even remember her?"

Arms crossed and mouth pulled sideways, she said, "Seriously? All Mom wanted was to know what happened to the baby, and you just want to know about the pretty girl?"

She was back on that again. Her words made me even angrier this time. I considered Courtney to be a 'pretty girl', and right at that moment it seemed wrong to use that term for Allie. It also bothered me that Iris assumed all I cared about were looks. If that were the case, I would have lost my virginity the day before with Courtney in the barn. Thinking about it made me cringe. "Do you honestly think I'm that kind of guy? Besides, Allie was born in the 70's and she is now dead. So, can we drop that line of attack, please?"

"Attack? Whoa. I am definitely not attacking you, John. Chill." She leaned back over to click a tab and bring a map into view. "So, to continue explaining what I spent hours last night finding out for you," she gave me a stern look, "The last known residence for Jim's parents, Silas and Esther Billings, is somewhere here." She pointed to the map in an area of eastern Kentucky so dense with mountains that there were no towns listed anywhere around it.

"How do you know that?" I felt torn between amazement and skepticism.

She zoomed in on the map and a town name popped up to the east of it, Riceville. There wasn't really a town. She said, "I know it because I looked up the address and there is only one Rock Biscuit Road in Kentucky, so I'm pretty confident this is the place."

"But there's not even a house." I took control of the mouse and zoomed in closer. The road wasn't even a road, just a yellow line the map service had drawn seemingly arbitrarily into the woods.

"There has to be a house because that's their last known address. It's probably under the trees or something." She turned to lean on the desk and looked at me with her arms folded in determination. "I think we should go."

"Go where?" I looked up at her in disbelief.

"To talk to them in Kentucky. We don't have to say who we are. We'll just pretend we're writing a book about the effects of murder-suicide on families. Maybe they'll tell us where the boy is. Or, maybe we'll luck up and he'll be there."

As off the wall and risky as that sounded, my instincts were to get in the truck and hit the road in that direction. I would have loved to go to Kentucky just to get the hell away from the farmhouse. But, I was reluctant to believe it would get us any more information. If it was so easy, Mom would have done it herself. I decided not to voice my skepticism.

"Okay, we'll go. But when? Today is Christmas Eve. Dad is coming in tomorrow. I don't think we'll be able to go until Wednesday."

Iris tapped her chin. Her fingernails were deep red like her dress. She must have just painted them. I considered that maybe freshly painted nails made girls tap stuff a lot. Finally she said, "Well, I'm okay with Wednesday. I just don't want anyone finding out about it before then. Are you sure you can keep a secret?"

"Oh, absolutely."

Part Three

Angelina

19

December 25, 2006

The inside of his truck smelled like a brand new pair of shoes. I wasn't sure if I liked it, the strong leather smell reminded me of Silas's belt. But the colored lights on the dash were nice.

He didn't say a lot at first, just grunted and said, "Shit!" a few times as he tried to get his truck out of the snowbank. When the truck finally broke loose, we slid in a reverse swish. I grabbed hold of the door as best I could, terrified we would skid right off the mountainside. He yelled, "Woo-boys!" Then he laughed as he moved the stick on the floor. We went forward, this time on the actual road.

It didn't take long for him to start talking.

"So what the hell happened to your face?"

I didn't say anything, terrified I'd say the wrong thing. I wasn't sure which of Silas's rules, if any, applied off the mountain. I was risking making this man angry by not answer him. When he didn't respond negatively to my silence, I thought it was a good plan to just keep my mouth shut entirely. I didn't want anyone tracing me back to Silas.

"Can't you talk?" I saw him glance at me, but I didn't want him to look at my face so I turned more toward the window. "I don't know what I should do with you; where were you going? Have you got kin around here? I can drop you off wherever you want as long as it's not past Louisville."

There wasn't anybody. I thought it, but I didn't say it.

He continued, this time more to himself, "Shit. You ain't talking. What the hell am I supposed to do? I can't put you out. I can't take you to my house. My Daddy'd shoot me for bringing you in, he ain't happy with anything I do. I go bringing you in he'd get his damn forty-five and I'd either be homeless or dead."

After a few more minutes of silence I felt the back of his hand gently slap my arm to get my attention. With instinctive fear, I jerked my head around to look at him, expecting a punch or a hard slap. I was sure my disrespect had pushed him too far. But he just scanned my face between turning his head to watch the road. He looked worried.

He asked, "Why are you looking at me like that? You think I was going to hit you? Is that what happened to your face? Somebody beat the shit out of you? Damn. Are you scared of me? Ain't nobody ever been scared of me. But, I know how you feel. My Daddy had me looking pretty close to how you look and Mommy wasn't any help. She'd say, 'Better get used to it Em, suck it up. You want to be a man, don't you?' No, I ain't going to hit you, let's just get that straight right now."

He spoke to me as if he cared what I thought and felt. It hurt deeply. His kindness only accentuated the pain I had endured my whole life. I didn't even know how to respond to him. I found myself crying with shame and frustration. I tried not to let him see it. My head stayed turned hard away from him as I held my breath, trying not to sniff. Finally I had to breathe and I did sniff, but I tried to make it sound like a regular sniff and not a crying sniff.

He kept filling up the silence, "My name's Emory. I should have said that already. I was coming back from Granny Talbert's.

She lives over in Williamson, West Virginia. You know that place?"

My tears kept falling as I listened. The truck was getting so warm and the night was so black. There was nothing to see but the road with patches of ice and snow and the lights on the dash. I listened, feeling a stab with each mention of something new, something I didn't know, places I had never been, and relationships I had never had. I reached up and pulled the brim of my hat low so he couldn't see my eyes.

He continued, "Williamson is just east of here. It ain't far from Louisville, really. But Daddy didn't want to see Granny Talbert. She's Mommy's granny, really my great-granny. She can't stand Daddy." He laughed to himself. "She's the only person in my family who actually likes me. Do you believe that?" He paused, and I assumed he had glanced at me for an answer which I didn't give.

"She's dying. They called us all to come but I'm the only one of us to go. Daddy, Mommy, my brothers all stayed in Louisville. I guess if it was me in Williamson dying, they'd have done the same."

Finally, he had said something I understood. No one would come to see me if I were dying, either.

We sat in silence for a long time. There was only the sound of an occasional sniff, this time from him. "I'm sorry," he said.

I looked over at him, wanting to touch him to comfort him. But I didn't dare because I didn't know how I should act around a man. I didn't believe anything Silas had said, but I had nothing else to go by. I kept staring at him, fighting an urge to reach out my hand for his. I hated being so ignorant. I should have known what to do. I should have known. But I knew nothing. Tears were coming, and even they were a mystery. I didn't know if I should push the hurt down, or let myself feel what I need to feel. I turned to look at the window and the reflection of the dashboard lights.

When the sound came, I jumped. Loud music filled the truck cab, but was quickly turned low enough not to hurt my ears. A man was singing a song about a girl, "I had my fingers in her hair under the light of the moon, I didn't know where we were headed, but I was getting there too soon." Thoughts of Jute and Allie came to mind. They were the only reference I had for romantic love. I reminded myself that I had to get the letter to Jute. To do that, I would need to speak, whether or not it broke Silas's rules for women. I worried I would say everything wrong and Emory would lash out at me for it. But I decided to get it over with.

I looked over to see him staring intently at the road. I gently cleared my throat to test my voice. In response, he turned down the radio. I asked, "Can you please drop me off in Nashville?"

His eyes stayed on the road as they squinted in confusion. "Nashville ain't near here. Are you telling me you were walking to Nashville? On Christmas night in the snow with your face beat to a pulp... to Nashville?" He glanced at me in disbelief.

I turned away from him again. Shame of my ignorance had reached an unbearable weight. I wasn't sure if I could ever again bring myself to speak to him.

"I'm sorry," he said, "Don't look back out your window. Talk to me. Are you a singer? You going to Nashville to sing, is that it?"

The bizarre question pulled me from my self-pity. I looked back at him and wiped my cheeks, flinching when my fingers touched the swollen bruises around my eyes. I probably looked like a monster. I wanted to convince him I wasn't. "Oh, I never sing. I have always tried to please God."

He laughed loudly and it hurt, but I didn't look away. Happiness was so beautiful and it was all over his face. His hand went up in dramatic disbelief, "Holy fuck! Why is this my life? What the hell are you talking about? Haven't you ever heard of gospel music? And I don't think there's a country singer alive that hasn't put out a gospel album. It's all Jesus and pearly gates and one Bible reference after another. I personally can't stand it. Just a bunch of hypocrites singing songs about the Prince of Peace while treating real people like trash. Bastards." His happiness left as dramatically as it had arrived.

The silence was heavy until he broke it, "I'm sorry. I feel like I'm saying everything wrong. I just don't really know what to make of this situation. Where did you come from? I mean, why were you in that road? Are you actually a ghost or an angel or some sign for me to change my ways?" He took his hand from the wheel and touched my arm. "You feel real. You look real. But you sure as hell don't sound real."

His words cut. "I just need to get to Nashville, that's all."

"Well, I can't take you to Nashville because I'm not going that far. I can take you to Louisville; but like I said, you can't come home with me. You got money?"

"No." I said. "But wherever you let me out, just point me toward Nashville and I will walk. I thank you so much, sir."

A less heavy silence filled the space between us. I watched the lights reflect on the road ahead. The landscape had flattened somewhat.

He exhaled. His voice became almost a whisper, "I don't want to get into your business. I don't like people in mine. I can tell by looking at you that you ain't asked for whatever happened to you. I know whatever you went through that put you on that road was much worse than any of my troubles. If you want to tell me, I'll be glad to listen. But I won't make you. That being said, I don't want to get my ass thrown in jail neither. So I need to know right now, are you running from the police?"

I pictured Silas's head broken open all over his bedroom floor, but then I reminded myself that no one knew I was alive except Ms. Thorneagle and she surely wouldn't yet know Silas had been killed. So, it was technically not a lie that I said, "No."

"Okay," he took in a breath and let it out. "I know someone you might be able to stay with for a day or two. If you want to wait, I'll try to see what I can do at work to get a day off and I'll drive you down to Nashville when I can. It takes three hours to drive it. I don't think you ought to try to walk it, especially by yourself."

His solution sounded perfect, except the part about staying with his friend. I was terrified of having to interact with yet another new person, someone much more knowledgeable about what to do and say than I was. I thought about leaving right then, but convinced myself I could walk away any time if things went badly.

"Thank you." I said.

"Her name is Marcy. She's cool, handles weird shit pretty well. I think she's seen just about everything. So don't be nervous."

Those words became a chant in my mind, don't be nervous, don't be nervous, don't be nervous.

Emory turned the radio back up a little. A woman was singing. Her voice was high and broken, I knew no other way to describe it. She sang like I imagined my heart would sing, "Heaven fell, under my feet, I'm stepping so light, you are breaking me slow…"

His voice interrupted, "You'll have to give me a name, even if it ain't yours. I need to call you something."

Instinctively I almost said Perdy, but I managed to get out the word, "Angelina".

He laughed again, and put his fingers to the brim of his cowboy hat. "Perfect. We'll go with that. Nice to meet you, Angelina."

20

Emory had stopped talking and seemed deep in thought. I watched the road and tried to make out the words to the songs on the radio. The volume was low enough that I could still here the faint thumping of the tires on the road. The heat was the warmest I had ever felt and I wanted to take my coat off, but I didn't dare. I rested my head against the window glass and before I knew it, I was asleep.

The next thing I felt was his hand shaking my arm. "Wake up. We're going across the bridge in three minutes."

I opened my eyes and blinked a few times. Lights were everywhere along the streets, in high buildings, and along the bridge. It took my breath away. I leaned forward to look higher and unhooked the seatbelt to look behind me.

"Hey, put that back on!" He reaching across me to grab the belt. I caught sight of his eyes in the light. They were a faint green, the soft color of a lamb's ear leaf. His eyelashes were long and blond. His skin was so clean. He was concentrating on the road, holding onto the belt, unable to see me looking at him. I glanced at his hands in the light. They were the softest hands I had ever seen. Everything about him seemed newly made, like it hadn't known a day of trouble. I was still staring when I felt the truck go off the side of the road.

My head jerked up to see that he had driven onto a gravel access road which led to a snowy area beside the bridge. Reflections of the light from tall buildings across the river danced over the water.

"Sit back a minute so I can buckle this, will you?" His voice sounded a bit harsh, but when I looked at him he was smiling at me. "I'm going to guess two things, Angelina. I'm going to guess you ain't ever been off the mountain. And I'm going to guess he probably punched you in the face at least six times. Holy hell, you're a mess."

I slid back in the seat and sat up straight as he clicked the seatbelt in place. I looked across the river to the buildings and tried to feel excited again, tried not to cry. I felt his hand take mine. It was a kind touch and I wondered if he pitied me.

He said, "Bruised as you are, your eyes are just as blue as the lights on the bridge. I bet he thought he could steal that light like taking sapphires from a crown. I don't know the details, but I know you got out of the mountains. And, I didn't run over you. And, damn straight, you're here. And your eyes are looking at that blue light up there on that bridge because you are alive. So am I. I don't know about Granny. All I know is that sometimes nobody wants you to live but you do anyway. And it's beautiful to be alive sometimes. Sometimes it ain't. But right now, it is."

His hand squeezed mine and let go so he could move the stick on the floor. We backed up and drove up to the road again. In any other place, I would have thought more about the deeper things he had said. But the city filled me with awe and I had no thoughts at all beyond how a thing like that could have existed and I not known about it.

Fifteen minutes went by before Emory drove onto a street lined with small houses. They were small compared to the tall buildings, but huge compared to the trailer I had lived in. These houses were even bigger than our church. He slowed down and turned into a short driveway behind a little red car. There was a chain link fence around the small front yard.

"Sit here. I'll talk to her."

He opened his door causing a loud bell to ding repeatedly until he leaned back in and took his keys out of the ignition. A light on the porch flickered on. The door opened and a smiling girl stepped outside wearing a black bra and black panties. Her bright red hair was pulled up on top of her head like a big

August tomato. Her skin was nearly covered with drawings of flowers. She bounced excitedly a couple of times on her tiptoes before wrapping her arms around Emory. She was taller than him by an inch or two. She pulled off his hat and ran her fingers through his yellow hair before pulling him toward her. Her mouth covered his. She seemed to be trying to permanently attach herself to him. Her arms and legs moved around him and down and around him again.

I was curious to see how he would respond to her behavior. I watched intently as he leaned against the door frame and let her hands pull his shirt untucked. She had her mouth on his neck and her hands inside his shirt. His hands went to her arms where his fingers grasped her muscle. His head fell back and his eyes closed and opened again widely. His mouth was moving, saying something I couldn't hear.

She took a step back and listened. I watched her look deeply into his eyes and nod as he spoke. When he pointed toward his truck, she saw me for the first time. I wanted to hide, but there was nowhere to go. She smiled at me and raised her hand in a wave, even the palm of her hand had a flower on it. I raised my hand, too, and tried to match the wave she had made. She looked at Emory and nodded again before going back inside and closing the door behind her.

He came to my door and opened it. "She said you could stay, come on."

His hand was held out for mine. The porch light was bright and I was ashamed to put my rough and stained hand into his. Still, I didn't want to be rude. Silas's boots were heavy and clunky as I slid my feet out the door.

When we walked into the house, a wave of heat hit me and immediately made me sweat. It was terribly uncomfortable and only made worse by my full bladder. Marcy reappeared in a shiny red robe with a bluebird print all over it. She had fuzzy red slippers on her feet and white glasses on her face. the edges of her frames were adorned with sparkly clear stones.

"There's a bed in the room on the right," She pointed down

the hall behind her. "You can put your stuff in there and I'll get something to help your face feel better."

I put my hand up to hide my face, pretending to touch my bruises. I asked, "May I use your outhouse?"

Emory looked at Marcy as if I had just proved something. She gave him a quick nod and said, "Come on Angelina, I'll show you the bathroom. You'll love it." She took my hand from my face and pulled me to follow her. We walked a couple of steps down the hall and turned right into a bathroom. She said, "You just push that handle down when you are finished, okay?"

"I know." I said, feeling embarrassed. "We had one, but it never was hooked up." I immediately regretted blurting out something about my life. I couldn't look at her.

"Oh," she said. "Well, let me know if you need anything. I'll be in the living room."

I waited for her to close the door before I looked up at my reflection in the mirror. I pulled off my hat and stared at the stranger looking back at me. My face was swollen all over, but mostly around my jaw and lip. Shades of purple, blue, and black faded and blended around my eyes. Emory had commented on the color of my eyes, but I could barely see them.

I pulled off Esther's coat and folded it before dropping it onto the floor. Next I removed Silas's boots and pants, fighting a series of shivers as I tossed them onto the coat. I sat down on the toilet and stared at the clothing, hating it all, wanting to shred it until it was unrecognizable. Silas had stolen everything from me and left me with nothing but the breath I breathed, and only barely had I escaped with that.

All I could think about while I washed my hands were my callouses and cuts. Marcy's towels were more beautiful than any dresses I had ever owned. They were bright blue with yellow rose appliques sewn on them. My hands didn't deserve to be dried by them. I wiped my hands on the heavy sweater I wore, then pulled it off over my head. The movements of my arms caused the cotton fabric of my dress to tug on the wounds of my back. I tossed the sweater in the pile on the floor and turned to see the back of my dress in the mirror. It was a solid shade of maroon.

I couldn't go out there. I thought I could leave my story on the mountain, but I had carried it out on my back. I contemplated sneaking out the bathroom window and trying to find Nashville on my own. But I would surely encounter others, strangers eying me with pity or ridicule.

With the blue fedora pulled as low as I could get it, I stepped out into the hall and walked toward the living room. When I reached the corner, I stopped. Emory was sitting on the couch and Marcy was sitting on him, holding his face between her hands. She was kissing him again. I watched the back of his head fall to rest on the back of the couch. He must have liked it. But seeing it made me feel out of place.

The decision was nearly irreversible in my mind. I would pick up my things from the bathroom and go. I could never fit in with what was happening and I needed space to figure out the feelings I was having about it. But before I could turn, Marcy looked up and saw me. She stood up, still wrapped tight in her robe. "Oh. I didn't know you were out. Are you ready to see your room?"

Emory stood and picked up his coat from the arm of the couch. He looked at me uneasily, "I have to go. I'm already late. It's almost eleven and I can only blame so much on the snow. I'll see you ladies as soon as I can get back up here." His eyes held mine for a moment and I wished his expression wasn't so pained. He assured me, "You'll be okay here."

He put on his hat and walked out the door. I was surprised by how drawn I felt to follow him. But I didn't act on it. What right did I have?

Marcy smiled as she walked past me. I caught the most lovely scent from her, citrus and earthy. I knew my body smelled nothing like that. I turned, not so much to follow her as to hide the blood on my dress. From inside the back room she said, "It's a small bed. Pet will want to share it with you. She gets hair everywhere. Are you allergic to cats?"

Out of eyesight, it would have been the perfect time for me to walk out the door. But I didn't. I took quiet, cautious steps down the hall until I could see the orange cat lying on a yellow quilt. With a few more steps, I saw Marcy's back bent over an open dresser drawer. "Here's a nightgown if you need one. Take your pick, really. The drawer is full of them. Whatever you are comfort-"

She had turned mid sentence, but stopped talking with her mouth still open. She cocked her head sideways to the right and slowly walked in that direction, around and closer like the start of a spiral, until she was within arm's reach. She put a hand on the white sleeve of my work dress and gently held it while her head tilted a little more to see the back of my dress.

Her words were a whisper of shock, "Holy Jesus."

21

"I never ask, Angelina. As a rule, I respect others' privacy."
Marcy was talking through the shower curtain while I soaked in
her baby blue bathtub, dress and all. She talked on and on as if
afraid of the silence, or afraid I might speak before she got all
her words out. I wasn't sure which. "Em is amazing, and I love
him, but he doesn't read people very well. Most of the time he
thinks too badly of himself and too highly of others, so I can't go
by what he has said. He told me how he met you, and he told me
all kinds of wild speculations about what he thinks happened to
you. But I'm leaving it up to you what you tell me about that.
Still, Angelina, I need to say that I know you aren't an adult. I
just don't know what I'm going to do about that in your case."

"But, I am a woman." I said, trying not to think obsessively
about how far away I had left my hat in the other room. It still
held the letter.

"So you are eighteen?" She sounded skeptical.

"I just turned sixteen today, but I've been a woman since I was
twelve."

The curtain slid open and Marcy looked down at me. With
the light no longer filtering through the blue shower curtain, the
water looked much more pink. She said, "It's time to check you.
Sit up."

I sat up and hugged my knees while she pulled gently on the
fabric of my dress. It was still stuck in a few places. I said, "You
can cut this dress if you want. I have another one."

"There's no need." She pulled the stopper out of the drain. "Sit
tight."

When the water drained out, she plugged in the stopper and turned on the faucet again. She measured out some Epsom salt and let it fall into the water stream. She said, "Turn this knob all the way to the right when the water reaches here." She pointed to an invisible point on the side of the tub. After seeing me nod, she gave me a quick smile and left the room.

Thirty minutes later, Marcy came back. This time my dress pulled free. Marcy cheered and made a production of it, dancing around the bathroom, making funny faces. I covered my mouth and bit my lip so I wouldn't laugh. If I had ever even thought of acting that way, Silas would have scarred my bottom.

She said, "I'm stepping out of the room while you get undressed and dry off. Call me in when you're ready and I'll take a look at your back and make sure it's clean before I bandage it up."

She was gone before I could say anything, gone before she could see my eyes widen or hear my heart pound. Her words sounded very similar to what Silas would have said before my punishment. I knew the words probably meant something different to her. But all I could hear was Silas. I had no other references. So I did as she asked. I got out of the tub, took off my wet dress, dried myself, folded the towel and laid it on the floor, stood with my hands against the wall and my back to the door, legs apart. With a shaky voice that wanted her not to hear me, I said, "I'm ready."

I heard the door open, then immediately close again. Through the door she said, "Angelina, what are you doing?"

"Am I not doing it right?" I wanted to cry with frustration, but I worried she would be mad.

"Doing what right?"

"Standing so you can inspect me."

I heard the door open again, slowly. I heard the sound of her fuzzy slippers slide a little with every small step toward me. Her hand touched a place at my spine, a place without injury. "How long?" she asked.

I didn't understand. "What?"

"How long had it been going on?"

"I don't understand what you mean. Do you want me to do something different? Is this not right?" There was no point trying to hide my tears. I was too disconnected, too lost to find strength in any semblance of truth. The only truth I felt I had was that I was foolish, ignorant, stupid, repulsive, evil, and unwanted.

"Look at me," Marcy took my hand and gently pulled me around to face her. She kept her brown eyes locked on mine. "Never do this again. Never, do you hear me?"

"What did I do wrong?" I wanted to look away, but her eyes demanded I not.

"Nothing. You did nothing wrong. Other people have done wrong. Your body is yours. It isn't mine, it isn't your Daddy's, it isn't your Mama's, it doesn't belong to anybody but you." Now her eyes had tears, too. She wiped them away briskly. "If I ask you to do something and it feels wrong, like I'm stealing something away from you, don't do it. I would never want that. If you think I have asked for that, I'm telling you now I never would. If anyone else makes you feel like they are asking for that, say no."

"Yes, ma'am,", my head swam with contradictory thoughts. Saying no had never been an option. Refusal to do what I was told would have only caused more problems. I wasn't sure if I believed it could be that easy.

"Now just turn around and stand there, upright. I'm going to put some ointment on your back and wrap it up, that is all."

I turned my back to her. She gathered my long wet hair and laid it over my shoulder. Water dripped down my stomach as she patted my back with a towel. She rubbed thick gobs of something that felt like cooking fat on my cuts. It hurt, but physical pain was something I had learned to handle with grace. By the time she had covered most of my back, the pain had lessened.

"I'm going to wrap gauze around you to keep the medicine on while you sleep. I'll pass it to you on the right and you can wrap it around your font and pass it back to me on your left. Ready?"

We made quick work of getting me wrapped. As she helped

me pull a long white nightgown over my head, a beeping sound came from somewhere in the house. Marcy opened the door and ran out. I wasn't sure if I should follow her. But I couldn't resist when the distinct smell of chocolate cake wafted in. I found her in the kitchen, which was red and white with cherry decor everywhere. Black iron trivets hung on the wall. She was pulling a baking pan out of the oven, wearing two round, red, cherry shaped mitts. After setting the cake on the stove, she tossed the mitts into a drawer and turned to smile at me.

"Surprise! Happy Birthday!"

"But, it's Christmas…"

"Okay, did I hear you wrong when you told me you turned sixteen today? You said that, right?"

"Yes, ma'am."

"And just guessing by everything I know about your day, which isn't a lot, but enough to guess, you did not get to celebrate it."

Obviously, it was not a universal understanding that babies born on Christmas should be locked away with shame. The realization wasn't surprising. It was actually a relief. There was so much to learn and Marcy seemed safe enough. I decided I should divulge a little more.

"No, I didn't celebrate." I said. "Thank you."

"Come on, I have another surprise." She took my hand and led me down the hall. I couldn't imagine what it was. She had found out it was my birthday only an hour earlier. We stepped into the room on the left, which had a sewing machine on a white plastic table, a mannequin, and shelves full of fabric.

"I'm going to make you whatever you want. A new dress? Pants and a shirt? A fancy ball gown?" She wrinkled her nose up and made a silly face. "I love to sew. It's how I pay rent. I can make anything you want. And little lady, you need clothes."

"A dress?" It came out as a question, but I meant it as my answer. Excitement pricked at my heart.

"Great! Do you see anything on these sketches you like?" She pointed to a cork board with drawings pinned to it. All the clothing in them seemed tight and impossible to work in. Sensing my hesitation, she said, "Why don't you let me come up with something I think you'll like, just for you?" She must have noticed I looked no less apprehensive. She said, "Don't worry. I don't always walk around in my underwear. I wear it to bed, and Em has seen it a hundred times. I promise, whatever I make for you will be suited for your taste, not necessarily mine. It will be appropriate for your age, too." She gave me a hopeful nod.

Considering that I had no idea what 'appropriateness' meant anymore, whatever she came up with would surely be better than the stained items in my leather bag. I said, "Thank you. That would be something I could really use."

Marcy bounced on her tiptoes while her hands made tiny little claps in front of her face. "I just need to take your measurements." She took a measuring tape from the table and quickly wrapped it around my body in various places. I held out my arms like I had done years ago when Esther used to make my clothes. Marcy said, "I am so excited! Now, let's go see if the cake is ready for frosting."

Back in the kitchen, she gently pressed her hand on the top of the cake. "It's still too warm."

"I like it warm." I said, trying out a new, uncharacteristically non-cowering voice.

Marcy kept her eyes on the cake and shrugged. "Alright."

She opened the cabinets for two plates. They were mismatched, but both had flowers in the center. She cut two huge pieces of the cake and sat the plates on the bar. "You can have the white trillium, it's my favorite."

"Thank you," I said, taking a seat on the barstool near the plate with the familiar white flower. My first bite of cake was warm, nearly hot. The chocolate flavor became more intense as I held it in my mouth. I didn't want to chew it because I didn't want it to be gone. My eyes rolled up behind my eyelids. It was bliss.

"I hope you like chocolate."

"I love it," I said with my mouth still full. I swallowed and said, "I haven't had cake since I was eleven, before-" but I stopped myself because I didn't know what to call Esther or even if I should be talking about her at all.

"Before...?" Marcy turned to look at me, pleasure in her eyes from eating the cake. I thought maybe I could tell her everything at that moment and she wouldn't care enough to remember. She seemed lost in a chocolate cake dream.

"Before she died... Esther... she made cakes."

"Was Esther your mother?" Marcy kept eating, not looking at me.

"I thought so until today," I set my fork down, feeling sick from eating after having gone so long without food, or perhaps for another reason.

"Mmm," she nodded with her mouth full of cake. She patted her lips with a napkin and swallowed, then swiveled her chair to face me. Her voice was soft. "Does that have something to do with why he hit you?"

I shook my head. "No. That was nothing new. It was always the same until I became a woman. He didn't want me to get pregnant. None of it had to do with Esther."

Marcy frowned with tight lips. I searched her face for how I should feel about what Silas did. How would the world see me, see him, see my life? She said, "I bet he told you it was your fault, right?"

Not wanting to tell her every bad thing Silas said about me, I put another fork full of cake into my mouth and refused to look at her. She kept staring at me, though. When I had eaten the rest of my cake, I had no excuse not to look back at her. I felt miserable both physically and emotionally.

She must have noticed and decided to let it drop. She said, "There's a spare toothbrush in the bathroom drawer. Before you go to bed, do you want me to braid your hair like it was before?"

Relieved she had changed the subject, I said, "No, thank you," and got up to leave the room.

22

December 26, 2006

When the bed moved, I awoke. The sunlight was blinding. Panic washed over me. I shouldn't have still been asleep when the sun was up.

"I didn't mean to scare you." Marcy said.

All the memories from the day before came at me with knives. I must have had troubled expression because Marcy shook my arm, "Wake up, sweetie."

I blinked a few times and focused on her bright orange-red waves of disheveled hair. It framed her face and fell to the image of a bouquet of calla lilies unfurling on her chest.

"Did you paint that?" My voice was raspy and in need of a drink. I put my fingers to the petals of the center white lily and felt only her skin. It had been dyed somehow.

"It's a tattoo," she said, taking my hand and holding it. It occurred to me then that perhaps I shouldn't have touched her. But she didn't seem phased. "A needle permanently inserts the ink into the skin."

"But why?" It was beautiful, but seemed painful to have done.

"Well," she looked up to the ceiling for a moment and then back down at me. "I usually tell people that I get them because I love flowers, which is true. But, the whole truth is, I got the first tattoo because I wanted to feel like my skin belonged to me. For the first seventeen years of my life, I hated my skin. It had experienced some terrible things and even when it was no longer experiencing those things, it still felt the memories. My skin remembered everything."

Marcy allowed me a moment to process her words. I thought about what she had told me the night before when we were in the bathroom, how my body was my own and it was my choice what I did with it. Those ideas were so new and hard for me to understand. But I wanted to understand.

She slowly took a deep breath and let it out before continuing, "I used to want to stop feeling the memories so badly that I would cut myself. See?"

Her hand took mine and moved my fingers across the skin on her arm where inked tattoo bracelets formed vines and flowers near her wrists. Ridges of scarred skin rippled beneath my touch. The scars I understood more than her tattoos. She said, "I don't recommend it, kid. Hating yourself, even in parts, is never going to get you past what has happened in your life... not saying you do hate yourself. I hope you don't. I just know a lot of people don't fare well after abuse."

Abuse. What Silas had done to me had a name. I felt less alien knowing I wasn't the only one. But it hurt to hear Marcy talk about it so tragically. Only a few weeks ago, I had been convinced that the things he did to me were saving my soul and making me righteous. Now all the words used to describe my life were tragic. It made more sense logically, but I felt pangs of anger at having been made a fool. I had worked very, very hard to attain a goal that was itself evil. I felt the familiar guilt whirring through my veins.

I wondered if Marcy's abuse was like mine. I asked, "So, someone took away your name and made you believe you belonged to them, told you in order to be holy, you would have to do everything they said?"

Her eyes held confusion and sadness. "No, Angelina, it was different."

I waited for her to explain, but she didn't. Her mouth pulled sideways in thought. Finally she said, "So, I really came in here because I wanted to show you what I made last night."

She went to the hallway and stepped back in with a blue dress in the exact shade of blue as my hat. I sat up in the bed, feeling my bandages tug at my back. I ignored the pain. "It's beautiful!"

"I made this, a coat, and a pair of pants which you will need to try on before I can finish them."

"Did you not sleep?"

She laughed, "I don't sleep at night. Which brings me to the second reason I am in here. It's my turn in the bed. I'm going to change your bandages, feed you breakfast, then put you in front of the TV."

"What's a TV?"

Marcy's head fell back as she laughed loudly. "Oh, my, Angelina. You are going to school this morning."

"School?" I shook my head in confusion, but had to smile at how hard she was laughing.

"Yes, TV school. We'll start with Carl Sagan and Cosmos. It will Blow... Your... Mind." Her hands went to her face then out into the air with wiggling fingers like an explosion.

"Even more than tattoos and staying awake all night to make dresses?"

Her arms wrapped around me, "Yes," she said into my hair. She held me for a long time, long enough for my tension to ease. She held me until I stopped anticipating that she would touch me more, until I knew she wanted nothing. It was only kindness.

23

Marcy slept for hours then took a shower. She walked into the living room wearing a yellow robe; her hair was wrapped in a yellow towel. She plopped down on the couch beside me before she saw my tears. Surprised, she wrapped me up in her arms.

"Angelina, why are you crying? Have you been crying all day?"

"A little," I answered into the fluff of her robe.

"Do you want to talk about it?"

I stayed pressed against her, not caring if my voice was muffled, "He was just talking about our place in the universe, and I didn't know there was a universe. I didn't know there were places where kids go to learn about the sun and Earth. I didn't know anything. I'm so ignorant about everything. How will I ever catch up and learn it all?"

Marcy held me at arm's length so she could look into my eyes. "Believe me, no one knows everything, not even Carl Sagan. You aren't expected to know it all. Don't think of it like that. Just think about what you learned today and make every day like today. You're going to have so many like this, and it will be enough, I promise."

She smoothed my hair, but her words calmed me more than the touch. The future had never seemed more than a daydream, or thoughts of the next gardening season. But Marcy's words gave me something to hope for beyond that moment. I just had to keep going.

I leaned away from her and blurted out, "I have a letter."

Her head tilted with confusion. She said, "Do you want me to get it for you?"

"No! I mean, no, thank you. I was just telling you that I have it and that's why I'm going to Nashville."

She put a finger up to signal me to wait. "We have to have a discussion before you divulge anything to me, Angelina. I never turn anyone away if I can help. But if I want to keep helping people, I have to follow the law. And you being sixteen complicates that matter. At some point, soon, especially if I become aware of a crime being committed, I will need to get the police involved."

Seeing the horror on my face, she took my hands in hers and squeezed them gently, "Don't worry. I am not doing anything today. We're going to talk about a solution. You and I together are going to figure out a plan for you. Angelina, you need to find a safe place. You deserve that."

"You can't call the police," I pleaded.

"There is no way you will be in trouble, Angelina! It is obvious that whoever did this to you is in the wrong. They should be arrested and charged. If you choose not to report them and take your chances on your own and there's any trouble, the police could send you right back to those people."

"They can't because no one knows who I am. No one knows I exist." Tears welled up. "They pretended to be my parents but they were supposed to have killed me when I was a baby. They just kept me alive instead, told me lies and made me feel ashamed for being born."

"But don't you want to see them go to jail?" She seemed genuinely curious.

I couldn't answer. I didn't want to tell her what I had done. I worried she would call the police.

She saw how worried I was and took my hand in hers. She ran her thumb over the top of it as we sat in silence. No one spoke except Carl Sagan. Episode seven of Cosmos continued to play for the second time. I only pretended to be paying attention to it. I sensed she was doing the same.

After a few minutes I felt the tension leave. She gave my

hand a squeeze and let it go, "Do you feel like trying on those pants?" She stood and headed toward the hall before I could answer. I began to see that Marcy preferred having peace over finding out the truth about things.

I followed her into the sewing room. On the table laid the dress, a long heavy coat, and a pair of black pants.

"Slip these on." She knelt down with the pants held open. I stepped into them and felt the soft fabric stretch around my legs as she pulled them higher. These were nothing like Silas's pants. My legs felt like fingers in a glove. I liked the feeling, but wasn't sure if I should.

"They look good," she said, "How do they feel?"

"Good. But what am I suppose to wear with them? The dress?"

Marcy shook her head, "A blouse. I have a couple to give you if they fit okay. They should get you started."

The words 'getting started' gave me a jolt as I realized this really was a new beginning.

She said, "Step out," and pulled the pants back off. "I'll just add a zipper and they'll be ready. It'll just take ten minutes. You can stay in here or go back to Mr. Sagan."

I sat down in a black plastic chair near the door where I could watch her sew. She pulled the towel off her head when it kept falling forward over her eyes. Her red hair was still damp and looked less the color of August tomatoes and more like southern red oak leaves in October. Marcy was really pretty, but not as attractive as Emory. I guessed she was older than he was, but not by much.

"Are you going to marry Emory?" I bit my lip and waited for an answer.

Marcy didn't stop sewing. "No. We're just really close friends."

"Friends kiss like that?"

"Not normally, but sometimes. Kissing is one of my favorite things and Emory is in need of kissing. Why do you ask?"

"I just wasn't sure what to do with boys, really."

She twisted the pants to sew them from a different angle.

"Emory would love to hear you say that."

"Don't tell him what I said! He would think I'm so stupid!"

"Angelina, I'm not going to tell him anything. I just meant it would make him feel good to know you think of him that way."

"I don't!" I covered my face with embarrassment. "I wasn't saying I wanted to kiss him."

"Him." She turned to look at me and said it again, "Him. You obviously have no idea Em is trans. He completely passed. I keep telling him he's handsome, but he never sees what I see. Maybe he would believe you."

"He's very handsome." I couldn't possibly have turned more red, "But, I don't understand what trans means."

"It means he was born with a woman's body, but he is really a man. He's been working on changing his body for all the seven years I've known him. He has put up with a lot of shit from his parents about it. It's a long story that you don't need to know, at least, not from me. Just know that it would mean a lot to him that you see him as a man, which he is, in fact."

"Oh, I had no idea." I contemplated how it might happen that a woman's body would become a man's body. I thought of how Marcy's tattoos required a needle, and I concluded that becoming a man must be a lot more painful.

She folded up the finished pants and laid them beside the coat. "I'm starving, do you want a grilled cheese sandwich?"

"Breakfast was more food than I usually eat in a week! How can you be hungry again?"

"Alright, Angelina, a new rule for you to learn: Never question a woman about her hunger."

It was a confusing rule but I nodded. She laughed as she walked out of the room.

24

Marcy and I had been sitting on opposite ends of the couch with our feet up toward each other for hours. A quilt was spread over us in colors of violet, indigo, and lavender. Pet was curled up asleep on Marcy's side. We were watching Nova videos about everything. Marcy said it was science, but I didn't see how that single word could encompass all that information. My favorite subjects were the universe and time. Both were far greater than I ever imagined.

"You were right," I interrupted the show. "I think my mind has exploded."

Marcy laughed. "I told you. I've watched all these multiple times and I still get chills." We turned back to the TV. She said, "I should probably go stitch up some more things for you."

I put my hand on her leg through the blanket and shot a glance at her, "Don't."

She never replied because there was a knock at the door. Marcy got up and looked through the window to see who it was. When she opened the door, Emory walked in with two flat boxes.

"I brought pizzas! One margherita, one pepperoni. I hope these will work." He smiled at me, his eyebrows raised questioningly. I didn't know what he was talking about, so I didn't say anything. I just stared at his face and tried to see him as a woman. I couldn't.

Marcy walked up and took the pizzas before kissing him on the cheek. She turned away from him and winked at me.

Emory said, "Your face is looking so much better. The swelling has gone down a lot."

I had looked in the mirror every time I had gone to the bathroom. I appreciated his positivity, but I knew it still looked bad. My entire face was bruised. But he was right, the swelling had decreased substantially.

Marcy walked back from the kitchen and slid her hand into Emory's. Her other hand pulled off his hat, tossed it on the couch, and moved fingers through his hair. "Someone was telling me earlier that you are quite the handsome man," she said before kissing his cheek.

I felt like I shouldn't be watching, so I stood up and went into the kitchen. I had chosen a slice of the tomato pie and was carrying my plate to the bar when I heard the bedroom door close. The TV was left on in the living room. I could have turned and watched, but I faced the bar and ate while listening to commentary about Einstein's equation.

As I finished my second slice, the bedroom door opened and Emory walked quickly, angrily into the kitchen. He leaned on the bar on the opposite side of me, looking piercingly into my eyes. Marcy walked in soon after, quietly. Her hair had been let loose from the braid I had given her earlier, stray waves fell to her face.

"What did she tell you about me?" His teeth were clenched.

Marcy turned her back to me and pulled two plates from the cabinet. She spoke without looking at us, "Em, I don't know why you are making such a big deal of it. What matters is that she didn't know, she never suspected. I thought you'd be thrilled."

Emory spun around to face her. His hand raised and his finger jabbed in her direction as he spoke, "That is the point, dammit! That is the goddamn point! I finally get my body to a place where people can't tell and you fucking tell them I'm really a woman. You fucking tell it! What about that seems right to you? How does that help me?"

Marcy calmly put a slice of pepperoni pizza on her plate. "Angelina thinks you are a handsome *man*. Hear that and forget the rest of it."

I could see the back of his neck turn red and I knew she had embarrassed him. I felt embarrassed, too, but my face was too bruised to show it. Emory turned back to me, "So, Marcy says I should forget it, but can you? Can you forget what she told you?"

The truth was that I couldn't imagine a time I would forget such a thing. It had been quiet a revelation to me. It gave me insight into the relationship between Jute and Allie. Maybe Jute was like Emory. Or maybe Allie was. I didn't know how these things worked, but I was determined to understand it.

I answered Emory's question with a shake of my head. "I don't want to forget it."

Emory threw his hands in the air and spun around to say something to Marcy, but she had already moved to sit beside of me.

He turned back toward us and said to her, "See! Do you fucking see?"

Marcy looked at me apologetically, but didn't seem very worried. She said, "Yes, I do see. Do you see? She's sixteen, Emory. So, it's not like anything was going to happen between the two of you. And I am thinking she had probably never heard of anything queer in her life."

"So I'm just a puppet show? It's okay to out me for the good of society?" His hands were still motionlessly pointed toward me as if attached to statue arms.

My voice broke when I said, "I have a letter..." It was my second attempt to talk about it. But, I didn't know if I should go on. I was interrupting their argument, but it seemed relevant.

They both blinked at me as their faces softened. I was glad to see it. I decided to keep talking, "I found it in a hatbox. A girl named Allie wrote it to a girl named Jute."

No longer blinking, they both became a bit wide eyed. Their expressions made me feel uncomfortable, like I shouldn't say more. Maybe I had said too much, but it was good to get the words out, to not be the only person carrying the weight of it. I added, "Allie is dead now. I think Jute would really want the letter."

"Are you talking about Jute Duren?" Marcy asked.

"Yes!" I screamed and hugged her so tightly, "You know her! I am so happy!"

"She don't know her," Emory said snidely, "Not personally anyway. She just knows of her." He glared at Marcy while asking her, "Hear that? Jute Duren! So, do you still think Angelina don't know queer?"

"Stop it, Em! She's sixteen, so no she doesn't. That would have to be one very detailed letter..."

"Well you aren't helping at all by acting like it's a thing you have to warn people about."

"Oh, my God, Em! I was not warning her! Jesus Christ! I was telling her because I was so happy for you I couldn't hold it in! I'm sorry already!"

My attempt to sidetrack them failed. They were still arguing and pretending like I wasn't there. Maybe I shouldn't have been. The urge to leave had come and gone like summer rain, but now it was flooding like springtime.

Emory spoke with calm, but his eyes were still a bit wild, "Which am I, Angelina? Am I a man or a woman?"

His demanding eyes reminded me of Silas's and I didn't like the feeling in my stomach. I was afraid not to look him in the eyes and answer him properly, "A man, sir."

Marcy snorted before laughing. She stood up and walked over to Emory, wrapping her arms around him. "I win," she said and began kissing him on the mouth.

I don't know why it made me angry, but it did. They weren't interested in anything other than whether or not Emory was perceived as a handsome man, which he was. He was a very handsome man. I had even imagined kissing him like Marcy kissed him. Watching them together made me blush with more emotions than I knew existed. I couldn't just sit there. I went to the bathroom and locked the door behind me.

No one came after me. No one knocked on the door to check on me. Even through a long shower, no one had even jiggled the door knob. I turned off the water and dried off as best I could. My bandages were soaked and needed changed. I didn't want to ask Marcy for help, but I knew I needed it. I took a deep breath, wrapped a large sky blue towel around me, and walked into the living room. No one was there. I walked down the hall and noticed the door to Marcy's room was ajar. Stepping closer, I saw Marcy's naked back, clearly visible from the hallway. She was sitting on the bed, moving her hips which were covered by a quilt. I was mesmerized by the detailed flower garden tattooed on her back. It almost looked real, as if I could escape up the footpath through the center. I wanted to look at it closer, notice each flower, but I was startled by the sight of hands sliding around her sides and pulling her to lie down. Emory.

Without a sound, I stepped into the sewing room where the stack of clothes had been laid out hours earlier. I picked up the dress, felt the soft creamy fabric and imagined how heavenly it would feel on my skin. But, my skin was still ripped open. I didn't want to stain the beautiful things Marcy had made for me. So, I chose to put on the newly laundered work dress with the blood stains. I had to reminded myself that it was clean, just stained, and would be fine. I slipped on the warm coat Marcy had made. I only needed boots.

The thought of putting on Silas's boots again made my limbs go numb in protest. But I didn't see another option. I laced them up and stood, put the leather strap of my bag over my head and shoulder, and picked up the blue fedora from the sewing table. The letter was still tucked safely inside. I put on the hat and pulled it low. The night promised to be cold and I had fewer layers of clothes, but I couldn't stay in that house another minute.

I didn't know why it mattered so much to me, why it had hurt more to see them together this night than it had the night before. But I felt an overwhelming sense of loss. I wanted a love like Allie talked about in her letter to Jute. I had to admit that I'd started to feel a hope to love Emory that way. I wanted to understand what if felt like to kiss him. Those feelings were already confusing, but seeing him and Marcy together assured me there was no hope in those dreams. I didn't belong there.

I opened the front door and stepped out into the night, careful not to disturb them.

25

Which way was east, which was west? I thought back to our drive to Marcy's house. We had driven though the city, so I assumed the city was to the east of me. I could still see the city lights in the distance despite the glow of the streetlights overhead. I decided I would walk in the opposite direction, hoping it would take me closer to Jute.

Walking away into the unknown was much different in Louisville than it had been in the mountains. Some of the houses and buildings I passed had windows lit or people sitting outside, smoke billowing up from something they held to their lips. I saw people move in the shadows between buildings.

I kept my hat pulled low, my hands in my coat pockets, and my arms held close to my body. The night air felt just as cold as it had two nights ago. I missed the added warmth of Silas's pants, but thinking of them made me a little sick.

From my right, a deep voice called out, "Hey, Baby!"

I stopped and turned to see only shadows and an old building with broken windows. Then I thought I saw something move in the shadows. I squinted to make out what it was, but saw only blackness. So, I resumed walking.

The voice came again, this time from close behind me. "I said hey, Baby! You not answering a man when he speak to you?"

Images of Silas flashed in my mind. I didn't turn around, I ran as fast as the over-sized boots would allow. I heard laughter behind me.

"Run, bitch, run!" Laughter came from a different voice, then two or more together. I couldn't tell. I just ran. I was afraid of what they might do to me, but also what they might see. Nothing about me was normal, nothing about me would fit into this outside world. As I ran past lit windows and the lights of passing cars, I thought of the mountain and the garden. I thought of feeding the chickens under the willow tree in summer and the smell of honeysuckle growing on the fence. I considered going back there. I could bury Silas's body and clean his room. My mind worked frantically to figure out how I could get back, how I could make it work if I lived on the mountain alone. I didn't want to go back, but I had no faith I'd ever fit in anywhere else. I was consumed by all the thoughts pulling my heart in so many directions.

A loud horn and the squealing of tires snapped me out of my thoughts. I stepped up on the sidewalk, realizing too late that I had apparently crossed a road without looking for traffic. The car's horn continued to blare angrily after passing. I looked around me, trying to find a safe place to gather my thoughts. There was no obvious place, so I turned left and kept walking until I came to a short iron fence around an old cemetery. There were lots of large old trees inside which reminded me of the willow. I decided this was good enough. I could find a place to sit and formulate a plan.

I had only taken a few steps past the entrance when the sound of an engine approached. I stopped and stood very still, hoping it would pass and no one would notice me. But when light flooded the field of graves in front of me, I knew someone had turned into the entrance.

I started running again, wishing I could pull off the heavy boots and run faster.

"Stop!" It was a familiar voice. Emory called out his open window, "Angelina! Wait!"

The lights went dark and the sound of his feet on gravel got louder as he approached. I had almost made it to a tall monument surrounded by trees near the exit when he grabbed my arm.

He was out of breath, "Stop…," he panted, "We need to talk."

I was out of breath, too. It was all I could do to stay standing and not crumple onto the ground at his feet. I wanted to lean into him and cry, but I also wanted to get away so I wouldn't have to look at him. He led me over to a bench and sat with me, his arm pulling me against him.

"I'm sorry I acted like that in front of you," He said with his cheek pressed to the top of my head, "I wasn't mad at you, I was mad at Marcy. When we saw you were gone we both felt terrible. We shouldn't have argued in front of you. Please come back to the house. You can't be out here alone."

"Alone? You mean like I was in the house? I don't feel right being there, seeing the two of you..."

"You saw us in the bedroom? Aw, shit. Angelina, we didn't know. I told Marcy we should hold off, but once she gets started and... I'm sorry. If nothing else, come back so she won't worry. I swear we won't do anything to freak you out. I know you're already freaked out by what I am."

A breeze rustled the limbs of the trees overhead but never quite made it low enough to chill us. I shivered anyway. I didn't want to go back to the house, but Emory wasn't understanding why.

"I don't think bad of you, Emory. I don't think bad of Marcy either. I'm just not... I just don't know anything about what you are doing or how I fit into it all. I don't have a place in it."

I felt his body relax, "Angelina, you're sixteen. You shouldn't have even seen me and Marcy like that. There should be no place for a girl your age in any of that."

His words validated my fears. I really didn't belong, not with them or anyone. My mind drifted back to the mountain. I wanted to go back so badly, escape this foreign world where people touched for pleasure, kissed and laughed, knew about stars and the universe, had everything and knew everything. The experiences I had since leaving the mountain revealed to me the full breadth of my wounds beyond the physical, and just how ignorant and alone I was. Before, I could find small and secret joys. But now, with every wondrous thing I learned, I was also reminded of the abuse which caused me to be ignorant of it in the first place.

"Hey," he said, after I had been silent too long, "I'm not saying you aren't pretty or that if I was younger I wouldn't be attracted to you. I mean, your face is kind of a mess right now." He squeezed my arm and laughed a little, "But your eyes, Angelina, prettiest eyes I have ever seen. Some boy… or girl… whatever person you want, someday they're going to give you whatever you ask for. You ask for the biggest whale in the ocean and they'll start building a giant boat big enough to haul it back to you. I swear, you have so many good things ahead of you. And hey…" he touched his hand to my chin and pulled my face to look at him. "I don't want to admit it, but Marcy was right to tell you about me. You just don't know how much it means to me that you thought I was a handsome man."

I felt my face blush and wanted to pull away, but I didn't. His eyes were shining. The look on his face was intoxicating. I leaned into him, hoping I could kiss him the way Marcy kissed him. My lips touched his and my body felt warm all over. His hands cupped my face. He sighed a warm breath onto my lips before he pulled away.

"I'm twenty-five, I can't do this," his eyes were looking so hard into mine that I couldn't process his words. He said, "Touching you is illegal."

I fought not to cry. I blinked back the tears. "I don't understand why. I am a woman. I have been a woman since I was twelve! I've been touched all my life, and now that I finally want to be touched, you tell me it's illegal."

Emory gently wrapped his arms around me. "You shouldn't have been. It was wrong of him, Angelina. He was cruel. And, I'm so sorry I can't comfort you the way you want me to. I just can't. I care about you too much. I want you to have whatever is left of your childhood. I want you to have a chance to be a little girl."

"I will never be that, Emory," I sobbed, "Look at me!"

"I know it feels that way now, but you will. It's all going to get better. But your life is a giant clusterfuck right now and the last thing you need is me and my shit life meshed with yours. Just please come back to Marcy's for tonight. I'll call in sick tomorrow and get you to Nashville. Then I'll get the hell out of your life and you'll be better for it. I'm nobody, Angelina. You'll see when you get out in this big world."

"You aren't nobody, Emory. You are in my life because of fate, and you are helping me get a very old letter to its rightful owner." I hoped he'd recognize how important he was. I thought he and I could fulfill my calling together; it would have become *our* calling.

"A divine plan for mail delivery? Is that what you believe?" His eyes were a bit too amused for my liking.

I nodded. "It's better than believing in nothing."

Part Four

John

26

December 26, 2006

The sound of Montgomery scratching at my door woke me. I blinked a few times to orient myself. My room at Dads' was nothing like my room at Mom's. The walls were a pale silver color with bars of light and shadow from the sunlight filtering through the blinds. My bed, dresser, and desk were all heavy black metal. When they had built the house, Dads had been into industrial decor. I hadn't stayed in the room often enough to worry with changing it over the years. Now it had grown on me.

Montgomery scratched again.

"Go away," I mumbled and tossed my pillow toward the door. Not surprisingly, it didn't do any good. Montgomery just barked a few times before scratching again.

The door opened and Dad Tracy stepped in with puffy eyes full of sleep. His head was bowed to look at Montgomery. With high pitched baby talk, Dad said, "What you want? You want in to see your brother John?"

"Not funny, Dad."

"No?" He looked up and smiled at me, immediately losing all

signs of exhaustion. I was in no mood to deal with his charming good looks. It was annoying.

"Can you get that dog out of here?" I turned to face the wall.

The mattress sank with Dad's weight as Dawson's voice bellowed from downstairs, "Monty!" A few hand claps were followed by a whistle. Montgomery's claws scraped the hardwood floor as he ran off in hopes of going outside. I figured he wouldn't stay out long because it was so cold out there.

"He's gone," Dad stated the obvious, "So, what's going on?"

"About what?" I covered my head with the pillow I hadn't thrown. Why did parents always corner their kids while they were half asleep and want to talk about *things*?

"Maybe we could talk about this girl, Courtney?"

I groaned with unbearable annoyance. "Oh… My… God, Dad! She was just some girl that wanted to fuck her way into your world. You know, like everybody else. How is that a surprise to everyone but me?"

"Ah," he said. I felt him lie down behind me. He was probably staring up at the industrial chandelier, a sphere of metal strips encasing delicate blown glass orbs, each containing a tiny bulb. I had been with him when he bought it in New Mexico when I was eleven. It had been my first trip on the road with him. Every time he came in my room after that, he stared up at it.

Minutes passed and he said nothing. The room was made especially silent by the pillow I still pressed to my ear. Eventually, I felt my heart rate slow. I felt my body relax. I felt myself stop wanting him to leave. Being aware that my defenses had fallen only made me more bitter. I wished I wasn't, but I couldn't help resenting how much time he spent away from me. I never saw him, yet when others looked at me, all they saw was him.

"People are shit," he finally said.

I took the pillow from over my ear and tucked it under my head. "I didn't say that."

"I know, but it's true. They're mostly pricks. I'm sorry you have to deal with an inordinate quantity of them."

I sighed, "So, you aren't on Mom's side?"

"Whoa," he pretended to sound scolding, "I am always on your Mom's side."

"Great."

"Seriously, John. She's just worried that you might need someone to talk to, is that so bad?"

"Yes, when she says it in front of Iris! And she's probably telling all those crying women my business!"

"No, believe me, she's not telling anyone your business. I think she prefers those women to never see you as a person with sexual thoughts. Honestly, I don't think she's ready to see you that way herself. You're her little bee-bee boy." He mocked her voice perfectly.

"Shut up," I kicked back until I hit the side of his leg. "You're being weird."

"Alright, no more playing. I'll just say it all and get it over with. I'm sorry you have to deal with shit because I'm famous. I'm sorry you have to deal with shit because I'm gay. I'm sorry you have to deal with shit because your mom has a house full of very sad-for-a-good-reason women. But no matter how sorry any of us are, it won't change your reality. All I can say is, you are a great kid... a great boy, almost a man. I have never known you to be unkind or self-serving. I have no doubt that when you do finally have sex, you will handle it as you do everything else in life, with more regard for your partner than for yourself. That includes protecting each of you from complications like STDs or pregnancy, which obviously the latter does not apply to you directly, but I assure you it would apply to you secondarily." He took a loud breath and let it out. "So get clear consent, use condoms, use kindness. If your partner is drunk, their consent is null and void, hands off. Follow those rules and whatever you do sexually is your business. I'm not getting involved and I'll try to make sure your mother doesn't either. That being said, you can ask me anything. I am impossible to shock. Try me."

My face was red hot with embarrassment. But, I was thankful he said it all without asking me anything or requiring me to look at him. He slapped my side just before he sat up, "I take your silence to mean you have no questions at this moment. I need to go pour some coffee. Want me to make you a cup?"

I shook my head, still staring at the wall. I felt his weight leave the bed, but just before his footsteps went into the hall, I turned and stopped him, "Dad?"

"Yeah?" He leaned back in the room with one hand on the doorknob.

My face was still red from the talk, but I had to ask, "Was I named after Allie?"

His smile dropped to a worried frown as he stepped back into the room and shut the door behind him. He rolled the desk chair around so he could sit and face me. "Did Mom say that?"

"No. Iris."

"Ah." His head leaned back, his gaze hung on the chandelier again, but not for long. He looked back into my eyes, "The thing with Allie was complicated. But, yes, you were named after John Lennon and Allie Vining. She was the love of your mom's life."

So it was true, and no one had bothered to tell me. But Iris knew. Probably everyone knew. "Doesn't anyone think I should have been told that before now?"

His hands gripped his knees and he nodded as he stared at the floor. "I do. I'm sorry. But, you just grew up so fast, John. I could never have told you when there was any chance you would repeat what I said to her. It was really traumatic for her after-"

"I know," I cut him off, "I found a news article about it. I had to read it from a newspaper because no one in this family wants to tell me anything."

"So you know Mom watched Allie die? And you know Mom nearly died as well? And you know that Allie saved your mom's life the year before? And you know that Allie was and still is the only person your mother has ever loved that way? Ever." His voice was sharp and starting to crack, "And you know, from that news article, that Allie's son is now in the hands of her abuser's family because Allie's family was completely destroyed by that same abuser? Every goddamn day Mom thinks about that baby, did you know that?"

"No!" I sat up and screamed at him, "I didn't know. But whose fault is it that I don't know?"

"It's my fault!" He was screaming back at me, "Because I don't want your mother hurt! I don't want to talk about things that hurt her because I need her to function so she can be a mother to you and not fucking go all to hell over a woman that didn't deserve her! I should have never encouraged it. I live with that regret, John, but I am not going to wave her pain in her face by having our little boy constantly bringing up Allie's name and breaking her heart all over again."

"Well how broken is it if she can just send all Allie's stuff to the barn? I think she's probably over it." I watched him for a reaction. I was still trying to figure out why Mom had done that. His face went blank for a moment as he tried to process what I had just said.

"She did what?"

"She had me take a box of Allie's stuff to the barn and some other crap so Iris could have the attic room. That's how I know about her. Iris didn't just start telling me stuff. She knew you and Dawson told her not to talk about it. But, she kind of didn't have a choice anymore."

"Oh," his eyes held thoughtful concern. "That's unexpected. I don't know what to make of it. Did Mom say anything about the stuff, or give you instructions to take special care with it?"

I shook my head. He shook his in response before running his hand though his short wavy black hair.

"Damned if I know," he said. "It's been nearly sixteen years ago, so maybe that wound has healed and she's moving on. But, let's still not mention it, okay? If you want to talk about it, just come to me. I promise I won't scream at you next time."

"Yeah," I said, smiling, "You're the worst."

He smiled back at me, looking as handsome as a Calvin Klein ad. Why couldn't I have just a few of those good genes?

27

When I finally made it downstairs, Dawson was at the stove, flipping bacon with a fork. I had intentionally cut my shower short because I was anxious to get to Mom's house and talk to Iris. We had planned to drive to Kentucky the following morning. I was worried I had made it riskier by bringing up Allie to Dad.

"Food will be ready in ten; drink you some coffee," Dawson's voice cut through my thoughts. Dad was sitting at the bar reading Alternative Press magazine. It was the "Most Anticipated Albums of 2007" edition.

"Are you in there this year?" I asked while pouring coffee into a black mug.

"Nah," he said, "I won't have another album out until 2008. Tour lasts until summer, then I'll have a couple of months to get some songs together. Then I'll have a few more shows this fall, so we won't be able to record until sometime in November."

"You better get to writing old man," Dawson twisted to look over his shoulder and winked at Tracy. "Right now you got nothing."

I let out a laugh into my coffee cup making steam rise and warm my face. Dad glared at me for laughing, then shifted his eyes to Dawson's back. He deepened his voice, "Oh, I wouldn't call it nothing."

I nearly choked as I tried to swallow the coffee in my mouth. I coughed to clear my airway and said, "Your son is in the room! Your son is in the room! Attention, people!"

They both laughed. Dawson came over and hugged me,

slapping my back a few times. "Sorry, John. We'll stop flirting with each other... for now. You want fried eggs or scrambled?"

"Neither," I said, "Just pile a plate full of bacon and I'm good."

Dawson's smile dropped, "You can't eat just bacon, kid. I'm going to scramble them, your usual, and they'll be so damn good, you'll eat every last bite on your plate."

I rolled my eyes at him. He just winked at me, ignoring my disrespectful behavior, and walked back over to the stove.

Tracy changed the subject, "What do you want to do for your birthday? We're only nine days away."

This question always hit a nerve. Every year, Dad was usually out on the road and everyone else was in celebration-overload from Christmas and New Years. I had stopped asking to go back on the road with him years ago because it almost never worked out. Trying to accommodate it seemed to stress everyone. I tried to think of the least intrusive thing to request for my birthday, but I came up with nothing. I just said the first thing that came to mind, which was probably the most intrusive. "We could all go on a short vacation to a place where no one knows who you are."

He sighed and sat his magazine down, his finger stayed stuck between the pages to mark his place. His eyes searched my face and displayed a range of emotions as if I had just rubbed salt in a wound. Finally he said, "I'll see what I can do."

When the food was ready, Dawson made my plate for me like I was still a little kid. I did appreciate that he piled on extra bacon, though. I wasted no time eating it. I thanked Dawson, then grabbed my coat.

"You going to Mom's?" Dad asked.

"She'll want the tree taken down," I explained. "You know she hates to have decorations left up after Christmas."

He picked up his magazine again, "Okay. But we're making pizzas tonight and watching Contact. Be back by 6:00. Tell Iris to get her butt up here, too."

I nodded my agreement to Dawson because Dad wasn't looking. Dawson raised a fork full of eggs as if to say *be off.*

I walked out the door and immediately wished I'd put on a

hat. The wind was gusting hard with jabs of icy air that seemed to whip through the hillside and hit me from all directions. I made quick time getting through the field to the farmhouse. I went in through the back door which led directly to the hall. The heat from the wood stove was heaven.

Iris was already in the living room pulling ornaments off the tree. The little girl was helping while the mother wrapped red candles and placed them in a box for storage.

"About time, John," Iris teased. "We've nearly worked you out of a job."

Smiling at the little girl, I said, "That's because you replaced me with such a good worker. I don't think I can keep up with her."

Finally, the little girl gave me a full smile. Sometimes I did win over a guest, but only in time for them to move on with their lives.

We had all the ornaments off the tree and had begun to pull off the garland when something occurred to me.

"Where's Mom?"

Iris shrugged, "She hates doing this kind of thing. I think she's in the back office."

I handed her the ring of garland and walked off in that direction. With an uneasiness, I opened the office door. She wasn't there.

"Mom?" I quietly called for her in a tone just under the allowed limit. I made my way upstairs thinking she might have been working in Iris's room. But on my way to the attic door I passed my room and saw her on my bed. She was sitting there with her hand over her mouth, tears in her eyes, and Allie's photograph in her hand.

I froze. I wished I could do more than stand in the doorway with my mouth gaping open in fear, dread, and regret. I couldn't decide if I should walk in or walk away. I stepped one foot in front of the other until I made it to her side. I sat down and put my arms around her. Mentally, I gave myself hell for not hiding that photograph better. I had left it under my pillow, which was stupid. But I had just forgotten about it.

"I'm sorry I took something of yours."

"It was never mine," she could barely speak for crying. I had never seen her so unraveled. "She left me. That's all there is to it. She left me and she's gone."

I took the photo from her hand to put it on the nightstand. As soon as it left her fingers, her other hand went up to cover her face. Her sobbing was loud, louder than I was ever allowed to be. I put my arms around her and hugged her as tight as I could. All her pain was my fault. Now I just wanted it to stop. I wanted to make it better, make her stop crying.

"I'm so sorry, Mom! I should have left it in the barn."

She shook as she cried before she began to sniff and try to pull herself together, "Yes, John, you should have left it in the barn. It needs to be put away. I've spent so much time trying to understand why she came to me, but now I don't even think it was me she came to see. She just wanted away. All I was to her was a place away from something worse. That's all I am to anybody, just a place away. I'm sorry. I shouldn't say that to you."

Mom gently pulled out of my arms. She stood and looked down at me. Her eyes were red, her face puffy, her hair a mess. She put her hand on my cheek and I could tell she felt guilty, but she said nothing. She left. I listened until I could no longer hear her feet on the stairs.

I looked over at the photo of Allie on my nightstand and tried to blink back my own tears. More than anything, I was scared I had hurt mom and Dad would have been right about her, that she would spiral out of control and not be the mom I knew. It would have been my fault if that happened.

I said to the photograph, but mostly to myself, "How can she still get so upset after all these years?"

It seemed ridiculous to me. I wanted to put together a list of all the reasons her emotions were unjustified, present those reasons to her, and make her understand how wrong she was to feel them. But, my mind kept going back to what Dad had said about Mom. She had so many unanswered questions about Allie and about Allie's baby. If I could find the answers for Mom, maybe it would bring closure and ease her pain.

Iris had been right that we should find him. I knew it for certain now. But I also knew there was no way Mom would allow us to do what we were planning. We would have to spend the day as if what I had just witnessed had never happened.

When I stood up, I realized just how shaken I was. I slid the photo of Allie into my wallet, vowing never to let it out of my sight again. Then I went back downstairs to help Iris. She was already outside with the ladder leaned against the side of the house.

I pretended to be mad, "Hey now, don't get any ideas. Pulling off the wreaths is my job!"

Iris tested the ladder by giving it a few shakes. "Nothing says only John Duren can climb ladders. I think I got this, but I won't argue if you want to hold the ladder."

Honestly, she was better built for the job than I was. She was small and agile, making her way up and down the ladder in twice the time it had normally taken me. In less than an hour, we had pulled all the greenery from the house and had it piled in the field for our annual New Year's Eve Bonfire.

As we put the last boxes of decorations in the shed, I quietly asked Iris, "Are we still on for tomorrow?"

"Yep," she whispered back.

"I need to talk to you about Mom, but can't now. Dads want you to come up for a movie tonight at six. We can't talk then, either. We can talk in the morning, maybe leave at sunrise? Tell them we're going to Memphis to see that friend of yours."

"You mean Trish? You know Dad is friends with her mom, right? And what's the reason we're saying you're going?"

"Because I need to get my mind off Courtney?" I cringed at the sound of the lie.

"Courtney, huh?" Iris raised an eyebrow. "If you say so."

Mom stayed in her office for hours. Iris had asked where she was, but I gently shook my head and hoped she knew to stop asking me. As lunchtime neared, we warmed up the left overs from Christmas dinner and fed everyone lunch. There was a group therapy session scheduled for three o'clock and I wanted to be out of there before then. If Mom was pulling herself together, I didn't want the sight of me to remind her of that morning. I loaded the dishwasher while Iris swept the dining room. After that, I told her I was leaving for Dads' and reminded her of the movie Dads were planning to watch.

"I'm going to get things ready for our trip to Memphis tomorrow," she said convincingly. "I'll be up in a couple of hours."

"Okay," I said, my single word wobbled under the weight of the lie.

I grabbed my jacket from the stool by the door and went out to the porch before putting it on. Whatever it was Iris and I were headed into, there would be no backing out. Thinking about Mom holding the photo of Allie confirmed it. The can of worms had toppled over, wide open.

28

December 27, 2006

Going in the house before we left for Kentucky wasn't an option. I didn't want to wake Mom. Seeing me would have only made her sad or curious. Either scenario would have been bad. I set to work scraping the frost off Iris's windshield and hoped she would show up before my fingers turned blue from the cold.

I had all the ice cleared off and was sitting in the passenger seat for fifteen chilling minutes before I saw her walk around the corner of the house. She must have come out the side door, which was smart because it didn't creak like the front door. She was wearing a red wool coat that looked like a dress and a matching wool hat. She had on black leggings and knee high patent leather black boots. She opened the door of the car and nearly fell over when she saw I was sitting inside it.

Her voice was a high whisper, "You scared the daylights out of me!"

I said, "You scared me, too. I thought I saw Santa Clause coming around the corner."

She closed her door before turning to give me a stern look, "Don't comment on my clothes, John. You and your hillbilly-fabulous style have no place in that kind of conversation."

Her expression was a prize, I loved getting her riled. I smiled at her while I pulled the seatbelt over my shoulder and clicked it in place. "I'm kidding, Iris. You look stunning, like the brightest star in the night sky, like holly berries, beautiful and poisonous, like-"

"Stop before I poison *you.*" She started the car. I was thankful her VW wasn't as loud as Greenman. We had already told Dads we were going down to Memphis today, but there was no point waking Mom. If anyone could have recognized I was lying, it would have been her.

Before we got out of Nashville I told Iris about Mom finding the photo of Allie and how she had reacted. I watched Iris's face to see how she would feel about it, if it would be the same way I did. Iris listened intently. Her eyes squinted, deep in thought.

"What if she's right, John? What if Allie really didn't care about her?"

I had been thinking the same thing, but hadn't wanted to say it aloud. There seemed to be multiple sides to Allie. There was the Allie responsible for the poetry, the Allie in the photograph with her beautiful blue eyes, and the Allie responsible for hurting Mom. It seemed Mom found it easier to reconcile Allie's death by seeing her as the leaving kind. I couldn't fault Mom for that, but I also couldn't accept that was all there was to it. I said, "You read the notebooks, too. I just don't think Allie could be that heartless."

"Some girls will fool you," she said, and the implication stung. Was she talking about Allie or Courtney? I didn't want to talk anymore.

Iris drove like we were late, speeding five to ten miles per hour over the speed limit at all times. She also sang incessantly. The CD disc changer was stocked with every genre. When it was Rascal Flatts, I sang, too. But when it was Rhianna, I had no idea what the words were, so I just listened to Iris belt them out off key.

By the time we neared Lexington, we had been on the road three hours. We stopped at Magee's Bakery where Iris sent a text to Dawson saying we were almost to Memphis, making sure to point out that we had stopped for breakfast. I felt too nervous to eat. I bought a small bottle of milk and sat at a corner table. Iris came over a few minutes later with a country ham biscuit for me and what looked like a pecan danish for herself.

"Eat, skinny boy," she said, tossing the food down in front of me before settling into the chair across from me.

"Hey, I'm getting bigger," I defended myself, putting up my arm to flex my muscle. My heavy coat made the gesture moot.

Iris clicked her tongue at me and shook her head. She was holding back a laugh and I felt anger wash over me. Seeing my face turn red, she let out a small laugh into her coffee cup. She swallowed a drink and said, "John, you need to take yourself less seriously. You're fine like you are. As soon as you believe it, you'll stop trying to prove it, and won't be getting all bent out of shape when someone teases you... namely, me."

"You think I'm *fine*? Just fine?" I teased, pretending I wasn't nervous. I didn't want Iris to know I was becoming more stressed the deeper we got into Kentucky. I took a big drink of milk, hoping it would settle my stomach.

"Yeah, John, fine. If I say anything better than that about you, it would be weird. You're my brother and all. Take it as a compliment, which is how it was intended." She bit into her danish and her eyes rolled up in pleasure, "Damn this is *fine*."

"You are not even funny," I said before picking up my ham biscuit and mimicking her euphoric bite-taking. Barely keeping the crumbs from tumbling out of my full mouth, I said, "Damn this ham is sexy."

We both laughed, being intrusively loud, drawing a few stares. She shushed me and wagged her finger at me like it was entirely my doing. "That is no way to impress a woman. You're being gross."

I shrugged and took another drink of milk. "So, what's the plan? Are we just going to knock on the door and hope a teenage boy answers it?"

After swallowing a bite of danish, she reached into her purse and pulled out a notepad. "I wrote down some questions to keep us on track. I thought we could pretend we are writing a book about life in eastern Kentucky, just to assess if telling the truth is even an option. Obviously some people in this family had violence issues, but surely a violent person wouldn't have been allowed to adopt the baby."

"If it's family, Iris, I don't think it matters." My stomach tightened again and I could tell from Iris's expression that she felt anxious, too.

"Probably so," she conceded. "Let's make sure we park the car for a quick getaway."

"Having second thoughts?" I said teasingly, but I secretly hoped she would decide to go back home.

"Yes." She drank a sip of coffee. "But if we don't do this, no one else is going to do it. I think we owe it to Mom to try to get some answers. If nothing else, maybe we can get a photo of the boy, let her know he's okay."

"That sounds like a great job for me. I'll snap a photo and you can do all the talking."

"I agree. The less you talk, the better." She took another bite and jotted something on the notepad, leaving me to wonder if she had intended to insult me.

We finished eating in less than thirty minutes and were back in the car. Iris cranked up the music and drove back up on the interstate like we were in an IndyCar. I realized then that I was the farthest I had ever been from a parent. I had been to far away places, but never far away from adult supervision. Yes, Iris was an adult, technically. But she didn't act much differently than my school friends.

Within an hour, the landscape had become more dense with trees; the hills grew steeper. I felt twisted up inside and couldn't get my mind off Mom's tears. If she was still torn up about losing Allie, I could only imagine what it must have been like for Allie's son. Or did he remember her at all?

When Iris turned onto the road which our map indicated would lead to the house, my heart felt so tight it might have stopped pumping. I thought I would vomit. I must have looked sickly because Iris reached over and patted my shoulder.

"You okay?"

"No."

The Beetle moved slowly, maybe because the road was

narrow and rough, or maybe because Iris felt as terrified as I did. Our GPS predicted we would arrive at our destination in one mile. We rounded a curve and came to a police car with its lights flashing. It was parked alongside the road leaving barely enough room for us to get around it. As we did, I could see the taillights of an old truck which had evidently crashed down the embankment.

"I hope everyone is okay," I said.

"Yes, me, too," Iris mumbled, focusing her eyes ahead in preparation for anything.

The road narrowed to a single lane before the pavement ended. Sparsely graveled dirt continued. Iris maneuvered the car carefully around ruts and large rocks, jostling us so much that I felt certain I would lose my breakfast.

"This feels like a bad idea," I said, placing a hand on the dash to try to steady myself. That didn't help.

"There's no place to turn around now. We'll have to go all the way. Maybe it won't look so bad at the top."

My instincts said it would look worse. I was becoming less terrified and more angry at Iris. Blaming her felt justified. At least there was a cop not far off behind us if things went terribly wrong.

The road topped a hill then flattened, becoming more like the path through the field back home. It was mostly dried grass as it curved around a bend to the other side of the ridge. As the landscaped opened up, it was clear that things were worse than either of us had imagined.

29

The tips of branches hung low over the road at the tree line. Red and blue lights reflected off the spindly twigs hanging so low they scraped the roof of our small car. We emerged into the yard to see three police cars parked in front of a tiny trailer, its door streaked orange with rust. Two police officers began walking toward our car.

"This is not good," Iris mumbled and pushed the buttons to lower both our windows.

An officer approached my window because it was closest, "Step out of the car, please."

"What's going on?" I asked, opening the door slowly and easing out.

"Why don't you tell us? Can I see your I.D., please?" His tone was even and gave no hint to the accusation his words were implying. He bent to look through my open window at Iris, "Ma'am, I need you to step out of the car, also. I'll need to see your I.D."

I removed my learners permit from my wallet and handed it to him. While he looked it over, I read his name tag, Kite.

"Well that's unexpected," he glanced from the card to me and back again a few times. He motioned with a tilt of his head of the other officer to take a look. That officer did the same slow double-take. "You related to Tracy Duren?"

My face felt hot and sweat beaded up on my forehead. My fingers ran through my hair to get it out of my face. I tried to remember to breathe. Iris spoke up, "Yes. And I'm Iris Dawson, a friend of the family."

"Well, well," said the other officer, Officer Crumbly. "What brings you two up here to see Mr. Billings?" Something about his question seemed off, like it was a joke we weren't in on.

Iris stuck to our previous plan and did the talking, "We're here looking for his grandson. We just wanted to know if he was doing well. Our mother, I mean, John's mother has wondered for years what happened to him. We wanted to surprise her with some answers. It looks like we came at a bad time."

Both officers stared at her, planning their words carefully, "What significance is his grandson to her and what makes you think his grandson is here?"

Iris spoke with impressive calm, "He was brought to Mom's house about sixteen years ago, on the night his mother was killed. He was just a few months old. She never saw him again, never knew what happened to him. I did a records search and found that Silas Billings would have been his next of kin. We figured we'd start here."

Officer Kite said, "So this is your first time on this property?"

We both nodded insistently. I began to worry that whatever news we gleaned about the boy would not be anything Mom would find comforting.

A white van pulled into the yard, snapping off a few low branches. It parked beside a police cruiser. An older man in a suit stepped out. Both cops gave him a quick acknowledging wave. "Gentlemen," He waved back. "I assume he's inside?"

"Bedroom," Officer Kite replied to the man before turning back to us, "I have to make a call before I can let you leave. We'll need to take a statement and may be contacting you again. It's protocol with homicide investigations."

"Homicide?" My voice pitched too high and awkward for a fifteen year old boy. I wished I had left the talking to Iris.

Officer Crumbly nodded in response as Officer Kite walked off toward the house. "We're still gathering evidence. It seems Mr. Billings didn't have a lot of friends or family. No one seems to know much about him except to stay off his property. Evidently you kids missed the memo on that one."

"So, he lived alone?" Iris reached into her purse and pulled out the notepad, the printed copy of Jim's death certificate, and a copy of the news article about the night Allie died. "I don't know if this information will help, but it's what we used to figure out where to start looking for the boy."

The officer took the papers and glanced over them. "Interesting. We've only been here an hour, haven't gathered much evidence yet. We're State Police, here to assist the county, so I'm not familiar with Mr. Billings. Can I hold onto these?"

"Sure," she smiled more sweetly than was typical.

He smiled back at her before his mouth pulled into a line of seriousness, "Still, it's kind of strange you kids would show up now." He glanced at each of us for our reactions to the statement. I'm sure I looked ill. I was too nervous to look at Iris. A heavy silence settled in as Officer Crumbly scanned over the documents. Officer Kite came back with a County Officer. His plain nylon tag was embroidered with the name Jeff Scott. He nodded a greeting, then explained that we were not suspects. "However, because of the unusual timing of your presence here, we'll need to take a statement from you to account for it."

Officer Kite took a clipboard and motioned Iris to walk over to his cruiser. Officer Scott stayed with me.

In giving my statement, I spared no detail. I told him about the notebooks, the photograph, Mom crying, scraping the windshield this morning, waiting on Iris, the ham biscuit, and my nausea as we approached the Billings' property. I barely took a breath. I wanted to leave no doubt that we were there for the reasons we said we were there, and had nothing to do with killing anyone.

As I signed my name to the bottom of the form containing the information I had given, the door to the trailer opened and the older man walked out. I heard him say, "I can understand that his head might have been injured from the accident, but someone else caused the final blow. It appears his pants were opened to expose himself prior to his landing on the floor. So, we're looking at blunt force trauma at the moment, but I think there's more to this. It should be an interesting case, boys. Let's load him up."

Officer Kite walked back over with Iris by his side. He spoke loud enough for everyone to hear, "Alright kids, get out of here. We have work to do so we can all get off this mountain before that cold front moves in," I noticed how shaken Iris seemed. He patted her shoulder, "Expect we'll be in touch."

The car seats were ice cold, but that wasn't why I couldn't stop shivering. As we passed the wrecked truck again, Iris slowed down to a stop. I leaned over her to get a better view of the accident. It looked bad enough to nearly kill a man. I wanted to believe the accident was to blame. I didn't want to tell Mom that Allie's son was a murderer.

Iris stopped gawking at the wreck and turned to look forward. That was my cue to settle back in my seat. She pressed the gas and said, "I think we have time to drive through Felicity, Ohio."

"Seriously? Why would we do that?"

"We're already close, relatively speaking, we might as well see the town where they lived."

I eyed her skeptically, "For what reason?"

"I just want to see it, get a feel for what it was like living there. I'm trying to understand what kind of relationship Allie had with Jim. Maybe someone will know where to find their son. Isn't this mystery driving you crazy?"

"No, but you are."

I wouldn't have called it a mystery. It was a nightmare with no clear meaning. I just wanted to go home because I felt we were digging ourselves deeper into a pit we couldn't climb out of. But I was her passenger, so I went wherever she wanted to go.

30

Iris flipped down the car's sun visor where a CD holder had been attached. She slid a folded paper out from a pocket and tossed it onto my lap.

"We'll go to the cemetery first, get that out of the way before the sun goes down." She paused while I unfolded the paper to see a map she had printed from the Internet. Dots made with a yellow highlighter marked where, I assumed, she wanted to go.

"What are these other places?"

"Allie's mother's house, her mother's grocery store where Allie had worked, Jim's house, and the church they attended."

"How did you find out all this?" It was a little creepy that Iris had been able to dig so deeply into their lives; or possibly the creep-factor came from knowing we were now searching for a murderer.

"Just believe me when I say I know how to find what I'm looking for, John. I don't like to snoop; but if I need to, I know how to do it quickly and successfully."

I thought of all the times I had caught her in my room and my face felt hot with embarrassment and anger. I looked out the window, not wanting any part of her plan.

She drove in silence for a while before turning up the radio. She tuned the dial to a local station playing bluegrass and twang so unapologetic for its mountain roots that even Nashville would have cringed. But I liked it, even if I wouldn't have admitted that to my school friends. There was something about the high pitched longing of Ralph Stanley's voice that pulled out all a person's pain. Listening to east Kentucky radio meant hearing a lot of other similar voices, all distinctly Appalachian, all new to me.

"Do you like this music?" I finally asked, but felt it was a stupid question. She had chosen to listen to it, after all.

"It's not my favorite, but I like it okay. I'm trying to get my mind wrapped around this area."

"You're talking like we're in a different country. We're just a few hours from home."

"Let me have my adventure," she said without further explanation.

We pulled into the town cemetery as afternoon turned to evening. I had fallen asleep in the car, so Iris had to slap my chest to wake me. I sat up and rubbed my eyes. She parked the car in the center of the cemetery. "We'll need to walk around and find their graves."

She got out and started walking to the far end, glancing at every marker as she passed. I went the opposite direction toward the entrance and did the same. Fifteen minutes of searching seemed much longer with the cold wind picking up. I was relieved to finally hear Iris call out that she had found it.

The headstone was rather plain. It had the word BILLINGS carved in large letters, underneath were the words *He Will Rise*. A small stone marker was situated above where Jim's body was buried. His name, birth date, and death date were carved there. A new arrangement of artificial poinsettias had been place in the planter by his head. But above where Allie's body was presumably buried, there was no marker, no flowers, no mention of her name.

"Are you sure she's here?" I asked.

Iris didn't answer. She stared at Jim's stone plate as if she might kick it loose and smash it to bits. Finally, she said, "Yes." Then she marched angrily toward the car.

"Where are we going now?" I ran to catch up.

"It's Wednesday, church will start soon."

"Ah, Iris!" I whined like a baby and immediately stood taller to make up for it. "Let's don't."

"I want to see the motherfuckers," she spit the words.

"Who? Who are you mad at?"

We reached the car together. She slapped the roof and laid her head on her arm. I couldn't tell if she was crying, but if she wasn't, she was close to doing so. She spoke into her sleeve, "The least they could've done was put her name on the goddamn headstone!"

"Who are 'they?' Everybody in her family died!"

"Silas wasn't dead. Jim's mother wasn't dead." She raised her head to look at me; the fierceness in her eyes was frightening. "A whole congregation of church goers didn't die. Someone paid for the Billings stone, and someone paid for the plate by his head. The bastard has two stones. Two! And not a word about Allie. Even the quote, He Will Rise, is all about him. He. Not her. Jim didn't deny that to Allie, John. The church denied that to Allie. And we're going to go there and I'm going to find out why."

"How is that going to help anything? You keep changing our reason for coming up here. We can't fix the past, Iris. And it's so late already. We should just go home."

"No," she opened the car door and got inside. I either had to get in with her or find another way home.

31

We skipped all the other places marked on her map and headed straight to the church, which was south by the river. I had hoped no one would be there and the doors would be locked. But seeing a few cars in the parking lot told me to prepare for disappointment.

When I pushed the latch on the main doors and they opened, a soft groan of irritation escaped me. I wished Iris would have come to her senses and driven us home. She could have easily passed by the church and we'd have been on our way back to our normal, well... kind of normal lives. But she had stopped, and the doors had opened, and the sounds of music which had been faint in the parking lot hit our ears like a blast of unwanted joy.

I closed the doors behind us and we stood in a foyer at the back of the church. The stage was visible from there. Rich blue carpet covered the sanctuary floor, up the stairs to the stage, and all the way back to the baptistry. On the stage stood a young boy playing a violin, a teenage girl with braids playing a clarinet, a dozen ladies being led in song by a woman wearing a purple scarf over her hair, and somewhere off stage a piano played. Having been around music all of my life, I picked up on the sour notes of the clarinetist, as well as the masterful nuances of the pianist. I was so mesmerized by the mismatched group that I momentarily forgot why we were there.

I remembered our mission as soon as a tall, thin, old man stepped around the corner of the sanctuary and made his way to us. He was smiling an exaggerated smile. His whole body looked stretched out; his wrinkled and translucent skin hung in places and seemed pulled taut in others. His hair dyed black hair swooped broadly over his male pattern baldness. A large gray age spot rested on his chin like spilled food just beneath his thin lips. His wide smile twitched into a pucker before pulling wide again. "May I help you?" His eyes held a spark.

Iris said, "We're here to-"

"I was speaking to the young man," he interrupted her without even looking at her. He kept his shining eyes on me, his mouth still struggling not to twitch back out of his forced smile. In my mind, I cursed Iris for putting me in that situation. I didn't know what to say to him.

"Uhm, we were just driving by and stopped to stretch our legs, heard the music and thought we'd come inside to listen," I lied.

"Lovely," he said, eying me suspiciously but still maintaining his smile. "God is doing amazing things with them, isn't He?"

We all stepped closer to watch the musicians, whom I no longer cared to hear. I just wanted to leave. The song ended and everyone on stage shifted restlessly. The clarinetist licked her reed and momentarily stood on one leg, then shifted to the other leg. The violinist kept his eyes on the lady with the purple scarf. From our new location, I could see a tall boy at the piano. He stretched out his arms to crack his knuckles before shaking his hands. He cracked them again, shook them again, then cracked them again.

The lady with the microphone said, "The congregation will be here soon. We need to get this down. Everyone focus-"

"I need to go to the restroom," interrupted the boy at the piano.

"You just went," the lady snapped at him. "And so let's start with the second-"

"I need to go to the restroom," he interrupted again. The lady ignored the boy and continued speaking to the choir. The boy raised his voice to be heard over her, "I need to go to the restroom. I need to go to the restroom." He began to bounce on the stool very much like a toddler would if in need of a toilet.

"You are breaking the rules, Gabe! God is not pleased!" She yelled at him.

He stopped bouncing, looked straight ahead and placed his hands back on the keys. He played; his fingers worked through an amazingly difficult string of notes without error. The lady stomped down the stairs to his side where she physically held his hands up from the keys. Even though she was not speaking into the microphone, we could all hear her say, "That is not the piece! You are still breaking the rules. We're doing this one!" She jabbed her finger at a page in an open book of music, "Play this when I say."

As the lady walked back onto the stage she said to the other ladies in the choir, "He will be the death of me, yet!" They all giggled or murmured, but the two musicians stood meek and still. She said into the microphone, "Everyone, again on three. One… two… three."

While they played through the entire piece again, I glanced over at Iris. She was no longer fuming with anger. Her expression was a mix of curiosity and disbelief. She caught me looking at her and leaned over to whisper, "She's a bit of a tyrant, don't you think?"

The tall man stepped forward at the sight of us whispering, his fake smile still firmly in place. "Is there a problem?"

"We're fine," I said just before the piano stopped playing.

We all looked to the stage where the woman screamed, "What now?"

"I need to go to the restroom. I need to go to the restroom," the boy repeated.

The tall man shook his head and sighed, his fake smile twitched and faded.

The woman responded to the boy, "I see we are not going to finish until you do. If you must, go on. But expect to be punished later for disrupting, young man."

The boy stood and walked with stiff legs, arms swinging as if in a march. His eyes fixated on the top edge of the wall, glancing only briefly to look where he was walking. When out of his peripheral vision he caught sight of us, he stopped walking, nearly stumbled, and glanced at us nervously. His hands went up to shield the sides of his face from our view, or us from his. He inched past us cautiously though he was at least three inches taller than I was. I turned to watch his resumed march out of the sanctuary, curious about how such a grown looking guy could act like such a little kid. Had these people done that to him?

Seeming to read my mind, the tall man said, "That boy was cursed at birth." He sounded apologetic, as if to make clear the boy was not a reflection of the church as a whole. "That's what happens to the children of Jezebels. They come out of the womb with twisted hearts and minds."

Something about the words he chose made me think of Allie. I felt renewed sympathy for her that she was ever involved with those people. Just hearing how they spoke of one another cut to the bone and I didn't even know them. It was obvious why they refused to give Allie a headstone. She wasn't worthy in their eyes. I could have taken Iris's hand and left at that moment, satisfied that we had learned everything we needed to know. But instead, I asked the old man, "Is that why you refused to have Allie's name placed on her headstone?"

His eyes widened before squinting to examine us. "Who?" He asked rather convincingly.

"Allie Billings, she used to be involved with this church. Why is her name not on her headstone?"

"I am not familiar with such a person," he straightened his back, "I've never heard of her. Perhaps you should ask her family?" The spark returned to his eye.

"She doesn't have any," Iris put her arm around me and stood very close in hopes he would address us both.

"Oh?" He raised a hairy eyebrow, "What a shame. Was she a friend of yours?"

"Yes!" Iris pointed her finger at him, "Allie was loved! She deserves to be remembered as the beautiful person she was!"

The woman with the purple scarf materialized by our sides, "Is there a problem, Mr. Grathes?"

"Nothing," he waved his hand in the air, "I will handle it. I believe you should check on sir pianist."

"Yes," She seemed suddenly flustered and walked quickly out of the sanctuary.

"Well," said the man we now knew to be Mr. Grathes, "We are not the provider of headstones. But, we *are* the saver of souls. I certainly hope this woman benefited from our services, though I don't recall her ever coming here. We always try to turn sinners into saints, but not all will make it to the pearly gates, I'm afraid. Freewill is the downfall of many. You have my condolences. May I walk you out?"

"No need." Iris pulled my arm toward the door. I had never been so ready to get out of a place.

When we were back in the car, Iris looked visibly shaken.

"What's wrong?" I asked.

"That place," she shook her head, "There's something... I can't quite put my finger on it."

"It was bizarre," I forced a laugh. "I'll be glad to get home, won't you?" I crossed my fingers she would say she was ready to go.

"I guess," she said, "But I think we should try to raise money and get Allie's grave marked."

"Great idea!" I breathed a sigh of relief that we were finally going home to Nashville.

Part Five

Angelina

32

December 27, 2006

Marcy came into the bedroom around six o'clock that morning. She lifted the blankets and slid into bed behind me. Carefully, she draped her arm over me, kissed my head through my braided hair, and nestled her head onto the pillow. She hadn't known I was awake, but I had been for quite some time. Waking up just before dawn was something I had been required to do most of my life. I listened to her breathing slow and the intermittent sounds of snoring.

I closed my eyes again, not wanting to leave the warmth of her body or the safeness I felt. She was complicated, but kind. My mind drifted from her to Emory. He was also complicated, also kind. He had brought me back to Marcy's the night before and made me promise I wouldn't run off again. He and Marcy promised the moon if I would just stay long enough to get me to Jute. It was strange to be begged to accept the thing I wanted most in the world. Of course I agreed.

My thoughts turned to kissing Emory. I remembered the feel of his breath on my lips. I knew he said I shouldn't, but I wanted to kiss him again. I wanted to do it better, do it like Marcy had, make his head fall back in pleasure. I imagined it over and over again. I hoped there would be a chance on the way to Nashville; maybe he would pull over to look across a river and tell me how blue my eyes were. Warmth filled me as my thoughts carried me deeper into a dream.

I had fallen asleep, but my eyes flew open when I heard the front door bang shut. The room was full of sunlight. I marveled at the peace I had felt, how deeply rested I was.

"Angelina!" Emory sounded breathless as he ran into the bedroom, "Come on, we have to go. I've got to be home by five o'clock and we have quite a drive ahead of us."

"Let the ladies sleep!" Marcy groaned and covered her head with the blankets.

I climbed out at the end of the bed. "I overslept, I'm sorry. Give me five minutes to get dressed."

Marcy's muffled voice came from under the covers, "I laid out your clothes on the sewing table and packed your new things in your bag." She pulled the blanket down so I could see her squinting eyes, "There's a few surprises."

I was too focused on getting ready to think much about surprises. I shut the door to the sewing room and saw a newly made outfit folded beside a pair of short boots. The pants were blue like my eyes and fit as perfectly as the others she had made. The blouse was sheer with flecks of mauves, browns, and blues and came with a blue camisole to wear underneath. I dressed in the sewing room, and was impressed by the comfort and beauty of the clothes.

While in the bathroom brushing my teeth, Marcy gently knocked on the door. I opened it before I spit the toothpaste into the sink. I quickly rinsed my mouth then said, "I'm almost ready."

Marcy smiled at me, amused. She held my face with one hand while her other patted my lips with a towel. "Be still. I'm going to put a little make-up over your bruises." Her hands worked quickly and softly over my face to smooth liquid, then powder. She brushed on a little color. I was worried the end result would have me looking as painted as she made herself; but when I turned to look in the mirror, I looked nothing like either of us. My bruises were barely visible and it was hard to stop staring at my raspberry lips. Some minor swelling still had my face looking unnaturally puffy, but overall her work was astounding.

"Wow, thank you!" I hugged her.

She wrapped her arms around me, "You deserve all good things, Angelina. I wish them for you today and always."

We walked into the living room. Emory already had my bag over his shoulder. He took my hand and led me out the door. When I climbed into his truck, I looked to see Marcy on the porch hugging herself for warmth. I raised my hand and gave her a wave. In just a little more than a day, I had changed so much. I felt so much older despite the wishes of Emory and Marcy that I feel younger. I felt like I could conquer the world. With that thought, I laughed aloud causing Emory to glance over at me before he started the engine.

"I guess you're excited to see her?"

"I was just thinking about how much smaller the world feels already."

"Well, tell me that at the end of this three hour trip."

He backed out of the drive and headed past streets of houses, old buildings, parks, and eventually onto a busy road with lots of traffic all headed in the same direction.

"If you're hungry, there's a few granola bars in the glove box." He pointed. "We'll grab lunch in Nashville before we head up to the Duren farm and try to avoid getting arrested."

"Why would we get arrested?" I pushed away visions of Silas's body.

"Trespassing on private property. You can't just walk onto someone's land, especially when it's owned by Tracy Duren. Technically, we could be shot for that."

I didn't know a lot about the outside world, but I had trouble believing that was true. My mind did not see Jute or her family as the shooting type. However, it did cross my mind that they might be inordinately protective. I started contemplating backup plans, different ways we might get the letter to Jute if we couldn't hand it to her face to face. Ideally, we would be able to just drive up to the house. Maybe we would have to sneak in on foot. Maybe I would have to leave the letter somewhere to be found by her, which was not an appealing thought. I had so many questions to ask her. I desperately wanted to actually meet her.

The drive was not as bad as Emory had predicted. It was much better than walking. He stopped at a deli just outside of Nashville. We shared the largest sandwich I had ever seen. Emory ate all of his half and part of mine. I was nervous and I didn't talk much.

It didn't help ease our tension that many of the people coming in and out of the restaurant turned their heads to stare at us. I was already feeling self-conscious because my hair wasn't braided and put up in public. It hung in waves from the braids I'd worn the night before. I worried it was vulgar, as Esther would have described it. But other women had their hair down and no one stared at them.

I reminded myself that I had assumed wrong about many of the world's moral expectations. I tried to let it go, but I also sensed that Emory was bothered by the staring as well. He looked stiff and defensive. I patted his knee to comfort him, but he pulled it away and gave me a look of warning.

We took our to-go cups of tea to the truck where we both relaxed out of the public eye. He said, "We're only fifteen minutes away. Are you ready to meet them?"

I shook my head no, "I don't know how to be ready for this. Let's just see what happens."

33

The gate was huge. The fence was huge, too. Its well-maintained iron bars were beautiful and impenetrable. We drove until the road dead-ended by the river.

"Damn it!", Emory protested. He struggled to get his big truck turned around. When he finally had us facing back toward the road, he sat idle with his hands on the steering wheel. He seemed to be staring off into the thoughts in his head.

"What do you think we should do?" I stared at him, worried, but found his gentle eyes distracting. I remembered when I thought he was capable of hitting me. Now I knew the only part of me he could ever hurt was my heart.

He shook his head, still thinking. "This is bullshit," he groaned in frustration before slamming the gearshift down. His tires spun out, kicking up dirt behind us then squealing on the pavement. After revving the engine one more time, he coasted back to a slow roll. He still had no answers.

"Are you sure this is the place?" I asked.

He snapped, "Yes! I'm sure." He glanced from the road to the fence. "I'm sorry. I'm just pissed off. I hate being locked out, all the damn time."

I suspected he wasn't just talking about fences. "I'm sure they're just trying to protect themselves."

"I know. I'd be the same way. If I had their money, I'd probably make the damn thing electric," He reached up and pulled the brim of his hat low with determination. "We'll see if we can get in on the other side."

Emory hit the gas again, jerking the truck forward and my

head back. He steered the truck side to side, driving nearly into the grass along the road. I wasn't sure what he was doing, but I could tell he was becoming increasingly upset. I put my hand on his shoulder.

He moved away, "Don't do that. You don't need to baby me. I said we'd get in, we will get in."

As we approached the turn for the gate, Emory sped up a little then slammed on the brakes, sending the truck skidding into a twist that landed us facing the gate. It scared me nearly to death, but when it was over I realized it might have been intentional. I hoped it was, anyway.

"Are we just going to ram it?" My hand clung to the handle above the window.

"No. I'm thinking."

Before he could form a plan, a police car came from the direction of the dead end. I was confused as to how that was even possible. Emory looked startled. The car stopped behind us, blocking us from backing out. A very large man in blue jeans and a brown leather jacket got out of the driver's side and approached the truck. Emory muttered, "Shit."

The man tapped his knuckle on the window so Emory lowered it.

"Can I help you?" the man's deep voice was calm, but serious.

"We were just lost," Emory lied.

"Tell me a lie again, son, and I'll call backup. I'm not on duty, see. I don't want to have to deal with harassment on my day off. If you want to see him, buy a ticket to his show. Don't come up here bothering the ladies."

Emory's face turned red and his mouth clenched tight. I knew little about him, but I did know he hated when people assumed bad things about him. I thought I better intervene before he said something we wold both regret. "I have a letter I need to get to Jute Duren. It's from Allie Vining."

The Officer's expression was unflinching. He stared straight at me, not speaking for what seemed like eternity. Finally he said, "How did you come to have such a letter?"

"I found it in a hatbox," I almost left it at that, but I could tell it wasn't enough. I added, "Allie was my mother."

His mouth turned down briefly. His words came quietly, full of warning, "Don't lie to me. Do you understand me? This family means everything to me and I will not tolerate-"

He was interrupted by another voice coming from the car, "What's going on, Dawson?"

"Stay in the car!" the officer ordered the man. I heard the car door slam and assumed his order was ignored. Emory stared up at his rear view mirror then pushed a button to lower my window. He must have observed the man approaching my side of the truck. I turned to see him, broad shouldered and beautiful. As he looked at me, his mouth fell open in shock.

"Damn it, I said stay in the car!" the officer screamed again. "You can't encourage these people!"

The man didn't look at the officer at all. His eyes stayed locked on mine. His voice finally came, like a whisper, "You can't be real." His hand reached out and gently touched my hair.

I was overwhelmed by the unfamiliar feeling of being recognized. I struggled to say the words, "I have a letter for Jute... from Allie."

"Oh my God," he exhaled the words and struggled to breathe his next breath. He put both hands to my face and held it between them. "Oh my God, how is this possible?"

The officer said, "Tracy, what's going on? Talk to me!"

"She's Allie's. I don't know how she is here, but there's no denying whose she is. Look at her," now he was laughing and looking at the officer, "Look at her eyes and the shape of her nose and how she holds her mouth more to one side! Unbelievable!" But then his face lost its glow and his forehead wrinkled with concern. He nervously ran his fingers through his dark hair, "Dawson, we have to get her out of here before Jute sees her. She can't just go up to the house. We need a plan, something to ease Jute into this. We need to know what's going on."

"But you have a plane to catch, as in right now. We should be driving, right now."

"I can't. I'll cancel. Jute can't handle this alone. I'm not sure she can handle this at all."

The officer, who I now knew to be Dawson, looked worried. "You're serious," he said. "If you're right about her, I agree."

The man nodded.

"Okay, then. I need you all to follow me to the house."

As the men walked back to the police car, Emory and I dared to look at each other. I felt an excited sense of accomplishment, but Emory looked wild-eyed with terror. After the police car moved enough for him to back out, Emory said, "That was Tracy Duren. Holy shit! And we're going to his house. This is fucked up, scary as hell!"

"I thought you liked him."

"I do, on the radio. But, I don't know him. I don't know how he's going to judge this situation." Emory didn't mean the situation with me, he was referring to his secret.

"I'm sure they'll like you. You're amazing." To ease his mind, I offered, "I won't say anything about what Marcy said."

His shoulders tensed, "See, you don't see me the same."

"I just see you better now," I said, "I mean, I wouldn't mind being married to a man like you."

He snapped, "Well, you can't be. Stop trying to act all grown up. You still have a couple of years as a kid, enjoy them."

It was always the same excuse. I was a kid, not an adult. But I knew in my heart his real reason for not wanting me had nothing to do with my age. I was the ignorant girl from the mountains, ruined and scarred by abuse. He probably wanted a perfect girl, or just a girl not so terribly flawed, something I could never be.

We followed the police car down a winding dirt road bordered by an electric fence. At the top of a steep hill, just as the road made a sharp right curve, the police car pulled off the road and up to the fence right . Tracy got out and unhooked the electric wire so the car could drive into the field. He motioned for us to follow. We pulled in and stopped behind the car to wait for Tracy to reconnect the fence. He then jogged up to my door and opened it.

"Scoot," he said.

Emory made room on the seat by raising part of the center console so I could sit in the middle. My leg was pressed against Emory's. My face felt hot and my hands were sweaty. Tracy slid in beside of me, smiling. He waved his hand for Dawson to go.

Emory put his hand on the gear shifter between my knees. As he moved it, his wrist brushed my leg. For a moment I forgot where I was. I kept my eyes on his hand as it rested on the gear shifter knob. I felt a completely new level of desire for him. I wanted him to slide his hand over onto my knee. I knew it was wrong, but I wanted it anyway.

"She won't be satisfied until you've told her everything," Tracy's voice was calm, but it still startled me. I looked up to see he was staring at me and appeared to have been for some time. "You can't just tell her a little. She deserves answers."

"But, I don't know everything," I felt like I would be a disappointment. I heard Silas's words echoing in my mind, telling me I was worthless. They would all eventually see I could offer them nothing. With an apologetic tone, I said, "I was hoping she could tell me everything."

We came to an iron gate which looked the same as the fence we had driven around earlier. Its elaborate curves and swirls seemed out of place running through a cow pasture. The gates opened automatically. Just beyond was a three-story brick house with a separate white wraparound porch for each level. A smaller fence circled the house and kept in a small, jumping and barking dog. We parked outside the garage.

Dawson got out of his car and quickly came back to open Tracy's door, "You need to call Dink right now and confirm he's available to fly you out tonight. Go take care of business and I'll see these guys in, just go."

Tracy gave me a wink and patted my knee. "Don't go anywhere," he said, sliding out of the truck and running in through a garage door.

34

"Coffee?" Dawson held an empty mug in our direction.

I said, "No, thank you, sir."

Emory said, "Please."

While Dawson prepared their coffee, Tracy's eyes scanned me from across the table. He was still staring after Dawson brought us each a mug and sat in the seat beside him. Dawson said to me, "I made you some hot chocolate. It's the microwave kind because we were out chocolate. I hope it will be good enough."

"I've never had it, but it sounds wonderful. Thank you."

"I'm sorry." Dawson looked embarrassed." If you're used to having it made with real chocolate, you'll be disappointed."

"No," I shook my head, "I've never had any kind of hot chocolate."

Dawson looked sideways at Tracy. Concern rippled between them. I wasn't sure what was so bad about never having had hot chocolate. Dawson finally cleared his throat and looked back to me. "Can you stay the night?"

"Yes," I said immediately, with an embarrassing level of excitement.

Emory's voice was low and shaky, "I can't. I have to get home by five or my dad will kick me out."

"Ah, fuck it," Tracy said nonchalantly, "Let him. Besides, how old are you? Twenty-five? Twenty-six?"

I could tell Emory was tense. I tried again to comfort him by patting his knee under the table. He jerked his leg away for the second time that day. His face was red and his teeth clenched as he stared down into this coffee. He seemed to be pulling himself into a ball.

"He's twenty-five," I offered, trying to bridge the expanding gap of silence between Emory and our new acquaintances.

My words didn't help. Emory was obviously angry or extremely stressed about something. He put his hands on the table and stretched his fingers wide before pulling them into fists then brought them up to his forehead. He ran his fingers through his hair a couple of times, but never looked at any of us.

"Man," Tracy sat up and let his arm rest on the back of his chair. He shifted a little toward Dawson. "My dad locked me in a hotel for years after he realized I was gay, wouldn't let me leave the place. The best day of my life was the day I left that son of a bitch and never went back. As a matter of fact, it was Allie driving the getaway car."

Hearing her name made my heart skip a beat. Tracy had all my attention, but there was no response from Emory. He kept his head bowed, propped up by the palms of his hands. I watched Dawson and Tracy stare at each other again, subtle signs of silent communication passed between them. There were a few slight shrugs and face twitches, a shake of the head, and finally Tracy pushed his leg forward and kicked Emory's boot.

Emory looked up alarmed. We could all see he had tears in his eyes. Tracy said, "You know why you're upset? Because your Dad is a dick."

"Hey," Dawson puts a hand out in front of Tracy as if to call off a fight, "Don't insult the boy's dad, man."

Emory started wiping his eyes and tried to process what was going on. He looked at Tracy with both curiosity and fear.

Tracy leaned forward and held Emory's gaze so he dared not look away. "What is it you want out of life?"

If I had not been staring at Emory's lips, I wouldn't have understood his faint words, "I want in."

"First you have to get out," Tracy countered.

Emory exhaled a sigh of resignation, but all I could do was hold my breath. Before hearing Tracy's words, I had not realized just how much Emory and I had in common, or how much our story was like Tracy's. Maybe every child suffered. That thought came tethered with heavy sadness. Tracy glanced at me as if he could read my thoughts. Surely he could not. I forced myself to think only about hot chocolate and took a slow sip.

Dawson's chair scraped the floor as he stood, "Let's take a walk, Emory, and let these two discuss that letter. You can decide later if you want to stay. Don't let Tracy push you around." Dawson winked at Tracy, but Emory was too focused on the table to catch it. He didn't move except for his knee nervously bouncing up and down. Dawson tried again, "There's a shooting range out back, want to go let off some steam?" Emory looked up with surprise. Dawson said, "Tracy won't shoot with me, he thinks he's too uptown. Come on."

It worked and I marveled at how easily Dawson had pulled Emory out of his shell. But it didn't take long after they left for me to realize I was left alone with an intimidating man I barely knew for an indeterminate amount of time. He stared at me again and made no effort to hide that he was staring at me. I tried to ignore it, taking sips of the hot chocolate which had turned cold. But finally I had to break the silence, "So are you Jute's brother?"

"What makes you say that?" His voice gave nothing away.

"Your last names are the same."

I braved a glance at his eyes. They were gleaming with a joy I couldn't understand. "She's my best friend and the mother of my son. Do you really not know this?"

I shook my head. "I don't know a lot of things. It's a long story."

"I bet." Silence fell again, yet his eyes stayed glued to me. I couldn't shake the feeling he already knew everything about me, even what I was thinking at that moment.

My words just slipped out of me like a sigh in my sleep, "No one knows I'm alive." I cupped my hands around my mug but it provided no warmth. Tracy said nothing, still. It was unsettling. I had no idea what he expected of me. "They lied to me," I tested the waters for a reaction. "They said I belonged to them." Now tears were filling my eyes and I felt ashamed that I let them be seen. I couldn't bring myself to look at him.

He slid into the chair in front of me where Dawson had been sitting. His hands reached out and covered mine around the mug. He said, "I remember when Social Services took you."

"I don't know what you mean," I looked up at him.

"Social Services took you the night your parents died. We don't know a lot about what happened to you after that because your parents had a will which did not include us." He leaned back in the chair again and scanned my face for clues.

"No. That was Gabriel, not me."

"Well, I figured you had changed your name, and… changed in a lot of ways. But it's okay here if you want to be called Angelina. We never even knew your name was Gabriel anyway."

It took a few moments of replaying his words in my mind before I realized he thought I was like Emory, born with the wrong body. "Oh… Oh, no. I'm trying to find Gabriel, too. I found his birth certificate in Silas's closet. And a lot of other papers," I reached into my leather bag and plopped the bundle of documents onto the table. They seemed remarkably dirty on the polished wood. I pulled the ribbon and the papers slid out of the stack in various directions. Tracy picked them up randomly, his eyes squinting and scanning.

"Now I don't understand," he kept his eyes on the papers.

"I'm not sure, but I think Gabriel is my brother."

"Then why didn't Allie bring both of you that night?" His pitch raised as he struggled to make sense of it.

"Because I was given away after I was born."

"To whom?"

"Silas, Jim's father."

"Why?" He leaned in again.

"He was supposed to kill me."

"No way!" He screamed it as he stood up and started pacing. "You have to be lying." He chopped through the air with his hand as he spoke, "There is no way Allie would have allowed that. How could she stoop that low? Or did she have a choice? That son of a

169

bitch." His face was hot with anger. "You can not tell Jute this. Don't you dare tell her this!" His hands pushed through his hair and laced behind his neck as he looked to the ceiling in concentration. "So why didn't Silas kill you?"

"I... I... don't know. Something to do with my name, my real name, Angelina. Esther stopped him. Esther was Jim's mother. They always called me Perdy, so I didn't even know I was Angelina until... " I couldn't say the rest. Guilt and shame paralyzed me.

Tracy leaned over the table with his hands cupping the edge of it. He looked down at me as if he could see right through to every image in my brain. "So, you said nobody knows you're alive, but Silas and Esther are somebody, aren't they?"

"Yes, but-"

"But they know you are alive. That isn't no one." It sounded like he thought I was caught in a lie.

I swallowed and tried to breathe, my head felt light and dizzy. I opened my mouth to speak but nothing came out. I feared they were going to have me arrested. If they found out what I had done, I would never be allowed to see Jute. Tracy could give her the letter, but would he? He seemed afraid of what the truth would do to her. I thought maybe I was I wrong to come there.

Tracy sat heavily into the seat across from me, grabbed my hands in his, "I don't like not knowing the truth, Angelina. You can tell me anything. We run an abuse shelter, well, Jute runs it. But sometimes Dawson and I get involved. So, I promise you that whatever you tell me will not shock me or make me think less of you. It's safe. No one can get you here, but I need to know if we should expect someone to come looking for you. I want to help you, but I need to know everything."

"But I don't know..." Tears were sliding down my face before I could stop them. "I barely know anything at all. I was lied to my whole life, called Perdy because I was a pretty little girl, I guess, like a pet. They said I was theirs and I had to do whatever Silas said because he was the man of the house. I had to learn to be a good girl, a good woman. I had to prove Satan wasn't in my

170

heart," saying the words made me feel like I was back at the trailer. I could feel Silas's eyes on me from behind. I felt his hatred. I felt him wanting to rip me apart. I couldn't say anything else. I glanced up at Tracy. His jaw was set hard with rage. I was unable to comprehend that his anger might be for anyone other than me. "I tried," I pleaded with Tracy not to be mad at me, "I did everything he asked. I felt the Holy Ghost. I felt it. I know Satan has left me now. Silas didn't believe it, but it's true. I'm not evil."

He moved chairs again, this time sitting where Emory had been. He had turned it sideways so he could take my hand and pull me over to him. I sat across his lap, his arms wrapped around me, "I know. I know." He comforted me. My head rested on his shoulder and his head leaned onto it. The energy of his huge presence wrapped around me like a mother hen might protect a chick. His arms pulled me so tightly to him that I felt the wounds on my back break open again. I convinced myself I could take the pain. But he squeezed his arms around me again and the pain was too great to hide. I gasped and tried to rein in the sound of my groan.

He pushed me off of him in alarm. "I'm sorry," he said, wide-eyed. I felt lightheaded with emotion and had to hold onto the table to stand. Tracy stepped behind me so my back was to him. I thought about what Marcy said, that if anyone asked me to do something I didn't want to do, tell them no. I didn't want him to see my back, but it was too late. Blood had soaked through my blouse.

35

Three walls were white. The fourth wall, the one with the window, was the color of a blue jay. A nightstand was by the window. The metal lamp which sat on it had a stained glass shade; the panes were shaped like the tips of blue jay feathers in colors of white, turquoise, sky, and navy. The furniture was simple. There was a bed made of metal piping, bent and linked symmetrically. The blanket was gray, but soft like an animal's winter coat. The room felt purposefully empty, unintrusive, a listener.

Emory set my leather bag, with all the papers haphazardly thrown back inside of it, onto the bed. He turned to face me. His eyes scanned my face with worry, a very different look than they had held the night he said my eyes were beautiful. He stepped closer and wrapped his arms high around me, careful not to touch my back. His fingers swirled on the back of my head to soothe, massaging through stands of hair to my scalp. I laid my head on his shoulder, feeling drained.

"I have to go, Angelina. I'll be back, though. I just need to get my things out of my parents' house before they realize I'm leaving for good. I think you'll be safe here, lucky really. They already care more about you than most of us are ever cared about by anyone."

I wasn't sure if I believed Emory. Dawson had showed me to this room after failing to get Tracy to calm down. There had been much discussion about what to do with me. Tracy didn't want to leave me even though he had a concert the following night. Dawson had calmly and consistently reminded him that I would be fine. Tracy had reminded Dawson that I could not, under any circumstances, meet Jute without him present. Nor, according to Tracy, should I be allowed to leave, because my leaving without meeting Jute would be worse than meeting Jute without Tracy. He had been a little frantic. Dawson must have felt it would be easier to calm him if I was sent out of sight.

"I'm scared."

"I know, baby," Emory kissed my head through my hair, "But Dawson is going to make sure everything is done according to the law so justice is served. Please, do what he says."

The thought of justice being served did not put me at ease. I knew what I had done. Killing Silas had felt necessary at the time, but I also knew it was wrong according to the Ten Commandments. Thou shalt not kill. It was a clear rule which I had broken. I should have just run away without killing him. But, visions of myself trying to survive the journey without a shred of clothing made his killing seem even more necessary. It had been a choice between Silas's life or my own. Still, maybe I should have died righteous instead of surviving with the blood of that evil act on my hands. I reminded myself that for all I knew, the story of the Ten Commandments was as fake as my name being Perdy. It didn't really matter what I believed. The world would judge me according to whatever it believed.

"There are nurses coming," my voice was as unsteady as my strength to stand. I felt lightheaded. I wanted to close my eyes and escape into the darkness of sleep.

"Yes," Emory said, "They are coming to help you. They are going to gather evidence to make sure they can show your side of the story. I won't lie, Angelina, it won't be easy. They have to see your body and touch your body in uncomfortable ways." His arms held me tighter. "You are lucky. Not every woman is believed from the start."

Lucky, there was that word again. It was the last word I would have used to describe anything about my life. But the phrase that bothered me the most was *every woman*. Did every woman have a need for a moment like this? If that were true, then there must be many men in agreement with Silas's beliefs. How many men were there who believed women are full of Satan and must be punished? I found myself, again, longing to be on the mountain without Silas, with just the chickens and the garden and myself.

"What if I tell them no, like Marcy said to just say no if I don't want someone to do something?"

"They won't force you. You always have choices, Angelina." He let go of me so he could look at me. "You could leave right now. It is a choice. But, I can't lie and tell you it's an equal choice. You have to think about what is best for you. Right now I think it's trusting these guys to take care of this."

I looked into his eyes so I wouldn't miss his reaction and said, "What if I'm guilty?"

He smiled, but I could see hurt in his eyes, "Some choices are difficult choices with unfortunate consequences. I don't know what you've been through or what you've been made to believe, but I've never met anyone more innocent in all my life." He swallowed hard and blinked his eyes to keep them dry, "I wish you could have met my Granny Talbert. She was the kind of woman who could see right to the heart of people. If she had met you, she would've known and made you believe it. You're an exceptional girl."

I hugged him, "I'm sorry, Emory, I didn't know you had lost her already. Why didn't you tell me?"

"There was no reason to mention it, until now. I'm okay, really," he pushed me away and held my shoulders at arm's length. "So, you hang out here, alright? I don't want to drive all the way back down here this weekend and find you've disappeared into the night."

"I'll stay and wait for you." My heart was overflowing with ache and want.

"Don't do it for me. I'm nothing for you to be focusing on right now. Just focus on healing up." He let go of me and took a step back. After giving me a quick nod, he picked up his hat off the bed. He adjusted it down low toward his captivating green eyes. He smiled a bit awkwardly then walked out of the room. I wanted to go after him, but old habits were hard to break. He said to wait and I didn't want to disobey him.

Not long after Emory left, the nurses arrived. Officer Grant, a thin lady with short, white hair, came in with them. She explained why they were there and what they would be doing, but it was too much for me to process. Too many new words were squeezed in with familiar ones. We went downstairs and out of the house to a very large van. Officer Grant opened the back doors to reveal an awe inspiring amount of medical equipment inside. There were two beds, cabinets, and a sink. Movable lights were attached to the ceiling. I tried to imagine what Mrs. Thorneagle would think of such a vehicle, then decided surely she knew of such things. Maybe I was the only one so ignorant.

Officer Grant said, "Ms. Shaina Emmerson is our Sexual Assault Nurse Examiner and Mrs. Heather Matthews is here as your Sexual Assault Advocate. They will answer any questions you have," she looked from me to them, "I'll wait inside the house while you ladies finish up." She smiled encouragingly and left.

Ms. Emmerson's skin looked brown in the shadows and golden in the light from the van. Her skin tone was similar to Dawson's, but her skin shone like silk. Her beautiful lashes framed large eyes. Her long hair was braided into uncountable braids and pulled back into a ponytail. A clear, shimmering gloss painted her lips and glistened with every word she spoke. Everything about her seemed soft, thoughtful, and kind. "We're going to ask you a few questions before we do the exam, Miss Angelina. Do you have a last name?"

"It should be Billings, if I even have one. I have no records."

"Since we don't know what it is legally, I will indicate your last name is unknown. What I need now is for you to tell me everything that happened to you which caused your injuries, and any other information you feel is relevant to that event."

Injuries, there had been so many. Surely she didn't want me to tell her about every single time he hurt me. I wasn't sure where to start. I stared at her eyes, trying to discern what she

175

wanted from me.

Mrs. Matthews cleared her throat and pushed a spiral of red hair behind her left ear. Her fingers were pale and tipped with pink paint the color of wild roses. Her voice came unsteady at first, but was gentle and sweet, "If you have questions, don't be afraid to ask. Ms. Emmerson is only collecting information to tell your account of events. She isn't here to judge you in any way. And I am here as an advocate, a friend. It's my job to make sure you know what your options are and to listen. Neither of us are here to judge. You should also know you have a say in what we do here. You can tell us to stop at any time; but the more information you give us, the better we will be able to represent your side of events. Let's just take it one thing at a time, though. Does that sound okay?"

I nodded, but I was still unsure.

Ms. Emmerson clarified, "I'm only asking what happened so I will know where to attempt to collect DNA and make sure I have a record of all your injuries. I can assure you, Angelina, I know this was not your fault. None of this. It's normal for assault victims to feel shame. I understand. But, you need to believe me that I am not judging you. I'm here to help you begin to heal."

Mrs. Matthews leaned forward to squeeze my hand. "Would it help to start with the last thing that happened, or the first thing?"

"I don't remember the first," It was difficult to speak while holding my breath.

"Can you tell us about when the first episode took place?" Ms. Emmerson asked.

"I don't know how old I was, but my first memory is of being told not to cry, ever. I remember thinking something was different, what he was doing, and that's why I cried." Ms. Emmerson jotted notes onto a yellow pad of paper before giving me an encouraging look to continue. But I wasn't sure how to break down my entire life into a few sentences.

"Why don't we move on to what happened to your back?"

"It was a belt."

"Through clothes?"

"No. He had ripped off my nightgown."

"Who ripped your nightgown?"

"Silas."

"Any injuries from that?"

"It had caught on my neck before I moved so it wouldn't choke me. Then it came off. So, maybe."

"And the injuries on your face?"

"He punched me. Silas punched me."

"How many times and please point to places of contact?" Ms. Emmerson was still writing as she spoke. Mrs. Matthews had been holding my hand but let go so I could point.

"I'm not sure how many times. Here, here, here, on the side here, and I had turned so back here and my shoulder, too."

"Any other touches?"

"He pulled my ankles. He was going to..." I couldn't say it.

"So he pulled your ankles, and were there other touches?"

"Not this time."

"What day did this happen?"

"Christmas morning."

"Were there any other injuries from this day?"

"When I was running away, I fell down an embankment and landed on my elbows and knees."

"Did anyone else have contact with your injuries?"

"A lady named Marcy bandaged them, and Emory hugged me." I felt my face grow hot and hoped they couldn't see it.

"Any penetration before you ran away or after?"

"What do you mean?"

"Did anyone insert a body part or object into your vagina, mouth, or other orifice? I'm sorry to sound so technical. But I have to ask." Ms. Emmerson waited for a response as Mrs. Matthews picked up my hand again and cupped it between hers.

Images of Silas flashed briefly, images I had locked out of my mind for years. They came like lightning, so quick that I had no time to protect myself. I tried to push them away, my head getting light and dizzy. My mind swam toward what it hoped was darkness, I needed to get to the black. I needed to get out of my body. I needed it now. But I couldn't get there. Tears were falling, out of my control. I could control nothing. My memories kept coming, flooding me with images of Silas's fat fingers, things in his hand, his short shriveled penis. The images wouldn't go away and I couldn't get into the black. The sound of Mrs. Matthew's voice muffled in through the noise of my brain and I hated her for it. I wanted her to stop talking so I could get away, into the darkness. I thought, if she would stop talking and slap me, or tear at my skin, or punch me, maybe it would send me over. She was no help at all.

I slid off the bed and onto the floor. With all my force I slammed my head against the boards. My brain buzzed, but it was not enough. I wanted to do it again, over and over. Before I could make contact a second time, her hands pulled my head up, keeping it from slamming down. My head was held tight against a chest, stiff fabric covering soft breasts and the smell of coffee and something else, something floral like summer. Arms wrapped tight, tight enough to become an escape. I breathed in deeply the unfamiliar smells, letting their newness carry me away from what I wanted to forget.

Mrs. Matthews' words kept coming, finally making sense to my ears. She had me in her arms. "No more words. You don't have to speak. No more words. It's okay. You can tell us no and we'll stop. You don't have to speak. Shhhh."

Part Six

Jute

36

December 28, 2006
12:47 a.m.

Allie's hand moved over my hip. The distinct feathery touch of her fingertips was unmistakable. I didn't remember undressing myself. I tried to open my eyes, but was paralyzed in my sleep. I tried to relax and focus on the feel of her fingers as they rippled over my ribs, five separate gentle touches of skin and the tips of long fingernails. I held my breath when her hand slid over my breast and lingered to feel all the years of changes that had occurred. Would she still find me beautiful? Had she ever?

"I love you." It was Allie's voice. It was so clear, and yet impossible. I fought to open my mouth to speak, to open my eyes and look at her, but sleep held me captive. I felt my own tears flood out past my eyelids.

I thought, "I love you, too. I love you so much." I thought it over and over, desperate for her to hear me.

Her hand moved to my face and ran through my hair. I felt her lips brush mine. I sighed with pleasure, my mouth finally able to move. I had broken free, my eyes sprang open to see her, but I saw something else instead. Above me hovered the nightmare I had thought was over. The vision seemed just as real as Allie's touches had seemed in the dream. The corpse floated in the darkness, its skin hung from its muscles in decay. I frantically blinked my eyes and pressed my palms into them to make the vision end.

Tears came, again. I had cried so much since finding Allie's photo, more than I had cried in all the last decade. Now not only had thoughts of her returned, but also my nightmares. They had stopped when I had become pregnant with John, so many years ago.

Thoughts of John filled me with panic. Were the nightmares returning because I had disregarded him, pushed him out of the center of my heart now that thoughts of Allie had returned? I needed to check on him. Maybe the sight of him would help me focus on the person I had become, not the me I used to be.

I slipped my feet into my house shoes and went to his room. The door was still wide open. There was just enough light coming in through the window to see him sleeping face down on top of all his blankets. He was still dressed in his clothes, even wearing his coat. His feet hung over the edge of the bed, still in his shoes. When I untied them, they were so cold and damp I assumed he'd not been home long. I looked at the clock, it was nearly one o'clock in the morning.

"John," I whispered, giving him a gentle shake. He didn't answer. I took his coat by the sleeve and gave it a gentle tug, trying to pull it off without waking him. The left arm was easy, but I had to lean over him to pull the coat from his right arm. I had nearly pulled it free when he awoke, startled.

"It wasn't me! It wasn't me!" He shoved me off the bed and I tried to catch myself with my elbow. I hit the floor and my shoulder screamed in pain, but I fought not to indicate it. Silence settled before he said, "Mom?"

"Yes. I was checking on you and saw you were still in your coat and shoes." I was proud of my ability to keep my pain to myself.

"I was just really tired," He explained.

"We all are sometimes," I pushed myself up off the floor with my good arm and went to him to feel his forehead. He didn't feel like he had a fever. I sat on the bed beside him and heard him sigh with protest. I ignored it and said, "I'm sorry for how I acted earlier. I shouldn't have let you see me like that. You are probably wondering what all that was about."

"You don't have to explain it to me, Mom. I know more than I want to know about the whole Allie Vining mess."

Tiny pin pricks stabbed my heart, then multiplied and radiated through my body. I didn't want John to hate Allie. It was one thing for me to view her memories as bittersweet, but hearing his disdain for her was like a punch in my gut. Guilt washed over me. I should have never acted the way I had in front of him.

"It wasn't her fault, John," I patted his arm to comfort myself more than him.

"Well, it doesn't really matter now. Just be glad we're not involved."

His response was confusing. What exactly was he glad not to be involved in? Domestic abuse in general? Did he know more about my history with Allie than I thought? Did he read the notebooks? What part of them would make him not want to have her in our lives? Every way I tried to explain his words still seemed wrong. The only thought that felt even close to rational was that John knew something I didn't.

Part Seven

John

37

December 28, 2006

The light filling my room was magnified as if the Earth was a million miles closer to the sun. I looked at the clock. It was past noon. I blinked a few times until my eyes could adjust to the brightness. I knew with the perceptiveness of a ten year old that there was snow on the ground outside my bedroom window. It explained the brightness. But, unlike a ten year old, I had no desire to jump out of bed and verify my suspicion. My mind was numb with thoughts of the events from the night before.

Our trip to Kentucky and home by way of Felicity, Ohio had left many more questions than answers. I wished we had gone the hell home from Kentucky, but I had no control over that. Now Iris was hellbent on getting Allie's name on a marker by her grave. I probably should have been glad. Getting her name carved into a rock seemed much more appealing than tracking down a murderer. Thinking about it while safe in my room, it seemed odd that Iris hadn't brought up the murder while we were at church. Maybe she felt there was no point, those people didn't exactly seem very knowledgeable or cooperative. I bet they had stayed within ten miles of that town all of their lives.

Being home in Nashville had never felt so good. We had arrived back just after midnight. I don't even remember crossing the Tennessee line because I had passed out asleep. I had managed to make it to bed somehow. Then the next thing I knew, Mom had come into my room, waking me up, acting weird, and talking about Allie.

I exhaling a loud groan into the silence of my room, hoping to drown out the memories playing out in my head. I had no reason to be awake and no ability to go back to sleep. The last thing I wanted to do was see Mom. The next to last thing I wanted to do was see Iris. I decided my best plan was to avoid women all together.

I picked up my cell phone and called Eugene.

"This is awesome!" He screamed into the phone instead of saying hello. He must have seen my number.

I had to laugh, "Eugene, my man!" I tried to match his excitement.

"Hey, you coming over? I got fifteen classic monster movies for Christmas! MONSTER-A-THON!" His voice boomed.

"Eugene, you're fucking sixteen years old!"

"So?" I imagined the shrug he probably gave.

"Yeah, you're right. Sounds cool. Why don't you bring them over and we'll watch them in Dads' theater room? I need to get out of this girl house."

"Awesome!" He bellowed his words again.

"Call me when you get here and I'll open the gates."

"Give me an hour. Dad will need to drive me over in the truck because of the snow."

"Sure."

I ended the call and realized I hadn't even looked out the window to see how much snow was on the ground. I stood up, still dressed in yesterday's clothes, and peeked out. Everything was white, covered in at least three inches of snow. The tree branches weren't sagging from the weight, so I figured the roads weren't too bad.

I pulled off all my clothes and tossed them on the bed, got dressed in clean ones because I didn't really need to take a shower just to watch movies with Eugene. Jeans, a blue long sleeved t-shirt, and a plaid button up flannel shirt over it was good enough.

Mom was sitting in a chair in the living room, reading a book with a coffee mug in her hand. A couple of other ladies were on the couch, one reading the newspaper and the other sorting through a pile of receipts on her lap.

I cleared my throat and startled Mom. Seeing me, she put her mug down and started to get up. I held my hand out for her not to move, "I just came to tell you I'm going to Dad's, okay?"

"But you were gone all day yesterday." She looked hurt. This whole thing with Allie had made her even more annoying.

"Yes, and I want to be gone all day today."

"Iris wanted to talk to you," she looked like she expected an explanation.

"Well, I don't really want to talk to her. I'm just going to hang out with Eugene. He got a few movies for Christmas. We're going to watch them. There's nothing for you to worry about."

"Right," she mumbled and looked back to her book, "Go on, but try to be back at a decent hour."

"I'll probably spend the night," I threw the words out hoping she'd just nod and keep reading.

"There will be more snow this evening. You should really be here," she gave me a firm look.

"Come on, Mom! I'm just going to be on the hill with Dawson!"

The lady sorting receipts looked at me over the top her glasses, which were barely clinging to the tip of her nose. The extra attention pissed me off more than it should have.

Mom said, "Have you asked Dawson? You don't know if he has anything planned."

As usual, she used Dawson to get out of arguing with me. Of all my parents, Dawson was the most likely to call me out for doing shit. But I knew he wouldn't mind me staying there. "Fine.

If he doesn't want me up there, I'll come back here. Eugene and I can watch Hope Floats in Iris's room or something." I rolled my eyes.

She watched me grab my coat from the rack and walk out the door. I slid it on after I was outside. A gust of wind caused my muscles to flinch and tighten. It was so incredibly cold. I jogged back up the porch steps and leaned back inside the door to grab my gloves from the table there.

"Button up!" Mom called after me as I closed the door again.

38

Dawson's car wasn't parked by the garage. I assumed he was working and was happy about that. He had told me I was welcome any time, and this was any time.

Montgomery wasn't outside, though. Maybe Dawson forgot to let him out, or maybe he left him inside because it was so cold. I expected he would be glad to see me so I could let him out for a minute. I opened the gate and ran up the porch steps. The door was locked. I had a key of my own, but had forgotten to pick it up off my dresser before I left. I ran back down the steps and through the snow to the pool fence. I opened the gate and flipped open the end of one of the bars where a secret compartment hid a tiny magnetic box with a spare key inside. I took off my gloves to get it out. The metal felt like ice on my fingers.

I ran back through the snow, more anxious than ever to get inside and get warm. I turned the key and pushed the door open. Montgomery flew out of the house before I could even step inside. I thought it was strange that Dawson didn't have him kenneled while he was away, or at least put in the bathroom.

I kicked the snow off my shoes a couple of times on the threshold before stepping into the foyer. Once inside, steam caught my eye. A plate of scrambled eggs sat on the kitchen bar, still hot.

"Dad!" I called, wondering where his car was parked. "Dawson, is it okay if I hang here for the day? Hello? Are you here?"

I heard nothing. I went to the closed door of his bedroom and knocked. When no one answered, I pushed it open. The bed was made and there was no sign of him. Something was wrong. I couldn't think of any reason why he would leave a hot plate of food on the bar and disappear somewhere where he wouldn't answer me.

"Are you in the bathroom?" I called as I went to check the master bath. The door was open and it was empty. I checked the other two downstairs bathrooms. He wasn't in either. I kicked off my shoes so I wouldn't track mud and snow onto the carpeted upstairs. All the doors on the second floor stood wide open and all the lights were off. Too much had happened in the last couple of days for me not to feel terrified. I kept telling myself that Dawson was okay. He was probably in the upstairs bathroom or maybe he was in the theater wearing headphones. But then why the steaming plate of eggs? I shuddered and ran up to the third floor.

"Dad!" I called, really wanting him to answer. There was only one door that was closed. It was the door to the blue jay room, the room Dad Tracy slept in when he was in the middle of writing songs. I thought of it as the isolation room because no one was allowed to interrupt him.

I exhaled with relief. Everything was clear. Dad Tracy was home and Dawson was at work. But then why was he not answering me?

I stood at the door and tapped lightly with the back of my knuckles. "Dad?"

Silence.

I turned the handle cautiously, hoping I wasn't interrupting his creative process. I managed to push the door open without a single disruptive sound. He wasn't in there. On top of the bed was a leather bag and a pile of loose papers. Laid out on the pillow was a blue dress and on top of that was a matching hat. These were definitely not Dad's things. Maybe they were Iris's. Mom said Iris had wanted to talk to me and I hadn't seen her that morning; maybe she had come to Dads' before I did.

"Iris? Are you here?" I turned and looked around the room. No one answered me. I was frustrated by the realization that every tiny thing I tried to do turned into a huge ordeal. I sat on the bed and picked up the top paper. My heart stopped, completely froze like I might never breathe again. It was the birth certificate of Gabriel James Billings, the son of Jim and Allie. I now knew his name, and as soon as I read it, I remembered the lady at the church calling the pianist 'Gabe'. My face flushed hot with panic. If Iris had gathered those papers, it meant she was still investigating something I wanted no part of. And if she was at Dads with them, had she already told them what we had done?

"Iris!" I screamed as loudly as my voice would go. Still, no answer came. "Where the fuck are you? This is not a joke, Iris! I swear if you don't come out I'm going to call your Dad and tell him everything and then we'll both get our asses kicked." Still nothing. "Damn it!" I kicked the bed post and it slammed against the wall.

A woman's scream came from under the bed. I nearly jumped out of my skin, then screamed in unison. I had found her, but I was pissed off at her for nearly scaring the life out of me. Her charades weren't the least bit funny. Hearing her crying under the bed felt briefly like justice served until it stopped sounding like Iris at all.

I dropped down to lie on the floor and lifted the edge of the quilt to see under the bed. A ray of light shone across a familiar face, cut and bruised. Allie Vining. I screamed like a toddler. My eyes stayed fixed on her face as I screamed again. She screamed back at me. We screamed until it became ridiculous to continue. Obviously, she wasn't a ghost. Obviously, I somehow injured a real girl. Obviously, I needed to stop screaming and apologize.

I swallowed and took a deep, steadying breath, "I didn't know you was under here. I'm sorry I kicked the bed. Are you okay?"

She had covered her face with her hands and wasn't answering me. One of her fingers was held stiff in pain. When I had kicked the bed, she must have been holding the leg.

"I'm sorry," I tried again, "I didn't expect anyone to be under here. Why *are* you under here, anyway?"

Her hands stayed pressed to her face, "You can't see me," she sounded like a little girl.

I almost laughed, but I didn't want to hurt her more. "I assure you, I can see you."

"Well you aren't supposed to," her voice was muffled. I flipped the quilt all the way up onto the bed so light filled the darkness where she hid. She was wearing a ratty old nightgown with stains and holes. For sure, she made a very believable ghost.

Trying again, I said, "I've seen a lot of things this week that I wasn't supposed to, but none of them screamed about it. I'm pretty harmless. Come out of there."

I pushed off the floor and stood waiting. All the pieces of the puzzle were flashing in my mind, but I couldn't even begin to put them together. I wanted the girl to come out and explain where the pieces fit. She obviously had something to do with it. Then I would know and could be done with the whole thing.

"Your eggs are getting cold," I switched tactics to persuade her. "Want me to eat them for you?" That way of teasing would have worked for Iris, but I wasn't sure if I was gaining any ground with the girl under the bed.

She said nothing.

"How about this?" I questioned, "What if I told you I know a secret about Gabriel? Come out and look me in the eyes and I'll tell you what I know."

I heard her body shift. I looked out the window to give her privacy. She would want a chance to slide out without me staring at her in that falling apart sleepwear. Before long, I heard her voice behind me, small and timid. "I'm out."

I turned. The light from the window lit up her eyes like sky blue crystals. She was not a ghost, not a ghost at all. I couldn't find words. I could only stare at her, thinking how much she looked like the photo in my wallet, how blue her eyes were, how her head tilted with curiosity just like a girl waiting to be kissed. I was certain my mind was slipping away from me. She, her presence in my Dads' house, and all I had been through were too much to process.

She asked, "Who are you?"

That was supposed to have been my question to her. But I just answered her, "I'm John. This is my Dads' house."

"You're Tracy and Jute's son?" she leaned in to look closer at my face, turning her head and stepping to the side to see all of me. "I am in so much trouble," she added.

"Me, too. You have no idea." I let out a nervous laugh because it wasn't easy being eyed at so thoroughly.

"Your mom isn't supposed to know I'm here until Tracy gets home and we can go together."

This was a valuable clue. "I won't tell her. When is Dad coming in?"

"Sunday," she stopped staring at me and walked to look out the window. "If I don't get taken away before then."

Now I could stare at her without her seeing me. The light through the window permeated the thin cloth of her gown, making visible more of her than I should have been allowed to see. A contrast of emotions were triggered by the sight of the purple bruises on her shoulder and the silhouette of her breast. Her vulnerability made me uncomfortable. There were questions I should have asked her, but I was afraid to know. I already wished I knew so much less. At least my feelings of guilt had lessened with the realization that Dads were hiding things, too. I reasoned that Dads probably had everything under control. I told myself I no longer had to worry about finding all the answers to questions I didn't want to ask. Iris would have handled the situation much differently. But she wasn't there.

"What's your name?" I asked.

"Angelina," she said it like a question.

"How old are you?" I stepped beside her.

"Sixteen."

"Gabriel killed his grandfather." The words were like a splinter pulled out of my sole. There, I had said it.

"What?" she turned to me lit up with alarm.

"The cops are looking for him now, but I think I know where he is."

Her head jerked away to look out the window again. Her blue eyes were so wide I could see the snowy landscape reflected in them. I stared, waiting for her to say something, or so I told myself. The truth was that if I had not kept looking at her, I would have stopped believing she was real. Whatever else there was to be said about Gabriel, I was too distracted to care.

39

The phone vibrated in my pocket with an incoming call from Eugene. I accepted the call, but before I could greet him, he said, "Open Sesame!"

"Hold on, I have to go to the box." I glanced at Angelina. She was still staring out the window. I left her and went down to the back door where the control box was built into the wall. I pushed the green button. I informed Eugene, "It should be opening."

"Yep," he said, "Dad's letting me out here. I'll walk the rest of the way. The truck almost didn't make it this far. The roads are terrible. Do you think your Dad can take me home later?"

"Uhm," I knew that would likely not be an option, "Maybe you should just plan on staying the night. Tell your dad not to worry about it."

"Okay. See you in a few."

We ended the call. I opened the back door and called for Montgomery. He came running from the other side of the wrap around porch. He wasted no time getting back inside and headed straight to the kitchen where he barked to be fed. When I got there, Angelina was sitting on a stool eating her cold eggs. She was still in the tattered gown. I filled up Monty's bowl with dry kibble and returned the bag to its spot under the sink.

"So," I began hesitantly, "my friend, Eugene, is coming over to hang out and watch some movies in the theater room. You're welcome to watch them with us, I mean, if you like monster movies. He's kind of a movie geek."

She stared at me, or through me, her mind obviously working in overdrive. She chewed slowly, deep in thought. She gave no indication she planned to respond.

"It's up to you about the movie thing, but you probably should change out of that gown."

She looked down at herself, then back at me, "It's all I have."

"But, what about the blue dress?"

"It's the only dress I have that isn't stained and I'm saving it for when I meet Jute."

It was an odd thing to say. I promised, "We're not going to do anything to ruin it."

"I already ruined my blouse yesterday," she started crying which set me on edge because I didn't want to have to tiptoe around her like all the women at the shelter. I held my breath and listened anyway. She continued, "Tracy hugged me too hard and my back started bleeding again. I couldn't get the blood washed out. He said he'd take it to a cleaner, but blood never comes out. I don't want to ruin the clothes Marcy made."

I was so sick of everything revolving around battered and bruised women. "Well, look, you can't wear that thing you have on now. It's incredibly inappropriate. I mean, it's see-through. I can see everything!" I was yelling at her and I hated myself for it. I told myself I didn't care, and I hated myself for that, too.

Eugene spoke from behind me, "See everything about what?"

I turned around about the same time he laid eyes on Angelina. He looked terrified, but that's how Eugene had always acted around girls. With Angelina behind me, I couldn't see her response to him, but I imagined she thought he was a bit odd. Most people did. Eugene was wearing a yellow Godzilla t-shirt under a heavy black trench coat, which was too short in the sleeves and left open to make room for his belly.

Expecting to see her gawking at him, I turned back to look at Angelina. She was staring nervously at Eugene, but had made no attempt to cover herself. She seemed a bit in shock. Eugene was kind of out of the ordinary, but I never thought of him as scary. She looked at me for a cue about what she should do.

I rolled my eyes and pulled off my plaid shirt and wrapped it around her. "Go upstairs and Eugene and I will get you some clothes."

"We will?" Eugene was saying from behind me. "How, man? We can't drive anywhere." He kept talking, asking, speaking words that I didn't process because all of my mind was locked on watching Angelina run up the stairs. "Who is that girl?" was the next thing I understood from him.

"A girl Dads are helping. I just found her this morning."

"What happened to her face?" Eugene's lips were contorted with empathetic pain. He put a hand up to scratch his head deep down into the curly pile of hair he was growing.

"You need a haircut, man," I said.

"I'm growing it out."

"I've heard you saying that since we were nine years old. Every time it gets this long, you shave it. Want me to get the shears?" I knew how to push his buttons and hoped to get him off the subject of Angelina.

He looked a little dejected and I felt guilty. "You sound like my mom, she makes me shave it when I can't comb through it anymore."

"I'm just teasing you. Forget it. Besides, we have to walk down to the barn and get a couple of bags of clothes for her." I had pointed up the stairs to indicate which her I meant, as if there was a doubt.

"Let's ride the sleds down!" His dejection was replaced by enthusiasm.

"Whatever," I shook my head like I was really too mature for sleds. But the truth was, sledding was an awesome idea.

We made it down the hill in less than a minute and loaded a bag onto each plastic sled. On our walk back up, I saw her looking out the window at us. Her braids were let out and her hair laid in waves in front of her. I figured that was her solution to hiding a see-through gown, but having her hair down also made her look less like a little girl and more like a teenager. She put her hand up in what could have been a wave, or maybe a sign to stop.

I put my hand up, too, and smiled. Eugene saw me and

looked up to see her waving. His hand shot up as well, waving side to side.

She met us at the garage door, her arms crossed over her hair and her gown.

Eugene and I were both shivering from the cold. I said, "I don't know for sure what's in these bags. It's clothing, but it may not fit you."

"*What?*" Eugene protested. "You mean we might've done all that for nothing?"

We carried the bags to the laundry room where there were racks with hangers and a table for sorting. I dumped the contents of the bags onto the table. Dresses, dresses, and more dresses overlapped each other. All were brightly colored, all were vintage, solids and prints. I picked up a yellow dress with ruffles and held it up to see what she thought about the size.

She had tears in her eyes, "They're so beautiful."

"We'll go out and let you try them on," I elbowed Eugene and motioned for him to follow me.

"But I don't want to mess them up!" She protested.

We were already out of the room. "Mom was going to throw them out. It won't matter if you do." I shut the door.

40

We were in the theater room watching the opening commentary at the beginning of the movie, Frankenstein, when Angelina opened the door and flooded the darkness with light from the hallway. She was wearing a red maxi-dress, obviously from the 1960's. It had bell sleeves, a low cut v-neck, and hugged her body in a way that made it more alluring than the nightgown.

Eugene whistled and I fought the urge to lean over and slap the back of his head. I sunk lower into my seat and I said, "Shut the door and have a seat. We're watching Frankenstein."

Angelina closed the door and made her over to us by the light of the giant screen. She walked in front of me, smelling kind of like the barn. She sat beside me, not on the other side of the armrest, but beside me on the same large section of seating usually occupied by one individual. Of course, Eugene was sitting on the other side of the armrest, so it sort of made sense she'd fill up that space between us. But, it was a big room with three more rows of seating. She could have sat anywhere.

"Do you have a blanket?" She looked at me apologetically.

I got up and went into the hall, retrieved a soft indigo blanket from the linen closet, and came back without missing much of the movie. I didn't really care anything about watching it, anyway. Eugene might have been able to watch the same monster movie fifteen times in a row, but I couldn't.

I dropped the folded blanket onto her lap and sat back down beside her. I didn't want to insult her by moving to a different seat.

"Thank you," she stood up and let the quilt unfold in front of her, then sat back down before turning to place her feet over my lap. I looked at her like *what the fuck*, but she didn't notice. She settled in with her head leaned over on Eugene's shoulder. I was pretty sure this was the first time he'd ever been distracted enough to miss part of the opening scenes of a movie. I caught his eyes making their best effort to see down the neckline of that red dress. My face felt hot. I wasn't sure what this girl wanted. But she was acting more and more like Courtney with every passing minute.

We made it halfway through the movie before Angelina started crying. It was a thing girls did all the time, so I ignored it. But I couldn't ignore Eugene reaching over and taking her hand. I wanted to tell him to stop falling for it. I kept glancing over at her, looking for clues about her intentions. I began to doubt my theory that she was like Courtney. She seemed genuinely interested in the movies, both Frankenstein and King Kong. I felt guilty for assuming she had been hitting on us when she had just been making herself comfortable.

I was very uncomfortable after a couple of hours of not moving my arm off the back of the seat for fear I would touch her. The back of the chair had seemed like the only safe place to put it. But I reasoned that she had made herself comfortable and so should I. Hoping it would not be misconstrued, I let my arm fall across her legs. She stayed engrossed in the film and didn't respond at all.

Everything was going so well until Eugene had the great idea to watch the Exorcist. I suspected he had hoped it would scare her right into his arms. But it wasn't long until he realized he had overshot the mark. Within the first couple of minutes, about the time the little girl shoves her crotch at the adults in the room and screams for them to fuck her, Angelina ran out of the room in tears.

"Well that was a bad choice," Eugene mumbled to himself in confusion. "I don't know what's so scary about it, though. It was obviously fake."

"Just stick with the old stuff," I snapped at him as I ran out after her.

"The Exorcist *is* old!" He called after me.

Angelina wasn't in her room and I made sure to check under the bed with my eyes, not by kicking the bed. When I stepped back into the hall, I heard the sound of her crying. I followed it and found her in the bathroom. I opened the door without knocking, but regretted it when I saw her sitting on the toilet, her dress held over her knees, her hands fidgeting with a wadded up ball of toilet paper.

"Get out!" she screamed at me loud enough to rival Iris.

"Sorry!" I called through the door after I closed it. I meant it. "I was worried. Are you okay?"

"No!" she said, "Go away! You two are just mean and cruel and heartless. Leave me alone!"

"Hey, it wasn't my idea to put on the Exorcist, but Eugene didn't mean anything by it. He watches scary movies all the time. He's sort of desensitized to horror. He wasn't trying to upset you."

Eugene appeared about that time, a defeated look on his face. We stood in the hall listening to her sob. Then we listened to her flush the toilet. We listened to her washing her hands and it started to feel like we were invading her privacy. I worried she would walk out, see us standing with our ears to the door, and punch us both. I signaled to Eugene that we should head down the hall. We had just started walking away when she opened the door.

"Do you believe that?" She asked to the backs of our heads.

"Believe what?" I said as we turned around.

She looked furious, almost monstrously angry. She screamed at us in a way that must have hurt her vocal chords, "Do you believe little girls ask to be fucked? That the devil gets in them? Demons? Do you believe in demons?"

As tough as we had been during those movies, we were both frightened watching her. I shook my head as calmly as I could, hoping she would be convinced I did not believe in demons. But I knew Eugene did believe in them. I couldn't see what he was doing, but decided if he was nodding his head I was going to beat the shit out of him right there. I glanced over and saw his mouth gaping open. He wasn't about to lie, but he knew better than to tell the truth.

She stopped screaming, probably because it hurt. I watched her swallow hard before saying calmly, "There's no such thing as the devil. There's no such thing as God. It's all a lie to control people, make them do horrible things for salvation, but there is no salvation. If there is a Hell, we are already living it."

Tears streamed down her face. I pretended I didn't know why she said those things, but I did know. I had been around it all my life and I recognized the pain of abuse. For years I had made a point of turning and running in the opposite direction every time I saw any sign of it. But this time I didn't. I told myself to get away from her before it was too late, before her pain became my own, but I couldn't.

Eugene's voice shook and I was surprised he was crying, too. He said, "I hope you killed the bastard."

She said, "I did."

41

Eugene raised his hand for Angelina to give him a high-five. She flinched thinking he was going to hit her and I wanted to hit him. I glared at him as he slowly pulled his hand down and shrugged.

She stood there waiting to see what we would do or say about her confession to killing 'the bastard', whom I assumed was Silas. She had an expression of resignation on her face.

All of the answers I had been avoiding came crashing into my brain. I knew that Gabriel hadn't killed Silas, Angelina had. Judging by what we had just witnessed and the bruises, Angelina had probably been abused for a long time. Throughout my life, I had seen and heard so many women having panic attacks, paranoid delusions, night terrors, and near-suicidal breakdowns. I had watched Mom try to soothe them and bring them back to reality. They had terrified me when I was younger. But later, I resented them for always needing her. The sound of crying still set me on edge. But, I learned to tune them out, which had really helped me deal with the shocking appearance of Angelina when I first met her.

She was different, though. I had never met an abused woman who had killed her abuser. Those kinds of women never made it to the shelter. They usually made it to jail or were fortunate enough not to be charged and returned to their homes. Angelina was different. I understood why Eugene wanted to high-five her, misguided as it had been.

Eugene broke the heavy silence by asking me, "Do you remember that Halloween when we were thirteen?"

I dreaded hearing what would come out of his mouth. Social interactions were not his area of expertise. I gave him a hard look of warning, but nodded that I did remember.

He looked back at Angelina and started in on the story. "We were at Ray's house and he wanted us to help hang him up from a tree like an outlaw. He was dressed up like a cowboy with a gun holster and leather vest. Hidden under his shirt was a harness to hold him up, so he wouldn't actually die from the fake noose we tied around his neck. Once he was hung up there, he slumped over so his cowboy hat would hide his face. It looked real as fuck. Every time a kid came by, Ray would jerk his body around and make gagging sounds."

Eugene paused his storytelling to demonstrate. His arms and legs flailed around and his mouth opened up. His cheeks and body jiggled about and the most realistic vomit sounds came out of his mouth. It was too hilarious not to laugh, which was one of my favorite things about Eugene, along with his loyalty. He didn't let loose like that for everyone, though. I was laughing so hard I had to lean against the wall to keep from falling into the floor. I was doubled over and coughing, trying to catch my breath. I looked up at Angelina. She was fighting a smile.

"Then what?" She asked.

The sound of her voice brought Eugene out of his act. He tugged his Godzilla shirt to straighten it out and cover himself. "Well," he continued, "These three girls came by. You remember, John. It was Miranda, Anisha in the lead, and Courtney following behind. They were dressed up like the Three Musketeers, only with their asses hanging out of their skirts and their ruffled blouses unbuttoned down to their umbilicus-ess-ess-ess whatever," he winked at her. "I'm sure their mamas didn't know. They probably pealed off their angel costumes once out of sight of their houses. Any-who, Anisha calls out to Ray, 'I know that's you, Ray!' but he doesn't move. She says, 'My sister said you scared her, so stop trying to trick me'. But he still didn't move. John and I were sitting up on the porch by the candy dish and I swear I started to get nervous because Ray was so damn still. I thought maybe the harness broke and Ray was dead. He stayed limp as a corpse.

"Those girls huddled around and whispered and then Miranda says, 'Ray, I'm going to prove it's you!' So she walks up to Ray and yanks his pants down. He's wearing purple girl underwear and it didn't do a very good job at hiding his... you know. Anyway, the girls die laughing. They're sitting on the ground so they don't pee their pants because Ray has on girl underwear. But, see, Ray hadn't moved that whole time. He's just swinging from the force of having his pants yanked down. He's limp like roadkill. Finally those girls realize he hasn't even moved a twitch."

Eugene pauses, waiting for Angelina's obvious anticipation to reach its peak. Finally she whispers, "Was he dead?"

"Well Courtney was the first to notice. She stood up like she was about to run away, but couldn't tear her eyes off Ray's swinging body long enough. Anisha looked at the fear on Courtney's face and that made it all the more real, so she started screaming. I mean she was belting out one scream after another until Miranda shoved her back toward the direction they'd come. They took off running for their lives. We wanted to laugh. But by that time, John and I both were too worried. We got the step ladder out and John climbed up there, pulled the hat off of Ray. His head stayed all bent over, that motherfucker didn't move a hair. I was about to shit my pants. And all of a sudden he starts jerking around, twitching like he's having convulsions, gagging. Drool was dripping out of the corner of his mouth. John screamed bloody hell and had his phone out, going to call 911. Right about that time Ray starts laughing. Son of a bitch scared every damn one of us. That Halloween was fucking awesome!"

Angelina was shaking her head, but her eyes were shining. "Do all kids act like that?"

"Nope," Eugene stood tall with pride, "You're lucky to be with the coolest guys on the planet, and not just because it's snowing outside. Get it? Coolest?"

We all stepped into the nearest bedroom to look out the

window. Just as he said, snow was falling. We stood shoulder to shoulder watching the giant flakes blowing to the east. They were falling so heavily that I couldn't see the ridge or the barn. I felt my phone vibrating in my pocket. It was Mom calling. I didn't answer it.

"It's amazing," Angelina said, her eyes flitting about to take it all in.

"There was a cold front moving in," Eugene began another episode of geekery. I was sure he'd talk her ear off about weather, which was his first obsession before dinosaurs, both of which happened before horror movies.

I took the opportunity to walk down to the kitchen and called Dawson.

He answered on the second ring, "Yeah, John?" It was his standard way of answering, two words pushed together like yeahjohn.

"I was just wondering if you were going to make it home."

"Probably not. You and your Mom okay? This storm is going to be a nasty one."

"I'm at your house."

Silence. I knew he was probably freaking out and I couldn't let it go on. I said, "I've met Angelina. I don't plan to tell Mom. Eugene and I came up to watch movies. I found her then. We're fine, though, don't worry."

His voice was a whisper, but I could hear his relief, "I'm glad you're there, John. I was worried about her. She's been through a lot. She doesn't need to be alone in a big house in a snowstorm, especially if the power goes out. You know what to do right? Light the gas fireplaces. The one in the master bedroom is the best, y'all hang out in there if you need to. Go ahead and prepare supper just in case."

He made it sound ominous. Dawson was always overly cautious about emergency preparedness.

"I know," I replied, "I can handle it. I just called because..." I wasn't sure if I could say it.

"Yeah, John?"

"I did something you need to know about."

"Ah, yes, I know. If I had known what you kids were planning, I would have advised you not to go. Angelina gave us her account and I've already called the local police. They mentioned the two of you. There's nothing you need to worry about, except maybe telling your mom. I obviously haven't told her anything, yet."

I exhaled more air than I knew my lungs could hold. "So, you're taking care it?"

"I'm involved, yes. That's all you need to know, John. It's not your place to try to solve other people's problems, not your mom's and not Angelina's. We're going to get this straightened out. She's not in trouble, and as far as I'm concerned, neither are you."

"Thank you," I sighed into the phone. I couldn't have asked for a better Dad.

"Hey, be extra nice to her, please. Let her know I'll be home when I can get there and it's all going to be okay. Remember, she's been through a lot and a little kindness will go a long way."

As soon as I ended the call, I went to the kitchen and assessed the contents of the fridge. We still had left over ham from Christmas. I decided to bake some frozen rolls and hard boil some eggs. I was optimistic that we'd have power through the night and the preparations would be for nothing, but every few years Nashville had a storm big enough to put us in the dark for a few hours. There were no guarantees.

I thought about going back up to let Eugene and Angelina know what I was doing, but I needed time to think. Dawson had taken a lot of the burden off of me. Without the worry, my mind was free to feel curious. I now found myself questioning how she came to be in Dads' house. Who was she, really? She was certainly not just a girl seeking shelter. So many questions swirled in my mind.

I stayed in the kitchen until the eggs finished boiling and the rolls were baked. While the oven was hot, I placed some ready-to-bake sugar cookies on a cookie sheet and slid them in, set the timer for twelve minutes.

When I got back to the bedroom, I found them sitting on the bed, thumb wrestling. Their right hands were held together and Eugene had her thumb pressed beneath his. She leaned over as she struggled to free it. She was laughing. I stood in the doorway just to watch her.

Eugene let go, "Okay, I win again. Do you want to play another round? Or do you want me to teach you how to really wrestle?"

I cleared my throat, "I don't think she can wrestle in that dress, Eugene."

"Well, then I'll show her how it's done by wrestling you!" He stood dramatically and puffed out his chest like he was in the WWF. But he wasn't even on the high school wrestling team. Eugene had no idea how to wrestle and neither did I, but that had never stopped us. He went from standing tall to suddenly bent over and running with his head aimed at my gut like a battering ram. I put my hands out to stop him, but I missed. He plowed into me and nearly knocked me over, but I wrapped my arms around his head to steady myself and tried to bring him down instead.

"I will defeat you!" He called to the floor because he couldn't stand upright with my arms around his head. Unable to do anything else, he wrapped his arms around my waist and intentionally fell backwards, nearly throwing me to the floor behind him. I let go to catch myself and at that second he slid from under me and ended up on top of my back. He was much heavier than the last time we'd wrestled. I could barely breathe.

"Okay, you win," I managed to say with what little air I had left.

He stood up with his arms above his head in victory. Angelina clapped for him. It burned a little. But I knew how to regain their admiration.

I stood and straightened out my clothes before announcing, "I put sugar cookies in the oven. They'll be out in five."

42

It was 9:37 p.m. when the power went out. We had already eaten supper, made a second batch of cookies, and popped popcorn. We had been in the theater watching Tim Burton's Corpse Bride when the room went dark. Keeping the movie selections PG-13 had prevented any more breakdowns. In general, Angelina seemed to enjoy movies, just not movies about little girls possessed by demons. When the power went out and the room fell into dark silence, she gasped. Hours of watching scary movies had evidently had some effect on her.

I stayed calm and stood up. "I guess we should move down to Dads' room. I'll light the fireplace."

"How will we see to get out of here?"

I reached for her, hoping my hand wouldn't land inappropriately, and was relieved to feel her shoulder. I slid my hand down to hers, "Follow me."

The hall was equally dark. Montgomery met us there, pawing and brushing past my leg. "We're okay, Monty. Stay with us."

Angelina held my hand all the way to Dads' room. She was reluctant to let go when I had to light the fireplace. Once lit, I turned to see she and Eugene were still standing where I had left them. They were holding hands, too. For a moment, I just stared at her. The flames threw orange light and flickering shadows across her face. Her eyes were wide with worry, but no longer because she feared us.

"I'm going up to my room to get a couple of sleeping bags. Eugene and I will sleep on the floor here and you can have the bed, Angelina. I'll get you some of my pajamas, too. Do you want some, too, Eugene?"

He rolled his eyes, "I think I'll need to wear Dawson's. I don't think I can fit in your shrimpy clothes."

I had never known Eugene to make fun of me, at least not to hurt me. I told myself he was just commenting that he needed a bigger size and nothing more. I pointed to Dawson's closet with the flashlight then handed it to him.

I headed up the stairs to a closet at the top where I retrieved another flashlight, then walked into the blue jay room. I wished I could have said why. I had intended to go to my room, but at the last second I turned into hers. I sat on the bed by the papers, picked them up one at at time. The musty smell of years of dust filled my nose. Most of the papers were not interesting at all. There were birth certificates, death certificates, recipes, jotted down wedding dates of someone else's ancestors. But one in particular looked nothing like the rest. It was written on heavy paper, folded once, with a smudge of water over the blue ink. It said, "*Her name is Angelina. I'll leave her here. If you find her alive, please finish. I can't. -Cynthia.*"

It was obvious Angelina had been left to die. That fact made it seem even more miraculous that she was in Dads' house. She had escaped. She had survived. But I didn't know exactly from what experiences she had survived and escaped. They had obviously been traumatic. But somehow she had ended up where she was needed most, here, to give answers and closure to my family. In return, I knew without a doubt, my family would consider her part of us. The thought caused an uneasiness in my stomach. I was ashamed of it, but there was a nagging wish that she had never come. She was already tied to everything my mother cared about, most of it had been kept from me. I wasn't sure where I would fit into it all once everything was out in the open. I had only known about Allie for a few days. It wasn't like I had grown up with all of this on my shoulders like the rest of the family had. Even Angelina knew more than I did. If her presence in our lives turned out to be bad, for everyone or just me, there would be no way to go back to how we were before.

I set the paper on the bed and went to my room. There, I grabbed pajama pants and a few t-shirts. I brought extras so she could choose. When I got back to Dads' room, Eugene and Angelina were sitting on the bed, cross legged, staring into each other's eyes. He was wearing Dawson's gold silk pajamas that Tracy had bought for their fifteenth anniversary.

"Staring contest," Eugene announced, "Don't mess me up, man."

"Dawson's going to mess your ass up if he sees you in his anniversary pajamas!"

Eugene broke his stare and jerked his head around to see if I was serious. Knowing I was, he hopped off the bed. "No, I think I'll change." He took the flashlight from my hand and disappeared into the closet.

I smiled at Angelina, "I brought these." I plopped them on the bed beside her. "Pick whatever you want."

She chose pale blue fleece pants and a yellow t-shirt. I fought back a laugh. I had told mom those were girl pants when she had bought them. Mom insisted pale blue was handsome on men. Maybe so, but I felt validated seeing Angelina choose them.

She said, "I need my bandages changed. Can you help?"

I didn't even know she had bandages. I broke out in a sweat. "Sure," I said as my voice cracked.

She took a flashlight from the nightstand and walked into the master bathroom. I heard the cabinet doors open and close, then she carried a box and a towel back into the room. "Mrs. Matthews left this here for me. She said I needed to change my bandages at least twice a day. I'm a few hours late. I hope they aren't stuck." She placed the box on the bed and turned her back to me. She pulled the red dress over her head. I told myself I should look away. She was naked except for a giant white square of bandages taped to her back. Her curves were those of a woman and didn't match her childlike innocence.

I thought I heard Dawson's voice in my head telling me to be extra nice, give a little kindness. He was right. I knew she was making herself vulnerable, partly due to ignorance. It was no time to feel what I was feeling for her. But, I couldn't turn it off. I resolved to try to ignore it.

"Do you want me to stay standing up or would it be easier if I lie down? Mrs. Matthews put them on with me lying down, but just tell me what you want me to do."

I wasn't sure which would be easier, but I felt I personally needed to sit down. "You can lie on the bed," my damn voice broke again. I pushed my hair back out of my eyes and tried to think about ice fishing in Minnesota, or changing the oil in Mom's car, or anything else that was the opposite of a naked girl. I turned off the flashlight so she could get positioned without making my situation worse. "Tell me when you're ready."

Eugene's voice came from the closet as he walked back into the room, "Ready for what?"

I flipped the light back on and Eugene screamed, "Ack!" in surprise, definitely not horror. His eyes were all over what my eyes were trying not to focus on.

"I'm changing her bandages. Hold this." I handed him the flashlight. He was wide-eyed and possibly in shock. He slowly approached the bed as if sneaking past a wild bear in the woods. I almost laughed. I was incredibly thankful he was there, even if he was now wearing Dawson's silk robe he had just received for Christmas.

Eugene sat on the pillow by her head and shined the light directly on her back, not that keeping the flashlight from shining on her hips made them not visible. The fireplace light still flickered an orange glow.

I tried to peel the tape away from her skin with my bitten down fingernails. I tried to be as gentle as I could, but it was difficult to get my short nails under the tape. I had plenty of time as I worked to think about what might lie beneath the gauze. When I finally got the tape loosened, the gauze pulled up easily, revealing gashes and bruises that made the wounds on her face seem like nothing. Scabs had formed, but the skin around them was red and slightly puffy. I had enough experience with injuries to know it was an early sign of infection.

After putting on disposable gloves, I put lots of ointment on my fingertips and smoothed it gently over her skin. The wounds ran from just beneath her shoulders all the way down her back to her waist. The thin latex of the gloves provided little barrier between my skin and hers. I told myself not to think of it as her body; I was just touching skin. I was being extra kind and refusing to think about touching her. Eugene kept quiet for the first time since he had arrived. I knew exactly what he was feeling. Nausea.

I pulled off the gloves and tossed them onto the towel before placing clean gauze pads over her back. I taped them down the way it had been before.

"All done," I said, letting my eyes scan what parts of her skin were left visible. Scars scattered about like she had been in a war. I picked up the pajama pants she had chosen and stood, holding them, waiting for her to be ready to take them. Eugene switched off the flashlight. Angelina sat up on the edge of the bed as my eyes adjusted to the darkened room. The firelight danced across the front of her body like a magical spell keeping me from looking away. I had never been so close to naked breasts before. For a moment, everything else in the room disappeared.

She looked up at me expectantly and the light in her eyes brought her whole body back to my attention. I had forgotten I was holding her pajama pants. I could have handed them to her, but the thought never occurred to me. I dropped to my knees and held them for her to step into them, feeling more comfortable bowed down in front of her. I kept my eyes on hers because I didn't want to make her feel uncomfortable by staring at her nipples again. She covered her smile with her hand and put one foot at a time into the pants.

"I'm not a child," she said.

I opened my mouth to say *I know*, but nothing came. My willpower was faltering. I wanted desperately to touch her. My kindness was in question. My thoughts seemed perverse. I had tears in my eyes for her, but also a little for me. I couldn't understand why this was so difficult, or if she had intended it to be so.

I pushed myself up from the floor and tossed the yellow t-shirt onto her lap. "I know you're not a child," the words finally came. I walked off to the master bathroom and closed the door behind me, shutting off all the light from the bedroom.

43

I took a shower in total darkness with the last remaining hot water, knowing that using it made me sort of an ass. But, I needed an excuse not to go back out there. I stayed under the water in the dark, steam making the air thick. I made quick mental stabs at figuring out what I should do next. Nothing I considered seemed entirely right. I didn't know her. It all came down to that. I expected she would slowly be, if not already, injected into every aspect of my life. Was I really supposed to know what to do with all that information in the few hours we had spent together? Most of that time had been spent watching movies or listening to Eugene talk about when we were kids.

The water went cold and then ice cold. My skin pricked up with goosebumps as I groaned loudly in exasperation. I hit the knob to turn the water off. I dried myself with a towel and tried not to knock things off the counter in the dark. I realized I had left my pajamas outside in the bedroom. "Damn it!" I whispered. I tied the towel around my waist. On the way out I nearly tripped over a stool, the banging around made it sound like I had fallen on my face. I opened the door and could see, in the dim light, Eugene and Angelina lying on the bed making shadow puppets with the flashlights like they were six years old.

Eugene was making his dinosaur shadow say in a fading to silence voice, "An-juh, juh, juh, juh, juh..."

Angelina's dinosaur puppet was facing his, saying, "Eu-juh, juh, juh, juh, juh..."

They both snickered. Eugene said, "Hold my flashlight, I'll make a bat."

It was a strange feeling to walk half-naked into that room and be ignored. Before, I had dreaded their eyes on me. But I had also thought about the hours I'd spent working out and thought I looked pretty good, at least, I hoped so. I mean, I hadn't set out hoping they would look at me, but there I was, vulnerable to their stares, anxious about their reaction. But, neither of them glanced at me.

I sat on the edge of the bed and grabbed my underwear, slid it on under my towel, then tossed the wet towel in the floor by the fireplace.

"Hey," Eugene said, "it's juh, juh, juh, John." Angelina shined both lights on me and I cursed myself for having wished they'd notice. "Damn, you've been working out," he said, "You make me look like the Blob."

Eugene stuck his hand in the beam of light and tried to make a blob shadow on me. I quickly pulled up my gray pajama pants, which required me to stand up out of the beam of light. Angelina moved it, though, so I couldn't escape it. I pulled on a white t-shirt then seamlessly leaped to take the flashlights away from her. I turned them off and set them on the nightstand hoping she'd leave them there.

Eugene asked, "What now, John? We could tell ghost stories? Or we could play hide and seek? Or we could play games on our phones."

"Angelina doesn't have a phone. And we should probably save our batteries." I sat on the bed in the narrow space left beside Angelina's body. "What do you want to do?" I asked her.

She was still in the black shadow of my vision left over from the flashlight beams in my eyes. I felt her fingers curl around my wrist. "Can you tell me about your mother? What do you think she will think of me?"

There was nothing I wanted less than to talk about my Mom. My defensiveness made its way out of my mouth before I could reconsider, "Why don't you tell me about your mother instead?"

She was quiet for a moment, long enough for me to start feeling like shit for putting her on the spot. Finally she said,

"Until Christmas, I thought a woman named Esther was my mother. She died three years ago. I only found out on Christmas Day that Esther wasn't my real mother, Allie was."

I recognized that Esther was Jim's mother's name. "How did you find out?"

She let go of my wrist and crossed her arms as if cold. "I was looking for the Bible because I was trying to learn to read Silas' favorite passages. I thought he'd be pleased, but it was stupid of me. He wouldn't have ever let me read. But, I accidentally dropped a hatbox onto the floor. Inside one of the hats was a letter from Allie to Jute. I hid it in my room. The next time Silas went out, I looked for more letters. I found all those papers you saw on the bed. Silas walked in and caught me with them. He told me I wasn't his daughter and told me my real name. They had always called me Perdy because Esther said I was the prettiest girl she'd ever seen. Silas said I had been brought to him to be be killed, but Esther spared me. I didn't want to believe my life was a lie. But when I saw the paper with my name, Angelina, written on it, I had to believe it was true."

Eugene said, "So you've only been called Angelina for four days? I bet if someone called your name on the street, you wouldn't even know to look. And then if they say, 'Hey Perdy lady!' you would turn your head." He snickered about his hypothesis.

My eyes had adjusted enough to see she was amused by Eugene and not offended by what, to me, sounded inappropriate. Still smiling, she said, "Your turn. Tell me about Jute. Do you think she'll like me?"

"I don't know," I shrugged. "She runs an abuse shelter. There's abused women around 24/7. Abused women seem to be her favorite type of people."

Angelina's face struggled to hold its smile. I had obviously insulted her. I couldn't say that I completely regretted it at that moment. I felt like I needed to dislike her for reasons I couldn't explain. I tried to push my uneasiness away and not act like a jerk.

I offered, "I don't mean that's all she will see in you. She'll see Allie. She'll probably love you like you were her own daughter."

"Would that make me your sister?" She asked, smiling for real now.

Thinking of her as my sister made me even more nauseous than I had felt seeing her naked. Comparing the feelings those two things ignited was a dangerous path to walk. I tried to push all those thoughts away, but first I had to answer her, "You wouldn't be my first sister who isn't really my sister."

"Oh, Iris!" Eugene interjected. "Wait until you meet her, An-juh, she don't take any shit from John. She's tiny, but can be scary. It's hilarious to watch."

"Did you just call her An-juh? Giving each other pet names, huh?" I tried to sound like I was playing around.

"It's okay," Angelina said, "I don't care what Eu-juh calls me."

I rolled my eyes. "It sounds like you're call him huge."

"Don't be a dick," Eugene said to me through his laughter. I couldn't tell if he was really upset, nor did I care. When had he become so confident in front of girls? Not that Angelina was a normal girl.

"Whatever." I didn't want to talk to either of them any more. I went over to the floor where I had dropped the sleeping bags and untied the black one. Realizing I needed a pillow, I picked up a flashlight from the nightstand and walked down the hall to the linen closet to get a few extras. By the time I got back to the room, Angelina and Eugene were lying nose to nose, staring again. He was saying things in a whisper and she was giggling. I threw a pillow at them, then another. I tried not to sound irritated when I said, "Have some more pillows."

I dropped my pillow down by the sleeping bag and eased myself into it. Sleep was the only place I knew where Angelina couldn't insert herself. But no matter how hard I tried, I couldn't make myself fall asleep. The constant whispering and giggling was worming into my brain and keeping me awake. Finally they were silent long enough for me to reach the edge of a dream. In the dream, I had Angelina in my arms in a dark underground walkway. I was carrying her sleeping body. I felt like I was carrying a ghost. The only light available was emitted from her white flowing gown; ripped shreds of it hung down and moved as I walked. Not only was there no breeze, but my lungs were heavy with the stale and moldy air around us. I didn't know where I should be taking her, but I kept walking until Eugene's snoring woke me from the dream. I opened my eyes to hear another of his loud rumbling snores.

I listened to him snore for about five minutes before I couldn't take it anymore. Usually, Eugene's snores didn't bother me. We had spent the night together many times. But, I had never gone to sleep mad at him before. I wasn't even sure why I was mad at him at that moment. I just found everything about him and Angelina to be annoying.

I got up to let Montgomery out. He hadn't asked, but I was doing it more for myself anyway. The rest of the house was incredibly cold. Once Montgomery was let out, I decided to light all the other fireplaces in the house. In Mom's farmhouse, we had to have at least a little heat going during winter or the pipes would freeze. Maybe it was different at the big house, but I wasn't sure and didn't want to risk it.

I lit the fireplaces in the formal dining and living rooms first, then closed a few doors to areas I didn't need to heat. The last fireplace I lit was in the third floor master bedroom which had a study attached. Dad Tracy usually slept in it while he recovered from jet lag because it was away from the rest of the house. I knew as soon as I walked in there that I wouldn't be going back downstairs. Once the gas logs were burning, I pulled all the blankets and pillows off the bed and made a place to sleep in the floor by the fire.

Thoughts of our isolation came in waves. I was ambivalent about it. I was glad to have time to process what was going on with Angelina before I had to deal with Mom. But I was worried I would never be able to figure it all out in time. In time for what, I didn't know exactly. It just seemed like things were changing so fast, so drastically, my mind couldn't keep up.

The snow was still coming down, though more sparsely. The image of falling snow was a wonderful thought to have as a distraction. I pictured what the woods must look like outside in the dark, with large white flakes tumbling through the air and weighing down tree limbs. I drifting into sleep.

44

December 29, 2006
12:01 a.m.

A wet nose touched my hand and I awoke, startled. It was Montgomery. As soon as I realized it was the dog, I also realized I had forgotten to let him back in the house. I sat up, overwhelmed with guilt. I rubbed his head for a moment before he crawled under the blankets beside me. He was not only cold, but a little wet. I shoved a blanket between us so he would warm up without making me cold and stinky.

"Settle in, little guy," I whispered as he wiggled around to get comfortable. Once he was settled, I turned over with my back to him. That's when I saw Angelina sitting on the edge of the bed, staring at me.

"He was barking. I got up and saw you were gone, so I let him in. He ran straight up here to find you. He's an excellent hunting dog."

"I can't believe I forgot about him." I propped myself up on one elbow. "Thanks for letting him in."

"Why did you leave?" She slid off the bed, moving closer, her eyes squinting to examine mine. With the firelight behind me, my face was in the shadows. She picked up the edge of my blanket and slipped under until her shoulder touched my chest and her hips touched my thighs. She was on her back, staring at the flickering shadows on the ceiling. My hand had been resting on the floor before being wedged between my stomach and her ribs.

I kept my mouth closed until I knew I could actually get words out of it. Finally, I answered by lying, "I left to give you some privacy."

I braved a look at her face. Her eyes held confusion, but her mouth turned up in a polite smile. "Why would I need privacy?"

"You know, you and Eugene were getting along so well."

"He snores so loudly," she giggled. "I couldn't sleep. Do you think he'll mind if he wakes up alone? I mean, if you don't mind if I stay up here with you and Monty."

"He'll be fine."

"I am so thankful to you and your family for letting me stay in your house."

"Technically, this isn't my house. I live with mom in the farmhouse."

"She has a farmhouse? Is there a garden?" She turned slightly toward me, scooting a bit higher to look into my eyes. More of her body brushed mine before she settled onto her back again.

I answered, "We have a garden by the house, a field we lease for hay and sometimes horses, a pond for fishing, and a couple of barns."

"We only had a garden and some chickens, a small barn and a church on the hill." She crossed her arms over herself. "I liked being in the garden."

I pictured what I could remember of Silas's land, how the mountain seemed to be swallowing it up. The trailer was small and rusty with a couple of cracked windows. I hadn't seen a barn or a church, couldn't imagine where they would have been, but I believed her. "I like to work hay with Ellis, the guy who leases the field."

"What is leasing?"

"It's like renting. Ellis agrees to pay a certain sum of money for a specific amount of time, usually a year, to use our land. Ellis and Mom agreed to a ten year lease last year, though, because he had already been leasing for so long. He raises horses and sometimes brings them to our fields. Mostly, he uses it for hay. A small section he uses to grow pumpkins for his grandkids."

As I spoke, she stopped looking at the ceiling and began watching my mouth move. When I finished, she was quiet and still. I glanced into her eyes for a moment, but had to look away.

"Is it okay if I touch you?" she asked.

My brain said no, absolutely not. The ideas her question triggered were all terrible, huge mistakes, points of no return. Feeling the heat of her body, I wanted to say *you're already touching me*. Her question confused me and I couldn't decipher its meaning through all the pornographic images bombarding my brain. Halfway into a panic attack, my answer slipped out before I knew it. "Okay."

She turned to face me, placed her arm over my side and pressed her head against my chest. I let out a small sigh of relief at the apparent innocence of her motive. She was probably just cold. I rolled onto my back, my arm holding her close to my side. She moved her hand to rest on my chest. I pulled the blanket securely over her. In my head, I repeated the phrases: *keep her warm, she's cold, be extra nice, this means nothing*.

She sighed with contentment and shifted her head around to find the perfect nook. She spoke full of sleepiness, "Do you know who you're going to marry?"

My heart was already racing because of her proximity, but now it raced in fear of her reasons for asking such a bizarre question. "I'm only fifteen," I tried to laugh.

"I'm sixteen. I'm going to marry Emory," she explained, snuggling into my shoulder even more.

My heart turned into an enormous, pounding, slow-motion jackhammer. I spoke carefully, "Who's Emory?"

"He almost ran over me when I fell from a cliff. But, he ended up bringing me here, to Nashville. He's very nice and handsome. He has pretty green eyes the color of lamb's ear. Do you know that plant? I kissed him once, but he made me stop because he said I'm only sixteen and shouldn't kiss someone who is 25. Do you think that's true?"

My face was hot and sweat was pouring out of me. I needed

to move around, but I couldn't move, and I didn't honestly want to move. Ever. I steadied my voice, "Yes, I guess it is true. Adult men shouldn't kiss sixteen year old girls. And..." I hesitated, but said it because it needed to be said, "I don't think you should be naked around boys of any age."

She propped herself up on an elbow to look down at my sweaty face. Her eyes were full of worry. "I did something wrong?"

"No. I mean, yes... sort of. You didn't mean to do anything wrong. Eugene and I are nice guys. But not every guy is going to be nice. Some might try to take advantage of you."

"Take advantage of me?"

"Yes. Touch you. Without you wanting them to touch you." I wished she would put her head back down on my chest and stop staring at me. Having her so close had been comforting, unlike the spotlight of her eyes on me.

"Oh. I wouldn't have taken off my dress in front of anyone. It's just, you were going to change my bandages and I trusted you not to hurt me. But honestly, I'm just not used to having a choice. There's so many new things I have to learn." She nervously scanned my eyes.

"Are you saying you haven't had a choice about being touched or having privacy? Either way, in both cases, you always have a choice no matter who it is. I hope you know, right now, you have a choice about how close... how close we are."

She smiled with understanding. I then realized something about her. The best way to ease her mind and make her smile was to explain something she wanted to learn. Angelina was a very curious person with a shocking lack of experience outside of the hollow where she was raised.

"Have you ever kissed a girl?" She asked.

"Yes." I tried not to read anything into the question.

"What else? I mean, what is normal to do next?" Her eyes lit up with anticipation of discovery.

I wondered if she was asking because of this Emory guy. Was she planning to seduce him? Giving her answers was becoming more complicated by the second. In my mind, I built a brick wall for me to beat my skull against. The thought of explaining sex, not just the physical aspect, but also the social implications, was making my brain crack. But I kept a straight face and tried to keep my terror from showing.

"Angelina," my voice broke, pleading, "I don't think I can tell you everything."

"Who else should I ask? I want to know so I don't make a fool of myself in front of Emory. When I was staying with Marcy, I thought she wanted me to do what Silas expected me to do, but she got upset about it. I know it wasn't right." Her tears welled up until finally they fell, sliding from her face, falling onto my neck. The sensation was perfectly annoying and distracted me from thinking about the places her body touched mine. I welcomed it, but hated to see her so upset. She said, "Please tell me what is normal, John."

I ran my finger over the track of tears on her cheek to keep more from falling. I thought carefully about what I should tell her. I wanted to say something to make her believe she had control over her own body. "Normal is to do what feels good to you, only as much as you want, and not worry about what other people expect." I realized after I spoke that I wasn't being entirely honest. If I believed what I'd just told her, I would have kissed her right then, because it was what I wanted. "Actually, Angelina, I guess it's best to form a relationship with Emory so you can discuss this with him. You need to know how he feels and decide, together, what comes next. But you shouldn't do anything you don't feel comfortable with."

"But I've already discussed it with him and he says I should be a kid and not try to rush things."

"I guess you should respect that, then," I felt completely selfish in saying that, but I really hoped she would take his advice.

"How can I, when I know I'm not a kid? I'm a woman. I mean, I'm older than you are, John, and I look at you and I don't see a kid. You're obviously a man and so how am I not a woman? How

227

can he not see that?"

"Maybe because it's illegal for him to see you as an adult?"

"That's just stupid," she said, and laid her head back onto my shoulder. I wrapped my arm around her shoulders and smoothed back her hair. I could tell she was silently crying because my shirt was getting wet. "Sometimes I just want to go back to the mountain and live alone. I'm never going to figure out how things work down here."

"Yes, you will."

She sniffed and steadied her voice, "Do you think Jute will want me here?"

I was thankful the subject had changed, "Absolutely. She'll kick me out of my room and move you in, never let you out of her sight, probably force feed you large amounts of organic, homegrown, vitamin-rich foods."

"You're joking. She's not going to kick you out," she insisted. I felt her smiling.

"She might, with or without you in the equation. She already said I should move up here so Dads can talk to me about girls." I kicked myself for bringing that up.

"What about girls?"

"Oh, nothing, really. Mom just heard I had some trouble with this girl, Courtney. She didn't know the whole story. So, she just assumed a lot of stuff that wasn't true and freaked out about it."

"What happened with Courtney?"

"My dad, Tracy, is famous. It has always been a problem. Some people want to be my friend, but a lot just pretend so they can get close to my dad. Courtney was one of the latter. I didn't know that at first. I really wanted it to work out with her. I tried to treat her right. So, when she started going a little too fast, I tried to slow it down and she lost her cool, started accusing me of being gay and in love with Eugene. Then she insulted my dads. She revealed the person she really is and I wanted nothing more to do with her. But Mom doesn't know all that. She just worries I'm going to mistreat her, always worried about how I treat them, never how they treat me."

"What did Courtney do that was going too fast? Was it like when I kissed Emory?"

"Sort of," I lied.

"What is slower than kissing? If kissing wasn't okay, then what should she have done?" I knew she was asking for herself as it pertained to Emory.

"It wasn't kissing, okay? It was a lot more."

"She was touching you without your permission?"

"Bingo." I hoped she'd be satisfied with that explanation.

"I never thought about men dealing with that. I mean, men say the Bible gives them power over women. What would make a woman think she has the power over a man?"

"Oh, believe me, women have a lot of power over men," I chuckled, but then regretted the comment.

"How?"

I wanted to say the first thing that came to mind, which was that men will do anything for sex. But that was objectifying, and it would have been dangerous for me to insinuate to Angelina that being objectified was a good way to have power. That was exactly what Courtney believed and I didn't like it. Another reason not to be flippant was that Angelina would hang on every word. She would take it to heart. I spoke thoughtfully, "I guess if a man really loves a woman, or if any person loves another person, they won't try to overpower the other. They would want to feel equal."

"So you're saying that by kissing Emory when he didn't want me to, I denied him power over himself?"

"Well, no," I sighed. She twisted everything I said into a lesson about Emory. "I don't think you were aiming for that. And he told you to stop and you did. You did nothing wrong. Kissing isn't that big of a deal, Angelina. Most of the people I hang out with have kissed lots of people, except maybe Eugene."

She raised up on her elbow and looked down at me with surprise. I continued, "I mean, I'm not saying you should kiss lots of people. I'm just saying you shouldn't feel guilty. It's a pretty common thing people do when they're getting to know a person

229

of interest."

She looked at me very intently, from one eye to the other. I could tell she was biting the inside of her lips by how they pulled sideways. She was contemplating what I had said, which was worrisome. I contemplated it, too, trying to predict what conclusions she would make.

"Can I kiss you, then?" she whispered, staring at my lips.

I could have never predicted those words would have come out of her mouth. I nervously licked my lips, which was not helpful. My mind was a whirlwind of caution battling desire.

She explained, "I think you are a person of interest."

I exhaled all my used oxygen and with it came the word, "Why?"

"Because my mother loved your mother. That makes you a person of interest."

It was not the answer I wanted to hear. It stung a little, to be honest. But I couldn't deny that it was a legitimate reason, for her, if not for me personally. At least there had been no mention of Emory. I yielded my power to her, not sure if I'd ever get it back, and breathed out the word, "Yes."

She leaned down and pressed her lips to mine, holding them motionless as the seconds passed. I kept my lips still and let her kiss me, or what was more like a resting of her lips on mine. We were in dangerous territory already and I had to fight the urge to kiss her for real. She pulled away slowly and looked into my eyes, "Like that?"

I suspected she was practicing for Emory. I was, in a way, being used again. But the rules she was playing by had been set by me. I was the one who had said kissing was no big deal. I couldn't blame her. "Not exactly like that," I whispered.

"How?" She was staring at my lips again, contemplating how to get it right. I felt self-conscious about them, licked them nervously again. She leaned down and kissed my bottom lip, then the top. A wavy curl of her hair slid over her arm and onto my cheek. Her weight shifted as she placed her hand on the other side of me, holding herself above me as she kissed me this way again and again. After a dozen strategically placed pecks, she whispered, "Like this?"

To answer her, I would have had to open my mouth. It was a risky thing to do. I mentally prepared myself to answer. Behind my teeth I practiced the tongue motion to say the word 'yes', so that when I eventually opened my mouth I'd be able to quickly get the half-lie out before closing it again. My plan failed because my delay in answering had caused her to assume she was still doing it wrong. She leaned in again and gently bit my bottom lip which caused a sigh to escape me before I could rein it in.

"Good?" She breathed. Her gentle, steady kisses moved to my cheek toward my ear, her hair falling over my face.

"Angelina, you can't do this to just anyone. I didn't mean for it to sound so common, so ordinary. This isn't a good idea to do with people you have just met."

"I won't," she said, kissing along my jaw bone toward my chin. I wished I had shaved. When she had nearly made her way back to my mouth, she let the weight of her chest rest on me so her hands could brush her hair back over her shoulders. She looked down at me and smiled, "Am I getting close?"

"What are you trying to get close to?"

"Doing this right."

"What is right?" I didn't want to talk anymore.

"That's what I'm asking you." Hurt and frustration flashed in her eyes. "Was I being stupid?"

"No," I pushed a loose strand of her hair behind her ear. "Do it again," I said like a fool.

She leaned down skeptically as if she believed I just felt sorry for her. This time, I kissed her back. The pain it caused my ego to know she was kissing me and thinking of someone else was worth it just to keep that hurt look off her face. I let go of my pride, told myself to just enjoy the moment, however short lived it would be. My hands went up to the back of her head, my fingers pushed through her hair. I pulled her close, pressed my tongue gently through her lips until it found hers. She mimicked my motion until I felt her take over, kissing me with a

231

desperation I hadn't expected.

I pulled her away from me so I could kiss her chin, along her jaw, and onto her neck.

She sighed and I felt her shiver. "Do you feel that?" She breathed.

"What?" I mumbled into the salty skin of her neck.

"The Holy Ghost. I feel it, John."

Part Eight

Angelina

45

December 29, 2006

He asked, "What does it feel like?" as if he had never felt the Holy Ghost before.

Honestly, I wasn't sure if I had either. I knew the euphoric feelings I had during intense prayer, but the feeling I had with John was different. His hands were in my hair and his sighing breath warmed my ear. I forced the words out with shaky breath, "It feels like the entire universe is crashing through my veins." With those words, I realized this was not the Holy Ghost. Nor was it a demon. It was life. It was what Carl Sagan had called star stuff. It had been electrified by John's touch.

"I don't think it's the Holy Ghost," he pressed his lips to mine again. His hands moved to hold my face gently between them. "This is a very bad idea," he spoke through the kiss.

It was confusing to hear. How could this divine feeling be bad? I knew how I felt, but I didn't know how he felt. He seemed to like it. However, his comment made me think perhaps he thought it was evil. The whirring in my brain went silent and I stopped kissing him. He relaxed his head back onto the pillow and looked up at me with eager and concerned eyes.

"Why do you think it's bad?" I wanted to know.

"Maybe it isn't. I don't know. I don't know what you want. I don't know why you're kissing me. And if my parents find out... I don't even want to think about the consequences."

"Is this what you mean by going too fast?" I felt self-doubt creeping up.

"Maybe. How do you feel?"

His question ignited me again. I didn't have words for the feeling. I definitely didn't think it was too fast. Still, I worried that he did. "I like kissing," I replied, thinking of Marcy's similar reason for kissing Emory. I leaned down and kissed John again, this time placing my leg over his the way Marcy had done with Emory. I remembered the image of her beautiful bare back as she sat over Emory in the bed. I wanted to do that, too. Marcy and Emory were just friends to each other, so it must have been fine in my situation with John.

I slid on top of him and sat up, closed my eyes and imagined my hair was red. I imagined my skin was covered in beautiful blooms and vines in every shade as I pulled the t-shirt over my head. The warmth of the fire came in waves across my skin, erasing the chill but leaving my skin tight and goose pimpled.

"What are you doing, Angelina?" he arched away from me, repositioned himself, and relaxed again. I felt him beneath me. I don't know why it was surprising to feel his erection so distinctly. My heart quickened and I convinced myself it was only excitement. But it continued to increased until I had to admit I was afraid. I kept my eyes closed tight and thought of lily tattoos, rose tattoos, a garden path, Emory's pale green eyes, the sound of snow falling on snow, anything but what was beneath me. I couldn't hold the bad thoughts back, the thoughts of Silas, images of his wrinkly penis. Memories flooded in. The sound of Silas calling me a sinner, a demon, commanding me to come clean. Come clean. And then the darkness swallowed me.

The next thing I knew, John pulled me up from him enough to slide out from under me. I opened my eyes. He was on his knees in front of me, holding my face in his hands.

"Look at me! Look at me!"

I did. I opened my eyes and saw his distraught expression, his hair had fallen forward in a swoop above his long eyelashes, the orange glow of flames danced across his worried face, his full lips were shut tight. They were no longer offering kisses. I had gone too fast, too soon. He was probably angry.

He touched his thumb to my lips and said, "Don't rush. You'll figure all this out when it's time." His eyes were wet as he blinked to clear them.

I pleaded, "I'm sorry. I went too fast. Are you mad?"

He touched his forehead to mine, "Yes. I'm mad at myself," he smiled. "Put your shirt on and lie down. You need to rest and I need to grab a clean pair of pants." He registered my confused look, smiled reassuringly, and kissed my forehead, "You're already perfect. Try to believe that."

He leaned away from me and pulled off his t-shirt, stood up with it wadded up in front of his pants, then walked into the bathroom. I heard the faucet turn on and his quiet cursing. I assumed the water was cold.

I found my shirt, put it back on, and snuggled up beside Monty. He wiggled up close to sniff my face, seeming to know my thoughts. If John had to clean himself, it was because I made him dirty. I was so tired. I was tired of the shame and my ignorance. I was tired of trying to figure out a world I would probably never fit into. I was tired of thinking at all. I closed my eyes and fell asleep before John returned.

46

Through the night, at least a foot of snow had fallen. I stepped out the door onto the third floor balcony. Icicles hung all along the edge of the roof. Judging from the position of the sun, it was late morning. I felt guilty for sleeping so long. As far as I knew, John had never come back to our nest by the fireplace. It meant that not once, but twice, he had slipped away from me in the middle of the night. I felt foolish for what I had done the night before. Remembering it made a warm feeling flood my body, but my mind knew I had crossed a line.

The outside air was calm, the sky was blue, the tree covered hills were beautiful. But the chill was intense and prevented me from staying out as long as I had wanted. I stepped back into the bedroom and tried to decide what to do. I didn't want to see John if he didn't want to see me.

I decided the best thing would be for me to go back to my room. When I entered the blue jay room, I was surprised to see Tracy sitting by the window, my papers in his lap, some on the nightstand.

"You're back early," I greeted him with a smile despite my apprehension.

He smiled automatically, still deep in thought. "Yes. I got back at four o'clock this morning. I have a few friends with big trucks and snow plow attachments. I managed to find one willing to help a friend in need in the middle of the night." He winked at me. "Neil was nice enough to swing by the police station and pick up Dawson before bringing us both home. This much snow is bizarre for Nashville." He glanced out the window. "How was your night?"

I didn't know what to say. There were many opposite truths. My silence brought his gaze from the window back to me. He looked worried. He asked, "The boys were nice, I hope?"

"Yes," I swallowed, "They made me laugh a lot. Eugene is really funny. And John made sure we stayed warm." I blushed.

"You've had a lot of excitement this week, and you still haven't met everyone. I'm going down to talk to Jute. I need to let her in on what's going on before I fly out again this evening. I'm not sure how she'll take it or when she'll want to meet you. John and Eugene are out shoveling a path through the snow in case she feels ready today. I hope they can keep you a secret."

I nodded, thinking there were other secrets I hoped John would keep. I didn't want everyone knowing how foolish I had been the night before. I asked Tracy, "Have you heard from Emory?"

"He texted me, said the snow was bad in Louisville but he plans to make it here by the time I leave this evening. I promised him a job and a place to stay. I have the job worked out with the tour company, but I need to look around for an apartment."

"Can't he stay here?" I cringed at my rudeness. "I'm sorry. I have no right to ask."

Tracy moved the papers from his lap to the nightstand and stood up, "He's a grown man, Angelina. He'll want his own place. How's your back?" He changed the subject as he walked around behind me. "Can I look?"

"John put new bandages on last night. None of the old ones stuck, so I think it's healing well." I felt him raise the back of my shirt a little and press the tape and a few places on the gauze.

"You should probably take a shower and clean the area. Dawson brought some wound cleansers from the station's first aid cabinet. When you're ready, one of us will come help you apply it."

"Okay," I felt like a burden. "I need to get some clothes from the laundry room first."

"We saw those and ran them through the washer and dryer

this morning. Where did you get them?"

"John got them from the barn."

"Ah," Tracy leaned his head back, "Well, maybe you should wear your new dress. We don't want to shock Jute too much."

I stared at him, confused.

He said, "Those clothes from the barn are ones she bought years ago for Allie in hopes she'd return one day. It was kind of foolish. I told her as much. But she kept buying them, even after Allie died. It was one way she dealt with the loss, I guess."

"I was hoping not the ruin my new dress," I explained.

"We'll find you something else, then. Maybe John has something unisex that will work."

I went into the bathroom down the hall and shut the door. I had been in the shower only a few minutes when Tracy knocked on the door. He called through it, "I have the wound cleanser. Is it okay if I apply it, or would you rather Dawson do it?"

"Can John?" I asked.

Tracy was silent for a moment before saying, "They're still shoveling the snow. But, if you aren't comfortable with Dawson or me, I will go get him."

I didn't want to be rude to the people sharing their home with me. "It's okay if you do it," I said.

"Are you sure? It's up to you."

"It's fine."

"Are you ready?"

I turned off the water and pulled a towel from the bar to cover the front of my body. I didn't want to make the mistake I had made the night before. "Yes."

He walked in, but I was turned away from him, so I couldn't see his expression. He said, "It's looking better." He took a towel from the cabinet and patted my back dry, then sprayed the liquid which stung a little, but I had expected it. "So John did a good job replacing the bandages last time?"

"Yes," I said, not wanting to elaborate.

"That boy might turn out to be alright one day," he laughed.

"Do you not think he's alright now?"

"I was being silly. He's a great kid. Don't you think so?"

"He's not a kid," I said defensively, thinking of myself, too.

"Sounds like you two got along pretty well." He stopped laughing. "Okay, I'm going to dab around the edges of your wounds so I can get the tape to stick." Tracy worked silently. It was too quiet. I worried I'd said something wrong.

"I know he's legally a kid," I conceded. "But, it's not like we aren't able to make our own decisions."

"Hmm," He pulled a strip of tape from the roll, "Are you trying to tell me John is not a kid, or that you are not a kid?"

"Both."

"Well, I understand completely. You are both old enough to take responsibility for your own actions. As far as we are concerned here, you are free to make your own choices. But whatever choices you make, we are all vulnerable to the legal and emotional consequences. So, we'd like for you both to think about that before making any major ones. Okay?"

It did make sense to me. If I chose to pursue Emory, I would be putting him at risk because of the law. It wasn't fair to him. "How old were you when you met Dawson?"

"I was nineteen."

"And how old was he?"

"He was twenty-six."

"See, there!" I was so happy, "It's not so bad."

"What's that?"

"Being in a relationship with someone much older."

He taped on the last gauze and gently pulled me around to face him. "When I was your age, I had a lot of relationships with older men. So, maybe I don't have a right to advise you not to do what I did. All I can say is that those relationships weren't what I thought they were. I was easy to manipulate because I didn't know how the world worked. Those men didn't care about me. They used me. Dawson was different. Plus, I was legally an adult when we became involved with each other. You owe it to yourself to wait, and be sure you know how someone really feels about you. If you care at all about the guy, you'll not try to talk him into doing something that could ruin his life."

I was grateful for his frank words, grateful that none of them held accusations of evil or prods toward living Holy. Tracy seemed genuinely goodhearted, telling me about his life as it related to mine. I put my arm around him in a half-hug while I held onto my towel with the other. "Thanks," I said.

It was settled. If I had to wait a couple of years to be in a relationship with Emory, I would wait.

47

Tracy left for Jute's house before noon. He had taken my leather bag and all the documents except the letter. I wanted to give that to her myself and tell her how much it meant to have a role in getting it there.

I'd been too nervous to eat breakfast. I stayed in the blue jay room, unsure of what to do. I couldn't even decide what to wear. All the dresses from the barn had been washed and were hanging in the closet. I tried on a few and discovered my favorite, a lavender and paisley print tunic with several strips of fabric sewn together in layers. It ruffled out when I spun around. But to wear it, I would have needed pants underneath. It was quite short. I thought of Marcy and wondered when I would see her again, if ever.

I pulled the covers up over my shoulders to keep them warm and tried to quiet my mind. I had so much to think about, important things like John's claim that he had seen Gabriel, and unimportant things like how badly I needed to brush my hair. My brain switched between the important and non-important things as if easing itself into a cold mountain stream. But I was never completely ready for the difficult problems I needed to tackle. I closed my eyes, just wanting to sleep again until Tracy came back to tell me what to do.

Finally, I did sleep. I napped long enough to dream I was on my knees scrubbing the church floor. I don't know how long I'd been dreaming when a knock came to my door. Anxious to hear what Tracy had found out, I called, "Come in!"

John opened the door and peeked around it. He saw me

sitting up in bed with the covers pulled up just below my bare shoulders. His mouth opened, but words seemed to stick in his throat. He blushed red and his voice cracked. "Where are your clothes?"

"I couldn't decide what to wear." I hoped he'd have a solution to offer.

"What about the clothes from the barn?"

"Tracy said not to wear those around Jute."

"What does he expect you to do?" He snapped.

"He said maybe you would have something." I felt nervous, wondering why John seemed on edge.

He stepped into the room and shut the door behind him. He held a couple of books close to his chest. "We'll figure something out, but first I wanted to apologize for last night, Angelina. I don't want you to keep avoiding me because of it."

"I'm not avoiding you, John," It was a half-lie. "I just have so much I need to figure out. I'm meeting your mom today."

"I know you have a lot on your mind, some of it I don't even know. I just don't want you to shut me out or be afraid of me."

"I'm not afraid of you at all. Is that why you're so on edge?"

John didn't answer. He scratched his temple thoughtfully, then decided to change the subject. "How's your back? Do you need help changing the bandages?" He walked over and put the books on the nightstand, then sat by the pillow. I stared at the closet doors as he examined my back for loose tape or soaked gauze.

"It's good," I answered, "Tracy changed the bandages this morning."

John's fingers ran along the top edge of the tape, but it didn't feel like a bandage check. Goosebumps rose up on my arms. He must have noticed because his hands slid from my shoulders down my arms and up again to warm them.

"What happened last night was my fault," he picked up the hairbrush from the nightstand and began gently working through the tangles in my hair. "I shouldn't have let any of that happen. I promise I won't let it happen again."

244

"Did I do something wrong?" I knew I had.

"No, Angelina. You didn't do anything wrong. I just don't want anything bad to happen between us." Most of my tangles were out of the section he was brushing, but he continued to brush it absentmindedly.

"Whatever bad thing you are worried about, it has to do with what I did. I did something, went too far, or something else. I don't know exactly, and you should just say it, John. I don't understand your implications and doublespeak. I need you to be blunt. Tell me how I was bad so I can be better."

He moved around to face me. "You aren't bad." His eyes searched mine. His words weren't helpful at all. I closed my eyes to try to stop the tears and let myself fall back onto my pillow. I was frustrated with his continued insistence that I'd done nothing wrong, yet I obviously had. I opened my eyes to see his face was feverishly red. He stared at my breasts which had come exposed when I had fallen back. I hadn't even realized it. He pulled the edge of the sheet up to cover them, the warm tips of his fingers radiated electricity through me. I caught my breath. He said, "You are so beautiful. Not just your body," he swallowed nervously and looked at my eyes, his fingers traced my jaw line. "You always try to do the right thing for everyone else. You're smart and witty. Everything about you is beautiful," his voice was now a whisper, "It's so hard not to touch you."

"You are touching me," I pointed out. His fingers were twirling a strand of my hair.

"I guess I am," He smiled. "I shouldn't be." He sighed, "I'm going to see if I can find you something to wear."

He walked out of the room, leaving me feeling isolated. Emory had not wanted to touch me because he said adults shouldn't be involved with kids. But John couldn't use that excuse. I started to suspect there was something wrong with me that made people afraid to touch me. Had Silas been right about me?

When John came back, he held a pair of jeans and a plaid flannel shirt with shades of blue. "Try these."

I swallowed down my feelings, a skill I had mastered, and focused on preparing to meet Jute. I said, "I hate to ask, but do you have any underthings? I could get dressed without, but…"

He blushed again, reminding me how uncomfortable I made him feel. "Wait here," he said.

I had no plans to do otherwise. When he came back into the room, he held out a black pair of mens underwear and a white tank top. I looked at him skeptically. He said, "It's all I have. Surely it's better than nothing?"

I didn't want to seem ungrateful. "Thank you," I said and slid out of bed to take them.

He quickly looked away from my body, then briefly glanced from the corner of his eye. "You have to stop doing that."

"I'm sorry. I didn't think about it because it's just you, John. It's not like you haven't seen me already." I took the underthings from his hands and slid them on. Both the underwear and the tank top were snug. I felt self-conscious. John and I were almost the same age. I shouldn't be too big for his clothes, but I felt my flesh stretching them out. I did not have the body of a child. "I don't know about it. What do you think?" I asked.

He glanced at me again from the corner of his eyes, then turned his head to fully look at me. He scanned me from head to toe and bit his lip, not saying anything. I felt so self-conscious I wanted to cry.

"Why are you crying?" He stepped forward and wiped my cheek.

"I just feel so… I don't know how to feel! I'm stretching everything out, trying to fit into it, and that's how I feel about everything." I covered my face with my hands and cried. The small issue about the clothes, which would have never made me cry before, had broken the floodgates open and all my worry slipped out into the open.

"I swear, Angelina, those clothes have never looked so good. My God, how can you not know how incredible your body is?" His hands held my waist, his thumbs nearly touching the underside of my breasts, "I have to fight not to touch you."

246

"You are touching me," I had to laugh after having said it twice.

He pulled me close and hugged me. His body smelled intoxicating. I relaxed into his arms. "Why do you smell so good? What is it?"

"My natural body odor," He laughed, too. "Actually, it's Dad's body spray. I stole some while I was upstairs."

"Because...?"

"Because I left mine at home. And because I had ideas I shouldn't be having."

"Do you ever really answer anything with the whole truth?" I laid my head on his shoulder and breathed in the scent on his neck, held it in, then exhaled. I was thankful for the distraction. I moved closer to his skin and breathed in the scent again through my nose and exhaled the warm air from my mouth. He sighed and it surprised me. He must have liked the feel of warm air on his skin. I made a mental note that the act brought positive results.

"You have to stop," he said, but made no motion to push me away.

"Why? If you like it..." I wanted John to feel good. I wanted him to not see me so negatively. Even though he said I should stop, he didn't seem to be upset. I pressed my lips to his skin and breathed in his scent again, then exhaled. This time I felt the warmth of the air inside of me. I leaned closer and kissed the skin beneath his ear. Surely such a small kiss wouldn't be too much.

"Dammit," He let the word fall out with his sigh. He grabbed my hips and pulled me against him. The force of it scared me. I leaned back to look into his eyes, hoping to glean what he was feeling. They were wet with tears. He looked away and let go of me. "Are you doing this to me on purpose?" He asked, covering his eyes as if the rays of the sun were blinding him, but the room was dim.

"Doing what?" I had done so little compared to the night before, yet he acted like I had done even more. I didn't understand. "Tell me, John! What am I doing that's making you angry?"

A knock came to the door and caused it to open. Dawson spoke before he walked into the room, "Everything okay up here?" He froze when he saw me, but immediately diverted his eyes and looked at John.

"I was helping her find clothes," John explained without being asked. "I was just leaving."

John walked out of the room. Dawson turned to follow him, telling me without looking back, "I'll give you some privacy to get dressed."

I could hear John's voice at the end of the hall saying, "It's not what you think! Just leave me alone!"

Dawson called after him, "John! I just want to talk!"

Then their voices faded to silence. More than ever, I didn't want to leave my room. I slid under the blanket again, still wearing only the underwear, and waited for Tracy to come back.

48

Tracy rushed into the room at two o'clock. I was in the middle of reading the first of two Harry Potter books John had brought.

"Get up," Tracy's voice was polite but urgent, "We have one hour and then I have to leave for the airport. We have to go. Now."

I placed the book on the nightstand. "John brought me clothes. I tried on the jeans, but they're too small. What do you want me to wear?"

"I think your back has healed enough to wear the blue dress. Put it on, quickly. I'll wait for you in the kitchen."

I did as he said and pulled on the dress. Then I brushed my teeth and hair, and slip on the pair of shoes Marcy had given me. Lastly, I pulled on the blue fedora with the letter tucked inside and made my way down the stairs. Tracy sat at the kitchen table, his knee bouncing anxiously. He smiled when he saw me.

"Ready?" He stood and picked up my wool coat from the chair beside him. He held it out for me. I put it on and he unnecessarily helped me button it. He seemed nervous.

"Dawson!" he called out, "We're leaving now. I'll call you." He took my hand and we headed out the front door.

A narrow path through the field had been cleared. As we walked along it, I thought of John and Eugene working so hard most of the morning. I felt guilty for not helping them. But maybe John wouldn't have wanted that. I couldn't seem to be around him without upsetting him.

The house came into view. It sat nestled among oak trees

with a fenced garden beside it. Snow glistened on everything. Smoke billowed out of the chimney. A cold gust of wind tugged at my coat and I couldn't wait to get inside. We made our way around to the front and climbed the stairs. Before we even knocked, a lady opened the door and wrapped her arms around me. She rocked me from side to side, saying through her tears, "I didn't believe him, but it's true! Look at you!" She stepped back and held my arms, her eyes were just like John's. The shape of her face and fullness of her lips meant she was undeniably John's mother. I smiled at her. She said, "Oh my, you even have her smile!" She pressed her thumb to my lips as a tear rolled down her cheek. She briskly wiped it away. "Come in! It's so cold out here!"

She took my hand and pulled me to follow her. She didn't let go until we were in her kitchen where sweet, cinnamon smells wafted up from the oven. A little girl sat on a stool at the bar. She looked at me shyly through the hollowed out bread crust from the sandwich she had been eating.

"We'll go to my office," Jute pointed down the hall and proceeded to walk that way. "Clara!" She peered into a room on our way down the hall. "Rolls are out in six more minutes. Would you mind?" I watched Jute nod and smile, then close the door.

Tracy and I followed her further down the hall. I couldn't help but think that her reaction to me, so far, had been nothing like what Tracy had predicted. Of course, I didn't know what had happened in the hours before I arrived. I wasn't sure how much she knew about me, or how she had initially reacted when he told her I was there.

She opened the door to a room with a couch, two chairs, and a small desk. I assumed she usually sat behind the desk, but walked over and sat on the end of the couch. She motioned for me to sit in the chair closest to her. Tracy sat beside her on the couch and gave me a reassuring smile. He took Jute's hand in his and squeezed it.

As she spoke, her eyes darted to mine and then away numerous times as if it hurt to look at them. "I hope you don't mind, but Tracy has filled me in on all that has happened with you. Some of it, perhaps you don't yet know. I just want to reassure you that I... we... all of us are going to make sure you never have to go through anything like that again." She forced her gaze to stay on my eyes. Hers began to fill with tears, "I'm sorry." She wiped them away. "You look so much like her."

"Would you like to read the letter?" I removed the hat and pulled out the folded piece of paper. When I handed it to her, she took it with uncertainty, then looked to Tracy. He put his arm around her and moved close to read it with her. She unfolded it and began to read. I had it memorized, so I read along in my mind. I watched the pain wash over her face as she read about Jim holding Allie captive, how she cared for Gabriel, and Cynthia taking her baby away. Jute's face softened when she read the part about Allie still loving her; but when she read how Allie feared for her life, Jute's hands shook.

"She knew he would kill her," Jute whispered, then leaned into Tracy and cried. "I'm sorry," her voice muffled into his chest, "I'm trying to keep it together."

"I know," Tracy said, rubbing his hand over her back, "You have a right to be upset about how she was treated. But we have to do something about what's going on now. There's a lot Angelina doesn't know."

Jute sat up and tried to compose herself. I was nervous. I hadn't given much thought to what would happen past the point of getting the letter to her.

Tracy said, "I'm sorry to speak so bluntly, but I have a plane to catch. I'm going to tell you everything we know, Angelina. It seems the police have uncovered a number of bodies on Silas Billings' property. Many are of infants, some are older. It's too early for DNA results, but we suspect one of them will prove to be Gabriel. Silas was the last known person to have custody of the child."

I was not surprised by the news of bodies on Silas's land. But I couldn't believe Silas would have killed Gabriel and spared me. I protested, "But John said he knew where Gabriel was!"

Tracy looked surprised. "Did he say where?"

I shook my head. "Silas had sons and Esther was never allowed to talk about them. The bodies are probably theirs. I don't know how many. They all died, as far as I know, except Jim. One of the bodies by the willow tree is Esther."

"Most were girls, judging from their clothing, infants. Maybe this is too grim for you to hear," he paused and waited for my response.

"No, Silas told me he killed Esther's baby girls and told her they died at birth." I said, "And considering all he put me through, they were probably better off."

"Oh, Angelina, don't say that!" Jute put her hand on my knee. "You got out. You made it here. We're going to find you a good family."

"You mean I can't stay with you?" Rejection twisted around my heart.

"For now, you can, but..." she paused.

Tracy picked up where Jute left off, "You'll stay with us for a little while. But, we have spoken with some friends of ours... do you remember Heather Matthews?"

I nodded. She was the Sexual Assault Advocate. Thoughts of the rape kit brought shivers down my spine.

"Well," Jute said, "her husband went to high school with Allie and me. His name is Casey Matthews. He always thought highly of your mother." She wiped a tear away, "They're both very nice people. They have no children. They live very close by. We've talked to them about you and we barely even had to ask before they said yes. They'd like to have you live with them, see how it works out for you."

Mrs. Heather had been so nice to me. I had no doubt about her kindness. But my heart felt shattered. "Why can't I stay with you?"

"You didn't do anything wrong," Tracy said. "I just think... we think... with you and John being so close in age, maybe it would be best if you were adopted elsewhere. We want to do what is right for you, Angelina. It isn't easy for us, either. We want you in our family, and you always will be, no matter who adopts you. You are part of us."

Tears streamed down my face. I had ruined my chances of being with them because of what happened with John. How did they even know? Did he tell them? I said, "It was nothing. I was just curious. I'm sorry."

"Angelina, stop," Jute's voice was firm, almost scolding. "I don't want you carrying guilt for anything you've done. That's what got your mother into that mess. Now stop."

I did. I stopped everything, even breathing, and just looked at her. She obviously wasn't angry with me, but what she said was not meant to be negotiable. She continued, and I relaxed with the familiarity of being told what to do, "We are not disapproving. We love you. We want you to be happy. Please, trust us, that what we are doing is for your own happiness."

"And for John's" Tracy added. "I don't think he will ever think of you as a sister."

It was then that I realized where I had gone wrong and why John acted the way he had. Even though we had joked about me being his sister if Jute took me in, I never really considered what that would mean in reality. He had expected us to one day live as siblings, and yet I had kissed him. Remembering his sighs and how his fingertips brushed my skin made me blush. I wanted desperately to change the subject.

I asked, "What if you find Gabriel?"

"I'll call John if it will put your mind at ease, but we aren't hopeful. There was no other family besides Silas to take him."

Tracy pulled out his phone and touched a few places on the screen before holding it to his ear. "No, it's not time yet. I just need to talk to John. Can you find him and put me on speaker phone so we can all talk together?"

After a few seconds, Tracy laid the phone in the palm of his hand and touched the screen with his fingertip. I heard John's voice come through. "Hello? Dad?"

"Yes. Hey, Angelina tells us you might know where to find Gabriel. Do you have any information?"

There were a few moments of silence before he spoke, "Iris and I went to Allie's church, the one where Jim was a youth minister."

Dawson followed with, "Yes, Iris told us you had gone to see about getting Allie a headstone, but it ended up being a wild experience and you left without finding out anything."

"Well, there was a boy there playing piano. A woman on the stage called him Gabe. He had some kind of nervous condition or something. He was just odd. A man at the church said it was because his mother was a Jezebel. I suspected it then, but wasn't sure until I saw the name Gabriel on his birth certificate."

Jute gasped and covered her mouth. "That's him," she said, "That has to be him!"

Dawson spoke, "But the boy has been in legal custody of Silas Billings all this time and the man never left the mountain."

"He left every Christmas," I offered, an epiphany washing over me. "He was gone all day, every single Christmas. That was Gabriel's birthday."

Now Tracy seemed convinced, but I felt like I was gasping for air. All I could do was try to breathe. My whole life, I had been banished to my room for the shame of being born on Christmas. Yet, it seemed Silas had made a special trip every year to go to Ohio to see Gabriel. Did they celebrate? I covered my face and cried.

"Dawson, call Felicity police and have them look into it. And if they come across a woman named Cynthia in the church, there may be reason to charge her with kidnapping, child abuse, and attempted murder. I'll fill you in when you get down here."

49

I watched the light of the scanner move under the lid. It buzzed to the right, seemed to jiggle there, and then whirred back to the left. It was the same with every document Tracy scanned from my leather bag. He was still making copies when the office door pushed open and Emory walked in. I jumped up from my chair and wrapped my arms around him. I had never been so happy to see someone in my life. Over his shoulder, I saw Marcy standing timidly in the doorway. She had a bag in her hands, her coat draped over it.

"You okay?" Emory asked into my hair.

I nodded. He hugged me, kissed my forehead, then pushed me back to scan my face.

"Your face is looking so much better."

Jute walked up and introduced herself to Emory. He gushed his admiration for Tracy and for all Jute did for abused women.

"We're a fan of yours, too," Jute said to him. "Thank you for taking care of Angelina and getting her to us."

"It wasn't just me. Marcy gave her a place to stay for a couple of nights," Emory motioned for Marcy to come into the room. She sat her luggage by her feet and shook Jute's hand.

"I was glad to do it. It was like a slumber party. We watched lots of Carl Sagan." Marcy glanced over to wink at me. "I used to take in a lot of homeless kids, runaways, I guess. Emory was the one to start it all."

I watched Emory's face flush red with embarrassment. I wasn't sure what about Marcy's words upset him. It didn't seem to take much to fluster him. Marcy noticed his blushing and decided to elaborate, "I had been running a tailoring business for about four years when I met him. I didn't know at the time that he was just seventeen. And I certainly didn't know that because of the clothes I made for him, he would end up homeless for a while."

"Enough," Emory said through gritted teeth, though he tried to smile afterward.

Jute put her hand on his shoulder and moved it in a comforting circle. "Don't worry. We're not judgy. If there's any place on Earth where it's okay to talk about hard times of the past, it would be here."

It was an odd thing to hear from Jute, knowing the lengths Tracy had gone to in order to prepare her to meet me. Maybe Tracy had been overly cautious, or he worked fast magic to ease her into the idea. She seemed to be handling it well enough, either way.

"I'll show you where to put your bags," Jute led Marcy out of the room.

I heard Marcy in the hall saying, "Thank you so much for inviting me."

Jute said, "Tracy thought you'd be good for her..."

Tracy's voice drowned out theirs. "We'll be ready to leave in just a minute." He placed another paper on the scanner.

"The roads are bad. Are you sure the plane will take off?" Emory asked.

"I've already confirmed it. We just have to get to the airport. I've called Neil to pick us up."

"My truck should make it. I'll drive us, unless you just want that guy to do it."

"That'd be great," Tracy pulled his cell phone out of his jacket pocket and made a call.

Emory was smiling now. He seemed to have forgotten about Marcy's over-explaining. His clear green eyes had a spark of joy to them I had never seen.

"I missed you," I said.

"I don't see how, with so much happening here! Tell me

something exciting you've done."

"Watched monster movies, baked cookies, got snowed in without electricity, and cried a lot."

His smile dropped, "Why were you crying?"

"I don't know. It's just hard to figure out what is expected of me, or to even know who I am. It's like I've just been born, but with all these scars and pain."

He stepped forward and held me again. I put my arms around him, too, and thought about kissing his neck, or breathing on it, or something to nudge him toward seeing me as more grown up. But before I could decide what to do, if anything, Dawson came into the room with a booming greeting, "Emory!"

Emory let go of me and jerked around to give Dawson a huge hug. Beside Dawson stood John, staring at his shoes.

Dawson said, "You haven't met my son, John. He's helping me crack a case today." The way Dawson said it, he made John sound like he was nine years old. John glanced up and gave Emory a quick smile and an even shorter handshake, then looked back down at his shoes.

Dawson walked over to the copier and tapped Tracy on the shoulder, "Hey, Tracy, I'll take over. You guys need to hit the road," Dawson looked at Emory, "I swear, the man is never on time. Never."

"Fine," Tracy said, handing Dawson the last few documents. He stood on his tiptoes and gave Dawson a goodbye kiss.

"Not in front of the kid," Dawson's voice was low and playful. Despite his cautionary words, he leaned down and kissed Tracy again.

I glanced over at Emory, embarrassed to have just been called a kid again. I didn't even registered with him. He was too caught up in gawking at the kiss. I wondered if that's how I looked the first time I saw him kissing Marcy.

Tracy gave Dawson a tight hug and then slapped his arm. "Hold down the fort," he said, then looked at Emory, "Ready?"

"Hell, yeah!" Emory said, "Can I help you carry your bags?"

"No, you're not my butler, Emory. Your job is to help set up the stage, and you don't start that until tonight. So until then, just be cool."

They walked together down the hall. I heard Emory say, "Thanks for getting me the job." Tracy replied with something I couldn't hear because they'd moved too far away.

Emory had left without telling me goodbye.

50

Marcy and Jute sat across one another at the kitchen table. They sipped coffee and talked about their past. I sat at the bar, devouring a cinnamon roll and a cold glass of milk. As I neared the last bite, I began to eat only nibbles, making it last longer so I could listen to all that was being said. I wasn't sure whose life was more fascinating, Jute's or Marcy's. Both shared, in candid detail, stories of their abusing fathers. Each, at one point at least, had been brought to tears just talking about it. But, neither described the type of suffering I had endured. Another difference between their abuse and mine was that they had an escape. With Jute, it had been Allie. With Marcy, it had been fashion design. I had really had nothing, other than meditative prayer, which was now decidedly useless without a belief in a deity.

Marcy and Jute seemed to forget I was in the room, or perhaps they wanted me to believe that. Talking around me might have been a way to talk to me without pressuring me to participate, which I really didn't want to do anyway. Eventually the conversation turned to Marcy's sewing and how she had been making clothes for transgender teens and adults for the last decade. Jute mentioned Allie's love of vintage dresses and I felt my face begin to burn. I thought about all those dresses in my closet and was very glad not to be wearing one of them. I felt like I had done something sacrilegious by wearing them at all.

Dawson came in and cleared his throat as if to make an announcement. The talking stopped and Marcy scooted her chair to face him. He glanced at them, then looked at me as he spoke, "They've located Cynthia Garrett. She has a boy named Gabriel living with her in the home once occupied by Jim and Allie. The Felicity police would like you, Angelina, to be there when she is confronted. They hope she'll be more likely to confess to her involvement in your kidnapping if she sees you. I think it's a good plan. But I'm going to leave the decision up to you."

The thought of coming face to face with Cynthia filled me with fear, and yet part of me wanted desperately to make her look me in the eyes and see that I was alive. I nodded.

"We'll have to leave now. Neil should be here any minute."

"Is John coming?"

"I haven't discussed it with him, but it's a good idea. He needs to give an official statement about what he saw at the church."

A short young woman with Dawson's complexion stepped around him, "Am I going? I was at the church, too."

"Fine. Tell John to pack his toothbrush and both of those boys need to get down here ASAP."

Ten minutes later, they arrived, overnight bags in hand. Eugene was by John's side, shifting his weight nervously from one leg to the other. John stared at the floor. Iris came into the room wearing a bright purple coat and matching purple beret, her dark smiling lips were covered in a shiny clear gloss. She looked so beautiful and confident. I remembered feeling that way myself when I had slipped into the dress Marcy had made for me. I suddenly had an urge to ask Marcy to make more clothes for me, but I bit my tongue.

"We'll be back tomorrow," Dawson said to Jute and Marcy. "This should all be over soon."

Jute got up and wrapped her arms around me, "I don't want you to go so soon," she whispered. "But this should be the last hard thing. After this, we should be able to get Gabriel and you can both get to know the Matthews. No one is going to hurt you again, Angelina."

I wasn't sure if I believed her. But I said, "Okay," to make her think I had.

Marcy gave me a hug just before we left. She kissed my cheek and I wondered if she had left red lipstick there.

Neil's SUV was parked in front of Jute's house. Dawson held the middle seats forward so I could climb into the back. John sat in front of me, which surprised me. I had thought he would sit beside me. Iris slid in beside John and Eugene sat beside her, leaving me in the back alone.

Dawson sat in the front. He said to Neil, "We just need to drop Eugene off at his house, then if you can take me by the station, I'll borrow a spare SUV to get us to Ohio."

"I can take you all the way up there if you want. I got nothing to do."

"That's a long way, Neil. But if you're up for it, I'll pay you."

"You just cover the expenses and I'll consider the adventure payment enough. I don't get to run around in the snow nearly enough, plus I get to help rescue a kid." Neil tipped his camouflage cap back and glanced at all our faces in the backseats. "You kids ready? Buckled up?"

I slid my seatbelt over, but Neil was already driving down the driveway by the time I had clicked it into place.

For the first few miles, I brooded over the way Neil had called us kids. I tried to imagine what Gabriel would look like, but I knew he wasn't going to look like a child.

51

Neil was driving behind a county police car and two Ohio State Police cars. John pointed out the church as we passed it. Cynthia's house, the house in which Jim and Allie had also called home, was not far from it. A line of trees along the road mostly hid it from view. We pulled into a driveway over a low wooden bridge covered with snow and ice. The ditch below must have been prone to flooding, but was now either dried or frozen. Across the bridge, a big yard opened up. The house sat nearly a hundred feet back from the road. It was bigger than Marcy's house, but not huge. The wood siding and the front porch had been painted white. All the lights inside the house were off. Our headlights beamed like spotlights. I felt oddly guilty about coming so late. It was nearly ten o'clock.

"Okay, everyone," Dawson called back to us. John's head jerked up as if he had fallen asleep. "The police are going to go in first. We'll go in after they motion for us. We don't expect trouble, but stay alert in case we need to dodge bullets." He smiled in a way that implied he was joking, but the shiver down my back didn't get the message.

I wasn't quite sure what they were expecting me to do. There hadn't been much said about it on the drive up. Iris talked about their trip to Kentucky and Ohio, telling all the details to Dawson. John kept his eyes on the landscape going by his window. He had only spoken occasionally to add more information or to correct something Iris had said. She had covered it fairly completely on her own, including how the coroner mentioned that Silas's pants were unzipped to expose himself. A sick feeling swirled in my stomach. No one looked back at me and I felt both thankful and forgotten.

As the reality sunk in that we were sitting in front of Cynthia's house, we were forced to address the reason we had driven all that way. I needed to know what to do.

Neil turned off this headlights. The police knocked on the door for the longest five minutes I had ever experienced. Finally, the door opened. I couldn't make out anything about the person at the door. The police spoke a few words before disappearing into the house, shutting the door behind them. I couldn't even see the color of the lady's hair, or if it had been a lady at all.

The SUV was so quiet that we could hear the gurgling of each other's stomachs. Only a few minutes had passed when Dawson's phone vibrated. We could hear the caller, even though he wasn't on speaker. "Ambulance has been called. Give them time to take the boy, then bring her in. We have enough for an arrest, but should make a case for all possible charges."

"Will do," Dawson said nonchalantly.

As soon as he hung up the call, I asked, "Is he hurt?"

Dawson twisted around to look at me, alarmed and worried. He probably hadn't realized we could hear every word. He forced a reassuring smile. "It's typical to gather evidence as soon as possible. He'll need a physical exam and to have any signs of injury documented." He hadn't answered my question, but I knew from hearing the call that he didn't know any more than I did.

I thought about my time in the ambulance, the rape kit, my breakdown, and how Mrs. Matthews had helped me through it. She had not forced me to do all the steps of the evidence collecting and I was grateful for that. She seemed like a very kind person, but nothing about her had made me think of her as my future mom. I found it hard to believe she would consider making me part of her family. Would anything change if this boy proved to be my brother, my twin? What if he had experienced abuse similar to mine? Would the Matthews family be willing to take in two traumatized teenagers, or would Gabriel and I be separated again after having just found each other? So many questions filled my mind. I lost track of the passage of time. It seemed like a blink of an eye and the ambulance pulled into the yard.

We watched the paramedics open the back doors, none of them looked like Mrs. Matthews or Ms. Emmerson. They looked hurried, precise, on a mission. A police officer exited the house holding the elbow of a tall boy, nearly a man. He was tall enough to be a grown up, but the way he walked and looked about the night sky seemed to imply he was younger than he appeared. An officer followed behind them and helped the boy into the back of the ambulance. In less than ten minutes, it drove away with the boy and a few paramedics in the back.

An officer motioned for us to come inside. I was the last to slide out of the SUV. John held the seat forward for me. For the first time since we left Nashville, he looked into my eyes. "Are you okay?" He whispered so low that no one heard him except me.

"I don't know," I said honestly.

He reached down and took my hand and squeezed it. His jaw tightened and he looked both anxious and defeated. I wasn't sure how much of the blame I held for that. We walked together, behind everyone else, to the porch. Just before we stepped onto the first step, John leaned over and said, "You're not what she thinks you are." He looked into my eyes so I would see he meant it. Then he let go of my hand and let me walk in front of him.

A woman was screaming at a police officer, "Where did you take my son? He can't be without me! He gets violent when he's afraid! They won't know how to handle him!"

"Is tying him to the bed how we should handle him, Ms. Garrett? Is that what you think the solution is? Judging from what I witnessed, he may have had a legitimate reason to be violent and afraid around you," said the officer. "But we can talk about that later, from your jail cell. What I want to talk about right now is a lady you might recognize. Angelina?"

I stepped through the front door in time to see her react to hearing that name. She was looking at the officer in shock and disbelief at his mention of it. When she turned her head to actually see me, she put a hand over her gaping mouth and nearly passed out. The officer caught her and helped her to sit on the couch. When she was able to hold her head up again, her eyes were filled with tears.

"How?" She cried. "How is this possible?"

"What makes you think it's not possible, Ms. Garrett?"

"Who is this person?" She pointed a finger at me. "This is not Angelina!"

"So you do know a girl named Angelina, but you believe this isn't her? What about this girl makes you believe she is an impostor?"

"She's pretending, for the trust fund. She's a liar if she says she is Angelina! Angelina is dead!" Cynthia had stopped being afraid and was simply angry. She had convinced herself to not to believe what her own eyes were seeing.

"How did Angelina die?" The officer asked.

"She was born dead. She was buried on Silas's property. She was never alive," her voice pleaded to be believed.

The officer handed her a copy of the note which said, "*Her name is Angelina. I'll leave her here. If you find her alive, please finish. I can't. -Cynthia*".

"Why?" She screamed. Her head fell back and she called up to the ceiling, or to God, or perhaps the soul of Silas himself. "Why did he keep this? Why!" She sobbed in despair. She cried for her own fate, ignoring that I was alive, that I had endured sixteen years of misery because of her.

My voice cracked when I spoke, but I made sure the words were loud enough for her to hear over her cries, "Did she know about me?"

"She? She!" Cynthia stood up, her face red with anger. Two officers grabbed her arms and held her from charging at me. "She was a whore! She didn't deserve him! He should have taken *her* to Silas to be killed! Jim had promised to marry me, but she got pregnant and he was forced to marry that little heathen." Tears rolled from her eyes. She took a seething breath and sneered at me. "He tried to beat the demon from her, but there wasn't any getting through. And then she said to him, if she had a girl she would name it Angelina. She thought naming a girl after an angel would make Jim forget how tainted it was. It was like Eve offering the apple to Adam. Jim nearly fell for it, thinking it was a sign from God. He remembered all those baby girls his daddy had killed over the years and he became weak willed. Jim started to doubt, but I told him he was a fool. That baby would have that Jezebel's sin in her veins. Jim didn't want to believe me." Cynthia puffed her chest out in self-righteousness. "But when he heard the whore calling out in the night, saying that lesbian's name, he knew I was right. And I *was* right. As soon as you were born, I planned to tie you up in a bag and toss you in the trash. But I thought I'd get caught, so I took you to Silas. He told me he killed you!" She screamed at me. "You destroy everything you touch, like the sins of Eve! You have no idea who your Father is, do you? Satan is in your heart. I see it in you. Look at her!" She commanded everyone in the room. "She looks just like the whore!"

She turned her eyes back to me and looked as if she would kill me right then if they'd let her go.

I swallowed the lump forming in my throat and hated her too much to let her see me cry. I steadied my voice, "He raped me from the time I could walk. You gave me to a man who raped me in the name of your god every day of my life until I became a woman at twelve. Then he tortured me in other ways, terrible and painful ways. If that gets your God's approval, give me Satan any day!" My steady voice had grown into a scream. Tears began to fall against my will. I hated her even more for making me cry in front of her, in front of everyone. I hated her.

"You're a ghost, aren't you?" Her eyes seemed distant and crazed, "You are not even real! Silas would have told me about you if you were real. Satan has his hand in this trickery! I will not disavow my God!" She called up to the ceiling again before beginning to sing a hymn, a song about Jesus in heaven which I had never heard. Silas had forbid songs of any sort. I had heard

Esther hum a tune now and then when he was away, a word or two was often sung between the humming, but never a full song. I thought of Esther with appreciation that she had been there to stop Silas from killing me, but I wished she had found a better life for herself.

The handcuffs clicked on Cynthia's wrists and she was led out the door.

Dawson said, "We'll give our statements here, then go to the hospital to see if they're ready to release Gabriel."

On the drive to the hospital, he called Jute give her an update. Then he called the Matthews to see if they were prepared to foster him. Much to my relief, they agreed to take us both. I imagined life as a part of a kind family with a father, mother, and brother. I wanted it so badly that it hurt to think about it. Everything I had ever wanted had been taken away or withheld to deprive me of pleasure. I hoped this dream of having a real family would be one I would get to keep.

52

By the time we reached the hospital, Gabriel's examination was complete. He sat on a bed in a room, waiting for us. The sound of our footsteps startled him and he spun around to see who had entered. When I caught sight of his eyes and the shape of his nose, I knew there was no denying our shared genetics.

"Hey, Gabe," Dawson spoke, "Are you ready to go and get out of this place?"

"Yes, sir." His voice was deep and full of projection as if he were speaking from a stage.

"Have you ever stayed in a hotel room before?"

"No, sir." His head tilted sideways then straightened.

"Good! It will be an adventure. Would you like to pick a friend for a roommate?" Dawson moved his hand around to indicate he could choose any of us.

Gabriel turned and pointed at John."I choose my friend from church. Church friends are good friends."

I noticed Iris roll her eyes, then she winked at me. I remembered she had said earlier that no one at the church would give her the time of day. Now Gabriel seemed to be ignoring her as well.

"No girls," Gabriel clarified.

"Okay. John will be your roommate. The boys will be in one room and the girls in another, alright? If we get there quickly, we'll have time to order pizza. Are you hungry?"

"It's Friday. I only eat on Saturday, Sunday, and Wednesday. I eat at the church. I use a fork and chew slowly so no one will stare at me. That is a rule."

"Well, you're in luck. It's almost midnight. So, it will be Saturday by the time we order our food." Dawson beamed, intentionally avoiding the revelation of Gabe's routine starvation. Dawson's words had been brilliantly calculated. Gabe became at ease. He stood up and hugged the paper bag he had been holding. We walked out, all of us grouped around Gabriel like a herd protecting him.

The ride to the hotel room was filled with nervous chatter. No one seemed to know what to say to Gabriel, so they tried to talk about everything except what needed to be talked about most. I thought about my ride to Louisville with Emory and how I hadn't wanted to tell him what I'd been through. At the time, I felt to blame for it all. I knew Gabriel probably felt the same way. If John's experience at the church was any indication, he must have grown up shouldering a lot of false accusations.

We made it to Cincinnati and stopped at a Hampton Inn and Suites. Dawson paid for two joining rooms for the men and a room across the hall for Iris and me. After he handed us a plastic card to swipe as a key, which was a very curious thing, Iris and I headed toward the elevator. "Hey," he called after us, "I'll call you when the pizza gets here, unless you don't want any. I know it's late."

"Call us," Iris insisted. I followed her, wishing I knew more about her. I hoped she would be as easy to talk to as Marcy had been. But Iris didn't seem very much like Marcy. Iris seemed like she had everything together and expected others to do the same. It was an expectation I couldn't meet.

When we reached our door, she sang, "Four nineteen…. no we can't talk at all," and then she laughed as she slid the card into the door labeled 419.

"We can't talk?" I asked nervously.

She laughed again in response as we walked into the room. "Hey nineteen? You know, the song about an old guy and a young prostitute?" She saw the confusion on my face and explained defensively, "I didn't write it, Steely Dan wrote it. The old guy tries to have a conversation with this young girl he has paid to have sex with him, but she doesn't know anything about the things that interest him because he's an old guy. So," Iris sang the line, "Hey nineteen, no we can't talk at all."

My gut instinct said she told the story to imply something about me. Maybe she, too, was saying I was too young for Emory. But he was far from being an old man. I tried to reason that it wasn't Iris's idea to have us in room 419, so it must have been a coincidence. But deep down, I was suspicious of her.

Iris plopped her bag on the bed near the window and said without looking at me, "I'm a goofball sometimes. Overlook it." She peeked through the curtain then turned toward me. "I'm glad we're rooming together. We haven't had a chance to talk much."

I thought to myself that she had lots of time to talk to me. She just hadn't done it. I didn't know how to respond to her sudden friendliness. Fortunately, I didn't have to say anything because she started talking again. "We had no idea you existed, but I guess you already know that. We went looking for Gabriel just to check up on him. I've been thinking about what we would have done if we'd come to Silas's trailer and you had been there, in the horrible situation you were in. Would we have seen you? Would we have even realized what was going on?"

It felt like she was rubbing salt in my wounds. Sure, maybe if I had waited a few days, they would have come and rescued me after sixteen years. Or, Silas would have killed me and I would have been buried in the yard by the time they got there. Where had they been my whole life? I knew I was just feeling sorry for myself and should stop. I breathed in a deep breath and let it out slowly.

"Am I upsetting you by talking about it?" Iris walked over and looked at me with great concern. She seemed sincerely worried.

"I'm just so tired. All this has been hard to process and I don't even know where I'm going to be tomorrow, much less a month from now.

"Well," she drew out the word as she pulled me to sit on the bed beside her, "I have a secret about part of that. I'll tell you if you promise me you won't tell John."

Her eyes sparkled and her mouth quivered a little as she tried not to smile. I was afraid to promise anything because I didn't yet know the secret. But she was dying to tell. It was all she could do not to blurt it out, so I felt obligated.

"I won't tell," I promised and hoped for the best.

"Did you know John's sixteenth birthday is Wednesday?"

I shook my head.

"It is and we're celebrating by taking a surprise trip!" She bounced on the bed and clapped, "Guess where?"

I wasn't sure what any of this had to do with me, and I certainly had no idea what place to guess. A week ago, I hadn't even known how to find Nashville, or that it even existed. I felt self-conscious again. What she said should have made me as excited as she was, but it hadn't because I was too ignorant. Tears started to well up and I looked away. She grabbed my chin and pulled me to look at her.

"Why are you crying? Don't cry! You're coming, too. You and the Matthews, and I guess Gabriel will come now that he's with us. Our dads and Jute are coming, and even Emory and Marcy! Don't cry!"

Hearing Emory's name made my heart leap. I really didn't care where we would be going, or when, or for how long. Once I knew he was going, everything changed. I beamed. She saw my smile and hugged me carefully as to not hurt me, then patted my back gently as if to say she hadn't forgotten I was injured. She seemed to know a lot about me. I wondered just how much she had been told and who had told her.

53

Iris and I walked over to the boys' room for pizza. We found them all sitting on the floor in front of the TV watching Back to the Future.

"It just came on," Dawson waved us over. We put a slice of pizza on our plate and sat at the foot of the bed. Iris sat by her dad and I sat beside her. I was closest to the door and could barely see the TV, but I could easily see the others. With the room lights dim, their faces were lit up by the TV screen. John glanced over at me, but quickly looked back to the TV when he saw I was looking at him.

Every now and then Gabriel would comment about something in the movie, saying in his expressive tone, "Inappropriate content!" or "That is a bad word!" But he didn't really seem bothered by it. He took bites of pizza and kept his eyes glued to the screen. A few minutes passed and he asked Dawson, "May I have more pizza, please?"

"Sure." The word was barely out of Dawson's mouth before Gabriel stood up and helped himself.

I watched Gabriel more than I watched the movie. I knew he had been kept hungry, but I wasn't sure what else had happened to him. He was thin, but had no visible signs of bruising. His long sleeved pajamas covered most of his body, though. I wanted to talk to him, but the time was all wrong. I remembered how Dawson had treated Gabriel in the hospital. I understood how important it was that we all try to make him feel comfortable. Asking him about his abuse would be counterproductive. And secretly, I wasn't sure how I would deal with finding out he had been treated well by Silas when I had been treated so terribly. I certainly wouldn't wish harm to him. I wanted the truth to be that he had been loved. I just wasn't sure if I was ready to compare my own experiences with his. Gabriel had already been the only one of us to be held against our mother's chest, to be loved by her. He may not remember it, but there's proof of her affection for him. For me, there was only a note proving she never knew I existed, a note which had been intended to cause my death.

By the time the movie ended, Dawson had fallen asleep in one of the beds and Neil had fallen asleep on a couch by the window. Iris was curled up on the floor in front of me. I couldn't tell if she was asleep or still watching the movie credits. She hadn't moved in a while. Gabriel was wide awake, having eaten four slices of pizza and downed a can of Sprite.

"We should probably get in bed," John said to him, changing the TV channel to one without programming. The static provided some light, but it was nothing Gabriel would get interested in watching.

"My bed isn't here," Gabriel said.

"I know. But we'll have to be like Marty McFly and sleep away from home."

Gabriel looked at me and Iris and I knew he was thinking about the scene with Marty's mom. I said, "We're going back to our room. It'll just be you and the other boys."

"You're a girl, so yes. You should sleep in the girl room." His voice projected like a TV announcer and I worried he would wake Dawson and Neil.

John explained, "But she's your sister, Gabe. Sisters are okay to sleep in the same room."

I glared at him for bringing up such a difficult topic at such a horrible time.

Gabriel said, "I don't have a sister. I have a mom and that is all the people in my family."

"Cynthia wasn't your mom. She lied. You and Angelina are twins and you will have new parents soon. Doesn't she look a lot like you?" John was pushing it.

Gabriel's face tilted, confused and thoughtful. He was quiet for a while before he said. "So I don't have to do my lessons if she is not mother?"

John shook his head in confirmation and placed a finger over his own lips to try to persuade him to quiet his voice.

Gabriel whispered, "Her lessons were bad. I did them wrong on purpose because I wanted to be bad. I didn't want to be good at those."

"Well, now you don't have to worry about it." John smiled, finally deciding not to get into the details any further.

Gabriel smiled widely. "I can eat all the food and go outside when I want and play all the instruments and sing on stage even if I can't keep my body still all the time?"

"I don't see why not, but you can't do it tonight. We need to sleep, all of us. Tomorrow you get to come to my house and I can show you my giant TV."

That did the trick. Gabriel jumped into the bed and pulled up the blankets.

"Do you like to sleep with all the lights off or some of them on?" John asked.

"All the lights off. Light is for awake."

"Okay, I'll turn the TV off. Then I have to carry my sister Iris to bed in the girl room. I'll be right back. Save room for me."

"Okay, friend." Gabe closed his eyes and pretended to immediately sleep, fake snoring and all. John and I both fought back a snicker.

John clicked the off button on the remote and set it on top of the TV. Then he picked up Iris. I opened each door for him. All the lights were off in our room, but moonlight shone in through the crack in the curtain. I lifted the blankets of Iris's bed so John could place her under. Her head rested perfectly on her pillow. I moved her bag to the chair so she wouldn't kick it off the bed during the night, or what was left of the early morning. It was nearly two o'clock.

John's face was lit by the sliver of moonlight as he stood

274

looking down at Iris. He seemed reluctant to leave.

I whispered, hoping to ease the awkward silence, "Gabe seems to be adjusting well, better than I did."

"He's witty," John looked up and smiled, "smart guy, but a bit odd. That's how I like my friends." He made no comment comparing our adjustment differences. He whispered, "I should get back. I shouldn't be here with you."

"Why?" My voice nearly rose above a whisper.

"Because Dawson said if we're caught doing inappropriate things, you may have to be moved to a foster home until the Matthews jump through all the paperwork hoops. Right now, my family is your foster family."

"But we aren't doing anything inappropriate. Did you tell them we wouldn't?"

"How can I make that promise to them?" He looked defeated, "I lose myself every time I look at you. Their rules fly out the window. All I see is you and I want to do what feels right with you. But I can't trust that. You haven't exactly been making good decisions, either."

"This is my fault." I felt overwhelmed and had to sit on the edge of my bed. I looked up at him, "I'm sorry I asked to kiss you."

"Are you?" he waited for an answer, but I didn't understand how to give one any different than what I had already said. Finally he said, "They told me you'll be staying with Mom for a while. I have to move in with Dads and you're taking my room, unless something changes because of Gabe. So, here we are. It's just like I knew would happen, they're moving you in and moving me out. You have ties to the person Mom loved more than anything. I don't. I was just an accident, an afterthought, something that can stay or go." He was looking around the room as if trying to distract himself so he wouldn't cry.

"I can leave. I didn't really come to stay. I only came to give Jute the letter. I'll just go, one night when everyone's asleep, I'll slip away and things will be like they were before."

"No you won't. You'd break Mom's heart. You'd have to be a

terrible person to put her through that. I'd never forgive you. Besides, it's not your fault things are the way they are. I've been locked out of her life for a long time, at least the most important parts of it."

I stood up and hugged him but he quickly pushed my arms away. I said, "I was just trying to make you feel better."

"You're just trying to make it more difficult. I'm sorry, but I had to let you know why I've been avoiding you and now you know. I should go."

He walked out of the room, leaving me standing there feeling lost. I couldn't understand what we had done that was so terrible. We had kissed, which John had told me was common, no big deal. Then suddenly kissing became a big deal. Now just hugging him to comfort him was off limits. We weren't even allowed to stay in the same house together. None of it made sense.

I went into the bathroom and slipped off my dress and hung it up on a hanger for the next day. Iris had packed an extra gown. She had laid it out on the edge of my bed, so I went back into the room to put it on. The blue cotton fabric stretched a little to fit my size. The snugness was a reminder that it didn't belong to me. But, I was used to wearing things that weren't mine, at least not originally; so I stopped feeling sorry for myself and climbed into bed.

Not two minutes later, I heard a quiet tapping on the door. I ran and opened it to see John standing there.

"I don't have a key," he looked distressed. "I knocked, but the TV is on again and they can't hear me. I think Gabe must be watching it. I was going to beat on the door and scream, but it's after two in the morning. I don't want to get us thrown out of here."

I opened the door wider to let him through. He dropped his voice to a whisper, "I'll sleep in the chair. I'm so sorry."

He went into the bathroom and I heard the shower turn on. I climbed back into bed and listened to the splashing water caused by his movements and the sound of his occasional profanity for no apparent reason. I knew he didn't want to be in the room with us. But, I felt comforted that he would be close if I needed him. I just hoped he wouldn't get in trouble for it.

When he opened the door, he had already turned off the bathroom light. The room stayed dark, but I could make out his shape as he walked to the chair.

"John..." I whispered loudly. I heard Iris shift positions. The light from the moon disappeared as he evidently pulled the curtains closed. Soon, I felt weight on the mattress.

"What?"

"Sleep here. They'll never know."

He was quiet for a moment, then said, "It doesn't matter what they know. It matters what they believe."

"Beliefs are almost always wrong," I argued.

"Really?" I felt him lie down. "What about my belief that you are a goddess?"

I quietly snickered, "There is no such thing. There is only star stuff."

"That, too." He exhaled a silent sigh, then turned his back to me.

"I'm glad you're here." I whispered behind him.

I felt his hand slide over to find mine, his fingers gave it a squeeze, "Go to sleep, Angelina."

54

December 30, 2006

When I opened my eyes, John was propped up on his elbow, staring down at me. "You snore," he said and smiled.

I looked up at the ceiling, blinked my eyes to clear the fogginess away. Through the wall, I heard the shower turn off and assumed Iris was in the bathroom. I looked back at John. He was wide awake and his shirt was off, which was distracting. I looked back to the ceiling.

"I don't snore," I insisted.

"Yes you do, little lady snores, like a sleeping barn cat." He laid back onto the pillow and stared up at the ceiling, too. "You should probably get ready to go."

I sat up. Memories flooded my brain, all out of order. "Where are we, again?"

"Cincinnati, Ohio. Look out the window. There's not much to see from here, but at least you can say you saw it: your third state."

I looked down and saw he was wearing jeans. "Don't people normally wear something other than jeans to bed?"

"I usually sleep in nothing-" He was interrupted by the sound of the bathroom door opening.

Iris stepped around the corner with a towel wrapped around her. She said, "He had his shirt on when I went in the bathroom. He's just trying to impress you with his big stwong muskles." She spoke with a baby voice, then laughed.

"Shut up!" John threw a pillow at her, but she dodged it.

She shook her head. "I'm gonna tell my Daddy."

John hopped up out of bed to go after her, but she made it to the bathroom and locked herself in.

Most of the morning went the same way. Iris and John made fun of each other, laughed, made fun of their dads and even Jute. I laughed so hard my face hurt. Their entertaining exchanges stopped when the phone rang. Iris answered. John and I were so quiet we could hear Dawson's greeting. Despite Iris's earlier threat, she didn't tattle on John. When Dawson asked if she had seen him, she explained he had been locked out of his room and slept alone in the bed by the window. She told the lie so convincingly that I almost believed it myself. I couldn't tell how well it went over with Dawson, though. The room was still quiet enough to hear him say, "Just like a trip to Memphis?" but I didn't know what he meant.

We were on the road to Nashville by nine o'clock. The trip home was an entirely different experience than the one coming to Ohio. Riding with Gabriel, who had expressed his preference to be called Gabe, made it more exciting because he was so easily excited. His enthusiasm became infectious and we all started to point things out to him, such as hawks in the sky, funny shaped signs, and truck trailers with interesting cargo. Gabe read almost every sign we passed. His word pronunciations seldom needed correcting. I felt ashamed in comparison. My ability to read aloud was still very limited. I would have never attempted to read the names of places which were unfamiliar and contained letter combinations with multiple pronunciations. Gabe didn't care. It was like he must read everything, or try, and couldn't contain his joy in doing so.

I was surprised at how little he seemed to think about Cynthia. But then I remembered how quickly I had pushed Silas out of my mind, at least when things were going well. He had still crept back in to cause self-doubt a number of times, but generally I easily accepted that he was not my real father. I had focused on moving on. But I knew, like me, Gabe likely had issues that would remain unresolved for quite some time.

We made it back by the afternoon. Jute had a meal prepared for us when we got there. She had made homemade fried rice with shrimp and chicken, sauteed green beans, and a spicy vegetable dish with mushrooms. I had never seen so many fresh vegetables in winter, but apparently it was common for people to have them. I wanted to ask how they were grown in freezing weather, but I didn't want to seem ignorant. Gabe refused to eat any of the food, insisting that he liked peanut butter on bread or apples. He also listed every other food he would eat, which was a total of twenty things, none of which Jute had prepared. He ended the list by saying, "And that is all". Jute smeared some peanut butter on a slice of wheat bread and he was content.

The Matthews were there, too. Mrs. Matthews seemed much different, less cautious with her words than she had been when I first met her. She laughed giddily as she embraced me and Gabe randomly throughout the night. I heard her comment to Jute that she was surprised Gabe liked to be hugged because some autistic people don't. I didn't know what she meant by 'autistic', but I thought it might have something to do with how particular he was. I decided to ask John sometime when Gabe wasn't around and there was no audience to witness my ignorance.

Mr. Matthews (or Casey, as everyone else called him) was as tall as Dawson. His blond hair was thinning, but otherwise he looked much younger than Jute. I wouldn't have guessed they were about the same age. Every time he caught me staring at him, he'd smile and wave excitedly like he hadn't seen me in forever. He was being silly. I found myself staring at him just so he'd do it again.

Marcy came up to me after dinner and asked if I was excited about the idea of having new parents, but I couldn't really wrap my mind around the idea. I told her it seemed like a dream and I wasn't sure if it was a good one or a bad one. She hugged me and gave me an exaggerated look of sadness. "Don't be so down about it," she said, "you are so incredibly lucky. I would live here in a heartbeat." She took a sip from her glass of wine and glanced back toward the kitchen.

"How was your night?" I asked.

She looked startled by my question, then gave a nervous smile. "Good. It's a beautiful place to be snowed in."

"Did you sleep in John's room?" I hoped I wasn't the only one invading his space.

"Why do you ask?" She sounded defensive.

"I heard I would be sleeping there. John's a little upset, I think."

"Oh," she exhaled with relief. "I thought you were implying something else."

"What sort of double meaning would 'sleeping in John's room' have?"

She laughed, "Nothing." She noticed my confused expression. "Never mind, sweet girl. I'm not going to be responsible for dirtying up your mind. There are things you don't need to know." She kissed my forehead and walked back into the kitchen to help Jute wash dishes. There was something about the way Marcy leaned in to whisper in Jute's ear that made me nervous. Was she saying something about me?

Gabe and John left with Dawson just before the Matthews left for home. Mrs. Matthews gave me a final hug and said, "You are such a miracle, Angelina."

From the living room window, I watched them get into their truck. In the silence of the house, I felt like I was floating with no ground beneath me. I whispered, my breath on the glass, "There are no miracles," and watched them pull away.

Jute, Marcy, Iris and a few other women were all in the kitchen rolling tiny sausages inside flat dough. I walked through on my way to John's room. "I'm going to bed," I said to whomever was listening.

"Did you say you're going up?" Jute asked, "Let me hug you goodnight."

She got up and so did Marcy, both hugging me tightly between them and laughing. I didn't feel like laughing, but their silliness forced it out of me . Jute said, "I'm so glad you're here, under my roof, and safe. Sleep well."

"Thanks for letting me stay." I squeezed her hand before letting go and walked upstairs.

To my surprise, I found a plastic bag lying on his bed. It contained new underwear and a couple of nightgowns. The gift touched my heart more than the hugs, and I felt a little ashamed by that. I had needed those items so badly and I hadn't even had to asked for them. Jute just knew. Or had the Matthews brought them? Maybe Marcy had. I wasn't sure. But I mentally thanked them all for being so good to me.

I took the bag to the bathroom and started the shower. I managed to peel off the tape and gauze without help. Having not felt pain most of the day, I was optimistic I could sleep without replacing them.

The shampoo smelled like John's hair. I missed him. I started to think of him and our complex situation. I thought of the unspoken rules I kept breaking, and how much it was hurting him, and how powerless I felt to stop it. I wondered if I had done the same thing to Emory. There was a missing piece, or maybe a hundred of them. I had so many unanswered questions, I couldn't even think of them all. I stayed under the water just a little longer than necessary, letting myself cry tears of both joy and despair. I felt like life was trying to make me a promise, trying to coax me into believing in hope. But I wasn't sure what I was supposed to be hoping for.

Dried and dressed in crisp, clean sleepwear, I slid beneath the blankets on John's bed. His pillow smelled like the shampoo and a hint of his sweat. The sheets smelled like the body spray he had used the morning he pushed me away. Had it really been only yesterday morning that I had breathed in his scent and kissed his neck? I remembered how he told me to stop, but I didn't because I didn't believe him, and then Dawson came. Because of that, John was forced out of his bedroom and I was moved into it. I wished John was with me, not at his dads' house, so I could talk to him and try to make it right.

I heard footsteps in the hall and then footsteps walking up some stairs on the other side of the wall. There must have been a bedroom above, in the attic. I marveled at how Jute had filled up that big old house, every single corner, with people in need of a safe place. She had given it all, even her own son's room. Was John so different that he couldn't even give up his room for just a little while without becoming upset? I realized it was different to give something freely versus being forced to do so. I also thought maybe Jute shouldn't give away things which weren't hers, that it really wasn't fair to John. I should have been the one to stay with Dawson if that's what John wanted.

Sleep wouldn't come. My mind couldn't reconcile the guilt of lying in John's bed against his wishes, much less the act of actually sleeping in it. I pulled back the blankets and got up. I wanted to find Marcy. She usually stayed awake until morning, so I imagined she was probably still in the kitchen preparing for the New Year's Eve party.

But when I got to the kitchen, the only light on was the light over the stove. The oven timer had ten minutes remaining, so someone had to still be awake and close enough to hear it. I peeked into the living room and saw her on the couch. She had her fingers laced with Jute's and they were kissing. I didn't want them to think I was spying. I cleared my throat and they jumped a little, let go of each other's hand and unnecessarily straightened out their clothing.

"We were just waiting on the last of the rolls," Marcy said, uncharacteristically self-conscious. She certainly never looked so guilty after kissing Emory.

"Uhm," Jute began, then pulled her lips tight as she planned her words. She said, "I should probably explain... Marcy and I have gotten... close... while she has been here. She has really helped me let go of lot of hurt I was holding like a crutch. We don't know what will become of this, if anything. Please don't tell John what you saw. Let us figure this out first, so he won't worry."

I nodded, not sure what else to do.

"Did you need something?" Jute's kind eyes implored me to tell her anything at all I might need from her.

"I just came down to tell you thank you for my underthings

and the gowns," I looked at both Marcy and Jute.

Marcy said, "I thought you might need them. I made Emory stop on the way down. You deserved something lovely."

I nodded and hoped I seemed happy enough. "Goodnight."

"Goodnight," they said in unison.

I crawled back into bed, surrounded by the feeling that John was with me, seeing me, knowing I had a secret he wasn't supposed to know. Iris had told me of a trip he wasn't supposed to know about. Jute and Marcy were… involved… in a way they didn't want him to know about. John even said he hadn't known about Allie until just a week ago. I felt bad for him, always in the dark, always left ignorant. If anyone knew how terrible it felt to be the only one left in the dark, it would be me.

I imagined myself telling him everything, imagined how he would handle it, knowing he would likely be hurt. I imagined myself kissing away his pain, imagined him pushing me away because they'd forbidden it. How could they have been so opposed to us kissing when they were doing it? Jute had said Marcy had been helping her, but it looked no different than what had happened between John and me. I figured they probably opposed it because they believed we were kids. I felt a fierce need to protest that assumption. I closed my eyes tightly, determined to drift off to sleep while dreaming of all the things I wasn't supposed to do with John.

Part Nine

John

55

December 31, 2006
New Year's Eve

I keenly felt her absence. I felt it when I woke up at 2:38 a.m. and again at 5:15 a.m. It was unshakable at 9:49 when it was too late to stay in bed on a Sunday morning. I thought about her, again, imagining her in the farmhouse, in my room, in my bed, asleep. Was she still asleep? I remembered waking up in Cincinnati and feeling her breath on my shoulder and her arm draped over my chest. Remembering it made me erect and made me sick. I didn't want to feel like I felt about her. Dawson had been right to warn me that getting involved with her might ruin her chances of staying with us, with Mom. I just needed to convince my heart and my body of what my head already knew.

To everyone else, Angelina was there for Mom and they all did what was best for Mom. It wasn't like Angelina came first, but at least she wasn't harmed by any of their efforts. I'm sure she was glad to be with us. It had to be like heaven compared to the place she had left behind. But weren't there hundreds of foster families? Couldn't she easily find a better home anywhere? So, it wasn't fair to argue that her life would be ruined if she was taken away to a different family. It would just be terrible for Mom. And it would be terrible for me.

A few days earlier, I might have even intentionally made it happen. I was so worried about being replaced that I could have sabotaged the whole thing before ever getting to know her. But, I had gotten to know her too well. I felt like I could see right through her blue eyes and into her soul and there wasn't a single imperfect thing about her. She wanted nothing for herself, expected nothing, was constantly thoughtful about how her actions affected others. There was a beautiful innocence about her that made no sense considering all she had been through. She had been horribly mistreated and abused, yet she was this amazing girl inside and out.

I found myself thinking about all the things I would love to show her. There were so many experiences I could give her. My fantasies went from passionate kisses to visions of watching her jump into the swimming pool for the first time, taking her to Elliston Place Soda Shop and watching her take her first bite of a butterscotch sundae, or taking her to see Dad in concert, which she may or may not enjoy. I didn't know what kind of music she liked, if any. I made a mental note to ask her next time I saw her.

As much as Dads wanted me to keep my distance from her, I knew it would be impossible for them to control it later that night. It was New Year's Eve and we would have our annual Christmas Greenery Bonfire. We would have a larger crowd than usual with the addition of Angelina, Marcy, Emory, Iris, the Matthews, as well as all the women staying at Mom's house. Aunt Drew and Devon always came, too. Boardgames would be set up in a couple of rooms, the kitchen table would be covered with snacks for foragers, and there would be unlimited alcohol for the adults. Supplies would be set out by the fire for making S'mores, roasting marshmallows, or hot dogs. There would be no way for anyone to know where everyone was at every moment. Surely I could find time alone with her.

I got up and looked out the window. The snow was nearly

melted; patches of grass were exposed, showing a map of every bump I liked to drive over. Rays of sun slanted from sparse clouds in a mostly blue sky, melting even more snow as time passed.

I took a shower and got dressed, then went down to the kitchen with my mind set on frozen waffles. Dawson and Gabe were there, popping mini quiches out of cooled pans. Judging from the smell, more were in the oven.

"For the party?" I asked.

Gabe looked at me, then to the ceiling, then back to me again, forcing himself to make eye contact, "Good morning, friend," he said. "We are making lots of party food with bacon which I like and mushrooms which are very disgusting and I don't like. We have thirty-six cooling and I helped cut the tomatoes with a sharp knife which is dangerous and should be very careful."

Dawson pulled the last two quiches from his pan and placed them on the table. "Yes. These are for the party. Gabe is interested in learning how to cook, so I thought we'd help your mom out with the snacks this year. I'm going to have you take these down once we're finished so she can set everything up."

"We're going to make donuts," Gabe said, "Mr. Dawson is going to teach me how to make them and we are going to eat some which is very cool."

He seemed incredibly content to be in such an unfamiliar place. "Do you like to cook?"

"Oh, yes. I like food very much, making food and eating food are very good. But I will not eat these quiches because they are for the party and they are very gross. But I can eat some donuts because Mr. Dawson said donuts are fine if I eat a few that I make."

He pulled out his last quiche and set it on the table. I asked, "Can I try one?"

"No! They're for the party!" His voice boomed and he seemed suddenly upset.

"It's okay. John can try one to make sure they're good. A chef should always try his food before he serves it to his guests."

Gabe looked nervously up to the ceiling, then turned his head from side to side. Dawson had explained to me that Gabe made certain repetitive motions to calm himself. They were called stims. Dawson and I waited for Gabe to calm down before saying or doing anything else. Finally he said, "I'm sorry."

"It's all good now," I changed the subject, "Which ones did you put together, Gabe? I want to try one of those."

He pointed to a row of quiche with halved cherry tomatoes on top of each. I picked one up and bit into it. It was flaky on the outside, fluffy in the center with delicious slices of mushroom and bits of spinach. With my mouth still full, I said, "Oh my God that's good!" It sounded like ahmahgahfashguh.

"See," Dawson tapped the back of his hand to Gabe's sleeve, "I told you if you followed the recipe exactly they would turn out perfectly, and you did it."

"I did it," said Gabe, putting a hand up for Dawson to give him a high five. I put my hand up, too, and Gabe slapped it with excited force. "High five, friend!"

"High five, Gabe!"

When we had all the quiches placed in boxes, I loaded them in Greenman. Instead of driving through the field, I drove around through the gates and took the road. I pulled up to the farmhouse and saw Emory's truck outside. That meant Dad was home. As soon as I had that thought, he stepped out on the porch and waved.

He came down and opened the passenger door. "Dawson called, said you'd need help carrying in the food."

The house smelled amazing, even better than it had at Christmas. Mom went out of her way to make every New Year's Eve special for us. It was also the one night of the year when she would get drunk. She wasn't the only one. There were always plenty of non-alcoholic beverages for the kids, just not a lot of adult supervision.

After setting the boxes on the counter, I looked around at all the food she and the other women had prepared. "This seems like a lot more food than usual. How many guests are coming?"

"A lot," Mom sighed happily. "Everyone who normally attends will be coming, plus we have five guests in the house, plus our new family." She winked at me.

A red haired lady walked into the room; I recognized her as the one who had arrived with Emory. She was wearing a sheer black blouse with a camisole underneath and black leather pants. Her tattoos were visible through the fabric of her blouse, floral designs covering nearly every inch of her arms. Her orange-red hair was pulled into a bun with two large cavernous rolls of hair held in place over her forehead, very 1940's. A sequins bluebird clip was pinned beside the bun. She had pushed the rockabilly look as far as it would go.

Mom let go of me and held her arms open in surprise toward the lady. "Marcy! Oh my God, you look incredible! I'm not going to let you help me now. I'll feel bad if you mess up your outfit."

"I have an apron," she explained, then unfolded it and put it on. It was red and covered with blond pinup girls. Mom helped her tie it, then brushed down the front as if straightening wrinkles, only there were no wrinkles. Mom was acting very strange, like she'd been unraveled and wound back up. I wanted to quiz Angelina about how Mom was handling things.

"Where's Angelina?" I asked, searching each face in the room for someone who might know.

Marcy pointed a long finger tipped with a candy apple red fingernail toward the hallway. "She was talking to Emory."

I entered the hall, but she wasn't there. I started up the stairs, but as I neared the top I heard her voice. I wanted to run toward her, but something in her tone made me stop out of sight to listen.

She was saying, "But we're meant to be together. Surely they'll understand and would never make you lose your job. And it's just a kiss. People kiss all the time, Emory, please...."

Emory's voice was low and hard to hear, "Angelina, you aren't listening. I love you, but not in that way. You're too young for me."

"But I won't be forever! In a couple of years I'll be eighteen!"

"Shhh! Keep it down, okay? Look, you really need to stop with this. You don't even know me. How you're acting is kind of scaring me. I don't have feelings like that for you."

"Scary?" The hurt in her voice physically hurt me, too, even though I understood why Emory said what he did. "I don't understand why you're saying that. If I did something wrong, I'm sorry."

"That's the thing, Angelina. You need to figure out how to act. If you don't believe me, ask Jute. Ask Tracy. You're just a kid, I swear. Please, just focus on you. Forget about me."

"I can't! I love you."

"Dammit!" He raised his voice, then spoke in a whisper. "You don't have to understand the reasons why, but you do have to stop this and it needs to stop right now."

I heard footsteps running and a door slam. I assumed it was Angelina.

I began walking up the stairs again just in time for Emory to pass by without knowing I had been listening. He didn't even glance at me on his way down the stairs. I found Angelina in my room, curled up on my sheets, crying.

"You can't blame him," I said, startling her.

She realized it was only me and turned away toward the wall.

"Did everyone hear that?" She asked.

"No. I think I was the only one… and Emory, or course." I sat on the bed and rested my hand on her hip. She was still wearing a nightgown. It looked brand new and I was happy for her.

"He'll like me one day, don't you think?" She asked, twisting to look at me. Her face was red from crying. I wanted to touch her face and wipe her tears away. I wanted to make her pain go away.

"I can't image anyone not liking you. But that isn't the point. You should just try to be happy, Angelina. You've been so sad most of your life. What's wrong with just trying to be happy?"

"How can I be happy when he says I'm scary and he acts like he hates me?"

She rolled back over and covered her face with her hands.

"Why don't you try to get dressed? You'll feel better."

"I will. But right now I just want to be alone."

I took the hint, patted her arm, and left the room.

56

Until ten o'clock, everyone had jobs to do. Games were brought to various foldout tables, food was laid out, the burn pile was formed, a tent was set up nearby, and a stockpile of fireworks were put on the ready. Every guest helped, but at ten o'clock, everyone stopped working and went outside to watch the lighting of the bonfire.

We all huddled in a group under the night sky. Dad Tracy tapped a glass to get everyone's attention. He began, "Two thousand and six was an amazing year. It began well, but it is ending even better, with new friends, new family, and a lot of healing for broken hearts. We are celebrating tonight, new beginnings and renewed hearts, new hope for tomorrow, and a release of all the pain we've held onto for too long. We, myself, Dawson, and Jute, wish for each of you, all the love your hearts can hold this coming year, because right now, that is the blessing we are experiencing in our own lives. With that, I will light this baby!"

He turned around and began lighting the fire. It took fifteen minutes before the flames really picked up. That was fifteen minutes that felt like an hour in the freezing cold. By then, some guests had already gone back inside, but those of us still out there cheered and whistled when the flames shot up high into the darkness. I stayed for nearly an hour, knowing eventually Angelina would make her way out. In the meantime, I had eaten two hot dogs and three S'mores. Gabe had the same idea, as the Matthews stayed with him and helped him avoid overcooking his food. He had trouble at first, but quickly learned when to pull his marshmallow out of the flames.

I gave up waiting on Angelina and went inside to look for her. The house was buzzing with noise, which was typical. Few people ever wanted to stay outside until it got closer to midnight; then they all flocked out there to see the fireworks, thankful for the heat of the burning greenery.

I didn't see her in the living room, so I walked toward the kitchen. I stopped myself before crossing the threshold. Iris was sitting on a barstool with her back to me. Emory was across from her. They had their hands held up to the other's, comparing hand size, perhaps. Emory was smiling, his eyes glued to Iris's face. He moved his fingers to entwine with hers. Iris's back straightened in surprise, then she relaxed and leaned toward him.

My first thought was to wonder what made girls like that guy so much. My next thought was how upset Angelina would be if she saw them. I cleared my throat, "Have you seen Angelina?"

Iris spun around to face me. Her face was sparkling with some sort of microscopic gold glitter that girls wore to the school dances. Her lips were hot pink. She was definitely not trying to get lost in a crowd. She looked stunning, more so than usual, even if I personally didn't like the thought of kissing girls who wore all that stuff. Emory obviously didn't share my opinion.

"We were playing Song Burst with Mom and Marcy earlier. You know how she loves that game." Marcy rolled her eyes and I realized her eyelashes had gold glitter stuck to them. "I don't know why Angelina even wanted to play with us. She's never even heard music, really. Emory said, when he found her, she didn't even know about gospel. You'd think they'd have at least played gospel up on the mountain." She shook her head.

"Yeah, well I'm sure that was the least of her deprivations," I said, walking past them toward Mom's office.

"Wait!" Iris ran after me and grabbed my arm. I turned in time to see her panic fade to a forced smile. She looked suspiciously nervous. "Uhm… maybe you should look for her by the bonfire. When she left the game, she said she was going to look for Gabe."

"I was just out there, but I'll go check again. Go back to… whatever you and that guy were doing."

"Oh my God, John, are you seriously suggesting there's something between Emory and me?"

"It was rather obvious he's into you," I sighed, annoyed, wanting to get back outside.

"Really?" Her eyes widened, "I just figured he was like that to everyone. I mean, he's so cute he could have any girl."

"Yeah, so I hear."

Angelina wasn't by the bonfire. Gabe was standing there with an empty stick in the flames. I assumed the Matthews had gone into the tent to get him something else to put on it.

"Have you seen Angelina?" I asked him.

"She was in the dark. I saw a thing move and I was afraid it was a bear so I froze really still and didn't move and looked at that spot where I saw it and it was Angelina walking. She scared me a lot." He laughed. "Does she want to come make S'mores? S'mores are very fun to make with marshmallow, graham crackers, and chocolate which I like the best because it is my favorite. Next is marshmallow which is my second favorite."

"Hi, John," Mrs. Matthews placed a hand on Gabe's shoulder to get his attention. She took the stick from him and topped it with a marshmallow. "This is really a great thing your family does. We're so happy to be here, and Gabe seems very happy to be staying with you for a while. We were just explaining that very soon he will be coming to live with us and his sister, too."

Her words twisted me up inside. "Speaking of her. I was just on my way to find her."

"Is she missing?" Mr. Matthews asked.

"Oh, no. We were just playing a game, kind of like hide and seek and tag combined," I lied, "She's really good at it. Gabe said she went that way, so I better go find her before she thinks I gave up."

I headed toward the barn, the only structure in the direction Gabe had pointed. If she had wanted to hide until she froze to death, there were lots of places on our property to make that possible; but I assumed she'd have wanted a little shelter. When I reached the opening, I quietly called her name. I heard a shuffling, but it was so small it could have easily been a cat or a rat.

"Angelina, is that you? It's John. You need to come back before you freeze to death."

"I'm not going to freeze to death," she said, then sniffled.

"Why are you in here?"

"Because I don't want to be around Emory."

"Either you do or you don't. You girls can never make up your minds," I knew before I said it that I shouldn't have been joking.

"It's not funny. Iris knows all the answers and she's pretty. He couldn't take his eyes off her. The only time he looked at me was to feel sorry for me because I don't know anything. They all did. They all looked at me like I shouldn't even have been there."

I followed her voice to the room with the pumpkins. She was sitting on a bail of hay. I reached in my pocket for my key chain flashlight and lit up her face with it.

"Stop it!" She covered her eyes. "I don't want you to see me like this."

"I've seen you worse, Angelina. Stop feeling sorry for yourself and get up. I have something to show you."

"What?" she was doubtful.

"Something that belonged to your mom."

"It won't matter," she said, "I have her clothes, her hats, her letter, her DNA-"

I cut her off, "Her eyes, her hair, her nose, and also her tendency to fall for boys who don't deserve her."

"What do you mean?"

"Come on." I leaned down and picked up an electric heater by its handle. It was just a small infrared heater I had brought to the barn years ago. I climbed up to the loft with it and plugged it into an extension cord still draped over the rafters. The red light sent a glow across the room and soon the heat was felt.

"Up there?" She asked, already climbing. "What's up here?

297

More clothes?"

"Your mother's poetry and writing. Pages and pages of it. This box is full of notebooks that belonged to her. Mom had them in the attic until last week. She asked me to bring them to the barn. I guess she was ready to put the past behind her. Now that you are here, I'm not so sure. She may want them back."

"I doubt it," she said, then clenched her jaw as if she had said too much.

"Why wouldn't she? She loved your mom. You'll see when you read these, like even before they were more than friends it was obviously a seed in her mind."

"John, do you ever wonder why they keep so much from you? Like, why didn't they tell you about Allie? Why didn't they tell you about me? Why didn't they tell you the police had already called them about Silas? And in just the last two days, I have been asked not to tell you things twice. Why? Having lived my entire life in ignorance, I hate it. I hate keeping the truth from people."

My stomach felt like it might lose all that food I had stuffed into it over the last hour. "What am I not supposed to know?"

"Well, one of them has to do with your birthday, so I'm okay not telling you that. The other one is that I saw Marcy and your mom kissing. They asked me not to tell you, but I don't think that's fair."

My face contorted into a look of repulsion, "That's disgusting. Why was Marcy kissing my mom?"

"It's not disgusting," Angelina slapped my arm, "You're awful! Your mom is a wonderful person and Allie certainly remembered what it felt like to kiss her. She must have been pretty good at it."

"Oh, God! Stop!" I covered my ears.

She pulled my hands down, "Okay, so maybe they had a good reason not to tell you."

"No," I said, feeling her fingers still wrapped around my wrists like chains, "I don't care if they kiss, I mean, not in the way they think I would care. I'm surprised more than anything. All my life, Mom has always been alone. I've never seen her date anyone. If she has finally found someone she likes, I'm happy for her."

"See, that's what I thought you would say."

She let go of my wrists and sat down by the box so I sat with her. I pulled out my favorite notebook, the one written nearly seventeen years ago when Allie first realized she loved my mom. When I read it the first time, I never thought of my mom as the person Allie was writing about. I couldn't picture it, believing Mom wasn't capable of that kind of relationship. Now I had to admit Mom was more than capable. She might have been doing it again at that very moment. I wasn't sure if I wanted to read the poems after all I had learned. But I was excited for Angelina to read them.

I held the flashlight and watched her blue eyes move across the pages. She said, "I started teaching myself to read this year, but it seems so long ago." She became silent as she read and processed the meaning of every word her mother had written. She turned page after page. I could have sat there holding that light forever just to witness the emotion in her eyes and know that none of it was from hurt caused by Emory or Silas.

57

"That heater makes it so hot up here," she sat the open notebook back onto the box. She stood and removed her long coat, revealing a rich purple party dress that could have come from the 1960s. She pulled the black flats off her feet and sat back down beside me, cross-legged.

"That's a pretty dress. Did Mom give it to you?" I pulled off my heavy denim jacket and tossed it over to where she had laid her coat.

"Marcy made it. She sews really well. She also bought me new underthings and a couple of nightgowns. I really needed those." She didn't look up from the page so she missed how much I was blushing. I felt like such a virgin, blushing over the mention of a girl's underwear; but then I reminded myself that I really was, technically, still a virgin.

I straightened my back and flexed my chest muscles a few times just to feel less like a little boy and more like a man.

She gave me a sideways look, "What are you doing?"

"Flexing to impress you," I bit the inside of my lips so I wouldn't laugh.

She snickered a little as she turned her head back toward the notebook. "Listen to this line." She read, "When she falls into me, she leaves nothing behind for anyone else. She falls completely. Yet I am held prisoner by my wrongs, am always held up by those chains. She is fallen, there, reaching up with her fingers setting fire to my senses, but I can never let go."

Angelina's voice quivered near the end. I looked at her eyes and saw how wet they were. I understood how she could relate to that poem..

"That's how I felt when I first read it," I whispered. But what I really wanted to tell her was that hearing it in her voice gave it a whole new meaning. I wanted her to let go of trying to be good enough for Emory. I wanted her to feel like she was already perfect. "Can I kiss you?"

"I thought you said that was a bad idea." She glanced at me quickly, then back to the notebook. I watched her eyes and knew she wasn't reading anymore. She was waiting.

I brushed her hair back over her shoulder and leaned in, kissing her on the neck as she had last kissed me. I leaned back and saw her eyes closed, fluttering a little, and decided she must have liked it. I got on my knees behind her and settled down close to her, wrapping my arms around her, and kissed her neck again. She sighed with pleasure and I nearly lost all sense of space and time.

The neckline of her dress fit close, leaving very little skin exposed. I unzipped the back so I could kiss her shoulders. She smelled like new fabric and the shower gel from my bathroom. I slid my hands to her knees and slowly pulled the hem of her skirt higher, feeling the soft skin of her inner thigh. I felt her stop breathing. I waited for the sigh of her exhale, but it came as a cry of sadness, nearing anguish.

"Stop!" She cried and moved away from me. She laid curled up on our coats. She saw that I was trying to read her face so she covered it with her hands. "You can't get behind me like that, John. I just can't."

"Okay," I whispered pleadingly, "I didn't mean to hurt you."

"It's hard not to hurt someone like me."

"I can handle the challenge if you can," I slid over beside her, desperate to repair the damage I had done. "Can I lie beside you, then?"

She nodded, her face still covered. Her dress was still slipped off her shoulders. "Do you want me to help zip your dress up?"

"In a minute," she peeked through her fingers then moved her hands to wipe her face. She stared at me as if studying a bizarre creature. Her eyes lingered on every feature of my face, yet I could not read the thoughts behind her eyes.

"What are you doing?" I asked.

"Recognizing how much you look like your mother."

I rolled onto my back so she couldn't see me anymore, "Really?" I asked, disappointed and frustrated.

She propped herself up on her elbow and looked down at me, "Yes, really. You do look like her in some ways. I can see why Allie liked her, even if you refuse to see it."

"Yes, and you look like Allie. A lot. Like nearly identical."

"Do you think it would feel the same?"

I should have asked what she meant by that, but I already knew. She had hinted at the idea before, that because we were the unrelated children of two lovers, somehow we were expected to get to know each other in that same way. But a lot had happened since Angelina first made this assumption. What I wanted, more than anything, was for her to see me as John, only John, not my mother's son, not her mother's lover's son, not a fill-in for Emory, not a kissing teacher, but to see me as a person outside of all those contexts.

I should have discussed with her how wrong it was to wonder such things. I should have told her my feelings and made her understand how bittersweet her words, her actions, her presence in my life had become. But I did none of those things.

"Let's find out," I said, my voice catching on the lump in my throat. I pulled her down to kiss me, quickly, before she saw the tears fall from the corner of my eyes. Her mouth and tongue explored like they had the first time I had kissed her, full of curiosity and thoughtfulness. She was trying to kiss me, which was not the same as really kissing me.

"Stand up," I said, pulling away from her. She looked apprehensive. "Trust me. I won't do anything you tell me not to do."

She stood and steadied herself as if she were lightheaded.

"Are you okay?" I stood in front of her and held her face in my hands. She nodded, not looking at me. I kissed her lips, trying to bring her out of herself. I didn't want her to be frightened or feel uncomfortable. I didn't want to be reaching up with my fingers, setting her on fire, only to have her never let go. I needed her to let go and fall all the way. I slid her dress down over her breasts, unaware that it would immediately fall all the way to the floor. I sent a mental thank you to Marcy for her wonderful dress design.

Angelina stepped out of it, obviously worried it would get dirty. I folded the dress and placed it on our coats, then went back to her. The sight of the red glow on her skin made me feel weak. I put my fingers through her hair and kissed her again until I felt her body relax.

"I'm going to make you fall," I breathed into her ear. I felt her quiver and hoped it wasn't with fear. There was a lot I didn't know about her. I didn't know the details of her abuse or what might trigger flashbacks like I had just caused. I decided it was safest not to touch her unnecessarily, not to run the risk of losing all my chances to accomplish what I had set out to do. I dropped to my knees in front of her, keeping my eyes looking up into hers. She watched me with curiosity. "You can close your eyes if you want, but don't forget it's me… John."

She moved her fingertips through my hair as I ran my hands up her thighs before pulling away her panties. I only needed them down just enough to taste her, and wanted not to waste time undressing her. I wanted no hesitation or doubts on her part or mine. Her scent was intoxicating, more than I could have imagined, like a drug leaving me desperate for more. She held an entire world of unexplored terrain and I wanted to know every nuance about her. With every motion of tongue or fingertip, I keenly listened to her breathe and sigh, memorizing what caused her the most pleasure. I wanted with great urgency, with a desperation, to make her let go of everything except the feeling between us. I wanted her to melt into me because I was already hers. I had no way out.

I knew it happened when her fingers tightened on my scalp and she pulled me tightly to her, bruising my lip against her, but

I didn't care. "John!" She cried, her legs shook and she collapsed onto my lap which was wet because I had already come long before she did. Her arms wrapped around my shoulders, her hair draped across my face. She was crying. I couldn't tell if she was happy or sad. I just let her cry and kissed the soft skin over her collar bone; but I had to intervene when I heard her begin to hyperventilate.

"It's okay," I whispered, sliding out from under her so I could hold her face in my hands and look into her eyes. She resisted looking at me, moving her head too far to the right or left and continued to try to get air. "Look at me, Angelina," I whispered, holding her head firmly between my hands. I quickly planted a kiss on her lips before she could turn away. While kissing me, she gasped for air a couple more times before her breath finally steadied. Her hands found their way to the back of my head and pulled me closer. She relaxed into my kiss, forgetting to try.

Above us, loud booms vibrated the atmosphere. Cheers went up in the distance as fireworks caused one explosion after another. It was midnight.

"Happy New Year, Angelina."

"Happy New Year, John."

58

First Day of A New Year
January 1, 2007

I dreamed of her all night. I didn't want to get out of bed at all. I could have stayed there all day, but Dad beat on my door around ten o'clock.

"Get up! I have a plane to catch and you're coming with me!" He sounded adamant.

My first thought was of Angelina. Normally, I would have loved to go with Dad. But I didn't want to be away from her.

"Do I have to?"

He turned the door knob and pushed open the door, "Yes. Get up and let's go. I've let you sleep too long."

"Why do I have to go?"

"Because we don't spend enough time together. Plus, there's a lot going on around here lately and maybe you're starting to feel like you aren't important. I don't show you enough how much I love you." He had a wide grin, but also tears in his eyes.

I felt guilty, but I still didn't want to go. I couldn't believe he was making me leave her. I thought they had probably sat around the night before, discussing how they needed to separate us. Me going with Dad was probably just part of their plan. I said, "You just don't want me to see her."

Dad laughed, not a snicker, but a full belly laugh. "You are so much like your Mom sometimes." He shook his head, "I have your stuff packed, already in the car. Neil's waiting, let's go-go-go." He reached down and grabbed my hand and jerked me to my feet. He walked to my closet and pulled out a pair of jeans and a washed-out purple Bonnaroo shirt that used to be his. He tossed them at me and I had to catch them so they wouldn't hit me in the face. I groaned at him, wishing he'd go away.

He left the room while I got dressed, but as I was sliding on my boots he came back with a hair brush and started brushing my hair.

"What the hell?" I sat up and swatted his hand.

"We have to go, John."

"I can brush it on the damn plane, then. Leave me alone."

He scowled at me then sighed. "Fine," he handed me the brush, "Do it in the car. Let's go."

Neil greeted me like an old friend, which he had never done before our trip to Ohio. But I guessed that trip had been life changing for all of us. I guessed I could sum up the entire month of December as life changing. But 2007 had arrived, a new year. I started thinking of her again, remembering when the fireworks had exploded over us and she had melted into me. I felt like crying because Dad was making me leave Nashville, and wanting to cry made me feel like a toddler, which I hated. I directed my anger toward Dad, giving him a sideways glare without telling him why. He didn't see it. He was too busy talking to Neil as we drove. Of all things, they were discussing the goat cheese stuffed dates Dawson and Gabe had made the night before.

Neil drove us right up to the plane which had already started its engines. We grabbed our bags and Dad ran up the stairs. I wasn't in as big a hurry, so I moped behind him. When I walked through the door and turned to my right, I was scared nearly out of my socks by people screaming, "Happy Birthday!"

The passengers weren't Dad's band like I had expected. They were my family, the Matthews, Gabe, Angelina, Emory, and Marcy. I was so happy to see Angelina that no one else mattered, except when I realized she and Emory were sitting together in the front right seats. Emory was by the window, which made me suspect Angelina had chosen to sit beside him.

I didn't have time to brood about it. Dad called out, "Okay, everyone sit down and buckle up. It's almost time to take off."

Everyone sat except Dawson. He walked up to us, worried, "Have you seen Iris?"

"Here!" She said breathlessly from behind us. "I had to stop and pick up John's gift. It took longer than I intended."

I noticed Emory was craning his neck around to see her. Iris scanned the seats until she saw him, then a look of disappointment washed over her.

"Okay," Dad said, "Y'all sit. We'll talk more about it once we're in the air."

Dad and Dawson settled into the front left seats. Iris and I chose the last available seats which were side by side in the back. She let me have the window seat, but I realized too late that I wouldn't be able to look at Angelina without Iris noticing.

In a seething whisper, Iris let out a string of profanity followed by, "What the hell does she think she's doing?"

"Who?" I asked, already knowing.

"Angelina!" She said under her breath, "He doesn't like her, John. She needs to back the fuck off."

My face felt hot with anger. Iris glanced at me and her eyes softened, "Sorry. But, seriously. She's a kid and he's grown. He can't have that kind of trouble, and that's all it is, trouble. She's going to screw around until she gets him fired."

"Dad is not going to fire him. He knows the situation."

Iris just shook her head and sat back in her seat as we felt the force of the plane lifting us into the air. Gabe held his hands over his ears. Mr. Matthews sat beside him and Mrs. Matthews sat across the isle from him. I wondered why they hadn't let him sit by the window; maybe they thought he would be afraid of being so high in the air.

Once the plane leveled off, the pilot announced we could take off our seat belts and move around. Iris leaned over, "Go swap seats with Emory!"

"No!" I really wanted to sit beside Angelina, but I knew she wanted to sit with him, not me. Changing seats wouldn't change how hurt I was.

"Fine, then I'm going to switch seats with her."

I grabbed her wrist and gave her a pleading look.

"Let go, John. She's not as fragile as you think she is."

Before Iris could get out of her seat, Dad stood up and faced everyone. "Well, John, are you surprised?"

I forced a smile, "Maybe more confused than anything."

"We're all going to celebrate your birthday on a private island, Cayo Espanto, off the coast of Belize! We rented the entire island for four nights. I would have rented it for the entire week, but the weekend was taken."

I couldn't believe he was apologizing for four days on a private island with Angelina... and my family, of course.

"Now, to start the celebration," he continued, "We're showing a little movie we put together of our baby boy growing up. He'll be sixteen on Wednesday. These past sixteen years have been the best of our lives," he glanced lovingly at Mom and then at Dawson. "Everyone should see the movie start on the screen in front of them. If it doesn't come on, let me know and we'll help you find a seat with a working one."

The screens flashed and the movie began with my name and birth date on a black background. That shifted into a photo of me as a baby in the hospital with Mom. She looked so thin and her hair was so short. If I hadn't worked so hard building my muscles, I'd have looked just like her. The movie consisted of short clips of home video, mostly one to two minute segments separated by snapshots taken over the years. I was newly aware of Mom's sling in the early photos, and the way she later held me with her left arm. The images were in chronological order, so the early ones showed me messily eating baby food, taking baths (much to my embarrassment), and laughing. Next was a short video of me taking a few steps with Dad's hands holding me up, the Christmas tree blinking in the background. Then there was a snapshot of my first Christmas with Iris on the floor beside me. She was ripping paper and I was chewing the corner of a present. The snapshot led to the video of Mom helping me open the gift I had been chewing. While the camera was focused on me opening my first Christmas present, little Iris started opening my other presents under the tree. In the video, Dawson came over and picked her up and took her out of sight. After that, there a photo of my first birthday with the Elmo cake and that terrible dark blue icing all over my face and hair.

Everyone laughed at my cuteness. I glanced up and saw Angelina's head leaned over onto Emory's shoulder. She was shaking, crying. He had his head leaned over onto hers to comfort her. I glanced back at the screen, a video played of Dad singing to me as I held a toy guitar. He was looking into my eyes, trying his best to get me to sing the words of "Beautiful Boy" by John Lennon.

Angelina didn't even need to look at the screen to have the words of that song cut right through her. I heard the pain in her cry, now loud enough that everyone noticed her. Rage built up inside of me. I wanted the movie to stop, immediately. All I could think about was how much it was hurting her and how my family had been so thoughtless to make her watch it.

Mom stood up and went over to her, took her hand and lead her out of the cabin. There was a private room in the back. I knew Mom was taking her there; at least someone else had realized what was happening. But it was too little too late. I stood and pushed past Iris who grunted when I accidentally stepped on her foot. By the time I got to the back, Mom had shut the door behind her. I knocked, but she wouldn't open it.

"We'll be out in a few minutes," she said.

"It's me, Mom. Let me in."

"I know it's you, John. Who else would it be? Now just go sit down and we'll be out in a few minutes."

I did sit down. I sat at a small table outside the bedroom and refused to go back to the group until I knew she was okay. It seemed to take forever. Fifteen minutes passed before Dad came back to check on us. Mrs. Matthews was with him. She tapped on the bedroom door and it opened like magic. Evidently, Heather Matthews was deemed important enough to be given access.

"Is everything okay?" Dad asked me.

I shrugged, still mad at him.

He took the seat across from me and glanced out the plane window. "I didn't think about all this when I made the video," he said. I couldn't discern if that was meant to be an apology.

"Well, you should have known. It's fucking cruel!"

"Hey!" He looked at me, shocked and hurt, "It's your birthday, John. I'm doing all this for you. I certainly didn't mean to hurt anyone. Can't you see that I'm just as upset as you are?"

I gave him a sideways look and then went back to watching clouds go by out the window. The door opened and Mom came out before closing the door behind her. She gave Dad the *give us privacy* look. He nodded and headed back to the front of the plane. Mom slid into the seat he had just vacated.

"Why are you still out here?" She asked as if it wasn't a loaded question. "I thought you'd want to finish watching the video."

"I wanted to make sure she was okay."

"Well, you know what?" Mom sighed, "You can't. Not now, not ever. As much as you want to protect her from ever being hurt again, she's going to be. That's how life is."

"Maybe so, but for fuck's sake, Mom, do we have to rub it in her face that we had a happy life while she was being tortured?"

"John, watch your language. I'm not out to hurt you or Angelina, or anyone else. I'm trying to spare you a lot of pain. You can't lessen her burden by carrying the weight of what happened to her. If you carry it, you'll just be multiplying the misery because it won't lessen it for her. It will just mean that now her pain has doubled and rests on the backs of us all. So, yes, we had a happy life. That's what you think. But I assure you, mine hasn't been a happy life except for the parts that involved you. Other than that, my life has been a wreck." Her eyes glistened with tears that didn't dared tip over her lashes. "Dads and I have done everything we could to give you a life we never had. We've protected you and doted on you and loved you the way we wished we'd been loved. We are not going to feel ashamed of that. I refuse to to apologize for how much we loved you then and love you now. I won't and neither should you."

"But what about Angelina?"

"John, she'll come through this. Give her time. She has to do this for herself. And..." she hesitated only a moment, "You can't make her love you. She either will or she won't."

I clenched my teeth at the mention of Angelina loving me, rather, of her not loving me. Mom was crossing so many lines. "Is that how you felt about Allie? Just let her go? She'll either love you or she won't?" I crossed lines, too.

The tears now slid silently down Mom's cheeks as she stared at me. I should have seen them as a sign to stop, but I didn't. "If you had gone after Allie, tried to save her, maybe this whole thing wouldn't have happened! And if you had looked into what happened to Gabe, maybe Angelina would have been saved a long time ago! But you didn't! You just stayed holed up in a place where you didn't have to think about them. You helped people who don't need you to love them, don't require you to risk getting hurt, strangers who mean nothing to us. You thought it would be enough to just love your own kid and not love Allie's kids, too. Maybe you were avoiding the pain of thinking about it. But now that pain belongs to Angelina. That pain she feels right now is partly your fault! You want to talk about everyone else carrying Angelina's pain? What about the fact that we *all* carry *your* pain?"

"Enough!" Dad was standing behind me. He stepped into view, his eyes sharp as lasers onto mine. "You are out of line! Your mother has been hurt in more ways than you will ever, EVER know. She has come out of a horrible situation and become an amazing woman who gives everything she has to others. You may not know the whole story, but that doesn't give you the right to make up hurtful theories and use them like knives to stab at your mother's heart. For your information, she didn't look for Gabe because a letter came to her a week after the shooting. It was in Allie's handwriting, dated three days before Allie's death." As Dad spoke, Mom laid her head on the table and cried, "It said, '*They think Satan lives in us because of you. No matter what you hear on the news, you can't come near me or my baby.'* When your mom discovered that Allie had signed a will that specifically named us both, as well as Dawson, forbidding us from adopting Gabriel, your mother was left with few options. Hind sight is 20/20 and of course we would have taken action if we had known what was really going on. But we thought the abuse died with Jim and the worst that could've happened to Gabe would be to grow up in a weird Christian cult. Your mom is already hurting, already blaming herself, already feeling guilty for every decision she has ever made except for you, John. You're the one thing that has gotten her through all this, so stop being a jackass and apologize."

He paused and looked at me expectantly. Then he shouted, "Now! Apologize right now!"

"I'm sorry," I said reactively, but the sentiment began to sink in. I hadn't known. So much was kept from me. I was angry about that, but I understood why. She needed at least one thing that didn't hurt, and that had been me. But now even I had become tainted with the weight of her past. I put my hand on her arm, the one her head rested against. "I'm sorry, Mom. I know you were trying to protect me. You did everything you could. It isn't your fault the world is such a shitty place."

Dad cleared his throat, possibly to mask his shaky voice. He said, "Go on back to your seat, John. I'm going to sit with her for a while."

59

The warm winds blew over Belize in stark contrast to the winter winds we had left behind in Tennessee. We were scheduled to be taken to the island by boats too small for us all to go in one. Dads and I were transported to our boat before Angelina deboarded the plane. Again, I found myself craning my neck to look for her. Even while speeding over the blue-green waters, I still looked back.

We arrived at a dock where we were greeted by the island staff. Dad explained there were seven houses on the three acre island of Cayo Espanto. The small overwater bungalow at the end of a short pier would be mine for the next four days. He and Dawson would be staying nearby in a two bedroom house where they planned to host a number of the celebrations. The Matthews would be staying in the other two bedroom house with Gabe and Angelina. Everyone else was free to choose, first come first served. Dad seemed to take a bit of pleasure in anticipating the coming race and battle of guests rushing to claim their favorites.

While we waited for their boats to arrive, we walked around the sandy ground beneath a plethora of palm trees. Dad said an investor had bought the island when it was nothing more than a sandy flat slab above water with a single palm tree on it. It was built up into a miniature paradise.

We were able to walk from one end to the other in under five minutes. We turned back, taking a slower pace to point out interesting features on all the other houses. As we passed the Casa Aurora, the house where the Matthews would be staying, they arrived by boat at their dock. Dads walked up to greet them along with the staff, but I held back. I didn't want Angelina to see me as I watched her. A look of amazement filled her eyes. The Matthews were very focused on Gabe as he removed his ear protection and rocked side to side with nervousness or joy, it was hard to tell the difference. When a wide smile stretched across his face, I assumed he was pleased. Angelina stood alone beyond them, turned to face the vast open water. I watched her arms stretch out as a warm breeze tugged her white sundress in all directions, whipping it high to expose what I assumed were the bottoms of a bikini. She let her head fall back to look up at the sky and feel the wind. He hair snaked wildly about. Watching her made me love the island even more than I loved home.

The boat carrying Mom, Iris, Marcy, and Emory passed by and Angelina dropped her arms, aware of it, and turned her head to watch it pass. The carefree moment had died. I began to dread the moment I'd be forced to be cordial when I was already overwhelmed with what had happened on the plane, not to mention all that had happened last week. I just couldn't pretend to be okay. I wasn't.

I walked back to my overwater villa, known as Casa Ventanas. My suitcase was there waiting. I put my things away, just to see what Dad had packed. There were no winter pajamas or long sleeve flannel shirts. Despite being the first day of January, the late afternoon temperature hovered around eighty degrees. I was glad to see I had a few band t-shirts and my favorite swim shorts. I unzipped my toiletries bag; all the usual items were there. But there was also a small box of condoms. I fought back an unexpected sense of rage. I wanted to immediately confront Dad about it, but I wasn't sure which one was responsible, maybe both. I should have been glad they were looking out for me, not forcing me to come to them; but the mixed messages were too much to deal with. Mom and Dawson both had told me to leave Angelina alone and at least one of my dads (I assumed) were giving me condoms. I thought back to the first time Dawson gave me a box of condoms. He had said, "The fact that I am giving you this should not be misconstrued as blanket permission to use them. I prefer you wait until you are twenty-six, got it?" He had winked at me, but I got the message. I still had one of those old condoms in my wallet. I was sure Dads wouldn't approve of what I had already done with Angelina. I zipped the bag up and walked out onto the porch.

There was a hammock hanging on the side of the porch toward the Matthews' villa. Their villa was much farther away than Dads'. I couldn't even see their dock, but my mind and heart oriented itself to where I knew she was. I climbed into the hammock so I could look out over the water, thinking I might see a few boats go by. Instead, I closed my eyes and wondered if Emory was with her. I wondered if Iris had hurt Angelina's feelings. I wondered if Angelina was lying in a hammock over there, wondering if I was thinking of her. I doubted it. I didn't want to thinking any more about the island, or what would happen. I just wanted to think of being with her in the barn on New Year's Eve, over and over and over.

60

The sound of whistling woke me up. It was the kind of whistling someone would do to call a dog. I thought it must be Dawson, but I heard Mom's voice, "John?"

"Out here." I stretched, feeling like I had slept for hours. I opened my eyes to see a dull amber evening sky. "What time is it?"

She walked around from the back of the porch, "This is lovely!" she gazed around at my view as if it was any different from wherever she was staying. "And to answer your question, it's a quarter past five. Do you feel better?"

"I'm fine," I rolled out of the hammock and wasn't sure if I'd spoken too soon. I felt stiff and made a mental note that lying in hammocks and sleeping for hours in hammocks were two different things. "I need to sit in a real chair," I said and made my way to the table on the back porch.

Mom sat with me, "Your dad brought over some instruments, even a keyboard for Gabe. They're going to start playing in a few minutes if you'd like to come over. I mean, I think you should."

"I don't know yet," I really didn't want to be around anyone.

"John, you can't stay locked up in this house all week, no matter how beautiful the view. Dad really worked hard to book this trip and make it possible for us all to be here together. He feels guilty for not being around much lately. If nothing else, go for his sake."

"I might, for a little while."

"That would be great. The staff will be serving dinner. I hear lobster is on the menu." She raised her eyebrows a few times, expecting my usual reaction. I forced myself not to show signs of excitement, even though I felt my stomach rumble.

I changed the subject, trying to sound nonchalant, "So where is everyone staying?"

"Well, the house that way," she pointed toward Dads' two bedroom villa, "Is Dads'. I am on the other side of them and then Marcy. At the other end of the island is Iris, and then coming back around are the Matthews' and then between the Matthews' and your villa is Emory."

Great. Emory was between me and the Matthews', how fitting. And I could look out from my side porch and see his house and dock. I'd never be able to imagine him gone. Mom frowned at me, "I don't know why you kids want to rush things. You know, I was in love with Allie for years before it became more than friendship. I think if we had rushed things, we might have never had what we did."

I glared at her, wanting to say all the reasons she was wrong, but knowing I'd hurt her if I did. I couldn't help but still believe that Mom should have wanted it more, went after it harder, given Allie no chance to doubt how much Mom loved her. As these thoughts raced through my mind, I realized I was making the same mistakes. I still danced around my feelings for Angelina, not wanting to hurt her. My ideas about love sounded really simple and foolproof, but in practice they became a little muddy and complicated.

"There's no way to know, I guess," I conceded.

"Angelina has a lot to figure out. Give her time. Don't do anything stupid," she winked at me. "I'm going to get dressed. I'll see you at Casa Estrella." She used a butchered accent to call Dads' villa by it's official name.

"That was terrible," I laughed at her.

"I'm happy to see you are so entertained." She was already walking into the house toward the front door. "Now bring that cheery attitude with you later."

I headed for the shower, which was open to the outside air around the top. I stood under the heavy streams of water beating onto my back and looked out over the island and the rippling water. I stayed motionless for a long time, trying to decide how to approach Angelina. Obviously, she had not fallen into me like I thought she had, nor had she let go of her desire for Emory. Maybe Mom was right and I should just wait, give her time to see Emory's flaws. But it hurt me, more than I cared to contemplate, that she didn't feel what I had felt the night before. After everything….

I pictured her on lap, arms wrapped around me, hyperventilating. It aroused me to think about it, but I questioned if I was even perceiving it correctly. Maybe I had hurt her and not known it. Maybe that's why she didn't want to sit with me on the plane.

I finished rinsing the shampoo from my hair and turned off the water. I dried off and laid across the bed with the towel over me, feeling a still warm but cooler breeze blow through the open house. I tried to think about anything except Angelina. The only way I would be able to get ready to go to dinner was to only think about the dinner itself. I would go, eat, and come back to my own villa, go to sleep, and be glad the day was over.

The sound of Dad playing some warm up riffs easily made its way into my room. I pulled on a pair of jeans and vintage Santana shirt from 1983. Mom had brought it home from the thrift store for herself but it was too big. She held onto it and gave it to me when I grew big enough. I felt like I looked pretty cool, but didn't really expect Angelina to think so. She knew nothing about music. I felt my mood improve when I realized I had been wanting her to hear Dad's music and could now mark that off the list of things to share with her. It wasn't the same as seeing him live at a concert. Perhaps it would be better. I imagined her eyes lighting up and I wanted to be there to see it.

I slid on the cowboy boots Dad had packed, thinking they would keep the sand out, and headed down the pier toward the island. My wet hair whipped around in the wind and I suspected soon it would look just like Santana's silhouette on my shirt. I ran my fingers through it multiple times to keep it from drying in a permanent flyaway look. I entered Dads' villa, thankful the wind could no longer reach it. A much more nuanced breeze blew through the house.

The Matthews were in the main room where Gabe sat at a keyboard. His fingers danced effortless over the keys, though the keyboard was curiously turned off. Mrs. Matthews saw my look of confusion and said, "He's listening to some songs Tracy gave him." She pointed at the headphones Gabe was wearing. "He wanted to practice with the keyboard off so he could better hear the songs." She beamed with pride as if Gabe was already her son.

"Is Angelina here?"

"She's in the kitchen with Jute and Marcy. But you can't go in there because, for one thing, there is no more room. The staff probably wish those ladies would come out here and let them be."

Just knowing she was there, and hearing no mention of Emory, was good enough.

After twenty minutes of guitar tuning and showing off his skills, Dad put his guitar on the stand and went over to tap Gabe's shoulder. "Ready to eat?" Gabe looked up a bit startled, "It's time to bring in the table for dinner. We'll play more as soon as we eat."

The island staff filed in to clear the room and set up a table and chairs. They motioned for us to take our seats. Dad sat at the end of the table, beside him was Dawson, then me, Mom, and Marcy. Mr. Matthews sat at the other end, then Mrs. Matthews, Angelina, and Gabe who sat in front of me. There was an empty seat beside him and then Iris sat beside of Dad. The staff brought out individual dishes for us all. I wasn't sure how they knew what we each liked, but I assumed Dad must have told them. I had a lobster tail with steamed broccoli on the side. Gabe's plate contained a halved peanut butter sandwich and apple slices.

"Wow, Gabe. That looks delicious!" I was sincerely happy he was able to get something he liked.

"And it's Monday. But I can eat because Mrs. Matthews says we have new rules that we eat three times in one day, every single day Sunday through Saturday. I like the new rule." He took a bite of an apple slice. "These are yellow apple slices, like Golden Delicious, which I like. Apples have names for every kind. I have tried six kinds of apples: Red Delicious, Rome, Gala, Jonagold, Cameo, and these Golden Delicious. I'm going to try a lot of others, maybe all of them."

"I like apples, too," I took a bite of my lobster which tasted like heaven and nothing like an apple. "I like sour apples like Granny Smith."

"Oh." He took a bite of his sandwich and chewed it very thoroughly before swallowing. He drank a sip of water and said, "Granny Smith is one I am going to try."

"Tell me what you think of it when you do."

"We had a crab apple tree," Angelina leaned over to join the conversation. "I used to eat those tiny sour things. I thought they were delicious."

"We had a crab apple tree, too!" Gabe seemed excited, but then the joy suddenly vanished. He shoved another bite of sandwich in his mouth and stared down at his plate. I wonder what memory was haunting him. I was trying to think of something else I could say to get his mind off it when I noticed Angelina's eyes shoot up toward the door.

I turned to see Emory coming through the doorway. He was wearing a navy blue plaid western shirt with pearl buttons, jeans, cowboy boots, and a cowboy hat. It wasn't the kind of thing most people wore on an island off of Belize. But Angelina, no doubt, liked what she saw. He pulled off his hat, his blond wavy hair still holding the shape of it as if he'd been out on a horse all day. After hanging his hat by the door on a peg intended for more summery wear, he glanced around the table until he caught Iris's eyes. He walked over and sat between Iris and Gabe.

"Sorry I'm late," he said mostly to Iris, offering no explanation.

A waiter brought him a plate of prime rib. He and Iris spoke between bites of their food. I stole a few glances at Angelina to see she was stealing glances at Emory and Iris.

61

Not a moment passed at Dads' villa that I didn't want to leave. When the tables were cleared, the floor was left open for dancing. Dad started the set by playing Merle Haggard's "Mama Tried". Emory and Iris began line dancing as if they were born out of the womb knowing how to step. Marcy jumped in next, already dressed for it in her polka-dot circle skirt and black halter top. Mom joined in, followed by the Matthews. Mom stepped out of line to pull Dawson into the act. By that time, Dad was playing another old country song. Gabe went over and sat at the keyboard, which was still not turned on, and began playing as if it were.

Angelina looked mesmerized by the crowd moving in unison. The steps everyone made were very basic, but then Emory and Iris began to add more complicated moves. Before the second song had ended, everyone had moved back to watch those two dance. I glanced at Angelina to see her bite her bottom lip nervously. I couldn't tell if she was terrified or intrigued.

When the song was over, Emory walked up to Angelina and put his hand out for hers, "Want to learn how?"

"Sure!" Her initial look of relief turned quickly to apprehension.

Tracy nodded at Emory and began playing Johnny Cash's "I Walk The Line", which was a slower song with a basic rhythm. Angelina was finding it difficult to keep in step because she kept staring into Emory's eyes instead of at his feet. It was painful to watch, so I didn't. I slipped off to the bathroom and waited just long enough to be forgotten before exiting out of the house entirely.

I went back to my villa where the music wafted in through the open windows. I pulled off my shirt and jeans before climbing into bed. I covered my head with a pillow, then another. I felt strange, not really sad, not really angry, but maybe a little of both. Mostly, I just felt disconnected and useless. I knew I was going to have to wait the whole thing out, do nothing until she got over Emory, but I didn't want to have to watch it happen.

My thoughts turned to safe, random things until I fell into a dream. I was riding in a convertible 1956 DeSoto with Johnny Cash (for obvious reasons). He was telling me a story about a guy that once tried to convince him that he'd sell more records if he dyed his hair blond. Suddenly his wife, June, was in the car with us and she had her hand on my knee.

That's when I woke up because someone was really touching my knee. I threw the pillows off my face and sat up. Angelina was sitting there, crying, holding a tall glass with some sort of tropical drink in it. In the moonlight, the drink looked blue or maybe green.

"I brought you one," She sniffed and tried to act like she wasn't crying.

I took the drink to smell it, lemons and something not intended for kids. She stood up and went to the dresser to pick up her own drink, which was already half gone.

"You probably shouldn't drink that," I cautioned, but took a sip of mine just to see how it tasted. I could barely taste the alcohol which explained why Angelina was downing hers so quickly.

"I don't want to hear anything else about what I should or shouldn't do," she sipped and swallowed, "I just had to get out of there, John. I couldn't stand looking at them one more minute." She walked back to the bed and raised the blankets before climbing in under them. She propped herself against the headboard so she could continue to take sips of her drink.

"Well," I cleared my throat and sat my drink on the nightstand beside me; then I took her drink from her hands.

"Why don't you stop for a minute and just talk to me about it." I leaned over her and placed her drink on the nightstand beside her. I caught the scent of her and hesitated, almost imperceptibly, before I sat back up beside her. I consciously kept a safe distance. I was determined not to fall into the same delusion I had in the barn.

"Emory doesn't like me. It's like fate brought him to me just to remind me how worthless I am."

"Fate?" I tried not to sound so incredulous. "What does fate have to do with any of this?"

"When I fell down that bank and landed in the road, he was right there to save me."

"He nearly ran over you."

"Nearly, but he didn't! He stopped and rescued me, looking like that baby angel on Esther's wall," She was obviously feeling the alcohol. "And he said my eyes were like sapphires in a crown. I felt something I had never felt before. And he made every good thing happen. What else is that, if not fate?"

"I thought you didn't believe in God anymore."

"This has nothing to do with God."

"You're talking about some magical force bringing you together with someone who looks like an angel; I think that has God's name all over it."

"No, fate doesn't have to be controlled by a god," she crossed her arms.

"Then who controls it?"

"Maybe we do! Maybe we're all connected by invisible lines." She picked up her drink again and took another sip.

"You seriously need to stop with that before you get drunk."

Her eyes widened in shock and she quickly sat the drink down. "What is that?" She looked at the fancy drink like it was going to attack her.

"Curaçao" I answered. She looked confused. "I read the menu earlier." She still looked confused. "It's alcoholic."

"Oh, no!" She seemed panicked. "The man let me take them. He didn't say anything."

"It's fine," I laughed, "They probably don't care. It's just, you should go easy on it."

"It's no wonder Emory doesn't like me. I don't know anything!"

"Iris doesn't know anything either," I never passed up an opportunity to make fun of Iris; we were siblings at heart.

"Now you're just being mean." She angrily yanked the covers back and got out of the bed.

"Wait!" I reached for her, but her feet had already landed on the floor. I scrambled to get out of bed and grabbed her wrist just before she reached the doors. "I'm sorry."

She turned and rested her head against me, crying, "I don't have anywhere else to go."

It hurt to think she was only with me for that reason. I wrapped my arms around her anyway. "Why do you like him so much?" Part of me didn't want to know, but another part of me hoped she would give me an answer that would convince me to let her go for good.

"I don't know. I just think he's beautiful and he was the first person to make me feel beautiful, too. Do you think, one day, I'll be good enough to make him love me?"

"You couldn't possibly be better than you already are," I swallowed hard, disappointed that her answer only drew me in closer. I wanted to make her feel beautiful and loved. I felt I had failed her.

"Will you kiss me?" She spoke into my chest, not even looking up into my eyes.

My mind screamed in anguish, wounded by the unfairness that she would probably think of Emory if I obliged her. I was a fill in, her imaginary friend, a ghost of her mother's lover who she only played with when she pretended to be the ghost of her mother. She had called my name in the barn, but she couldn't see the person associated with it. Tears burned my eyes, but I kept my voice steady, "Why?"

"Because I want to feel myself falling," she said. She loved falling, but not letting go.

My heart pounded painfully. I whispered to mask my shaking voice, "Like in the barn?"

I felt her nod. The sounds in the room were lost to the whirring in my brain. I felt lightheaded, but I managed to carry her back to bed. I didn't kiss her. I just watched her lie back and close her eyes. I pushed up her sundress and ran my fingers along the edge of her swimsuit, watching her body shake with anticipation. I reached up for her hand, "You don't need me," I said "Just touch here," I put her fingers on the spot.

"No!" She sat up alarmed. "That's not allowed!"

"By whom?" I hugged her against me so she wouldn't see how upset I was.

"I... I don't know... I just can't and... it wouldn't be the same. John, please..." her lips kissed the center of my chest where surely she felt my heart pounding. I wanted her to stop. I couldn't shake the feeling that she was thinking of Emory. The unfairness of it tore at me.

"Fine," I breathed a sigh and gently pushed her away. She fell back, eyes already closed. If she had loved me, I would have taken longer. I would have caressed every inch of her, teased her until she begged, made her call my name. But she didn't love me. To her, I could have been anyone. I pushed my fingers under her swimsuit, feeling how badly she wanted to be touched. She was so close already that I could have brushed my hand across her and caused her to come. I wanted so badly to love her, but at that moment, I also hated her.

I kissed her there, through the fabric of her bikini. I held her hips tightly and gently bit her and it was over. She came, saying my name, reaching for me but I was already standing. She turned onto her side and cried. I wanted to run out the door and never stop running, but there was nowhere to go. I wanted to not love her, but I couldn't stop. I sat on the bed in front of her and took her hand from her face. I kissed where her tears were falling. I promised her what I hoped wouldn't be a lie, "One day, you won't hurt like this."

62

January 2, 2007

Dads spent most of the day with me. We fished and took a guided scuba diving tour. Emory and Iris came scuba diving with us, but the Matthews did not. It seemed unfair to have to look at Emory for hours, watch him be amazed at new discoveries, when it should have been Angelina there instead. But, I was also glad they didn't both come. The last thing I wanted was to watch Angelina stare at him instead of the coral reef.

By the time we came back to the island, it was late afternoon. I showered and dressed for dinner, tried to prepare myself for what I anticipated to be a night like the one before. Angelina would sit at the table and stare at Emory and Iris until jealousy devoured her heart. There was no way to prepare for that.

I intentionally arrived late. There were two seats left available, side by side. I sat in the chair by Mom.

"Where's Angelina?" I whispered in her direction.

The waiter sat a plate of fish tacos in front of me.

Mom said, "She's not feeling well. Heather said she's been sick and in bed all day."

"Oh. I didn't know." I felt ashamed for not knowing sooner, though I also blamed them for not telling me. All day, I had imagined her having a good time with the Matthews, relaxing in the jacuzzi or fishing off the dock. I wondered if she was really sick, or if she was just avoiding Emory and Iris. I wasn't going to inquire further.

I took a bite of my taco and glanced across the table at Iris.

She was wearing a turquoise bikini with an oversized, multicolored, sheer cover-up. Her eyelashes were sparkling with blue metallic glitter. She sat a bit sideways, leaning toward Emory, taking bites of her salad during pauses in their conversation. I listened, but tried to pretend like I wasn't. He talked about his family's horse farm in Kentucky. Iris never used to care a lick about horses; but she sat wide-eyed, enthralled by every story he told about competing in dressage. According to him, he had amazing skills and won national competitions multiple years in a row. I hated him and was convinced he was lying. But I nearly choked on my bite of taco when he said, "So Dad was super pissed when I said I wasn't like the other girls. I knew for years before I said anything, but I couldn't keep hiding it."

I managed to swallow the food in my mouth and clear my throat inconspicuously. I glanced at Iris for her reaction, but saw none. She obviously already knew. She put her hand on his back and rubbed between his shoulders. She said, "Don't start thinking about your Dad. You'll just get upset. And we're not on this island to waste our time being upset." She leaned over and kissed him, not the kind of kiss meant to comfort. She kissed his earlobe and her fingers curled up into his hair.

I stopped looking at them. I turned to mom to tell her about scuba diving, just to serve as a distraction; but she was turned toward Marcy, taking a bite of red bell pepper off Marcy's fork.

I finished eating as quickly as possible then went to hide in the bathroom again. I couldn't wait to get back to my room, but didn't want to seem rude. I stayed long enough to listen to Dad and Gabe play through a handful of songs. Then I claimed to be exhausted and walked back to my villa. I briefly thought of walking over to the Matthews' house and checking on Angelina. But I didn't believe she was really sick. Whatever reason she had to stay holed up in bed, I wasn't going to question it.

I, personally, wanted to get holed up in my own bed.

63

January 3, 2007

The next day, Angelina finally came out of her house for lunch. She was wearing the same white sundress and I cringed at the thought that she hadn't changed her clothes in days. Her hair was braided and twisted into a bun. She didn't look like she had any energy to have done it herself, so I suspected Mrs. Matthews had put it up for her.

Angelina picked up her plate of fruit and yogurt from the table and carried it off toward their house. No one called for her to come back, but Mom watched her with a worried look on her face. She looked over at me; her eyes registered that I was worried, too. She put a hand on my knee to comfort me or perhaps to keep me seated. "She's just not feeling well, John. At least she came out for food."

"Yeah." I looked away so Mom wouldn't read my mind.

Dad stood and tapped a knife to his glass. Everyone looked up. "Dawson and I are taking a boat to San Pedro this evening to do some shopping. If anyone needs anything, let us know before you wonder off." He looked at me specifically, "John, you're coming with us."

I nodded, not really having an opinion one way or another about it. But as I gave it some thought, I decided I'd look for a gift for Angelina.

San Pedro was a surprisingly short boat ride away. But in the few minutes it took to get there, Dads had me laughing. For the first time since we had arrived, I was glad I had requested a family trip as my birthday gift. They had needed it as much as I did. After the boat docked, we stepped off and headed straight to a chocolate shop. Chocolate was Dawson's first love. Dad didn't care for it, but he had a gleam in his eyes as he watched Dawson excitedly choose at least a dozen varieties. After Dad paid, Dawson tucked the bag into the olive green satchel he had brought.

Next, Dad wanted to go into a handmade soap shop. The idea of a soap shop wasn't at all appealing to me; but once inside, I found it intoxicating. I started sniffing one soap after another. I was certain I wanted to get something for Angelina there, but the selection was mind boggling. There were soaps shaped like slices of cake, cupcakes, and banana splits. Those were cute but impractical. I didn't want to get a giant slab of something I liked only to discover she hated the smell. I decided on a sample bag with ten small squares of different scented soaps.

As we headed to the checkout, a display of jewelry caught my eye. In the center of a line of necklaces was one with a pendent made from a small geode. The rock was cut so that black and white swirls of granite framed the black crystals in the center which sparkled like a night sky. It was the universe beyond a swirl of clouds.

"Dad," I waved to get his attention. He handed the cashier his credit card to pay for the soaps, then held a finger up to signal he'd be over in a minute. I placed the pendent in the palm of my hand, shifting it so the black crystals sparkled in the light like stars.

"You want to get that for her?" Dad had walked up behind me.

"Yes." I didn't look at him, worried he would have a look of disapproval in his eyes. He walked back to the cashier and asked about the price. It was more than I anticipated. I expected to hear him say it was too much. But, instead, he was pulled out his card again and placed it in the cashier's hand. My face grew hot with guilt.

"I'll pay you back," I whispered when he made his way back to me.

"No, don't even think of it. Consider this part of your birthday gift." He put his arm around me and we watched the cashier place the necklace inside a padded blue box. "Even the box is pretty," he said.

We went into every shop we could get to before the sky turned pink. Dad had bought things for everyone, including another gift for Angelina because he said the soap and pendant were from me and didn't count. Dawson's satchel was full of small bags, plus he carried a sack of apples in his hand for Gabe. Dad carried a bag full of fabrics he bought for Marcy. He had spent a lot of money on the fabrics, but claimed it was worth it because Marcy had made so many things for Mom and Angelina. The only thing I carried was the blue box and the soaps, all of it tucked inside a sheer silver tulle drawstring back I had found at the fabric shop.

When the boat pulled up to the dock at Cayo Espanto, the island looked deserted.

"I guess we weren't missed," Dad said, laughing. "They're probably caught up in the island magic," he winked at Dawson.

"I think I'm going to skip dinner," I said, wanting to avoid witnessing any island magic, especially from Dads. Besides, they needed some privacy.

They thought nothing of my comment because none of us were hungry. We had eaten samples of various foods all afternoon. As I headed off toward my villa, Dawson said, "If you need us, you know where to find us."

I had no intention of needing them, nor interrupting them. After dropping the silver bag into a dresser drawer, I went out to the hammock and took in the twilight. I was no longer upset with Angelina. I knew I was likely being a fool, but it didn't matter at the moment. I was exhausted from worry and heartache. For just a little while, I wanted to pretend like she wasn't using me and could be swayed to love me, too.

The reflection of the full moon seemed to vibrate over the shallow ripples across the ocean. I gazed out over the night sky until I felt my eyelids grow heavy. I welcomed the feeling and the sleep it would soon bring. I rolled out of the hammock and went inside to bed, not bothering to shower. I piled up my dirty clothes on the floor and fell into the softness of my delusions that all was right with the world.

At a little after 1:00 a.m., Angelina slipped into bed behind me. I had my back to her and pretended to still be asleep. I shouldn't have, but her presence caught me off guard. I felt her body press against my back and her hand slip over my stomach to rest her arm on my side. I tightened my muscles instinctively, not wanting to seem flabby.

"John?" She whispered, "I can't stay long. I just needed to see you." She sounded desperate.

I didn't turn around, "What's wrong?"

"I don't know. I just can't sleep anymore. All day, I have wanted to get out of bed, but I couldn't. All I have done is sleep because being awake makes me feel sick, my chest aches, I can't breathe. I feel like I'm dying. And now that it's night, I can't get to sleep and all I can think about is being here. I need you."

She was crying. I rolled over onto my back and turned my head to look at her. The moonlight through the open house lit up the room like a black and white movie. The only color was the blue of her eyes, eyes which were pleading with me to make everything better. I suspected she had been having panic attacks. I opened my mouth to say so, but she leaned down and planted her mouth onto mine before I could get the words out. She kissed me hungrily. It was all I could do not to let myself get lost in it. But I was too worried.

She kissed down the side of my cheek to my ear, "John, I feel like I'm nothing. I'm floating away from everyone and they don't even notice. Please," She reached for my hand and placed it on her thigh under her gown, "make me feel wanted."

She kissed my neck and moved her body lower so my unmoving hand would be forced into the position she wanted it. "Please," she begged again.

Her skin was warm and naked and my fingers automatically

pressed against her. But my mind refused to release the remnants of my pain. I was being used again. "Angelina, we can't do this," now my voice was pleading.

She sighed at the movements of my hand as it contradicted everything my mouth was saying.

"I'm serious," I pulled my hand away and yanked her gown down to cover her. She groaned in protest. I explained, "This isn't normal. I can't keep filling in for Emory. If you want him, you'll need to either go get it or accept living without it."

"Emory?" She sat up and looked down at me with confusion. Her hair was wavy from being let loose from her braids. I wanted to touch it, but I didn't. She said, "What does he have to do with this?"

"I'm saying that maybe I make you feel wanted, but I'm not the one you want and it isn't fair. *I* don't feel wanted."

She bit her lip nervously and said, "I can make you feel wanted, too."

I said, "No," as she leaned down and kissed my shoulder. Her hand slid over my naked stomach and wasted no time wrapping her fingers around my erection. "That's not what I want," I grunted through clenched teeth. I couldn't help but wonder if she was touching me because she felt obligated, perhaps Silas had made her do that to him. I felt dirty and evil, as if I were the abuser. She might as well have been stabbing a knife in my heart with every stroke of her hand.

I grabbed her wrist, perhaps harder than I intended, and pulled her hand off me. "You have to leave," I said, clamping my mouth closed so not to say more.

"Why?" The question held a lifetime of pent up pain and rejection.

I tossed her hand loose from my grip and jumped out of bed. I went to her side and pulled her out from under the blankets. "Get out!" I was careful to keep my voice low so it wouldn't carry to the other villas. "Go home!"

"I don't understand," she cried as she pulled her arms close and hunched over as if I was going to hit her. That just made me angrier.

"Who am I?" I cupped her face in my hands and raised her head to look at me. She was crying, her mouth open, sobbing. "Who the fuck am I, Angelina? Am I a make-believe Jute to your make-believe Allie? Am I your toy to play with until the boy you love finally loves you back? Or am I John?" She pulled away from my hands and turned her back to me. I grabbed her arm and pulled her around again. "Look at me! If I didn't love you, I wouldn't have let it go this far. But I wanted to please you, so I let you pretend I was someone else, I let you practice for Emory, but I'll be damned if I'll let you pretend I'm Silas! How dare you think I'm like that sick bastard!" I let go of her because my hands were shaking with the most rage I had ever felt.

I picked up a glass from the nightstand and threw it with all my strength into the mirror over the dresser. The crashing sound of shattering glass was deafening. I let out a loud burst of profanity to drown it out, release the hurt I felt inside. When the room fell silent, I realized I was crying and Angelina was gone.

64

My Birthday
January 4, 2007

As soon as the realization of what I had done hit me, I pulled on my clothes from the day before and headed to Dads' villa. I needed to be as far away from my villa, and as far away from Angelina, as I could get. On a tiny island, there was no place far enough. I was surprised and relieved to find no one was awake. I pulled off my clothes and laid down on their couch, my heart racing. I stayed restless for the next hour, only finally getting close to sleep around 4:00 a.m.. I was dreaming I was back on the plane until the sound of screaming woke me. The distant, loud, screeching desperation in Angelina's voice was enough to wake the entire country of Belize. She was screaming my name over and over again as if she had found my dead body hacked to pieces. I struggled to orient myself and tried to figure out where the screaming was coming from.

Dads ran through the room and out the door before they even realized I was sitting on the couch. I ran after them in my underwear, not even bothering to put on shoes. I caught up with them as they reached the ramp to my villa. Angelina's screams were coming from inside. I breathlessly warned them, "There's glass on the floor, be careful."

Dad flipped on the light revealing shards of glass all over the floor between the dresser and my bed. Angelina was on the back porch, on the other side of the mess, still screaming my name out over the water. Dawson, the only one of us smart enough to have put on shoes, stepped over the glass as I called out, "I'm here!"

Angelina heard me and ran toward me, over the glass, and leaped toward my chest; her arms wrapped tight around me. "I dreamed I killed you," she sobbed. "I smashed your skull with a rock and you fell into the ocean. Blood ran from your head into the ocean until the water was red as far as I could see. I needed to see you, but you were gone. I looked everywhere and then I saw the blood on the porch and thought the dream was real!"

"I didn't fall," I hugged her, crying with her, knowing the blood on the porch was from her own feet. "I was at Dads'."

"Why are you always leaving me, John?"

"I'm not leaving you. I'm right here."

Not only was I there, but so was everyone else. They stood with gaping mouths, in shock at the sight of us. I was mostly naked, holding up Angelina whose feet were bloody. From the feel of her hands pressing on my back, her palms were bleeding, too. I held her tight, up high, trying to keep her feet off the dirty ground. She leaned down in mid-whimper and kissed me urgently then stopped to say, "I'm so sorry."

"It's not your fault. I shouldn't have yelled at you," I kissed her cheek and hugged her tighter.

I heard Mom speaking and caught sight of the light of her cell phone. She was calling for an emergency transport to the nearest clinic. She said, "Yes, Cayo Espanto. Yes. Thank you." The light from the phone went out as she flipped it closed; then she grunted and cried out as she flung the phone out toward the open waters. She nearly collapsed as she cried, but Dad caught her and held her. I was surprised by the sight of Dad leaning on her for support as well.

Everyone was in tears.

Mr. Matthews walked over and scooped Angelina out of my arms. He held her like a child, but she put her hands out to me and cried not to be taken away. I was suddenly acutely aware of my nakedness. I wasn't sure if I felt so bare because of my lack of clothing or because of the increasing space between her body and mine. I felt like a piece of me was being carried away.

I stepped to go after her, but Dawson laid a hand on my shoulder and pulled me back. He wrapped both his arms around me to keep me from pulling away. The Matthews walked toward the loading dock with Gabe behind them. He was unusually still, as if in a daze. I wondered what would happen. I wondered if she would be taken from them because of what I had done.

A boat pulled up to the dock less than five minutes after Mom had made the call. Dawson wouldn't let me go to tell her goodbye. I watched Mr. Matthews carry her onto the boat. Mrs. Matthews tried to convince Gabe to come. He refused to get on the boat, obviously in a state of panic. Mr. Matthews kissed his wife and helped her board, then he got back on the dock to stay with Gabe.

I watched the light of the boat as it carried Angelina off toward San Pedro. We all watched, still too stunned to speak.

I wouldn't see her again until Spring Break.

Part Ten

Angelina

65

March 16, 2007
Spring Break

Technically, I didn't have a Spring Break. I had a tutor/nanny, Ms. Jenny Printz, who came to stay with me while the Matthews' worked. Before they came home in the afternoon, they'd swing by and pick up Gabe. He went to a special school where he learned, among other things, how to properly interact with other people. Sometimes I felt like I needed that, too. Heather, who asked that I no longer call her Mrs. Matthews because it sounded too formal, said she would like for me to be caught up academically with the other Sophomores so I could go to a real school starting in the fall. Ms. Jenny Printz (say her full name, please) believed I would have no trouble being a high school Junior, even though I was still struggling with how to use a pen to form letters. She did it effortlessly with perfectly straight lines, but it was so new to me that I could barely write legibly. I doubted I would be ready for high school by the fall and wondered if Ms. Jenny Printz was just bad at picking up on other people's ignorance.

Because Cynthia Garrett had pleaded guilty to avoid a trial, we were no longer required to testify. To celebrate a seemingly easy end to the worst chapter in our lives, the Matthews suggested we accept the Duren's invitation to go away for Spring Break. I found that suggestion surprising considering how I hadn't been allowed to see John since leaving Cayo Espanto. I assumed Heather believed the solution to my nightmares of losing John forever was to make it a reality. She said she wanted me to stand on my own two feet, yet very few decisions were left up to me.

Our adoption, "if nothing goes badly", (according to the Matthews) would be finalized sometime during the summer. Heather assured us that it would be very unlikely for anything to get in the way. But just because something was improbable didn't mean it was impossible. I had obviously ruined my relationship with John. I really didn't know what to think of him and it made my head spin to try. After we had left the island, he mailed a package to me. Inside was a silver tulle bag full of soap samples and a blue box containing the most beautiful necklace I had ever seen. He had handwritten a note in his tightly spaced script, "The strings of the universe can not forever keep the stars from falling." By *strings of the universe*, I wasn't sure if he meant fate, or the way I had held onto Emory, or the way he made me feel in the barn. Maybe he meant it all.

I had hung the necklace in my window and refused to wear it. I didn't feel like I deserved it. But I had no problem using all the soaps. I'm not sure if he knew just how powerful they were, how every time I took a bath I would smell those divine fragrances and imagine he was right there with me. Once the soaps were gone, I stopped wanting to bathe, much to Heather's disgruntlement.

Whenever I asked to visit John, Heather would explain that it would be better for everyone if we stayed separated for a while longer. She said I needed to heal and then she would rattle off a list of the effects of childhood sexual abuse as if nothing in the world was more nefarious. I had done my own research on the

Internet, thanks to the laptop the Matthews had given me. I recognized myself in some of the effects on the list: Sleep problems, extreme fear and anxiety, depression, withdrawal, and my ever present interest in all things sexual. Some of the other items on the list did not apply to me, but I feared them, like suicidal thoughts and substance abuse.

I wanted to see John again as soon as possible, so I didn't resist the efforts made by the Matthews to find help for me. Heather had hired a therapist before we even got off the plane from Belize. Her name was Elise Vanderson, and I could call her Elise or Mrs. Vanderson; she didn't care which.

When the subject came up about going on Spring Break with the Durens, Heather suggested I talk to Elise about it. At first, I was ambivalent about bringing it up. I was used to the way Silas would take away everything that gave me pleasure and didn't trust people to know what made me happy. But I finally told her about John, everything there was to tell. I said not a day, or even an hour, passed that I didn't think about him. I was admittedly obsessed. Elise asked if I was obsessed with John or obsessed with proving his accusations were wrong. Elise knew, but John did not, that I went to him that last night because I realized he meant more to me than Emory. I had felt so unhinged and the only thoughts which calmed me were those of John. Maybe I had been selfish that night, but I certainly hadn't gone there because Emory wasn't available. I went because I wanted John.

I still wanted John. But that was the easy part. The hard part was trying to figure out how not to be so emotionally draining and psychologically damaged. I wasn't the only person in pain back in January. John suffered because of me and I didn't want to cause that again.

I had a number of folders set up on the desktop of my computer. One of them held files, lists of links, and documents all related to healing from sexual abuse. I had read everything I could find and settled on a few favorite exercises, the most important being daily meditation. Elise said it's common for survivors of abuse to shut their memories off and pretend like nothing happened. I was the opposite. I examined my own life like a specimen in a lab. Elise said I was unusually analytical and that would help me. I hoped she was right, because I could never be free from the pain I had experienced until I intentionally wrenched myself from it.

Sometimes Elise listened to me talk about my research with a worried look on her face; that's how I knew she really wanted me to get better.

It was a bit different trying to talk to Heather, maybe because I tried to talk to her about boys. She tried not to look terrified, but I could tell she was. She didn't really listen to what I asked so much as she answered the questions she was prepared to answer. She would advise me to enjoy being young and not rush things. "You've been hurt so badly, Angelina, it has impaired your ability to know when someone is abusing you. You must be very careful what you do, especially around boys." She would give me a stern look. "If you have any doubts about someone's intentions, you just come talk to me before you do anything. I'm not going to judge you. I will just help you do the right thing."

The tension in her voice usually succeeded in making me not want to talk to her about it at all. I would just go back to my laptop and save more files to my folder about boys, what they liked, what they didn't, photos of really cute ones. I wished I had a photo of John.

As badly as I wanted to see John, I was also apprehensive. I was afraid I'd once again see his pained expression and know it was there because of me. I wasn't sure if I could keep from crying the whole time. I had been a jumble of nerves just thinking about Spring Break. Not only was I worried about John, but Iris and Emory were going to be there, too. I would have to watch them snuggled up to each other happily by the fire, stealing kisses, having the kind of relationship I wanted.

No, I didn't need so much academic training from Ms. Jenny Printz about calculus or statistics. I needed to go to Gabe's learn-social-skills school because I had no idea how to build a relationship with John or if that was even possible after the mistakes I had made. Even interacting with the Durens, knowing they had seen how I had behaved, was something I couldn't quite envision. All I knew was that I was lonely and I had caused myself to be that way.

I pulled the necklace off the nail over the window and gazed at all the sparkling black crystals, like stars in the night sky. I asked myself, "What is it you want, Angelina?" Calling myself that name still seemed odd. My mind went blank, but suddenly an answer that felt right came to me. "I just want to be who I am, as if nothing terrible had ever happened to me."

That was going to be easier said than done. I slipped the necklace back into its original blue box and placed it in my cosmetic bag. Then I snapped closed my suitcase and carried it into the kitchen. I set it by the others at the door.

Heather was sitting at the kitchen table with Gabe. She was pointing to photos in a magazine and Gabe was identifying the emotion of the person in the photograph. Every time he spoke the word of the emotion, his voice changed tone to mimic the emotion. I giggled and he looked up at me. He smiled and looked back at the magazine. Now that he had an audience, he began answering with silly answers just to make me laugh again. Heather pointed to a woman smiling at her baby. Gabe said, "She is very itchy!" He scratched at his arm and laughed. He pointed to the baby, "Oh, he is afraid because there is a ghost-faced bat in his bed which means he is in Venezuela or maybe Texas!" Gabe threw back his head and laughed at his own joke.

"You're hilarious!" I laughed at his laughter because his joke was terrible. I considered that maybe the best thing I could ever be was a sister to him and anything else would just be extra. It was easy to fall back to believing in a divine plan even though I could no long believe in divinity. I continued to point to fate because it meant I wouldn't have to figure out all the answers myself. I could just say to myself, "I'm Gabe's caretaker and that's all I need to be." But the truth was, Gabe didn't need a lot of help. He was a bit awkward with his word choices and how he moved; but sometimes so was I. Overall, there was no question that Gabe was extremely intelligent and capable of doing nearly any task as long as the instructions were clearly given. I sighed, almost wishing he needed me more than he did. Like it or not, I was going to have to figure out what I was going to do with my life.

"When do we leave?" I asked.

"We're driving ourselves. No planes this time. We'll leave when Casey gets home around noon."

"I like planes," Gabe said, then guessed the emotion on Heather's face, "Unamused?"

She laughed, "Sometimes I think they lie about your deficiencies, Gabe. Homework is over. Go play."

To Gabe, *go play* meant go explore something. He was sixteen with the curiosity of a five year old. He loved exploring outside because so much of his life had been spent locked away. More than once, Heather had cleaned out his room to discover containers of dead insects, dried animal bones, various soils, rocks, and unidentified moldy objects. Gabe was as fascinating as he was fascinated and the Matthews loved him. They were amazed by his mind, tolerant of his needs, and obsessed with the acquisition of things to make his life better.

I, on the other hand, was deemed less needy, far less interesting, and given mostly lots of privacy and time with paid helpers. I watched a lot of TV and movies, and would pretend to be the actresses when I was alone in my room. I had to learn, somehow, what it meant to be normal. So far, mimicking what I saw on TV had only made me feel like a liar, and just a little bit nutty.

"Do we have time to go to the mall before we leave?" I asked.

Heather looked up at me as if a stranger had said those words. She squinted skeptically before seeing that I was serious. She said, "I... think so."

"Confusion!" Gabe pointed at Heather's face.

She sighed, "Only in the magazine, Gabe. The rule is, it's rude to call out the emotions of actual people."

66

The North Carolina house was not a resort, exactly. I was told it was the home of Tracy's musician friend. On the drive there, Casey explained with excitement that our visit was a rare opportunity because the guy was super famous and his house was shaped like a castle. I had never heard of him. Gabe hummed a tune which I assumed was associated with the guy. Gabe could hear a song once or be told something about music and remember it forever. But even with Gabe humming away, I couldn't recall ever hearing that song.

As we passed the giant house with castle towers made of small and large stone, I thought it must surely be magical. I had never seen anything like it except on television. Daffodils lined walkways and circled statues in the front yard. A breeze pushed through the flowers causing ripples of yellow, coral, and ivory as their little heads ducked and bobbed with failed resistance.

Heather said, "We'll be staying in the guest house. It has four bedrooms, so we'll have plenty of room." The driveway curved around the bend and a smaller house came into view. I liked it even better. The forest trees came up closer to it, nearly touching the porch; and the view of the mountains was breathtaking.

While the everyone took their bags in, I sat on the porch swing and reminisced about living on the mountain. Bittersweet tears stung my eyes. Seeing those endless peaks and valleys awash in the long shadows of a setting sun made me feel at home. It was how I used to feel when I would walk up to church to clean it on Saturdays. So many memories came flooding back, just the good ones like picking tomatoes, feeding the hens, spinning in my winter coat, getting caught in the rain too far from the house to make a run for it, and lying on my back in the church yard, watching clouds drift quickly out of sight, wondering where they were going and if I'd ever get that far.

I listened to the shuffling and chatter inside the house as everyone put their things away. I didn't even want to go inside. I thought, if it was warm enough, I would just sleep on the swing. I wanted to revel in the feeling of familiarity.

"Did you just get here?" John's voice was so quiet I almost didn't recognize it. He walked around from behind the porch and started up the stairs. My heartbeat deafened my ears. His hair had been cut shorter and he seemed taller, but perhaps that was because I was sitting down. The memories triggered by the mountains were nothing compared to the memories flooding my mind at the sight of John.

"We got here ten minutes ago." I slipped my shaking hands under my legs.

"Blue jeans, huh? Wow. That's new."

I pulled my hands free and rubbed them back and forth over the denim as if to warm my thighs. I hoped he wouldn't notice how badly my hands were shaking. "Heather took me to the mall to buy some new clothes. I was tired of my two fashion choices: Marcy's twin or Allie's twin."

He pointed to my suitcase, "Need help carrying your stuff inside?"

"I was thinking maybe I could sleep out here."

He laughed, "Of course you were." He cleared his throat and sounded more serious, "But I think they'll worry you'll run off in the night." John sat down besides me on the swing and picked up my hands to examine my palms. "Did you heal okay?" He maneuvered my hands around to catch the light from the window and touched the only remaining sign of a cut.

"It looked worse than it was, in all regards. I'm sorry I put everyone through that, especially you."

"All of that was my fault," He looked up into my eyes. "Maybe I should have just given you what you wanted."

The thought of it made my head light, but his guilty expression worried me. I said, "I was misguided and I expected too much of you. You had every reason to to be mad at me. I'm sorry. I promise I'll never put you in that situation again."

John searched my eyes. "Never is a long time."

I didn't know what he meant, or what to say. He must have read my nervousness because he stopped looking at me. He leaned back and gave a little push with his legs to set the porch swing in motion. I scooted to the end and put my feet up on the swing beside him. I stared at his profile, memorizing it. The breeze created by our motion cooled the warmth that had risen in me.

"You're making me nervous, staring at me like that." He glanced over, then looked away. "Since when did you become a starer?"

"Don't be nervous, silly. I just haven't seen you in forever."

"Or ever," he quipped.

He was back to accusing me of not knowing who he was. It hurt, but I knew I deserved it. "You're wrong," I swiveled to put my feet down, stopping the swing. "I came to your villa for you, John. I might have been wrong in a lot of things I did; but you were wrong, too. I wanted *you.*" I stood up and lifted my suitcase by the handle, "I have to go inside. I guess we'll see each other again some time." I couldn't force a smile because I was trying so hard not to cry.

He stood, "Are you sure we should? If all I'm doing is hurting you, I can stay away."

"Stop thinking I'm so fragile."

"Aren't you?"

"No." I switched the suitcase to my other hand. "I'm just naive, uneducated, green, and seemingly benighted which are all words I can now write despite having never held a pen before January. I have learned so much in three months. I'm not always going to be your backwoods and ignorant abused girl. It is entirely possible that you are the one who doesn't know the person you've been kissing. Fragile? No, I'd be dead if I were fragile."

He stepped toward me, "I didn't mean to— "

"Forget it," I waved my hand through the air and walked inside. "I won't stop loving you just because you're so nescient."

I stepped through the doorway and caught sight of his stunned expression as I closed the door between us. I leaned against it, feeling like I had ruined everything, again.

67

March 17, 2007

When I opened my eyes, I wasn't sure where I was. Waking disoriented was my morning routine, no matter where. Even after living with the Matthews for three months, I still felt lost every single morning. I rolled over and looked out the window, remembering I had chosen that bed. The window was the feature I loved most about that room. The loft bed had been built against a wide window allowing me to lie in bed and look out it as if nothing but the wilderness existed. The room was in the very top of the house, so looking out had me eye-level with the tops of nearby trees. The sounds of birds, so many birds, became more clear as I listened closely for each distinct sound. I wanted to get up, get dressed, and run out among the trees. Yet, I didn't really want to be out where I'd have to talk to anyone.

"Angelina? Are you awake now?" Heather whispered from the doorway.

"Yes," I didn't turn around.

"Jute is here to take Gabe exploring in the woods. They're going to look for a few different things... nature stuff, I don't know. She would like you to come, too. Should I tell her to wait?"

I really wanted to say no and I really wanted to say yes. "I don't know."

Heather climbed up the ladder to my bed. There was no room for her to sit with me, so she stood on the highest possible rung. "What's wrong?"

"I just don't feel like seeing anyone today."

"Oh," She thought for a moment. "It's just Jute and Gabe. They'll be so busy looking for bugs and fungi," she shivered dramatically, "they probably won't even pay any attention to you. You can just hang back a little and enjoy the woods. Come on, get up." She smiled and climbed down. "I'll tell her you're coming. Don't forget to brush your teeth so you don't have stink mouth."

I heard Gabe in another room, "I already brushed mine!"

"Not you, Gabe, your sister."

Sister indeed. Exploring the woods with Gabe began to sound like fun. I assumed there would be little chance of me running into John out there. I still wasn't sure what I could do to make things right between us.

I dressed quickly in jeans and an olive green t-shirt. I brought my jacket down just in case there was a chill. I went into the bathroom and looked at myself in the mirror as I brushed my hair and teeth. That was another new thing I struggled to mentally process, seeing myself so hyper-washed and cleansed, hair styled and sprayed, and wearing decent clothes. I had to admit that I liked how I looked much better than before. I smelled better, too, most of the time. But, Heather had accepted there were times I didn't want to bathe because I occasionally had flashbacks of Silas telling me to cleanse myself . I never knew when they would happen. Some nights I just didn't feel able to handle it.

I smoothed rosy lip gloss over my lips and rubbed them together. I had other new make-up, too, but I wasn't exactly sure how to use it all.

Jute sat with Gabe on a couch made of cut tree branches, very shiny tree branches. Everything in the house was wood, but it glistened with a sheen of glaze. I theorized it was a protectant, but it made the wood look plastic. I slid on my brown boots and began to pull the laces tight. They were men's boots because I couldn't find any sturdy boots in the women's department.

"I love those!" Jute said, leaning forward. "Heather said you picked out a few things at the mall yesterday. Those will be perfect for exploring the woods."

"What are we going to look for?" I asked, feeling excited now that I was dressed and ready to go.

"Well, the main goal is to teach Gabe how to identify some of the trees before their leaves come on. But if I find any cottonwood trees, I might bring back some buds."

"For salve?" I asked, excited to be able to contribute to a conversation for once.

"I thought I might make lip balm for the ladies at the shelter. Little things mean a lot." She looked like she missed being with them. "Well," Jute slapped her legs and stood up, "Let's go kids. We'll talk more once we're in the woods. We want to get out and back before lunch."

I didn't talk, really. I was still worried I'd say something wrong. I listened intently, though, and soon relaxed as Jute began pointing out plants. She could identify a plant by a single leaf pushing up through the dead tree leaves on the forest floor. She pointed out trees with pink tipped branches covered in newly formed buds, and an occasional bird. She explained tree identifying clues like color, bark thickness, and patterns. I found it interesting, but not nearly as much as Gabe did. His eyes followed the direction of her pointed finger as he nodded with understanding and enthusiasm.

Gabe had been very attentive to everything outside his body that day, but he often seemed to forget where his body existed within that space. He had misstepped a number of times and aimed poorly when he swatted away branches over the trail. He had a few scratches on his arms and face to show for it. So when we eventually found ourselves along a high cliff looking down over a valley, Jute immediately took Gabe's hand. It was no place to bring an accident prone, lanky teenager with sensory differences.

"Let's go ahead and turn back," she said. "We've filled three bags with goodies." Her voice held all the overdone excitement of an adult speaking to a toddler. "You can show Heather the sweet gum seed pods we found."

I said, "I'm going to stay here for a while." I wanted to look out at the view and enjoy the solitude.

Jute gave me a worried look then glanced out over the horizon. "It's beautiful," she said with a forced a smile. "I'll come right back to make sure you can find your way home."

"I can find my way."

"I'll come," She insisted, glancing again out beyond the edge of the cliff. "Don't get too close to the edge."

I sat on a rock and let my legs hang down. It wasn't as steep as it seemed. Just ten feet or so below me there was a flat protrusion of rock, ready to catch anything, or anyone, falling from my seat. I picked up tiny rocks and twigs and tossed them down as I strained my eyes to look farther out over forever.

68

Jute came back like she promised, this time alone. She smiled so widely when she saw me that it must have hurt her face. Her eyes teared up, too.

"There you are," she said breathlessly. It was a strange thing to say because I was still sitting right where she'd left me. She handed me a thermos. "I brought you some tea. Oh, and Heather had already made lunch, so she sent you a meatloaf sandwich." She pulled a brown paper bag out of her backpack and held it out, waiting for me to finish swallowing a drink of tea before I could take it.

"Thank you," I felt my stomach tighten with nervousness at the thought of us talking. I didn't know what to say. I was glad for the sandwich; eating gave me an excuse to say nothing.

"Did you know I met your mother in the woods?" She stood looking out over the valley.

It took me a moment to figure out she meant Allie, not Esther or Heather. "No, I didn't know that," I said, which was what I said about almost everything.

"Yeah. Mom married this... man... and moved us all, my sister Drew and me, in with him. Right off the bat he started abusing us. Not even twenty minutes went by before he'd destroyed my sister's toy which she had had since she was a baby. He told her it was time for her to start acting like a woman."

Jute didn't look at me for a response. I knew she was telling me that story because it was relevant to my life. I had already heard some of it the night she had been talking with Marcy. It made me sad for her, but it also brought up memories of what

Silas had done to me.

She continued, "I met Allie that night. I was supposed to be grounded, but I sneaked out and walked through the woods not knowing where I was going. I had no idea there was even a house up there. She happened to be outside in the dark, chasing down her dog to make him stop barking. She was so beautiful under the moonlight. I didn't know I loved her because I didn't know what love was; but looking back now I'm sure I did. I loved her from the minute I saw her."

"Do you believe it was fate?" I hated to bring up that word again, but I still often wondered how much of what happened to me was destiny.

Jute sighed and shook her head. "I can't believe that. If I believe there was some divine plan to bring her into my life, I'd have to believe there was a divine plan to take her out of it. There was nothing," her hand dramatically sliced the air, "absolutely nothing divine about Allie's death."

"But what if your mom didn't marry that man? You'd never have met my mother. And how did she end up out in those woods at the exact same time you were there? It just seems like fate played a part."

"If Momma hadn't married Earl, I'd not be nearly as screwed up in the head," she laughed a little and took a seat beside me. "Things would have surely been different, but I can't say if they would have been better or worse. Good things and bad things come in and out of our lives, always."

"But she was your one true love," I searched her face, trying to understand how she could deny that fate brought Allie into her life. Because of their love, Allie wrote a letter, and that letter had saved me from Silas. All of it fit together like a perfect grand plan. How could Jute not see that?

"She was my true love, yes. She was exactly what I needed and wanted without knowing I needed or wanted it. She was an amazing person, beautiful, kind, selfless to a flaw. I loved her more than I will ever love anyone. But all of that is true because of the choices she and I made along the way, how we chose to treat each other and see the world around us. So many little things built up what we eventually shared, like twigs in a nest. I hate to say this because hindsight makes it feel like blasphemy, but there is a chance I could have loved someone else just as much as I had loved her. I certainly couldn't now that I've known her and made a home for in my heart. But before that, there were probably other options."

"That just sounds so wrong, Jute. Let me ask you, what if Allie hadn't written to you? I would have never been saved. You just don't know how much reading her letter changed how I felt inside, gave me strength to fight. Without it, I would have never known to find you. And if Emory hadn't been there, how would I have gotten to you? I knew nothing about Tennessee or anywhere other than the mountainside where I grew up."

"Well, first, I'm glad you found the letter. I'm glad she wrote it. I'm glad everything worked out so you could escape and get it to me and find peace for yourself and offer me closure. ALL of those things I am so, so thankful for. But I don't look at you and see a girl unwilling to fight. The letter might have ignited something, but the ability to be lit up was already yours. If you think about it, you can probably see there were a lot of twigs you used to build up this nest." She smiled and took my hand. "My life is better because you came to us. I hope yours is better, too. But life can take many twists and turns and still come out okay in the end. I guess what I'm telling you, Angelina, is that life isn't planned out ahead of time. Tomorrow isn't set in stone. There is no fate waiting on you to be ready for things. Life just dances about, whirling, twisting, jutting, and throwing its arms around. Sometimes it even falls on its face. But none of it is planned or synchronized between us all like a movie on a screen. That means you'll have to step up and try to take a little control over what moves your life makes. You can't just sit back and watch it dance. I believe in the power of our choices. I don't believe in fate."

"But I never had a choice about anything." Frustration began building inside me again.

"You have plenty of choices now, more than most. You'll need to start tackling a few and figuring out what you want. You can run some ideas past me if you think talking about it will help."

Apprehensively, I said, "Well, I do often think about who I am, I mean, who I really am. I know I'm not the person I was on the mountain, but what will take her place?"

"Oh, you are still that girl on the mountain. Why do you want to shed her off like an old skin? She was strong, beautiful, pure hearted, and kind. She knew important things about surviving and hard work. You need her, and she was absolutely you, Angelina. Be proud of her. Don't define her by all the terrible things that happened to her."

"But I'm nothing like her now." I shivered.

"You are that girl, only now you're set free!" Jute stood and spread her arms out as if attempting to hug the horizon. "You survived a hard lesson in learning to walk on your own two feet. But now you're ready to learn to fly." She waved in a motion for me to stand with her. I looked terrified. She laughed and said, "Not really fly! I'm not going to throw you off the cliff. Just stand with me and feel the breeze, look at the beauty around you, and proclaim what it is you want to make happen next in your life."

"I don't know. Maybe get married and start a family of my own."

"No!" She screamed at me and stomped her foot before smiling and laughing, "Oh, heavenly day! You are sixteen. No! No! No! Boys smell bad and they're really, really no good at picking up their dirty clothes out of the floor. That's a horrible dream for a young girl. This may be the only time in your life when you can do fun things for no other reason than because they're fun. You don't have to work. You don't have to please anyone else, other than minding the Matthews, of course. You don't have to decide right now what forever will look like. This freedom you have now will kind of go away once you get a job or make yourself part of a team like a marriage. Don't squander it. Just have fun and make up for all the years you lost!"

"I don't even know where to start."

"Okay, so name three of your favorite things." She noticed my skeptical look. "It can be anything at all."

"Well, I like Carl Sagan a lot. I like plants and gardening. And... I guess the third would be..." I thought about John and my face burned. I shook my head that I couldn't answer.

"Hey, two favorite things is a start and those are both awesome. I had no idea you were so nerdy and earthy all rolled into one," she winked at me. "I mean that in the best way possible. Brainy people with big hearts can do amazing things for the world. So, you want to learn more about Earth and the Universe?"

"Yes! I've been reading Carl Sagan's books. But I have to stop often to research things to even know what he's talking about. I feel so behind."

"Don't think of it that way. It's actually a strength to recognize how much you don't know. Most people think they already have all the answers so they stop searching." She took my hand, "Don't put yourself down. Look at all these trees with their naked, twiggy branches. They're on the verge of completely transforming in just a matter of days. You'll be like that very soon, showing off all you've gained. I look forward to seeing you grow." She hugged me tightly and leaned her head against my hair. "Your mother would have been so proud of you."

69

March 20, 2007

I locked myself away in the guest house for the next couple of days. Even though my day out with Jute had been fun, I didn't feel ready to see anyone else, especially not John. After our conversation on the swing, I realized things between us had changed and not in the way I had hoped. He was still hurt over what happened on the island, and still believed I didn't know who he was. I wanted to make everything okay, but I was sure I could only make things worse. Until I figured out a plan, I didn't want to be around him and risk hurting him more.

The Matthews were worried by my refusal to leave the guest house. They didn't force me to participate in their outings, but they always left with an air of defeat. When they had gone to explore caverns on Sunday, I stayed home and researched local things to do with no intentions of actually doing any of it.

On Monday they slept in and then went over to the big house that night for dinner. I spent most of that time in my bed, wearing the same pajamas I'd worn for two days. I read magazines, finished the last five chapters of Harry Potter and the Half-Blood Prince, and searched the Internet for pictures of cute guys to place in my "Boys" folder. It was admittedly not my usual academic research; but I reasoned that I really needed to understand what to do about John. The best way to find something out was to research it.

When I wasn't hoarding images of brown eyed heartthrobs, I continued my desperate attempt to define myself. I had created a folder on my laptop labeled "Angelina" and stored images of things I liked, things that spoke to me for obvious and not so obvious reasons. I did a similar thing with the magazines, folding corners, reading and rereading articles about hygiene and etiquette. Yet I never actually went anywhere to practice.

What I really wanted was to stop trying at all and run off through the woods until my legs would no longer hold me up. What I wanted was to be completely alone in nature where it wouldn't matter if I didn't know what to do with myself. I wanted to look at the world with an invisible eye. I wanted to look through a telescope and see the stars, look through a microscope and see my DNA, but I didn't want to look in a mirror. Despite how it appeared to my new family, there really were things I craved to do. But I wouldn't let myself do anything until I had picked a me to become, one I could feel at home with. I was terrified about starting school in just a few months and being around normal kids. I didn't want to feel lost and confused about them *and* myself.

Around noon, Heather walked in, "Okay, girl. Enough of this. Get yourself in the shower before you start molding."

I sat up on my bed and saved the last image I had opened up; then I shut down the computer. "I do stink, don't I?" I smiled, not because I felt happy, but because I appreciating how lenient she had been with me the last few days. We were supposed to be on this vacation together, but I hadn't been cooperating. "Do you think it would be okay if I had my hair cut?"

Heather's face lit up with surprise. "Sure! Get ready and I'll take you into town. Gabe is with Dawson. They're preparing a *Grand Feast* for us all. Gabe gets so excited about cooking with Dawson. So while he's doing that, we can have some girl time." She clapped excitedly, "We'll get our nails done, too."

We were gone all afternoon. Heather assured me, when I had shown her the photograph, that the hairstyle would look good on me. She was even more enthusiastic after it was cut and styled. She couldn't stop gushing with compliments. It was definitely different, springy brown curls framed my face to my chin. It was shorter in the back, yet long enough to bounce. Heather had even allowed me to have pink highlights put on a few strands near the front. Instead of the color pink I had chosen, they ended up nearly red like beet juice. I liked it a lot, even better than I had expected.

The salon offered facials and Heather had insisted we have one, followed by a manicure and pedicure. I felt self-conscious about my hands, still rough and forever scarred. Heather's hands were pale and looked much younger than mine even though she was twice my age. Still, the manicurist made great improvements. I chose a pale pink color for my nails and opted for miniature white and yellow roses on the tips. She did the same for my toenails. I was mesmerized by how effortlessly she made the tiniest swirls and ended up with perfect roses.

On the drive back to the house, Heather said, "Wow, a few days ago you wanted to shop for clothes and now the hair and nails! Do you feel like a new girl?"

"Sort of," I shrugged, not wanting to admit just how different I felt. It wasn't so much about my appearance as it was an internal powerfulness. I had chosen to look the way I did and I felt confident that I could do it again. It was very liberating, and not nearly as scary as I had anticipated.

Heather sounded giddy, "I hope no one's outside when we drive by. I want them to be surprised when they see you tonight. It will be like your belated Sweet Sixteen celebration. Maybe we should stop and get balloons and a cake."

I laughed, "Does everyone celebrate as much as this family?"

"We're lucky," she quickly smiled at me, then looked back to the road, "I know we're able to do more than most. Life is unpredictable. I don't take it for granted."

"I'm glad I ended up with you and Casey."

"We're glad, too. You and your brother have been real blessings to us, as well as to the Durens. They love you kids a lot."

I thought about what that meant, and all the ways a person can love another. Jute worried about us. Dawson and Tracy went out of their way to share wonderful experiences with us. I had never dreamed I'd ever be treated as well as they all had treated me over the last three months. I was fortunate beyond belief to have them in my life. But there was one specific Duren nagging at my brain. I asked Heather, "How do you think John feels about me?"

"John, huh?" She smiled, "Well, he sure was worried about you after you left the island."

I felt sick to my stomach just thinking about that night. "I ruined his birthday."

"Well, he missed you, that's for sure. But, he wanted you to get better. I think he cares for you a lot."

"What makes you think so?"

"He's asked where you were every day since we got here. I think he would really like it if you took a moment to talk to him." She smiled reassuringly.

"But until this weekend, I hadn't seen him in almost three months. I don't even think he wants to see me or he would have tried harder."

Heather chose her words carefully. "I think I might have had something to do with that. After they got back from the island, I went to have a talk with the Durens, specifically John. I asked him to give you time, some space, to not come around for a while until you got well."

"So you confirmed to him that I'm broken?" I knew I was, but I desperately wanted not to be seen that way.

"He's probably the least likely, of all the people you know, to think of you as broken. I just wanted him to understand some of the effects of childhood sexual abuse and be able to separate out which parts were you, Angelina, and which parts were because of the pain you had gone through. I was worried he wouldn't understand because he's so young, but he surprised me. He really does care for you or he wouldn't have agreed to stay away and give you time. Now, here he is still letting you have that space. He could have been at our door every morning, but he wasn't; not because he's disinterested, but because he wants you to be well."

361

"I'm so ashamed. I was kind of mean to him for insinuating I was fragile. Perhaps he believed that because of what you told him. I don't know if I can go tonight. I keep saying the wrong things."

"Please go!" She took her eyes off the road to give me a pleading look then quickly returned her attention to driving. "There is nothing for you to feel ashamed about. They aren't strangers. They all know your story. And besides, if you want them to see who you really are, you need to go and show off a little. You look beautiful, so much better than when you were wearing the same old pajamas for a week straight. You also smell better." She leaned over and sniffed dramatically in my direction.

I gently slapped her arm and caught myself just before I called her 'Mom'. It wasn't the first time I had nearly misspoken that way. I wanted a mother almost as much as I wanted a self. But, Heather wasn't officially my mother yet. I could be taken away from the Matthews at any moment if the courts deemed it appropriate. I couldn't imagine a reason why that would happen, but lots of things had happened that I would never have predicted.

"So, are you going to go?" She brought up the question again just as we turned onto the long driveway leading to the houses.

"I still haven't decided." I looked out the window and noticed a few redbud trees had begun to bloom.

"What if I told you John has a surprise for you? He's kept it at his table every night. Don't disappoint him again." She looked at me with an exaggerated frown.

I sighed and changed the subject, sort of. "How old were you when you had your first boyfriend?"

"That depends on if you mean a serious boyfriend or Timmy in first grade. And if you mean serious boyfriend, do you mean we were both serious or just me?" She saw the confused look on my face and laughed. "Sorry, sweetie, but love is complicated and usually takes a while to get right. But, to answer your question, I had a boyfriend when I was eleven. My mom would drive us to see a movie every Saturday. Then his mom would pick us up and take us for ice cream before she drove me home. It was nice, but then I fell in love with my friend Vivian's older brother. That was a mess. After I finally got out of that situation, I was fourteen and started dating a boy named Rob and we got pretty serious. I'd say he was the first almost-like-grown-ups, mutual-affection kind of relationship I had with a boy."

"What is the difference between 'almost-like-grown-ups' and 'grown-up' relationships?"

"Boy, that's a loaded question." She thought for a moment. "Generally speaking, the almost-like-grown-ups relationships are more intense. They take you higher and crash you to the ground harder. They can do that because there's nothing much else to think about when you're young. First loves are very hard to get over once it ends. And a word to the wise for you specifically, Angelina, you know you are especially susceptible to going too far, too fast. Be mindful of that and keep it slow so you don't fall so hard, if you do."

Her mention of me falling made me blush and sweat. I looked back out the window and tried to think about trees again, but I couldn't. All I could think of was John's kisses.

70

Heather gave me a final head to toe look of approval before she and Casey turned to walk out the door. "Don't wait too long," she said. "Food will be cold if you're not there by seven."

Casey leaned down and whispered to Heather, "I still don't understand why she's not riding with us."

She touched his arm, "She's making a late entrance." She winked at me as they left.

I waited thirty minutes before leaving. I sat on the couch, opening and refolding the note I had written to John. It seemed silly, but I had read about it in a magazine. Apparently every girl alive had written a similar note to a boy when they had a crush on him. It had felt like the perfect thing for tonight. But then I started to have doubts about it. I sighed and shoved it into my tiny silver purse.

I changed shoes at the last minute for fear of falling in the heels I had been wearing. I slipped on pink flats which matched the pink in the scalloped tulle skirt of my dress. It was the fanciest dress I had ever owned, sort of like the prom dresses I'd seen, only much shorter. The layers of sheer pink and yellow gave it a primrose color. A shimmering silver glitter belt set off the skirt from the pink bustier top. I was able to wear the bustier style and still have my back covered to hide my scars by adding a cropped pink sweater. In the mall, I had asked Heather if she thought it was too much. She said it was perfect, much more age appropriate than the vintage styles I'd been wearing. She insisted on buying a silver hair clip and purse to go with it. At the time, I had no idea where I would wear the outfit. But she had said, "You wear it whenever you want to wear it. We're buying it because of how you'll feel in it and that's all that matters."

Just before leaving the guest house, I put on the necklace John had given me. It felt heavy, but not overly so. It was comforting to know I would feel it there against my skin, even if I didn't raise my hand to check for it.

The night air was unseasonably warm for March in the mountains. The occasional breeze held only a slight nip of coolness. I walked fast due to nervousness. A song I'd heard earlier on the radio played over and over in my head, something about "here comes the sun" and "it's alright". Gabe had said it was by the Beatles. I thought that was a really strange name for a band. I hummed along to the parts I remembered and it calmed me a little.

I felt like I was going to meet everyone for the very first time. Sure, they all cared about me already so I shouldn't have been so worried, but I was. Now that I had chosen everything about myself and couldn't *be* my upbringing, the opinions of others held even more weight. This wasn't Silas's abused child walking to dinner. This was Angelina soon-to-be-Matthews, herself.

As Heather had suggested, I let myself in. She knew I was reluctant, so she convinced me to come late and just stand back and watch for a while. She said to join them whenever I felt ready. If not for her plan, I'd have likely stayed in my bed, afraid to be seen.

The lights were off in the foyer and living room. I quietly stepped over to the shadows by the door which led into the dining hall. Five round tables were spread about the room with a service bar along the wall. The only light was emitted from candles placed on each table and along the bar. John sat at a table by himself, intently looking at his phone, flicking his fingers this way and that, obviously playing a game. Iris and Emory sat at another table by themselves. The Matthews sat with Jute and Marcy, whom I was pleasantly surprised to see. Closest to the windows sat Tracy, Dawson, and Gabe. Everyone's plate had food heaped high so I assumed they had just sat down to eat.

The low lighting helped me feel more comfortable. I wondered if that had been Heather's idea. It probably wasn't; she had arrived only a few minutes before I had. I took a deep breath, trying to steady my nerves, and watched the reflection of John's screen light up his face. He seemed so calm, but also lonely. I had nearly convinced myself to go sit beside him when I saw Emory scoot his chair back and stand. He bent (I assumed) to tell Iris where he was going. He started walking in my direction. I stepped deeper into the shadow and pressed my back straight against the wall of the living room and hoped he'd pass without seeing me.

He took three steps past me and swiveled around in alarm. "Oh, my God!" He whispered. "Angelina you scared the shit out of me." Then he stepped closer and looked me over from head to toe. "You look incredible!"

"Shh!" I put my finger up to my lips.

"Why aren't you in there?" He poked his thumb toward the dining hall.

"I'm not ready." Speaking made me feel even more sick to my stomach.

"Ah, I completely understand," he slid his hand into the inside pocket of his corduroy blazer and pulled out a small silver box. He opened it and showed me the ring inside it. "I'm about to vomit, I swear. Do you think she'll like it?"

"It's beautiful!" I took the box and lifted out the ring, turning it so the clear jewels sparkled in the dim candle light.

"It's a secret," he whispered and snatched it away from me, quickly putting it back in his pocket. I had never seen him so nervous. "I feel like I'm out of my league with her, you know. She's so gorgeous, my God! Look at her." He peeked back around the edge of the doorway and shook his head in amazement.

"I've seen how she looks at you," I offered. "She really likes you."

Emory exhaled, "I hope so. I might just fall down and die if she says no. But I don't want to regret not telling her how I feel." He looked at me again as if he just realized I was there. "So, what

366

has you so standoffish? I haven't seen you in weeks. It looks like you've been in a cocoon and come out a butterfly. You barely look like the same girl."

I smiled because that was what I had been aiming for, to be a completely different girl with a completely different life. "I feel like a new girl. I just don't know if they'll like this me."

"Hell, Angelina, take a look around. They're not going to judge you on anything superficial like what you look like. Have you forgotten who these people are?"

I leaned over and peered into the room again. I took a moment to glance at each face and think of the conversations I had had with each of them. I thought of all the articles I had read in magazines and all the photos I'd saved from the Internet. I tried to think of a single representation that matched any of the people sitting in the dining hall. None came to mind. They were all so out of the ordinary, extraordinary. An epiphany washed over me. I felt like it was so obvious that I must have known all along, but I really hadn't. I had never fully realized just how special they were, not just to me personally, but as remarkable individuals in a world full of sameness. I had perceived normalcy as the goal when the people I loved most were anything but that.

"No two are alike," I whispered to myself, but Emory heard me. He stepped closer and put his arm around my shoulders.

"I have you to thank for getting me here. I don't know where I'd be if I hadn't met you."

"You're such an amazing guy, Emory, you'd have found a way to this moment even without me."

He leaned over and kissed my forehead and I didn't blush. I didn't feel drawn to kiss him back. I just felt happy for him.

"You know," he said, "John's sitting by himself again. He's been just as holed up as you. You should go over and let him see you're here."

"I'm not sure. He may regret wanting me here."

"Oh, no he won't," Emory slid his hand to my back and gave me a gentle push. I nearly stumbled over my own foot. I glanced back to glare at him, but he had already walked away. I turned back to the room and saw everyone's eyes on me. Jute began to clap. Dawson whistled. I felt myself blush as everyone stood up and applauded, everyone except John.

71

I gave them a bow, feeling embarrassed and grateful for the dim lighting. I quickly walked over and sat in the chair beside John which put my back to everyone else. I was thoroughly flustered by the attention.

John pushed the button to turn off his phone screen and sat up straight in his chair, leaning slightly away from me. I started to doubt my decision to sit near him. I certainly didn't want to upset him. I tried to read his thoughts. His dark eyes still held a wildness and worry. He glanced into my eyes briefly before scanning my face, my hair, the sparkling silver hair clip, then down to linger on the necklace he had given me. When his eyes moved back to mine, they held a new intensity that wasn't there at first. His eyes were asking questions I couldn't decipher. I was afraid the necklace was making him think of the island and how I left it.

"I think you're in the wrong section," he said, "This is the nescient only table."

My own words had come back to haunt me. "You aren't nescient. I'm just an ass, a jerk, a meany, and a little shit."

He laughed, "Don't forget 'a freakishly alluring, tyrannical beast of a ravager'. I mean look at you…"

I laughed, but it was a nervous laughter because he looked at me so warily.

"Are you hungry?" He asked, changing the subject. "I'll get your food if you wish, madam. You can just hide here at the command post." He winked. "It seems you don't much like the stares."

"I recall someone else making a similar complaint not too long ago," I teased.

"Oh, that was a very long time ago, days and days. Where have you been, anyway?"

"Lying in bed, hiding from the world, wearing stinky pajamas, browsing the Internet, saving pictures of cute boys to my 'cute boy' desktop file."

His smile fell into a straight line. "Right. Well, I'll be right back." He stood up and walked over to the bar where a buffet of food was spread from one end to the other.

While John was gone, I slipped the note from my purse and set it beside his plate. He came back and put a full plate of food in front of me then walked off again. Seeing and smelling all that food made me feel hungry, but there was more food on my plate than I could ever eat. I poked a fork into some red skin potato salad with bacon and tasted my first bite. It was full of unexpected and delicious flavors. I hoped Gabe had learned the recipe so he could do it again at home. I was chewing my last bite of it when John came back and placed a tall glass of bubbly liquid beside my plate.

"Is that legal?" I asked.

He slid into his chair beside me with an identical glass in his hand, "Dads don't care. It's just one glass and we'll sip it slow... with our food, you know." When he set his glass down, he saw the note. "What's this?"

I blushed, not wanting to watch him open it. I stared at my plate and held my breath as I listened to the paper unfolding. In my peripheral vision, I saw him hold it closer to the candle to read it. He immediately laughed out loud, throwing his head back, then he bit his lip and snickered. I wanted to run away, but I didn't want to stand and have people stare at me again. John's laughter had probably already drawn everyone's attention.

As I sat there brooding, John got up and walked out of the room, returning not even two minutes later. He sat down and bent over my note, a pen in his hand. He wrote something, folded up the note, and handed it back to me. I took it cautiously, looking for a clue in his eyes. They sparkled with amusement.

I carefully unfolded the note, held it close to the candle and read over what I had written earlier.

Will you be my boyfriend? Circle yes or no.

John had written the word *maybe* and circled it.

I looked up in confusion and got caught up in the desire in his eyes. He wasn't laughing anymore.

"That was silly of me, wasn't it?" I asked.

"Yes," he pushed a curl away from my temple. "But I liked it. I have something for you, too. But you have to come to my room to get it. We'll go after you eat. Try the catfish and tell me what you think. Dad and I caught that today."

I wondered what he had in his room, thought about what I hoped would happen there, and decided I had best stop thinking about it. I took a bite of catfish and nodded my approval. Everything on my plate was delicious, but Dawson's food was always remarkable. "You're so lucky," I said about having Dawson as a Dad, but it applied universally. John was so lucky about everything.

He swallowed a drink, "It certainly is looking that way."

I took a sip of mine, too. The tiny bubbles fizzed in my nose as I inhaled the slightly fruity scent.

He continued, "Now if I can just keep you from breaking my heart." He downed the rest of his drink and set the glass on the table. "Ready?"

He offered me his elbow. I held his arm and felt his muscle flex. I wondered if he was trying to impress me. We left the room without the fanfare I had received earlier. But I felt certain they must have noticed.

John was staying in the only room in the tower closest to the guest house. He walked directly to the bed and sat, patted a spot for me to sit beside him. I was afraid if I moved I would fall down from shaking so much. He reached for my hand and pulled me to come closer and sit. I was convinced he was going to do exactly what I had hoped. As soon as I sat down, I leaned toward him and kissed him, sliding my fingers into his hair.

He sighed and leaned away from me. He said, "I thought you said you wouldn't put me in this situation again." But I wanted him too much to care. I leaned closer, pushing him back onto the bed. I had wanted to be with him for so long. I pulled at his shirt until it came untucked and felt the tight rippling muscles over his stomach. He was saying something between his sighs which I couldn't hear and didn't want to hear. I pulled at the buckle of his belt, wanting to make months worth of fantasies come true. I wanted to touch him, memorize him, taste him, and everything I knew to do to him.

I was completely taken by surprise when he grunted and pushed me away. "That's not why I brought you up here." He stood to tuck his shirt back into his pants and fastened his belt.

I sat up and stared at his body unapologetically, still wanting him, until my gaze reached his eyes. His worried expression made me want to hide, but all I could do was turn my head away and feel foolish.

He got on his knees and reached under the bed. He said "I have been wanting to give you this for a long time."

He pulled out a gift wrapped in a shiny metallic blue paper. I held it, still feeling the sting of his rejection. I felt undeserving of whatever was inside and I was reluctant to damage the beautiful paper.

"If you don't open it, I'll do it for you." He snagged a corner with his thumb and started ripping the paper. I dug in, too, a hint of excitement replacing my gloom. In seconds I held a black leather book in my hands. It was large and flat, and held many blank pages inside. I was confused.

"It's a scrapbook album. You put pictures in it to record your adventures, and not the kind you find on the Internet. Real ones."

My excitement faded. I had no photos.

John sat beside me and pressed the tip of his finger to my lips for me not to speak. "I know that look. You're thinking I'm being insensitive because I should know you don't have any photos. Well, I'm not insensitive."

He went to his nightstand and picked up a leather bag from

the floor beside it. He set the bag beside me and unzipped it. Once opened, it revealed a camera and lenses. He said, "Dad bought me a new camera. This is my old one. I'm giving it to my girlfriend."

He had a girlfriend? I then realizing why he had rejected me. Three months had been too long for him to wait and he had moved on. He was just being nice to me, like a friend.

Before my mouth had time to make the puckered pout it was moving toward, John laughed and pulled me up to hug me. "I don't have a girlfriend," he explained. "But I might have one if you will agree to my conditions."

I felt a mix of rage and comfort at the thought of John making rules for me. I almost preferred to think he had found someone else as opposed to making me jump through hoops. Sure, following rules was something I was good at and I wouldn't have to figure out what to do on my own. But I didn't want someone else making the rules for me anymore. I stepped back away from him so I could look into his eyes. I crossed my arms, "What *conditions*?"

"Before we do anything sexual, you have to fill up all forty pages of the scrapbook with photos you take with this camera. You can't cheat, so you can only fill up a maximum of two pages per event. When the scrapbook is full, I'll say yes to whatever you ask." He stepped closer and kissed the side of my head through my hair, breathing in the scent of it. "Whatever you want, anything you want, everything you want." With his hands on my hips, he pulled me against him and sighed, reluctant to let go. When he stepped back away from me, he made his voice sound formal and dry, "Do you accept the terms of my offer?"

He looked so cute standing there with his eyes pleading innocently like he hadn't just been seductively pressing himself against me. I wanted to take the camera from the bag and snap a photo of him, but I had no idea how to use it.

"Well," I pretended to be seriously thinking it over, "You would have to agree to show me how to use the camera. And when you say 'event', do you mean like… one page for when I brush my teeth, and one page for when I eat breakfast?"

His smirk dropped to a look of disbelief. "No! It has to be big things, things you've never done before."

I giggled because he fit that description pretty well. I could just fill up every page with photos of him.

As if reading my mind, he clarified, "And nothing sexual."

"I was just kidding!" I laughed.

"You need to stay off the Internet," he insisted.

"I can't. I need to research places to go and where to have 'events'." I winked at him. "But I really have no idea how to use that thing."

"Well, let's go for a walk and try it out."

"Will this walk count as an 'event'?"

"Oh, I think it might," He sounded like he had something up his sleeve.

72

"There's a bald at the top of the ridge. I'm going back to the dining room to tell Dads where we're going."

"Can you tell the Matthews, too? I should go back to the guest house and change my shoes. Will you wait for me?"

"Yes, but not forever. Don't change your mind and hide in your room without officially telling me to fuck off."

"I would never..." I smiled. But he looked like he doubted me.

I ran back to the guest house for my boots. I also pulled the blanket from my bed, the one I'd brought from Tennessee, and quickly folded it around my arms. I was full of anticipation and a happiness I had never felt before.

As I approached the big house, I saw John standing near the woods. He was smiling with his arms held open. The camera bag strap was slung over his head to his shoulder, resting diagonally across his chest. A tall glass was held in each hand. The one in his right was empty. He stood there like that the entire time it . took me to get to him.

When I reached him, I stepped into his arms and they wrapped around me. He said, "I brought you a drink."

I said, "I shouldn't drink it. Supposedly, I am susceptible to substance abuse."

"I guess you really do research more than just *cute boys*, huh?" He stepped back and took a few swallows from the drink I had just refused.

I asked, "How much of that have you had, exactly?"

He shook his head without answering and took a last drink before setting the glasses on the ground just off the path. He walked ahead onto the trail and I followed. We navigated the steep and rocky trail with only the light from a tiny key chain flashlight. We were so focused on our foot placement that we didn't even speak, other than John pointing out certain protruding rocks or tree roots. We managed to get to the top in only twenty minutes.

Once we entered the grassy bald, my heart sang at the sight of the view. With the new moon cloaked in black and no light polluting the sky, there were more stars twinkling above me than I had ever seen. I found myself walking in a tight circle with my head tilted back, trying to take it all in.

John set the camera bag in the grass while I spun in an awestruck circle. Before I knew it, he wrapped his arms around me and lifted me up off my feet. I looked down at him, surprised. He said, "Don't look at me, look up."

I did. I looked up at the sky and John began to spin me around. I couldn't focus on anything, but it was thrilling, even when I started to feel dizzy and my head began to wobble. About the time I had to close my eyes, John lost his footing and fell. I put my hands out to catch myself, but was too disoriented to know where to aim them. John landed on his side and I landed draped over him. "Damn," he groaned, then laughed.

With my head still spinning, I slid off him carefully to lie beside him. I looked over to see him smiling up the sky. I asked, "Are you drunk, John?"

"Not at all." He pointed upward. "Just look at that!"

I did. My head still felt like it was spinning, the sky seemed to move and jerk, slowly settling back to normal as my brain oriented itself. I had the blanket hugged to my chest and thought we should get up and spread it out, but I didn't want to move.

He said, "I've never seen so many stars!"

"Neither have I. There are over a hundred million in the Milky Way Galaxy alone. I'd say there must be a thousand visible tonight, which is relatively a small number, but wow they are beautiful!"

He sat up and looked down at me, still suspiciously happy. "A hundred million? Since when did you become such a nerd?"

"I've always liked quantifying things, if that's what you mean. I just wasn't allowed to do it because it might send me to Hell."

"Because you're just a stupid ol' girl." He pulled the blanket from my arms and stood to unfurl it. After briefly blocking my view of the sky, it settled to the ground. He sat down toward the edge of it to leave room for me. I made my way to him by rolling, holding my necklace to my chest. John found that amusing. "You're going to ruin your dress."

I hadn't even been thinking about that. "Oh!" I sat up on my knees and straightened it out, picked a few blades of dead grass from the tulle.

John laughed again and reached out to knock a few leaves off the back of the skirt. More than once, his hand grazed the skin of the back of my thigh. I felt it all the way up to the center of my ribcage where my heart beat with frantic anticipation.

"Ugh!" he groaned and fell onto his back. "Hell. No."

I ran my fingers over my hair to check for grass, then sat beside him. "Hell no, what?"

"Hell no, I'm not ruining this. Now lie down and don't touch me... or get something in your eye... or ask me to pick burrs off your skirt."

"I didn't!" I protested, but let myself fall back beside him, making certain not to touch him. "And besides, you were squeezing me and spinning me around. Isn't that touching me?"

"Yes, and quite a horrible mistake."

We settled into silence, looking up at the stars. The longer I looked at them, the farther away they seemed. I thought about Allie, my real mother, and I wanted to feel love for her. But her light was too far away for me to feel anything from it at all. I said, "It's like the stars have been there this whole time, seeing everything that has ever happened to us. I feel sort of lonely looking at them. It's like we used to be up there, shining, and then we fell all the way down here. The universe is expanding, you know. The distance of our fall keeps getting longer, yet our backs are to the ground and we're not moving at all."

I felt his fingers wrap gently around my hand and the electricity of his touch ran up my arm and burst into my heart. I whispered, "You're touching me."

"All this talk of falling," he whispered. We were silent and motionless. I couldn't determine what he was thinking or feeling, but his words lingered in my head, conjuring memories of his touch until I thought my dress would catch fire. His voice pulled me out of my daze, "I don't want to lose you," he said, "I mean... falling has its hazards." I turned my head to see him staring at me.

I said, "First loves are supposed to be the hardest. They're supposed to bring you highest and drop you the lowest, that's what Heather says."

"Then I don't know if we should be boyfriend/girlfriend. I can't stand the thought of you one day thinking of me and how much I hurt you."

"Someone has to."

"Hurt you? No one has to hurt you."

I sat up and looked down at him. "Someone is going to be my first love, John. Someone. If you don't think it should be you, then who?"

He covered his face with his hands and rubbed his eyes with his palms as he groaned in frustration.

I climbed to sit straddling his lap, facing him. I leaned forward to grab his wrists and move his hands from his face. He looked scared. I said, "According to my research about sexual abuse, it is very likely I will either avoid sex or be obsessed with sex. I think you know where I land on that spectrum."

His expression changed into one of both dread and desire. I didn't really want to say what I felt like I needed to say. But we needed to talk about it. He couldn't just make up the rules and expect I would so easily follow them. Finally he said, "But you don't have to be what statistics say you will be."

"But I know how I feel," I leaned down and kissed him gently. He tasted like the champagne. I felt him become aroused.

The weight of my necklace momentarily felt like it had come

loose from my neck. I moved my hand from his wrist to check for it, found it resting on his shirt where I unbuttoned the top button. With his newly freed hand, he pushed my shoulder away until I sat up.

"Just because you feel something doesn't make it a good idea to act on it. I don't want to be with you like this."

"Yes you do," I moved my hips to indicate the proof.

He sat up and pulled away from me, grabbed my arms and spun me around to sit on the blanket between his legs. His arms had crossed mine over my body, holding me tightly so that I couldn't move. "No!" He sounded angry and I remembered the night on the island.

I had promised him I would never put him in that situation again. Yet twice in the last couple of hours, I had forced him to push me away.

"I don't understand how you want to be my boyfriend but you don't want to have sex with me," I cried. "How was what I was doing such a bad thing?"

I tried to pull my wrists free from his grip, but I couldn't. His arms were crossed in front of me and left little room for me to move. He said, "It's not bad, it's just bad timing. I can't let you do this and think for the rest of your life that this is the only way to be a girlfriend. Now stop fighting me and look at the goddamn stars." He laid back on the blanket and raised my hands up over my head so he could still hold them. His legs squeezed my sides to hold me in place. My head rested on his stomach and I could still feel how aroused he was.

"I can feel you," I said as if it proved something.

"Look! Is that Jupiter?" He was attempting to change the subject.

"I think that's Sirius."

"Are you serious?"

"Shut up." I laughed at his horrible joke.

We laid there staring up at the stars, my wrists still firmly held in John's grip. The sky really was beautiful. The feeling of gravity pulling the weight of the necklace to my chest was comforting. It was beautiful, too. I tried to think of something about my life at that very moment which wasn't beautiful. I couldn't think of anything, except maybe a few pieces of myself. I still had work to do. I was obviously pushing all the wrong buttons with John.

I don't know how many minutes had passed before John said, "Do you want to take some photos?"

It was a perfect excuse to get free, but I wasn't sure if I wanted to be. "Not yet," I wiggled my body around as if nestling into a warm bed.

He arched his back to break contact with a particular part of his body and let go of my wrists to push me up. "Alright, we have to start working on that scrapbook because you sure as hell aren't going to make this easy on me."

"Why is that book such a big deal, anyway?"

"Because there's so many amazing things I want you to experience, places I want to take you, things I want to do with you," he eyed me warily, "besides sex."

"Can't we do both?" I moved closer and he scooted back.

"Yes, when you've filled up the book. By then, you'll understand, I promise. And it will be so good," he leaned forward and held my face between his hands, his lips were a nanometer away so that when he spoke his top lip brushed against mine, "better than anything you've seen on the Internet."

I slapped his arm. "Shut up."

Part Eleven

The Scrapbook

73

Spring, 2007

By the time the first photo was snapped, midnight had arrived to welcome the first day of Spring. Angelina stood over John while he snapped a photo of her with the stars lighting up the night sky behind her. The necklace was held in her hand like a captured bird. She finally figured out how to work the camera and snapped a photo of John. She had convinced him, after much effort, to take his shirt off. He was embarrassed, feeling not truly good enough to pose the way she had wanted. But he did it, thankful she was into learning how to use the camera instead of trying to talk him into sex. Not that John didn't want to have sex with her. He really, really wanted to.

Before leaving North Carolina, John put many miles on his Dad's car. He drove Angelina along the Blue Ridge Parkway to spend an entire day skiing near Banner Elk. She was reluctant to learn how to ski and complained that it was difficult. It took most of the day for her to feel confident on her skis. When it was time to leave, she complained about leaving too soon. He stopped on the way home and fed her a slice of pecan pie, literally, with the fork in his hand. He had bought it to share, but after seeing her reaction to the first bite, he decided to just feed her the entire slice.

The next day they went to Backbone Rock in Shady Valley, Tennessee, which was a longer drive. They fished for trout, unsuccessfully, in Beaverdam Creek before climbing up onto Backbone Rock for a photo. John drove her the few miles north to Damascus, Virginia just so she could add another state to her list of those she had visited. They vowed to come back the next day to rent bikes to ride on the Creeper Trail. But it rained that day so they stayed in North Carolina where they went into town for lunch at a Japanese Restaurant. On the way back, they stopped to have their photos printed. John helped her create her first two scrapbook pages using only two photos from the bald, a photo she had snapped from the ski lift, and a photo he had taken of her standing on Backbone Rock. She protested, saying that should be at least three pages.

Angelina's photos had turned out better than either of them had expected. She had taken many of him while he was completely unaware of it. She had taken macro images of spring flowers, the bark of trees, and had even captured a decent image of a blue jay on a redbud branch. When he looked at the photos she had taken, he felt he was seeing the world through her eyes and he wanted to see more.

John thought all of her photos really deserved to be in an album, but filling up the one he had just given her would have defeated its purpose. He went back out that night and bought her two more albums for the extra photos. The next morning he gave them to her, but also suggested she create a photo gallery on the Internet so everyone could see how good they were. He reminded her not to post any images of the friend and family in her life because people might try to use her to get to his dad. He said, "Welcome to the family."

That was their last night in North Carolina. He promised her he would take her somewhere new every Saturday. She kissed him goodbye before he could stop her. She said she looked forward to it. He found himself unable to reply. They drove back to Nashville on a Sunday and John went back to school the following Monday. Nothing seemed the same. Everything around him was viewed through the thought of Angelina going to school with him in only a few months. He walked the halls and spoke to friends with her imagined presence by his side. He wanted to show her everything.

Each week, by the time Saturday arrived, he had planned an outing to do something she had never done before. And while the Matthews took Gabe to church on Sundays so he could enjoy his time playing the piano, John and Angelina would sit in Jute's living room and organize their photos. They made quick work of it so they could then go up to John's Dads' house and binge watch all the shows John felt Angelina should see. They watched Star Trek, Dr. Who, and all the Harry Potter and Lord or the Rings movies. They sat in the front row so Angelina could lie down with her head in John's lap and still see the screen. He wanted to wrap the curls of her hair around his finger, but he didn't.

She had stopped trying to undress him, so John assumed she had lost interest. But, she hadn't lost interest at all. Instead, she had gained faith that John's challenge would make things better. By having so many positive experiences, which were not at all sexual, she began to know herself in a way she might not have otherwise. John began to know her better as well. She was intimidatingly intelligent and never missed an opportunity to point out the most bizarre, metaphorical observations. John had even started writing some of them down and adding them to a scrapbook he had started in secret. It was filled with nothing but Angelina. Her skill at stealthy photography had inspired him to do the same to her. It was easier for him to go unnoticed because Angelina was often pulled deep into her observations and forgot all else. He had closeup shots of her hands, her eyes, the necklace as it lay on her chest, her skin, her hair. His camera had outranked Greenman as the best gift his Dad had ever given him, because with it he could hold onto Angelina forever.

He knew the cards were stacked against him when it came to building a life with her. They were both young, their feelings for each other were intense and perhaps even flawed. They were surely going to crash and burn. He put it off as long as he could, convincing her to use only half a page per event. She obliged except for the day near the end of May when she and Gabe were officially adopted. That event filled the entire page, and she purchased another two albums to fill completely to commemorate the celebration. She gave one to the Matthews and one to Gabe. She signed her name inside each one: Angelina Matthews.

By the fourth weekend in June, Angelina had filled the scrapbook down to her final page.

The following Saturday, John never showed up.

Part Twelve

John

74

July 1, 2007

I heard her climb up the ladder and then back down when she didn't find me there. I held my breath so she wouldn't hear me. I had been sitting on a bale of hay in the junk room of the barn for hours. I had come there to cry in private, like a big baby. I couldn't have been more ashamed of myself, how I hadn't bothered to put on clean clothes, or shower, or shave. And there I sat with my head in my hands, taking only the most necessary breaths through my mouth because my nose was stuffy from all the crying I had been doing. I had been terrified she wouldn't want to see me, and even more terrified that she would. But now she was here, only a few feet away from me, she just didn't know it yet.

I heard a foot step onto the hay by the door and knew she had found me. She was probably looking at me right at that moment, but I didn't move. I just sat there and tried to breathe.

"You promised," she said, hurt. Her voice was no longer the cheerful, excited sound it had been only a week ago.

I had been such a fool to think I could have kept her from

getting hurt. I looked up at her with the intention of begging her to forgive me for failing her, but I couldn't speak at all. She stood there in the doorway wearing a yellow strapless sundress and matching yellow sandals. She looked like walking happiness, but her expression told a different story.

She asked, "At what point did you realize I wasn't what you wanted?"

I shook my head that she had it all wrong, but I didn't know what to say to her. I had become so afraid of screwing up that all I could do was sit there and watch the whole thing unravel while tears ran uselessly down my face.

"Say it!" She screamed at me as she stepped into the room. "Look me in the eye for once, John, for ONCE, and tell me the truth."

I shook my head again and could say nothing.

"You can't do this!" She screamed again. "You can't sit there like I broke your heart when I did nothing!" She walked closer, still screaming at me, "This is what it's like to play it safe, huh? So no one gets hurt? Look at us!" She grabbed my arm and pulled my hand away from my face. "You need to hurt me right now, you break my fucking heart right now. Tell me the truth this time! Tell me you don't want me. Tell me to get out of your life! Don't just sit there in silence, pitying me. I don't need your pity! I need you to just say I repulse you and —"

I stood up and kissed her, the pain in my chest caused by her words throbbed, slowly being replaced with a desire so great it scared me. It probably would have scared her, too, if she believed it existed. There was a reason I had kept the space between us. I was afraid of how badly I wanted her. I had hoped the space between us would allow me to see her flaws and decide she was not all I believed her to be. I had hoped she would see mine before it would hurt so much. But she turned out to be more than I could have dreamed.

I was afraid of how I felt about her. She had accused me of seeing her as a monster, but I was the monster. I didn't want to hurt her. I didn't trust myself to know if I had done so. I didn't trust myself to be so close to her. But it was too late. I was kissing her and feeling her shock and confusion turn into desire, like the girl she had been in North Carolina when I had made her promise not to touch me.

Lifting her, I pressed her back against the old wooden wall and felt her legs wrap around me. Her fingers moved through my hair, pulling me closer. I moved to kiss her by her ear and said, "I don't want to hurt you."

"You already are, John. Now make it worth it." She pulled the top of her sundress down and moved my hands to her breasts. I could have easily devoured her, but I held back.

"What if you have a flashback? What if you forget it's me?"

"I probably will," she breathed. "I'll cry. It'll hurt, damn it. But you have to give me something good, John, something to replace the bad. You promised."

"I can't fix you," I felt tears come to my eyes again, but my hands were in heaven. My body wanted my mind to stop resisting her.

"I'm not broken. Now don't ruin this. Keep your promises," She smiled and looked at me teasingly.

"There's still the last page." I countered, feeling a shift inside me, knowing I was going to give in anyway.

"We better make the last event a big one."

We became two stars colliding, emerging, pulled by gravity, spinning violently. We were a dance of self-destruction, metamorphosis, and rebirth. The final results would not be known for quite some time. With the summer sun beating down on the barn roof and sweat sliding down our skin, our apprehension and uncertainty made its final beautiful swirl before falling like dust at our feet. My resistance had failed.

She was a goddess and I was a peasant. I knew I'd spend every day trying to keep her love for me alive, knowing it was against the odds, but trying like hell anyway. Maybe she would end up breaking my heart, but the thought no longer filled me with trepidation. Scars could heal, but lost time could never be replaced.

I would never love anyone as much as I loved her. There would never be a final page.

Thanks

Thank you for reading Winter Suns, the final book in the Winter Seedlings series.

I owe a lot to my friends Charles and Myron for being so openly in love. I would like to say that what they have together is a normal love, like any other love. But it is actually a greater love, an enviable love. Though there are no characters in Winter Seedlings based on either of them, their way of caring for one another and making a place for that in their world has definitely influenced my writing of this series. Congratulations to them on their marriage in 2014!

Special thanks goes to Casey and Rita Eggers, as well as Rita's mom, for their overwhelming support and encouragement. I tried to make this book as enjoyable as the first. I hope I have succeeded.

Lastly, to my mom, I am still your "Little Girl" and cringe at the thought of you reading all the times I've written the F-word here. I know the only reason you're reading this book series is because it has my name in big letters at the top. Your unconditional support means everything. One day I might write a crime novel, just for you.

Follow my blog to find out more about my life, my writing, and upcoming novels.

https://julierobertstowe.wordpress.com/

About The Author

Julie Roberts Towe was born in East Tennessee and spent most of her life there in the foothills of the Appalachian Mountains. The beauty of nature is ever present in her writing. Now living in a North Texas suburb with her husband and four children, Julie returns home to Appalachia in her stories. She covers many diverse subjects in her writing, but particularly addresses topics relating to equality for women and the LGBTQI Community, acceptance of personal and cultural diversity, and abuse recovery. She writes to give birth to love. Look for her novella, Silencer, in June 2015.

Silencer

Suicidal thoughts had comforted Rhoda since she was a child. She never actually wanted to die. But that changed on a cool autumn day in 1969 when the lifeless body of her infant daughter was pulled from the banks of Clinch River. Distraught, Rhoda set out on a journey to get as far away from War Gap as she could. With bus tickets and the use of her exhausted legs, she made it all the way to Grand Saline, Texas. She fell on the ground in the middle of nowhere and placed a gun to her head. Only, it wasn't the middle of nowhere. It was one of the few farms owned by a Black family in all of Van Zandt county. It was also the location of a recent murder fueled by racism. Rhoda was in the wrong place at the wrong time, or was she?